The Bee Charmer
Ali Spooner

The Bee Charmer

Ali Spooner

Affinity
Rainbow Publications

2017

The Bee Charmer
© 2017 by Ali Spooner

Affinity E-Book Press NZ LTD
Canterbury, New Zealand

1st Edition

ISBN: 978-0-947528-63-8

Editor: Angela Koenig
Proof Editor: Alexis Smith
Cover Design: Irish Dragon Designs

Acknowledgments

I would like to thank my fans for following my stories, providing great feedback and encouragement. Writing wouldn't be so much fun without you. A special thanks to Barb Carpenter, Tinna Webb, and Gail Dodge-Hankin for beta reading the story. Thanks to Affinity, Irish Dragon for the cover art, and the team of editors, readers, and publishers who continue to help me grow as a writer.

Dedication

To Rhonda, always, and forever.
To Kiwi, you'll always be my Gyp.

Table of Contents

Chapter One

Lower Western Canadian Border 1867

Nat rode through the pouring rain toward the cave that she had been using for shelter for the past few weeks. The raindrops slid down the brim of her hat only to bounce off the leather of her saddle. Hardy, her buckskin stallion, exhaled sharply and shook violently to free his coat of the soaking raindrops. Each day he and his master grew more intolerant of the dreary weather, yearning for a less miserable climate.

They reached the clearing that opened to a large cave that she, Hardy, and Quincy her pack mule had called home for several weeks. The smoke of her smoldering campfire greeted her. Quincy, tethered at the rear of the cave, welcomed them home with a loud grunt. Hardy shook one last time in an attempt to rid his coat of the cold rain before stepping under the protective lip of the cave's entrance.

Nat hung her full-length range coat on an oak limb that had conveniently grown into the mouth of the cave. She placed the pelts she had recovered that day beside her coat and began removing the saddle and tack from Hardy. Fully mature at four years old, Hardy had grown into quite a loyal companion who served her well. Stretching the tack out on the rocks near the fire pit to dry, she picked up an old blanket and wiped the soaking wetness from Hardy's coat.

"Hello, Gyp." Her faithful blue-coated companion trotted up to her master and licked her face while she bent down to dry Hardy's legs. The dog provided protection for Quincy and Nat's belongings while she was out during the day. Nat buried her hands in the deep blue fur of the animal as Gyp continued licking her face. She hung up the blanket to allow it to dry and then attached feed sacks to Hardy and Quincy.

"Ready for some left over stew?"

Gyp's ears perked. The dog sat and watched with loving eyes as her master added dry wood to the fire. Nat settled the stew pot on the spit above the flames and sat back beside Gyp, waiting for their dinner to warm.

Nat reached inside a saddlebag and pulled out a chunk of dried jerky, tearing off a piece for Gyp and tossing it to the patiently waiting dog. "Good catch girl," she praised her canine companion and then tore a piece of the dried meat off with her teeth. Nat chewed slowly allowing the saliva to mix with the morsel to soften the spicy meat.

She removed her hat and let her shoulder-length black hair tumble down her neck. She laid her head back against her bedroll, watching the flames dance to life in the fire pit. Shadows licked the walls of the cave as she slowly surveyed the culmination of her last month's efforts. Mounds of pelts were stored near the rear of the cave to remain dry and secluded from anyone who might wander into the cave with thoughts of looting her bounty. It certainly wouldn't be the first time a fellow trapper took advantage of another to profit from their hard work.

After obtaining the final day's trapping and retrieving the traps, Nat would break camp to head to Seattle to sell her pelts, restock her supplies, and choose her next destination. This site had been very profitable, but she was growing weary of the endless rainy days and cool temperatures. She smiled. *Some time spent closer to the ocean will do us good.*

She let the contents of the stew pot start to boil before scooping up a portion for her and Gyp. The dog waited patiently for her meal while Nat slowly stirred the thick stew, allowing it to cool. The action made her sigh as memories floated into her mind.

Nat had been born eighteen years earlier in British Columbia as Nathalie St. Croix, the sole child of Nathan St. Croix, a Canadian trapper, and his wife, Nanya, a full-blooded Mohican woman. The family traveled the Canadian and US border together, trapping, hunting, and trading until Nanya died during an outbreak of influenza six years earlier. Motherless at twelve years old, Nat clung more tightly to the father she adored who struggled to teach her the ways of the world. Trapping, hunting, and fishing came as easy as breathing to Nat, but teaching her to be a woman was an impossible task for Nathan. He had always treated Nat like a son. Her slim, six-foot tall frame and androgynous features allowed her to pass as a young man in most settings, and so far, that had proved a benefit to Nat during most of her young life.

For five years after her mother's death Nat and her father trapped the Northern US and lower Western Canada. Nathan taught her everything he knew about fur trading and she was an adept student, learning quickly the skills she would need to survive in their rapidly changing world.

When war had broken out in the eastern half of the country, Nathan decided they would push farther west and away from the brewing turmoil that caused many families to head farther west as well. Often times in their travels Nat and her father had come upon a solitary wagon of greenhorns who had fled west to escape only to find themselves lost, starving, or besieged by illness. Other travelers had ravaged the supplies and possessions of the deceased leaving little evidence of those who had perished.

Her emotions grew hard in the vigorous environment where she was raised, but she could not hold back the tears which flowed freely down her cheeks after she and her father discovered a small group of wagons that had been razed. There were several burnt skeletons, mostly adults, but also several small children. They buried the remains to prevent further degradation by predators.

Nat, sitting on a rock next to Nathan and resting after burying the bodies, was listening to the whispering of the wind as a cool breeze picked up. A weak sound alerted her and she struggled to make out the source. Standing up and moving slowly through the debris, she kept changing direction with each new sound emitted. She knew that what she heard was the whimpering of a small animal and she soon traced the cries to a pile of discarded clothing. Nat crept closer and raised a partially burned shirt to find a tiny bundle of blue fur. She reasoned that in this harsh environment the mother must have abandoned her pup as the runt of the litter. It had been left to perish on its own while increasing the chance of survival for its stronger siblings.

The pup's barely open eyes peered up at Nat seeming to plead for her help. She bent down, cradling the small creature in one of her large hands, and her fingers stroked the soft fur. She walked back to her father to show him her discovery.

Nathan looked at the small pup in his daughter's hand and shook his head. "You know its chances for survival are very slim."

Nat's eyes glowed. "I'll do everything I can to take care of her so she'll live."

"Looks like we have another mouth to feed." He smiled. "Bundle her up and let's see if we can teach her to eat." He moved to set up camp away from the burnt-out wagons and started a fire.

Once the fire was roaring, Nat warmed some of the stew they had eaten the night before. She dipped her fingers in the rich gravy. Holding the pup in one hand, she smeared the gravy across its lips. "Try it," she said softly, encouraging the tiny animal to eat. Slowly the pup began to lick its lips, tasting human food for the first time in its short life.

3

Nathan watched the glow on his daughter's face and knew she felt encouraged that the pup would survive. Nathan, more of a pessimist than his daughter, worried that the pup would die. He helped her by dipping a small rag in cool water and pressing it to the pup's mouth. The puppy instinctively chewed on the rag, forcing out the water as her small knobbed tail wagged in Nat's hand.

Nathan finished setting up camp that night while he watched his daughter nurse the young pup. As he toiled, he offered a silent prayer for the pup to survive and become a much-needed companion for his daughter. Later he watched Nat and her small friend curl up next to the fire and drift off to sleep.

The next morning, Nat awoke to a soft warm tongue lapping at her chin and shiny brown eyes gazing up at her. She warmed up more gravy and a small chunk of otter meat that she mashed into tiny fragments and finger fed to the small pup.

After breaking camp, father and daughter mounted their horses and headed north to a cabin tucked away in the dense woods. During the ride, the pup snuggled under Nat's coat, reveling in her warmth and protection. Near nightfall, they reached the cabin and cautiously entered it. Stray travelers or vagrant animals were known to take up residence in trappers' cabins, so the first entry was always potentially dangerous.

They were fortunate to find that the last human inhabitant had left dry wood on the hearth and Nat quickly had a fire burning to light and warm the cabin. Nathan found several small lanterns and filled them with oil that they had obtained from the animals they trapped, and soon the cabin was ablaze with light.

Assured that the cabin was secure and safe, Nathan returned outside to begin to unload the packs and tend to the animals while Nat set up shop inside the cabin. She stored the pelts in a small room off the kitchen and unpacked their food and cooking supplies.

Nat portioned out flour and patted out biscuits to accompany the last of their trail stew. Tomorrow they would hunt, and with good fortune, they would have fresh meat for dinner. She hummed with excitement preparing their meal while the puppy bounced along behind her every step.

Nat was cleaning up the sleeping areas and preparing the rustic cots for slumber when Nathan brought in fresh water. She returned to the hearth smiling at him and found the biscuits browning nicely. She dipped out a small bowl of gravy and another small chunk of the meat and prepared it for the puppy. Meanwhile, Nathan dished up stew for them and added biscuits to each of their plates. Nat placed the bowl in front of the puppy before sitting down with her father to begin her meal.

"Have you given thought to a name?" Nathan asked.

"I was thinking Gyp, short for Gypsy."

"Well we are a group of nomads, so Gyp would fit right in."

"Do you really think she is going to make it?"

"From the way she is attacking that food bowl I would say 'yes'. I think I may have finally found someone who appreciates my cooking."

Gyp growled her appreciation of the meal and then drank fresh water from the bowl Nathan had placed by her food.

"Instinct is kicking in." He watched the puppy lap at the water.

Nat watched with pride as Gyp finished her meal. She broke off a portion of biscuit and dipped it into the gravy on her plate before dropping it in the pup's bowl.

"I want you to go hunting for some fresh meat in the morning, while I start setting the traps. I don't know about you but I am sick of otter stew." Nathan grinned.

"I could devour a thick T-bone myself."

"When we head in to trade next month, I promise you will have the biggest steak you can eat."

"That's something to look forward to then." Nat cleared the dishes and walked Gyp to the door. "We'll check on the animals and be right back."

Nathan smiled. "I'm lucky to have such a strong young woman for a daughter," he mumbled. Sure, he had always longed for a son when he was younger, but now he doubted that he could be prouder of anyone than he was with Nat. He waited for them to return and then he doused the lights before both of them retired for the evening to rest up for the big day ahead.

Nat woke first and put fresh wood on the fire before taking Gyp outside. She watched the puppy pounce on leaves that blew on the ground in front of her. Nat's laughter broke the silence of the deep woods. The seasons were beginning to change. She knew that the brilliant color of the leaves rapidly falling from the trees and the brisk chill in the air would soon give way to snowflakes and long winter nights. Nat would be glad to make it through the passes to Seattle ahead of the winter storms and take shelter somewhere less desolate. For the past few years, she and her father had spent the winter in a small rented cabin in south Seattle. There they would plan for the coming year and catch up with fellow trappers, sharing trends in the trading market and news of the bloody war.

Nat returned to the cabin and set the coffee kettle on the fire. She cleaned her rifle and loaded it while she waited for her father to stir. He walked into the kitchen just as she was pouring the strong steaming liquid into their mugs.

"Morning."

"Good morning. Did you have trouble not sleeping on the ground last night?" Nat teased.

"When you get my age, it takes a while to adjust." Her dad picked up his mug.

"I'll keep that in mind." Nat continued packing her bag for the morning's hunt.

They made small talk while they drank their coffee and then Nat stood and stretched one last time. "I better get moving if I am going to get any meat today. See you when you get back tonight." She picked up Gyp. "Sorry, my friend, but today you will have to stay inside." She placed the pup inside the woodbin on a warm blanket.

She kissed her dad on the forehead and picked up her bag and rifle.

"Good luck today." He watched her go out the door.

Nat laced her arms through the straps of her pack and shouldered her rifle. She walked through the woods with a stealthy silence looking for signs of wildlife. She had walked for nearly half an hour when she heard a buzzing sound echoing through the cool morning air. Her keen ears led her to the trunk of an old tree that was now home to a swarm of honeybees.

Approaching carefully, Nat caught a glimpse of a large comb overflowing with honey. Honey for biscuits would be a pleasant change for both herself and her father, so Nat propped her rifle next to the tree and lowered her pack. She took out a small strip of worn cloth and wrapped it around a long stick. She would have to work quickly to harvest the honey without getting stung, but the sweetness was just too promising to pass up. Nat removed a jar from her pack, and slowly spun the lid from its lips. She took one of her remaining few matches and struck it, careful not to waste the precious fire. She lit the rag, which burned slowly, fueled by the animal fat and oils, and created a plume of smoke which Nat placed into the hive. The bees buzzed angrily but fled the hive just as Nathan had taught her they would.

Nat worked quickly to cut off a large section of comb and slid it into the jar, and then she dipped the jar into the honey until it filled to the rim.

She wiped the excess from the outer rim of the jar with her finger and then raised it to her lips. The sugary taste locked her jaws as she adjusted to the taste. She quickly replaced the lid and tucked her prize into her pack.

She extinguished the cloth with damp leaves from the ground and picked up her rifle to move on before the angry bees returned. With a huge smile gracing her face, Nat continued in the woods, making a mental note of where the honey tree was located for future visits.

Another mile into the forest, Nat came across fresh tracks where a deer had passed earlier. She hoped he would be heading down to the small river that was a short walk farther into the woods. She crept quietly down to the river's edge and waited in frozen silence for her prey. Nat watched several rabbits hop to the river's edge for a quick drink and then dart back into the undergrowth when they heard a larger animal approach.

Nat watched a huge buck step confidently from the concealment of the forest to the river's edge. She calmly raised the rifle and put the buck square in her sights. A fine specimen indeed and one that would provide meat for them for many days she thought. Nat waited until the buck lowered his head to drink and then squeezed the trigger firmly. The shot rang true striking the buck in the heart and dropping him immediately.

Nat took the rope from her pack and walked to where the buck lay dead. She laid her hand on his neck and she could feel the warmth leaving his body in the cool morning. "Thank you for your sacrifice," she whispered to the animal, and then she tied the rope around his back hooves. Nat carried the animal to the nearest tree and, using the rope, hoisted him upward until he was off the ground entirely.

Nat despised the next part of the ritual, but she took the knife from her belt and slowly drew a line across the buck's stretched throat to bleed him and then made the deep incision down his belly to disembowel the beast and prepare his carcass for transport. This unpleasant task done, Nat walked to the riverbank to wash her knife and hands before making her way back to the cabin where she would get Quincy to carry the buck home. The coppery smell of blood filled the air and she prayed she could return before the scent reached another predator.

She gathered her goods and made her way back to the cabin. She left her pack on the porch and peeked inside the door to find Gyp soundly asleep in the woodbin and she quietly closed the door. Removing the tether from Quincy's back legs, Nat led the mule back to the river's edge to retrieve the buck. Quincy allowed Nat to strap the buck across his back and they returned to the cabin.

7

Nat strung the buck up into a tree once again when they reached the cabin and she began the task of skinning the buck with her sharp knife. She carefully placed the hide on the tanning wall on the end of the cabin and then began to carve the buck. She cut a large roast from the hindquarter and carried it into the cabin where she skewered it onto the spit and placed it over the flames for roasting.

Gyp watched her from the woodbin with sleepy eyes and then wiggled her whole body when Nat reached down to pick her up and carry her outside. Gyp trotted along beside Nat and sat watching her carve the rest of the meat before carrying it into a small smoke house to prepare for curing. Gyp watched her intently as Nat coated the meat with salt, rubbing it deeply into the tender meat before hanging it from the rafters by string and lighting the fire in the smoke house. The process would take days so Nat scoured the woods surrounding the cabin for firewood to keep the fire stoked.

As the afternoon sun faded, Nat finished her chores and cleaned up at the river's edge before she walked back into the cabin. She pulled the jar of honey from her pack and placed it on the table. The roast in the fire smelled heavenly while she rolled out fresh biscuits and placed them on the hearth. Nat checked the fire in the smokehouse, and she was playing with Gyp when she heard her father ride into the yard.

"What is that most heavenly smell?" He dismounted and walked toward her.

"I was lucky this morning and got a nice buck." She walked her dad around to the tanning wall and then led him into the smoke house.

Nathan was very impressed with his daughter's success. "I would say you were lucky," he agreed, placing his arm around her shoulder.

"I have a roast cooking and there is plenty of back strap to make jerky, and yes before you asked I saved the heart and liver too," Nat replied.

She knew that Nathan enjoyed making stew from the deer's heart, and if they could find some wild onions or potatoes, he would fry the liver as a special treat. Nathan taught her how to use every part of an animal so nothing would go to waste.

Nat helped her father care for his horse and together they walked into the cabin, Gyp bouncing merrily along behind them.

"I swear she has grown since this morning." He scooped Gyp up in his rough hands.

"She slept most of the morning so she's been full of herself this afternoon," she told him, scratching behind the pup's ears.

They walked into the house together and Nat started setting the table while Nathan checked the roast on the spit. "This looks fantastic." He took his knife, and sliced off several pieces of the fragrant roasted meat and carried them to the table.

Nathan sat down at the table and spied the jar of honey sitting next to the biscuits. "My, my, you did have a good day's hunt." He lifted the jar holding the golden honey, spinning the lid off and pouring a small amount onto his plate.

"I thought we could use a treat." Her glowing smile lit up the room.

"Indeed, you have prepared us a feast." He praised her efforts.

During their meal, they discussed plans for spending a couple of weeks in the cabin before moving on toward Seattle to do their trading and settle down for the winter. Both Nathan and his daughter were eager to make the trip and return to civilization, if even for a brief respite.

Later that evening, Nat dreamed of soaking in a hot bath and buying a new pair of dungarees and work shirt to replace her buckskins that were in dire need of a good airing out.

In the cave, Nat sat back against the wall and closed her eyes her hand instinctively going to her neck. She located a leather thong and traced it until she touched the large bear claw nestled under her shirt as the memory continued.

The days had passed quickly at the cabin, and two days before they intended to pack and hit the trail, Nathan went out ahead of her to check traps. Nat saddled Hardy an hour later, and followed her father's trail into the woods. Today's catch would be the last, and then they would pack to head out at first light for the long ride into Seattle.

Hardy's nostrils flared as they rode deeper into the woods and his muscles twitched with every sound. Every one of Hardy's nerves seemed to be on edge and his anxiety was slowly transferring to Nat. She patted his neck in an effort to calm him but even her reassuring words could not prevent the lather of sweat breaking out across his shoulders.

A rifle shot rang out in the woods from the direction where her father would be trapping, and suddenly, the relatively calm forest broke out in a riot of sounds. Nat drove her heels into Hardy's flanks spurring him to a full gallop as she recognized the bellow of a bear and heard her father shouting. Nat reached a clearing and could only watch as Nathan got off another rifle shot, striking the bear squarely in the chest as he charged, but not slowing the animal's advance. Nathan fumbled to reload as the bear, a full-grown grizzly, only three feet away from him, reared onto his hind legs.

Nat watched in horror as the bear advanced on her father, sharp claws striking out at him while rabid foam flew through the air. The beast roared, his anger echoing throughout the forest. She raised her rifle to take aim as the bear raked a large paw across Nathan's face and neck slicing through his skin like a knife through warm butter. Nat squeezed the trigger and her shot hit the bear behind its left ear driving the bullet deep into his brain. The bear did not fall. She ejected the shell and reloaded, preparing for another shot when she saw Nathan fall to the ground. Her next shot struck the bear straight in the heart and the bear finally faltered and fell beside Nathan.

Hardy galloped across the clearing and slid to a stop ten feet away from Nathan. Nat jumped off his back, still carefully eyeing the bear as she rushed to her father's side. The bear twitched and Nat shot him once again, then knelt down next to her father.

Blood gushed from her father's face and neck, his jugular severed, and the realization struck Nat with a crushing blow—there was nothing she could do to prevent her father's death. Nat sat beside him on the blood soaked ground and held his hand while she watched his life slip away. "I love you, Father." Nat watched him close his pain-filled eyes and pass into the next world.

Nat sat for hours, with her father's head in her lap in the death-filled meadow, until Hardy's soft lips brushed her neck bringing her out of her stupor. She managed to find her father's horse and struggled until she managed to drape his lifeless body across his saddle and then mounted Hardy for the ride back to the cabin.

She carried Nathan onto the cabin porch and bathed the drying blood from his body. She searched through their packs until she found a shovel and began preparing a grave for her beloved father. Shock overcame her while moving mechanically, carrying her father and placing him in the ground before slowly covering him with the freshly dug earth.

Nat made several trips down to the river's edge to collect rocks to prepare a mound over her father's grave and, as the sun slowly sank into the horizon, she placed the last rock upon the growing pile. She sat beside the mound and Gyp, who had traced her every step, crawled up into her lap providing comfort to her mourning master. The chill of the oncoming night forced Nat into the cabin and she sat before the fireplace, alone for the first time in her life.

Sometime during the night, Nat curled up in a ball in front of the hearth and awoke the next morning with Gyp cuddled in her arms. She walked outside to where she had buried her father to confirm that she was indeed awake and not living some horrible dream. Reality struck her like a brick as she looked down on the mound of stones that covered the last of her family. Tears slid down her cheeks and she wondered what would become of her now. Nathan had prepared her well for trapping and trading, but she never dreamed she would be all alone at such a young age.

Nat saddled Hardy and with Gyp trotting beside her, she rode to the clearing where the bear lay motionless. Hardy shied away from the smell of fresh blood and remained a distance from the prostrate bear, refusing to approach closer.

She dismounted and began the tedious work of skinning the large bear, removing the large claws, and tucking them away in a leather pouch. Grizzly claws were prized trading items as well as the bear's pelt, but Nat was certain she would never part with the hide of the animal that killed her father. Nat hated to waste any animal but she would be damned if she would taste the flesh of this beast, and once she finished her work, she set the carcass ablaze, purifying the ground where her father had died.

Hardy shied away from the bear's pelt when Nat approached so she rode back to the cabin to retrieve Quincy who would carry the pelt on his back. Once they returned to the cabin, Nat removed the deer hide that had finished drying and replaced it with the bear's hide. Nat cut a long strip of the hide and used it to bind the two pieces of wood together that she had fashioned as a cross to mark her father's passing. She had carved her father's name into the crosspiece with the year of his death and used a large stone to drive it into the ground at the head of his grave.

Nat spent the next two days packing her supplies and preparing for the journey to Seattle, carefully storing dried meat and other food supplies for the weeks of travel ahead. She made one more trip to the honey tree to salvage one final jar of honey for her trip, and that evening she used the last of her flour to make a batch of biscuits.

Sitting in front of the fire, Nat chose one of the bear claws and, using a tiny awl, bored a hole through the claw. Using a thin strip of the deer hide, she fashioned a necklace with the bear claw and slipped it over her head to rest just above her heart. In the days and years to come, Nat would caress the bear claw when thinking of her father and take comfort in this token of his life.

The next morning, Nat packed the animals before going to her father's grave. After a final goodbye, she turned to take the first step to her future.

She rode for three days, the journey taking her through the mountain pass just as the first snow began to fall and Nat was relieved to reach flat ground. When she encountered the dreary rains that plagued the area, sometimes for days on end, Nat knew she was close to her destination. She found the large cave, planning to rest there before the last leg into Seattle. After a few days, Nat would ride for two days into Seattle where she would have to make decisions on what path her life would lead.

The final days passed quickly, and soon Nat was facing the last night in the protection of the cave. Nat slept curled around Gyp that night, and the following morning she began arranging her packs for the last leg of her journey. Unsure of what she would do once she traded out her pelts, Nat was sure of only one thing. She would stick to the plan that she and her father had made to rent a small cabin and spend the winter months restocking and planning for their next journey.

Nat and her companions spent one last cold and damp night in the woods, and by noon the next day, she crested a hill overlooking the bustling town of Seattle. Nat sat for a moment and watched the people scurrying through the crowded streets, and with a final look over her shoulder back into the forest, she urged Hardy to move forward.

Chapter Two

Her first stop was the furriers, to begin negotiations on her pelts. Smithy, the owner, had always dealt fairly with Nat and her father, knowing they would only bring him the highest quality pelts, and he rewarded them handsomely for their loyalty. Smithy smiled warmly at Nat, a smile that faded quickly when he realized she was alone.

"Where is Nathan?" he calmly asked, placing an arm around Nat.

"He's gone, Smithy," Nat told him, the threat of tears choking her voice. "He was checking traps and was mauled by a grizzly."

"I'm so sorry to hear that," Smithy replied. "Nathan was a great man."

"Yes, he was."

"What will you do now?"

"I don't know for sure yet, Smithy. After trading I plan on getting a hot meal, a bath, and then hopefully rent out the old Johnson cabin for the winter before deciding what to do."

"Well, why don't we get you unloaded and you can go get some food while I survey your pelts," Smithy suggested as he walked outside with Nat.

Smithy noticed the bear pelt on the back of her father's horse and ran his hand through the course fur. "Is this the one that killed your father?"

"Yes it is," she answered. "A big son of a bitch he was too."

"Are you planning on trading the pelt?"

"No, Smithy, that one's a keeper."

"Well let me know if you ever change your mind, a pelt that size would carry a large price on the market."

"You can see what you can get for these," Nat told him as she took the leather pouch, which held the bear claws, and tossed it to Smithy.

Smithy opened the pouch and looked inside. "A small fortune I would expect. Some of these new greenhorns pay dearly for grizzly items and I am sure these will be a prize. Give me a day or two to get the best price for you," he added with a grin.

"I'll check into the Stillwater and drop in to see you in the morning." With a nod, she led the two horses and mule over to the livery.

"See you in the morning then," Smithy called out to her.

†

Nat gave instructions for her animals to be cared for and then, with Gyp on her heels, she headed to the Stillwater to get a room. Nat saw the clerk smile before it turned to a scowl eyeing Gyp. Gyp growled at the man and Nat gave him a frown, and he handed her a room key without comment.

Nat carried her packs up the stairs to her room and then she and Gyp left the room to find a hot meal. She stopped at the desk. "I'd like a hot bath in my room when I've finished with my meal." The man nodded and she walked into the dining room. She found a small table and Gyp sat at her feet. Nat took off her hat and her dark hair fell to her shoulders.

A smiling young woman approached her table to take her order. "What can I get for you?"

"The biggest steak you can find, well done with the works," Nat answered. She looked down at Gyp. "Also, a smaller steak, well done for my companion, too, please. You can hold her beans," Nat teased. She added with a chuckle, "They give her gas."

The woman rewarded her with a brilliant smile before heading to the kitchen to place the order. Nat looked around the dining room at the town folk and a few stray fellow trappers who had come in for an early dinner, and like her, were still rugged from the trail. Nat knew the hot bath would do wonders for her and she looked forward to it as much as she did to a hot meal.

The server returned with a steaming plate of fresh rolls and butter. "You look hungry, so I brought these out for you."

"Thanks, we're starved." She buttered a hot roll, pinching a bite off for Gyp. "We are both sick of my cooking too."

"How long have you been out?"

"What month is this?"

"November," the woman replied.

"Nine months then."

"That's a long time to be in the woods alone," the young woman commented.

"I was with my father until a few weeks ago," Nat replied. She added numbly, "He was killed by a grizzly."

14

"I am so sorry to hear that," the woman stammered and, blushing, turned to go.

"Thanks."

Nat ate a few more of the delicious rolls while she waited on their dinner. When the woman returned carrying two large plates of food Nat's mouth watered with one look at the steak. She reached for Gyp's smaller steak to cut it into smaller pieces.

"You start on your steak and I'll cut this one up for your friend."

"Thanks."

The woman sat down at the table to cut Gyp's steak.

Nat took a bite of the steak and her taste buds exploded with ecstasy, the warm juices and seasoning assaulting her senses. She moaned loudly and the young woman at her side blushed. "This is heavenly," Nat moaned. "My compliments to the cook."

"Why thank you, ma'am," the young lady answered. "Just be sure to save some room for dessert, I have fresh pies baked today." She stood to leave.

Nat set the plate down in front of Gyp and watched with delight as the young pup devoured the tasty meal before gnawing the bone. Nat returned to her own feast and the young woman brought out another basket of fresh rolls.

Nat cleaned the meat from the T-Bone and then, drinking from a mug of cool water, placed the bone on Gyp's plate. She saw the young woman approaching again with a tray holding several slices of pie. Nat chose a thick slice of apple which, incredibly, was still warm. She was nearly finished with her meal when a pair of men came stumbling into the restaurant. Even from a distance Nat could smell the odor of alcohol on the men as they plopped down at a table near hers.

One of the men pulled out a coin purse and dropped it onto the table as the server approached cautiously. "Come serve us, pretty lady," he said loudly. "We've just come to town from the gold fields and we're starving. Two of the biggest steaks you can find and a bottle of whiskey."

"We don't serve whiskey here," she told him.

"What about you? Are you on the menu for dessert?" He grabbed her by the wrist and pulled her into his lap.

His partner laughed. "I bet she'd be good for two rounds."

The server wriggled free from his grasp and slapped his face.

The angry man lunged from his chair to reach for her. Nat's hand had slipped down to her boot and she retrieved a long skinning knife before springing to her feet to step between them. She interrupted his assault by pressing a sharp knife into his throat, freezing him in his tracks.

"I don't believe your advances are appreciated here, sir. Maybe you and your friend should take your business down to the saloon," Nat growled.

"What business of this is yours?" The man's eyes reached up to meet hers as she towered over him.

"I'm making it my business." She added pressure to the knife at his throat. "Take your money and go before we get the law involved in your attack on this woman."

"I didn't attack anyone," he cried.

"She didn't fall in your lap on purpose with you holding her there against her will. I don't know any lawman who wouldn't call that assault."

The man glared at Nat. Fortunately, his partner had better sense. "Come on, Joe, let's go get us a bottle and something to eat where our gold is appreciated."

"That sounds like a wise decision." Nat eased the pressure of the knife.

Joe turned to snatch his coin purse off the table. "I'll be seeing you again later."

Just then, the hotel owner, Joseph, a towering tall figure, rushed into the dining room. "No, you won't. If you step foot in here again, I'll have you arrested for trespassing," he warned. "Now take your sorry asses out of here." He grabbed the man's sleeve to escort him out of the building.

When he returned, he approached the young woman. "Are you okay, Marissa?"

"Yes, I am thank you." She turned to look at Nat. "Thank you, too."

"No problem. I'm glad you're okay."

"I want you to stay here tonight, Marissa," the owner suggested. "They're hopefully just passing through and will be gone tomorrow."

She nodded and turned to Nat. "Can I get you anything else?"

"Will you send my bill to the front desk?"

"Yes," Marissa said before returning to the kitchen

When Nat finished the meal, she left several silver pieces on the table before walking to the general store to purchase a pair of dungarees and a soft cotton shirt.

When Nat and Gyp returned to the room, steam was coming off the tub. Anxious to strip down and soak in its luxury, Nat had just pulled off her top when the door opened and the same young woman from the dining room stood in the doorway with a pot of hot water.

The woman blushed again and quickly stepped inside before closing the door. "I'm sorry I didn't realize you were in here." She turned away.

Nat, who was naked except for the bear claw around her neck, said, "That's all right." Nat walked toward the tub, "I couldn't wait to get a bath."

She stepped inside and watched as the woman poured the steamy water into the tub. Moaning loudly once again, she soaked a washcloth in the hot water and handed it to the young woman. "Since you are here, could I convince you to wash my back? My name's Nat."

"I'm Marissa." The young woman was obviously embarrassed and began lathering the cloth with a bar of soap.

Nat lowered herself under the water and emerged with her black hair plastered to her neck. "Hmm, that feels great." Marissa stepped forward cautiously and bent down to place the soapy cloth against her skin. Nat watched in the mirror feeling the tight muscles of her back and shoulders begin to relax. "That feels fantastic." She bent forward allowing Marissa access to her entire back.

"How long will you be staying in town?" Marissa asked.

"I hope to rent out the old Johnson place for the winter…if it's still vacant."

"Well then, we shall be neighbors if you do. I live in the small farmhouse just down the road."

"I'm sure we will be seeing each other again then." Nat took the cloth from Marissa. "Thanks for washing my back."

"You're welcome. I hope to see you again soon," Marissa added, slipping quietly out the door.

"You can count on it." Nat sank deeper into the water to soak. She washed her hair and body then soaked until the water turned cool. She slipped on a new nightshirt and slid between cool clean sheets for the first time in almost a year. Gyp slept on a rug next to the bed and neither of them moved until the sun came up.

†

Nat and Gyp went downstairs to the dining room where they saw Marissa.

"Good morning," Marissa called while smiling sweetly. "What can I get you this morning?"

"How about some bacon and flapjacks," Nat requested.

"Would you like honey or maple syrup?" Marissa asked.

"Maple syrup and lots of butter, please."

"Coffee?"

"Lots of it, with sweet cream if you have it."

"We even have sugar cubes here." Marissa disappeared into the kitchen and returned a few minutes later carrying two large plates, one with bacon and flapjacks and another with cut up bits of egg, flapjacks and sausage. "I thought your pal might be hungry, too." Marissa sat the plate down in front of Gyp.

"Careful, you're going to spoil us." Nat grinned.

"You two look like you could use a bit of spoiling." Marissa patted Gyp's head.

"We could, but won't your husband get jealous if we start showing up at your place for breakfast every morning?" Nat asked, looking at the silver band on Marissa's ring finger.

Marissa looked a little shocked at Nat's comment and then stammered out her response. "I'm a widow." A blush rose on her face as she turned to get the coffee from the kitchen.

Nat felt like a total heel, but there was no way she could have known. It was her turn to blush when Marissa walked back to the table. "I'm so sorry for prying," Nat said.

"It's no problem. It's been three years now, and wearing the ring helps to prevent most of the men in here from making assumptions."

Nat didn't feel any more comfortable with the answer, but the smile in Marissa's blue eyes seemed to bore right through her, warming her to the bone. She was relieved when another customer arrived and Marissa left her table to seat him and take his order, allowing her to watch Marissa while finishing her meal.

Marissa made several more trips to Nat's table to refill her coffee before Nat was done eating. She left her a few silver coins on the table and sent a smile to Marissa before she left the building.

†

Nat and Gyp walked over to see Smithy and received a warm welcome as soon as they stepped inside the door.

"I was very impressed with this year's pelts, and I hope you will be pleased with the price," Smithy belted out. He grinned. "I lucked up on the bear claws, too. I found one Easterner who wanted the whole lot at quite a good price. I was just waiting for your approval."

Smithy led Nat into the office to go over the figures and Nat was surprised with the offer. The pelts and bear claws would net her over two thousand dollars, more money than most of the townspeople would see in years. Nat carefully reviewed the figures and then signed the sheet and handed it back to Smithy.

"This looks very generous."

"Good money for high quality."

"Thanks for the compliment," Nat replied.

"Nathan taught you well. So well, in fact, if you decide to settle down here instead of heading back into the woods, I would hire you in a minute."

"I might just have to think on that offer pretty hard." Nat turned to leave.

"Stop by later today and I'll have your money ready." Smithy walked Nat out into the morning sunshine. "Did you hear we had a murder in town last night?"

"What?"

"Some traveler from the gold fields was found floating in the bay with his throat slit and his coin purse robbed."

Nat felt the blood drain from her face. "I had a run-in at the hotel last night with a man who fits that description. I pulled my knife on him when he attacked the server. I swear I didn't kill him though."

Smithy frowned upon hearing the news. "I don't doubt you in the least, but the Marshall will probably want to talk to you when he arrives later today."

"That's not a problem. I'll still be at the hotel." Nat smiled weakly at him. "I'll see you later."

Chapter Three

Nat decided to ride out to the old Johnson place to look at the cabin before she would go make an offer to rent it for the winter. She walked into the livery and saddled Hardy, then headed out of town with Gyp trotting beside them. There was a definite chill in the air and Nat predicted there would be snow flying soon. If the cabin was still in good shape, Nat would rent it out and get busy preparing supplies for the coming winter months.

Nat was relieved to find the cabin intact. With a small barn and a smoke house, it served as an ideal place to spend the winter. Curious, she rode a few hundred yards farther down the road until she reached a newer farmhouse, which surely must be Marissa's home. Nat felt strangely comforted to know that Marissa was close by, an emotion that left her rather confused.

After Marissa had left her room last night, Nat lay in bed thinking how great it felt to have Marissa's hands on her and a rush of pleasant warmth came over her. The longer she thought of the other woman, the warmer she became and she felt a dampness growing between her thighs. Nat's fingers probed the wetness, thinking of Marissa, and she was soon trembling with pleasure. Confused by these new feelings and totally exhausted, Nat slipped into the most restful sleep she had experienced in a long time.

Nat returned to town, and once again left Hardy at the livery, and then walked back to Smithy's to retrieve her payment. She left the furrier and went directly to the bank to deposit the majority of her funds for safekeeping. She also met with Mr. Barker who owned the Johnson place and rented out the cabin, paying for all four months in advance.

She returned to the general store, ordered supplies she would need for the winter, and requested delivery to the Johnson place the following day. Nat had decided she and Gyp would spend one more night at the hotel and would move into the cabin the next morning.

The day slipped by quickly, nightfall setting in as Nat headed back to the hotel. She was disappointed that Marissa was not in the dining room, but ordered up another hearty meal from the hotel owner's wife.

20

Nat devoured pan-fried chops and fresh vegetables sharing the bones and scraps with Gyp who accepted her master's offering with licks from her soft tongue.

Nat took a large mug of spiced apple cider out to the porch where she sat with Gyp, watching large snowflakes begin to spiral down from the sky. Nat laughed as Gyp jumped into the air trying to catch the flakes before they floated to the ground.

"Quite a pup you have there." Smithy walked up to the porch and sat beside Nat.

"Yes, she is. Dad and I found her at a burnt out wagon site while working our way west. You'd never know from looking at her now that she was abandoned by her mother as the runt of the litter."

"Those usually turn out to be the best of the bunch," Smithy proclaimed.

"Well, I know I couldn't ask for a better companion." Gyp returned to the porch and laid her head in Nat's lap.

Smithy chuckled. "I think that feeling is mutual. I'm going to head in to get some dinner, but please don't be a stranger this winter."

"I'll stop in whenever I come into town." Nat watched the huge man leave the porch. She observed a man, not as large as Smithy, coming toward her. "Are you Nathalie St. Croix?" the stranger asked.

Nat looked up at the large man. "Yes, sir, I am."

"I'm Marshall Corbit and I understand you had a bit of a run-in here last night."

"There was an ornery cuss here, with a pal of his, giving the dining room server a hard time. When he moved to physically attack her, I intervened on her behalf."

"After the altercation, did you see the man again?"

"No, sir. He and his pal went to the saloon as far as I know. After I finished my meal, I took a long, hot bath and retired for the night. I didn't wake again until after sunrise this morning."

"He was found floating in the bay this morning with his throat slit and his purse gone. I understand you pulled a knife on him."

"To get his attention and stop his attack, yes, sir." She carefully reached into her boot and pulled out her knife to hand to him.

He took the knife to inspect it closely. "You said there was another man with him?"

"Yes sir, they both appeared to be traveling together, and had been drinking before they arrived at the hotel."

"Could you describe what he looked like?"

"Not a big man," she replied, lifting her hand to shoulder height. "He wore a scruffy brown beard and hair. Looked like he'd been on the trail a while, too."

"You just came in off the trail, too, is that correct?"

"Yes, sir. My father and I have been trapping along the border for the last nine months. We come here to trade our pelts with Smithy and to ride out the winter."

"Where is your father?"

"Dead." She hung her head. "He was mauled by a bear and died from the wounds."

"I'm sorry for your loss. The hotel owner backs up your story and says you never left the hotel last night. I may have other questions for you. Do you have plans to leave town?"

"I've just rented the old Johnson place for four months, so I'll be living there."

"I know of the place. Have a good evening, ma'am." He handed her knife to her and tipped his hat before stepping off the porch.

Nat finished her cider and retired for the evening. After a hearty breakfast in the morning, she and her traveling companions would move into the Johnson place and she would begin preparing their home for the winter. Her mind whirled with plans, prioritizing the tasks she would need to complete in the next few days. She walked over to the window and peered out to see that the snow had almost completely stopped. Hopeful that the first heavy snows would hold off for a few days, she yawned before curling up on the comfortable bed and drifting off to sleep.

✝

The next morning, Nat packed up her goods before heading down for breakfast. She was pleased to see that Marissa had returned to the dining room and decided that she must work most mornings, which Nat felt was a great way for her to start her own day.

Marissa approached her table with a warm smile. "What can I get you this morning?"

"Why don't you surprise us." Nat grinned as Marissa poured her a cup of coffee.

"Not a problem." Marissa spun around and headed to the kitchen.

Marissa returned a few minutes later carrying a steaming platter of fried eggs, bacon, and fried potatoes, along with a small plate with the same combination for Gyp. She set the plates down in front of Nat and Gyp and watched as the two devoured the food.

"This is fantastic," Nat praised, and Gyp raised her head long enough to lick her lips.

"I thought you might want something hearty. It's really cool outside this morning and this should help to keep you warm."

"This is exactly what we needed. We'll be moving into the Johnson place today so we have lots of chores to do."

"So we will be neighbors then," Marissa stated.

"Looks that way," Nat responded with a smile.

"I get off later this afternoon. Would you mind if I stopped in to check on you?"

"No, not at all. Feel free to visit anytime," Nat told her as she gobbled down another mouthful of the food.

"Okay then, since you'll be busy, why don't I stop by with some supper," Marissa suggested.

"That sounds delicious." Nat wiped the corner of her mouth. "From the looks of the weather I'm a few days behind in preparing for winter, so I won't take time to cook."

"I'll see you later today then." Marissa turned to walk back to the kitchen.

Nat finished her meal and then went to the desk to pay her bill before returning to gather her packs. Marissa was in the dining room when she walked down the stairs and Nat tipped her hat before leaving the building. Nat walked to the livery, paid her bill, then saddled Hardy and her father's mount, Buck, and packed her bags on Quincy. Nat mounted Hardy and they rode out of town as the sun was rising.

✝

It was a brisk twenty-minute walk to the Johnson place that morning, and Nat watched Gyp run ahead of her chasing different scents, but always returning to her. Nat thought that after they settled in the cabin for a few days, she and Gyp would do some hunting so she could begin her training.

Nat tied Hardy and Buck to a porch post, and unloaded the packs from Quincy, carrying them into the cabin before taking the animals into the barn. Nat unsaddled them and let the two horses and the mule out into a small pasture to allow them to graze on the remaining few patches of grass. Nat searched the woodbin and found barely enough wood to start a fire in the hearth. That would be her first task, to set in as much firewood as she could before the weather turned miserable. She could work on the inside of the cabin after sunset and in the dreary days ahead.

Nat took out her axe and walked into the woods behind the cabin. She didn't have to travel far before she located several fallen trees that were large enough to provide a good start to her stash. She took her coat off and began chopping the trees into three-foot sections, trimming the smaller branches and tossing them into a separate pile.

Nat worked for several hours before taking a break. Gathering an armful of the smaller branches, she walked back to the cabin and placed them on the edge of the porch. Stepping inside she picked up the water bucket and dipper and went to the well to pump a bucket of fresh cold water. Taking a long drink, Nat sat for a moment on the steps to take in the beauty of the fading morning. Clouds were rolling in and Nat felt sure they would receive more snow tonight. Prompted by the ominous clouds, she returned to the woods and began carrying logs back to the cabin.

Nat was busy splitting logs when Marissa arrived. Her quiet approach allowed her to watch Nat for several minutes. Nat had removed her work shirt while she split the logs and Marissa watched the ripple of muscles on Nat's back as she expertly chopped the wood into sections small enough to fit into the fireplace. For several minutes, she admired Nat's handsome features until Gyp walked around the edge of the cabin and saw Marissa. A short bark alerted Nat that she had company and she turned to find Marissa standing twenty feet away.

"Sorry, I didn't hear you come up." Nat laid her axe down and reached for her work shirt.

"I can be quiet at times," Marissa answered with a grin before walking up to Nat holding a picnic basket.

"It's good to see you again." Nat returned her smile.

"Why don't you continue here and I'll go in and get our meal set up and then come get you," Marissa suggested.

"You have a deal. I'm anxious to get some of the wood in today."

Marissa watched Nat stack a large pile of wood near the front door before stacking a pile of the logs at the south end of the cabin, away from the worst of the impending bad weather.

Marissa went into the cabin and placed her basket on the table before arranging a meal of fried chicken, biscuits, and cheese. She found plates and cups in the pack that Nat had set down near the kitchen so the table was soon set. She stepped out onto the porch and bent down to pick up the water bucket just as Nat stepped onto the porch.

"I'll get that." Nat reached for the bucket and, for a second, their fingers touched. Nat felt a bolt of electricity surge through her and, from the startled look on Marissa's face, Nat was sure she felt it also.

Marissa turned and held the door open as Nat carried the bucket and set it down on the table.

Surveying the meal Marissa had laid out for them, Nat said, "This looks fantastic."

"Just some leftovers from today's special, but I thought it would work."

"I'll take this kind of leftovers any day." Nat poured them both a mug of water.

Just as they were about to sit down to their meal, Nat heard hoof beats in the front yard and looked out to see a wagon from the general store bringing her supplies. *What horrible timing.* "Sit tight for a few minutes and I'll be right back."

Nat walked out to the yard to greet Jess who was making the delivery. "Let's just set these on the porch and I'll take them in later. Will you put the horse feed and hay in the barn for me?"

"Not a problem." The young man picked up the first of the large feed sacks and carried it into the barn as Nat started unloading the boxes of household supplies.

Ten minutes later, Jess headed back to town, allowing Nat and Marissa to finally sit down to the meal. "Oh, wait, I forgot something." Marissa stood and walked to the hearth to retrieve a jar of gravy warming by the fire.

"Now I know you are trying to spoil us." Nat picked up a biscuit and crumbled it into Gyp's bowl, added a few small chunks of cheese before pouring some of the rich brown gravy across the mixture. She set the bowl down in front of Gyp.

"You do love that dog, don't you?" Marissa asked.

"I guess you could say that." Nat patted Gyp's head. "She's all the family I have left. Go ahead, girl." She smiled as Gyp dug into her meal.

Nat picked out a drumstick and took a bite out of it, moaning loudly at the succulent taste, and then picked up a biscuit, broke it open, and poured gravy across it. She looked up to see Marissa watching her as she cut the biscuit with her fork before slipping a chunk past her lips. "Okay, that settles it. I'm sending you a bag of flour a week so you can make gravy and biscuits too."

A huge smile covered Marissa's face. "You know it is easier to cook for two, so you are welcome anytime." Marissa blushed.

"Careful or we will be at your door every day," Nat teased.

"I wouldn't mind that at all."

Several moments passed while Nat contemplated the last few statements and whether to make the next move. She was surprised when Marissa spoke.

"We could do some bartering here if you are interested," Marissa suggested.

"What did you have in mind," Nat asked slyly.

"Well, for starters, you need help putting in your supplies and setting up the house and I could use more firewood than what I have managed to collect. I noticed you were very handy with your axe and I'm pretty good in the kitchen, so why don't I help you tonight and you can cut me some firewood?"

"Hmmm, that doesn't sound like too bad of a deal, especially since you threw in this wonderful meal." Nat grinned.

"To sweeten the deal, I'll even toss in use of my bathtub at any time you want," Marissa added.

"Okay you got me with that one," Nat admitted. "Even if I do have to heat my own water."

"No sense in two women struggling if they can work together to make life easier for themselves."

"That's very true and besides, I smell much better after a nice hot soaking bath."

Having that issue settled they finished their meal in relative silence.

Nat then headed out to the barn to harness Quincy while Marissa remained inside to start on the kitchen. She led Quincy into the woods and used his strength to drag three large trees up to the cabin where she could chop them into lengths for splitting and minimize the amount of carrying she would have to do.

As Nat began her rhythmic chopping, Marissa hummed while clearing off the plates from their meal. Once done, she began putting away the stores of supplies delivered that afternoon. She smiled at Gyp trotting back and forth between the kitchen and the yard, following Marissa as she checked on Nat.

Nat removed her shirt as she chopped and hung it on the porch railing once again exposing the strength of her upper torso. Marissa would stop to watch her work for a few minutes before carrying in each box of supplies. She was amazed at how fluidly Nat moved, and took a moment to watch the sweat begin to soak through the undershirt and run down her arms. While Marissa sorted through the contents of the last box, she allowed her mind to wander, and imagined what it might feel like, wrapped in those strong arms. Marissa had loved her husband deeply, but even he failed to make her feel the way she did when Nat smiled at her, or the way her skin burned whenever they touched. Marissa had tried at first to deny her attraction to Nat, but fate would have its way with them, of that she was certain.

Marissa finished in the kitchen and moved to the small bedroom. She covered the feather mattress with the new linens Nat had purchased and then laid a fire in the hearth, lighting it to add some warmth to the room. She placed a small oil lamp on the table next to the bed and set the packs, which held Nat's personal belongings on the bed. Content with what she had accomplished, Marissa packed up her picnic basket and walked out onto the porch.

Sitting on the rail, she watched Nat work methodically. *She's such a natural for outdoor work,* Marissa thought as she observed her. Hard as she tried, she couldn't see Nat happy working inside all day, and yet it was difficult to imagine her spending months secluded in the woods while she trapped. Marissa sighed, louder than she had intended and caught Nat's attention.

"I have your kitchen and bedroom prepared." Marissa smiled broadly.

"Thank you. Tomorrow I'll go to your place and start on your firewood."

"There's no hurry. I have plenty to get me started."

"Understood, but a bargain is a bargain. Besides, after all this wood cutting I'll be in need of another bath." Nat grinned wiping her brow.

The sun was starting to fade so Nat stopped chopping. She stacked the wood she had cut while Marissa carried several pieces in to stoke the fires in the bedroom and the kitchen. "I will be home by midafternoon tomorrow and will bring us a light dinner." Marissa turned to leave then turned back. "I left a plate of food in the kitchen for you if you get hungry later."

Marissa gave Nat a gentle hug of thanks before leaving to walk the short distance to her home. Once there, she spent the evening straightening up her cabin in expectation of Nat's visit. Lying in bed that evening, she thought about how much they had in common. Both had suffered the loss of someone they loved and both were struggling to make their way in the world. Just as they had similarities, they also had their differences. Nat was tall, and well built, with a rugged handsomeness about her, while Marissa was more petite and better suited for more delicate work. *A good complement to each other* was her last thought before drifting off, with the feeling of Nat's arms wrapped around her ushering her into a deep sleep.

Nat sat in one of the cane-backed chairs and pulled off her well-worn boots. The physical exertion of the day felt good to her and she knew sleep would come easily tonight. She would be up ahead of the sun tomorrow to begin the routine all over again. Nat stood and took her boots with her into the bedroom, which was lit only by the small fire in the hearth. Using a piece of straw, she lit the small oil lamp and sat it beside the bed once again, unpacking her belongings and storing them safely away.

She noticed the bear pelt sitting on a chair and she decided that she would wash it thoroughly to get the wild smell from it, and then she would use it to warm her bed in the coming winter months. She made a mental note to pick up some fragrant soap on her next trip to town as she changed into a sleep shirt and slipped between the cool covers. Gyp jumped up on the bed and lay down near the foot of the bed, and within minutes, both weary travelers slept an exhausted sleep.

Chapter Four

The next morning, Nat shared the remaining chicken with Gyp and then poured some of her honey over the remaining biscuits. Washing her meal down with cool water, Nat dressed and began chopping wood as the sun slowly rose.

Nat worked for several hours, chopping wood and stacking it at the end of the cabin. By noon she had a sizeable pile, and was satisfied that she would have enough for at least a couple of months. Axe in hand, Nat went to the barn and hooked up Quincy, and together they walked to Marissa's home.

Nat reviewed the pile of wood and noted that Marissa was severely short of the split solid wood that would burn for hours. Nat made a small pile next to Marissa's door and then headed to the woods with Quincy.

She felled several large trees and, after trimming the branches, she cut the tree into sections small enough for Quincy to pull. Nat went to work on the sections, cutting the hardwood into lengths to split and was busily splitting the wood when Marissa came home.

"My, you have been busy." Marissa set her basket on the porch and bent down to pet Gyp.

"Just getting started." Nat stopped swinging the axe, and walked over to the porch and sat down. She picked up a file and began to sharpen the blade, careful to stroke the metal with even passes to bring it to a thin edge.

"Are you hungry?"

"Not too bad. You?" Nat responded. "I'd like to finish up here first if you don't mind."

"I don't mind at all." Marissa stood and started carrying the split wood over to the pile Nat had started and placed it on the stack. "You split and I'll stack."

"Fair enough." Nat resumed placing the large logs on a stump and splitting them into smaller chunks.

Two hours later, they finished splitting and stacking the wood. Marissa had an ample supply for the first few months of winter. She sat down on the porch, obviously winded from the physical labor.

Nat sat beside her and offered her a cup of cool water pumped from the well. "Here, this will help."

"Thanks." Marissa took the offering, savoring the cool water and taking it in small sips. "That is really hard work."

Nat looked at her, concerned that she might have become overheated. "It's just like anything else," Nat replied. "Takes some getting used to is all."

"Now I understand how you can eat like a horse and still remain slim." Marissa spoke softly.

Nat chuckled. "Dad always said work like a horse and eat like a horse so I guess he was right."

"Did he also mention anything about smelling like a horse?" Marissa wiped the sweat from her brow.

"That just comes naturally with hard work." Nat offered her hand to lift Marissa to her feet. "If you want to get supper ready, I'll take Quincy home and feed the animals."

"Don't forget to pick up some clean clothes so you can have the bath I promised you," Marissa reminded her.

"Oh, I haven't forgotten." Nat returned with a smile, and she left the porch heading for her home.

Marissa carried her basket into the cabin and set the containers of food on the hearth to begin slowly warming them. She ran a length of cord across the back room where the bathtub was located and placed a large sheet over it to allow Nat some privacy while she bathed. Marissa carried several large buckets of water, and dumped them into the tub, then began heating the water for bathing. A large container would be heating while they ate. When mixed with the water already in the tub, it should be enough to get Nat started on her bath while Marissa heated up another large container. Marissa placed a few dry logs in the fireplace, stoking the embers to heat the water faster.

Her mind drifted to the morning on her way to work and she remembered seeing Nat splitting wood. She could hear the rhythmic thuds made by each stroke of Nat's axe and smiled, envisioning the taut muscles that were rippling underneath Nat's shirt. Marissa quickened her pace eager for the workday to end. Now she couldn't wait for Nat to arrive.

Nat fed the animals and placed them in the barn for the evening. Snow had begun to tumble from the sky and she wanted her dear companions to be as protected from the elements as possible. She rummaged through an old pack that held soft, warm blankets, and covered each of the animals with another layer of protection. She then went into her cabin and located a set of clean clothing, a towel, and soap before heading back to Marissa's cabin.

Knocking on the door, Nat stood with hat in hand until Marissa opened the door.

"That was quick," Marissa said before guiding Nat to the kitchen. Marissa handed Nat the bucket and she compliantly walked out to the pump to draw a fresh bucket of drinking water.

When she returned, Marissa had the food set out on the table and took the bucket from her. She doled out cups of the chilly water for them. Marissa looked around the room and asked, "Where is Gyp?"

"She is waiting out on the porch. She hasn't been invited in yet." Her tone was deadly serious.

"Have you lost your mind? It's cold out there and you should know that Gyp is more than welcome in my home."

"It's not polite to assume anything." Nat let a mischievous grin curve her lips.

Marissa flung open the door and called to Gyp who trotted politely into the cabin and came to rest in front of the warm hearth. Marissa dipped out a large portion of pot roast, vegetables, and gravy for Gyp, breaking off chunks of corn bread and mixing it in with the rest. She carried the full bowl over to the dog and set it in front of her. Gyp licked her hand in warm appreciation for the meal. Marissa sat at the table and joined Nat at the table.

"How are you set for meat?" Nat asked while they were eating.

"I don't eat that much meat, and what I do I usually buy in town. We have a great smokehouse, but I just don't have the skills to hunt or the knowledge to cure meat."

"Well, it just so happens that your new neighbor is an expert at both, and if you will allow her, she can teach you."

"I just hope she has the patience of Job."

"I think she can manage one student." Nat smiled at Marissa. "I was hoping to do some hunting tomorrow afternoon if you would care to join me," Nat suggested. "I have seen signs that there is a rather large buck in the area that would put an ample amount of meat in your smokehouse for this winter."

"I do miss the taste of venison," Marissa admitted. "Thank you. I'd like to join you in the hunt."

Nat smiled. "I'll look forward to it."

"The first vat of water should be plenty hot enough to start your bath. Why don't you dump it into the tub and then get a fresh vat warming over the fire while the hot mixes with the cool and I'll clean up from supper."

Nat stood and followed Marissa's directions to the letter and then disappeared behind the makeshift curtain. She stripped off her clothes and lowered herself into the hot water. Nat slipped completely under the water, and emerged with her black hair draped along her neckline and began bathing, listening to Marissa bustling in the kitchen.

"Are you ready for some more hot water?" she yelled.

"Yes, please, whenever you get a chance," Nat responded, then once again ducked under the water to rinse her hair.

Marissa went to the hearth to retrieve the water and stepped quietly behind the bed sheet drape. Nat again made no effort to hide her nakedness. Marissa blushed profusely when Nat caught her gaze as she looked down at her. Marissa poured the hot water slowly to mix with the warm water left in the tub. "Would you like me to wash your back?"

"That would be lovely." Nat handed Marissa a soaped cloth.

When Marissa stroked the cloth across Nat's back in large circular motions, Nat felt herself relaxing fully under the caresses. Marissa finished and handed Nat back the cloth.

"You know there's plenty of room for one more in this tub." Nat had a hint of challenge in her voice.

Marissa stopped dead in her tracks. "Excuse me?"

"I said there is plenty of room if you would care to join me," Nat called out a little louder to tease Marissa.

"A nice soak would feel good." Marissa turned away. "Are you sure you wouldn't mind?"

"Not at all," Nat replied with a sultry smile.

Marissa, beginning to unbutton her dress, stood with her back to Nat before allowing it to fall from her shoulders and down her body.

Nat's heart raced as she watched the fabric drop and Marissa's milky white skin and soft curves come into view. She could feel a stone choking off her voice as Marissa pulled her blonde hair into a knot, turned, and stepped into the tub. Nat caught a glimpse of full breasts and the light down that was nestled between Marissa's thighs. She slowly sank into the hot water careful not to crowd her much longer body. Nat witnessed Marissa's distress on where to rest her feet and legs. She softly told Marissa, "You can rest your legs on mine."

Marissa gingerly lowered her legs onto Nat's and then laid her head back against the tub. "This does feel wonderful." Nat watched the warm water enclose her in its caress.

"A welcome reward after a long day of hard work." Nat watched Marissa relax. "I bet your feet ache something miserable after standing on them all day." Nat tenderly placed Marissa's right foot between her large hands, massaging it gently. As Nat's strong thumbs kneaded the sole of Marissa's foot she moaned softly and closed her eyes.

Nat watched the pulse throb wildly in Marissa's neck as she slowly lowered her mouth to softly kiss the tips of Marissa's toes. Marissa gasped before her eyes flew open. Nat watched her eyes clouding over with pleasure, each subsequent stroke of her tongue and lips bringing undeniable desire to Marissa's gently quivering body. "Are you chilled?" Nat asked innocently.

"Oh, for God's sake, no," Marissa stammered looking deeply into Nat's dark eyes. "Can you not possibly know how you are affecting me?" she whispered.

"Tell me." Nat let her lips caress Marissa's big toe.

"Your touch makes me burn with desire," she admitted. "A desire that is unnatural between two women, and yet I find myself drowning in need to be touched and caressed by you. You must think me crazy." Marissa's voice was full of concern.

"If it is madness then it is one that we share together." Nat ran her tongue along the toe before looking up. "Since our eyes first touched, I have wanted to take you in my arms and hold you close, and I ache to feel the touch of you against my skin."

Nat smiled as Marissa stared at her. "You've described exactly how I feel better than any words I can use about my own feelings." Marissa noticeably shivered. "We need to dry off before we catch a chill." She stood to step from the tub.

Nat stepped from the tub and let Marissa wrap her in a thick, warm towel before tying another around her waist. Reaching for an edge of the towel Marissa dried her hair before combing the thick black hair away from her face. Once done, she led Nat over to stand in front of the fireplace to take the chill from her.

A schoolgirl awkwardness threatened to overcome Nat as she reached down to take Marissa's chin in her fingertips before raising her eyes up to meet her own. The need in Marissa's deep blue eyes urged Nat forward and she bent down to place her lips against Marissa. Nat's head spun with the excitement of her first kiss. Her mind began racing

33

wildly when Marissa parted her lips and encircled Nat's tongue with her own.

Marissa's moans vibrated deep into Nat's mouth, causing her to shudder with spasms of need as her inexperienced body shook with pleasure. The kiss lasted for what seemed hours. They softly probed each other's mouth while their hands began to caress as they explored one another.

Marissa broke the kiss and took Nat by the hand, leading her through the small cabin into the bedroom where she pulled back the heavy covers on the bed. Her hands removed the large towel from Nat's waist, dropping it to the floor while admiring Nat's strong body. She gently guided Nat back onto the bed and then dropped her own towel and crawled into the bed beside her.

Nat rolled onto her side, propping on an elbow, and Marissa could feel Nat's eyes caressing her. She patiently watched Nat's eyes slowly survey the curves and valleys that Marissa knew were so different from the hard edges of Nat's figure. When Nat bent down, the bear claw lightly grazed Marissa's skin, raising goose bumps on her flesh. Nat's fingers traveled down Marissa's excited skin from her face, down her neck and chest, and further down her to the extent of Nat's reach, the path of her fingers burning a trail of blazing desire in Marissa.

Marissa pushed Nat back onto the bed, covering her mouth with a slow sensual kiss. Her fingers began to explore the firm angles of Nat's body, from her strong chin down to her small but muscular chest to the ripples of muscles across her abdomen. She knew that Nat was aching to be touched down in the hot, wet space between her thighs. It was the exact spot Marissa took painstaking care to avoid with her soft caresses. Instead, her fingertips brushed lightly over Nat's hardened nipples, knowing that her kisses were threatening to steal the breath from Nat's lungs.

Marissa trembled with the excitement rushing through her as she moved to lie partially on top of Nat. Nat's hands brushed through her hair and down her back as Marissa kissed her way down Nat's face and neck until her soft lips were only inches from Nat's erect nipple. She let hot puffs of breath tickle Nat's sensitive skin as she approached and then covered her small breast with her warm, soft mouth. While she slowly sucked Nat's breast, she let her hand slip between Nat's thighs before her fingers played in the soft wet curls.

Nat's breathing labored with each new movement from Marissa, and when she was finally touched between her legs, Nat feared she would faint from sheer anticipation. Marissa's fingers traced the same trail that Nat's had followed, discovering her blossoming womanhood, but the combination of Marissa's mouth on her breast and her fingers caressing her wetness were beyond anything Nat had ever experienced.

Nat could feel the tremors growing uncontrollably, deep within her, as Marissa's fingers parted the soft hair and her fingers slid deep into Nat's opening while her teeth nibbled on her sensitive nipple. Combinations of moans echoed through the small bedroom as Marissa's movements brought Nat to her first climax, her muscles convulsing in violent spasms, her mind reeling with pleasure.

Marissa removed her fingers slowly, and Nat watched her trace her lips with fingers damp from Nat's juices. Moving back up her body, Marissa covered Nat's mouth with another slow gentle kiss, sharing the taste with her lover for the first of many times to come.

Nat could feel the need vibrating through Marissa and rolled over on top of her. Using Marissa's example, she slowly explored the soft, contours of her lover's body. Marissa's cries of pleasure at first scared Nat, who feared she was hurting the woman, but soon enough the sounds became music to her ears and Marissa exploded in orgasm.

Nat lay beside Marissa and watched her breathing slow, her eyes communicating to her what Marissa's lips were unable to speak. Nat softly kissed her exhausted lover on the lips and then turned her on her side pulling the covers up over their bodies and wrapping her arm tightly around Marissa, holding her close as they quietly drifted into sleep.

Chapter Five

The next morning, Nat awoke to soft lips on her neck and she stretched her arms above her head and engulfed Marissa in her arms. Marissa moved on top of Nat and her lips softly caressed Nat's, welcoming her lover awake. She traced the outline of Nat's lips with her tongue, teasing her as her hips began to grind into Nat. Nat placed her large hands on Marissa's ass and held her close. Her own hips began to match her lover's rhythm. Nat's tongue reached out to meet Marissa, tip to tip, and their arousal continued to mount.

Marissa's hands moved down between their bodies and her fingers tugged gently at her nipples, which grew hard as her moans began to resonate. The heat generated by their bodies made Nat begin to sweat and she kicked the covers from atop their bodies as Marissa kissed down Nat's neck and her mouth covered her right breast. Marissa's tongue swirled around her arousal-darkened areola, twitching with excitement. Marissa's right hand cupped Nat's breast and she squeezed the small mound of excited flesh as Nat began to writhe underneath her.

Marissa, enraptured by the sensations of making love to Nat, knew this time that she would taste her lover. Her mouth blazed a trail of desire down Nat's body, and when her tongue reached the inside of Nat's thigh, she caught the scent of desire and her need to taste her grew unbearable. Marissa used her fingertips to part Nat's soaked lips and closely examined the soft folds of exposed flesh as she looked upon a woman for the first time. The tender touches of her fingers were driving Nat wild, and the small bud normally hidden between the soft folds had grown erect with blood, and Marissa stroked the top of it with her tongue. Nat's hands grabbed the bed linens as Marissa's warm breath teased her and her tongue lavished attention on her.

Marissa moaned at the alluring taste of Nat's desire and she hungered for more. Her tongue stroked the damp edges of Nat's entrance, making her tremble before her tongue probed deeper, entering the spring of Nat's wetness. She buried her face between Nat's thighs, feasting on her lover.

Violent convulsions ripped through Nat. Feeling the most unbelievable sensations of her life, she gasped for breath as Marissa continued to drink greedily from her. Nat erupted again and she coated her lover's face with her juices.

Nat pulled Marissa back up her body and tasted herself on her lover's lips when their mouths locked again in a fevered kiss. She rolled their bodies on the bed until she rested on top of Marissa pressing herself between Marissa's thighs and feeling the heat and the growing moisture. She was eager for Marissa to experience the overwhelming pleasure she had just felt, and she slowly kissed her way down her body.

When her mouth hovered above Marissa's mound, Marissa groaned and spread her thighs wider, inviting Nat to take her. Nat spread her soaked lips with trembling fingers, gazing at the beautiful flower that opened up to welcome her.

She bent her head forward, and traced the outer ridges and moaned loudly when the sweet taste of Marissa exploded in her mouth. Her tongue explored every inch of Marissa's outer folds and when she slid her tongue inside her opening, she felt the silky lining inside Marissa, and her mouth pressed deeper with her teeth grazing the swollen bud that was throbbing with pleasure. Marissa erupted, soaking Nat's face and grinding her hips onto Nat's waiting mouth. Nat's tongue continued to explore the depths of Marissa as her thumb brushed over the swollen bud and Marissa continued to writhe, gasping for breath as Nat brought her to peak after peak of pleasure. Marissa reached down, placed her hands on either side of her head, and lifted Nat's mouth to hers.

Nat lay beside Marissa looked at her lover with a grin making her dark eyes shimmer. "That was incredible." Her fingers slid up Marissa, raising goose flesh in their wake.

Marissa shivered. "That was the most passionate I have ever felt," she admitted. "There is something that draws me to you and I want to touch and kiss you all the time." A deep blush covered Marissa's face.

"Well I don't mind if you do." Nat felt suddenly very giddy and mischievous. Her fingertips drew small circles around Marissa's left nipple while licking her lips.

Marissa's breathing quickened and her heart was racing in her chest as she watched Nat's eyes devour her. Nat looked up and smiled, her hand creeping down, and her fingers slowly entering Marissa. She bit her lip to keep from crying out when three of Nat's long fingers sank deeply into her and touched a part of her abandoned for so long. Nat's fingers moved slowly in the velvety liquid and Marissa thrust her hips to meet Nat's fingers as desire filled her.

Nat's fingers drove faster to match the movement of her body and Marissa's cries of pleasure seemed to spur Nat on until she shuddered and her climax soaked the bed linens. Nat, sharing a kiss, kept her fingers inside and Marissa felt the muscles deep inside wrap around Nat's fingers. Her climax lingered. The slightest movement from her sent waves of pleasure through her and it was several more minutes before she relaxed enough to allow Nat to withdraw.

"I will not be able to walk if we don't get out of this bed soon." Marissa groaned and rolled over on top of Nat.

"Do you have to work today?" The sun had just started to rise.

"Yes, but only until lunch and then I'm off tomorrow." Her fingers played in Nat's hair.

"I'll do some work around the house then, and when you return, we'll go hunting if you wish."

"I have never been hunting before. You'll have to teach me."

"I can do that." Nat climbed from the bed to retrieve the fresh clothes from the kitchen table. She was walking stiffly but Marissa could see a big grin on her face. She was still smiling when she returned to the room to get dressed.

"That is a beautiful smile you are wearing."

"You make me feel beautiful." Nat slipped on her dungarees and then bent down to pull on her socks.

Marissa reached up and pulled Nat back onto the bed. "In case you haven't noticed, you are beautiful." She kissed her softly on the lips.

Nat was still naked from the waist up and Marissa needed tremendous restraint to keep from covering one of her breasts with her mouth to resume their lovemaking. Instead, she kissed her again and then climbed from the comfort of the bed and began to dress for work. She poured a basin of water to freshen up and then pulled on a soft cotton dress, knowing that Nat was watching her closely from the bed.

"Dress warmly today; there is snow in the air." Nat sat up and pulled an undershirt over her head, then placed her arms through the sleeves of her work shirt.

"I'm sorry I don't have time to cook you breakfast." Marissa blushed.

"The breakfast you gave me was plenty to hold me until lunch." Nat grinned wickedly.

"Would you mind if Gyp and I walk you into town?" Nat asked.

"I would love that. If you'd like, I can cook you breakfast after all."

"Well, I did work up an appetite from all our activity and I do want to spend more time with you." She looked at Gyp. "Are you hungry?" Gyp let out a short bark. "Well, I guess we are going to breakfast then." Nat chuckled and walked to the door. "Stop by the house when you are ready." Nat kissed Marissa softly. "I'll grab a coat and be ready when you get there."

"I'll be ready in just a few minutes," Marissa promised. Nat opened the door to a brisk wind swirling into the house.

†

Nat and Gyp walked the short distance to their home and were glad to get inside away from the chilling wind. She stirred the embers in the fireplace and tossed a few logs on them to keep the interior of the cabin warm. She walked into the bedroom and pulled her range coat over her shoulders, picked up a small coin purse, and tucked it away in her pocket. She looked over at the chair where the bear pelt sat and her thoughts went to her father. Today she would buy the lye soap to boil the pelt in. This would rid the fur of the wild smell and prepare it to provide warmth for her bed for the coming winter months.

With that thought in mind, she walked out to the front yard with Gyp and she laid a small fire that she would build to boil the pelt. She was kneeling down when Marissa walked into the yard. She looked up at the sound of her approach, and her dark eyes locked onto Marissa from beneath the brim of her hat. Nat scowled when she saw the shawl that draped around Marissa's shoulders, knowing the garment was not heavy enough to keep the small woman warm in the bitter wind. She would have to take care of that when she made it into town.

"Are you two ready to go?"

"Yes, ma'am, just waiting on you." Gyp sprang to her feet as they headed into town.

Gyp trotted ahead of them and dashed off the road following the scent of some animal that had passed through earlier. Nat smiled at the young dog, nearly full grown, who had proved to be a dear companion to her since her father's death. They walked together in silence and Gyp joined them just when they entered town.

"I have a few things to buy at the general store, but we'll stop by in just a few minutes."

Marissa, with her cheeks flushed from the chilly wind, gave her a brilliant smile. "I'll have some hot coffee waiting for you."

39

Nat returned her smile and watched Marissa walking toward the hotel before disappearing inside. "Let's go, Gyp," she said, and they walked down the street to the general store.

✝

Inside, the general store, Nat found a box of lye soap flakes and then went to the clothing section. She found a pair of dungarees and a wool sweater that should fit Marissa. It wasn't long before she found a buckskin coat with a lamb's wool lining that would work well to keep Marissa warm when they went hunting, and when she was walking to and from work. The merchant wrapped her purchases for her and Nat was on her way.

Gyp waited for her at the door, and rose to her feet when Nat emerged from the store carrying her package. They walked to the hotel and found a seat in the dining room. Marissa's smile lit the room when she walked from the kitchen to see them sitting in the dining room. She carried a mug of coffee over to her table. "What may I fix you two for breakfast this morning?"

"Have you got biscuits in the oven yet?" Nat asked.

"Yes, I do."

"Well, we worked up quite an appetite yesterday, so how about eggs, bacon, and some fried potatoes for starters, and then when the biscuits are done, some biscuits and gravy."

"I do love your appetites." Marissa had a slight blush as she turned to walk back into the kitchen.

Nat watched her go and was amazed at how much she craved Marissa. Nat had never had someone affect her so profoundly, and she felt a warm rush throughout her whenever she looked at Marissa. She sipped her coffee and pondered her thoughts while waiting for Marissa to return with steaming platters of food.

She and Gyp were the only patrons so far, so when Marissa brought out their food she sat with them while they ate. The impending weather must have kept the normal breakfast crowd tucked away inside the warmth of their homes. Nat enjoyed the quiet time spent with Marissa.

Nat and Gyp finished eating, and Gyp had placed her head in Marissa's lap while she and Nat talked. Nat watched Marissa's hand stroke Gyp's head and she remembered her soft touch as Marissa caressed her earlier that morning, and she felt the butterflies take flight in her stomach.

Nat paid for their meal and, with a short good-bye, she and Gyp walked back to the cabin.

✝

Nat placed the package on the small kitchen table and stoked the fire before returning outside, the box of soap flakes in her hand. She fastened a large metal pot above the fire pit and lit the kindling to start the fire. She made several trips to the well for buckets of water and, when she was satisfied, she poured the chips into the water and waited for it to boil. She walked into the bedroom and picked up the pelt. She carried it out to the fire and placed it in the pot of boiling water. Gyp sat next to her on the front porch, her head in her lap as they watched the snowflakes begin to slowly fall.

Nat's fingers were buried in Gyp's fur relaxing and allowing her thoughts to drift back to the day of her father's death. Her heart still felt the ache of his loss, but she knew that her father was watching over her and she took comfort in the love they had shared. Once she felt the pelt had boiled enough to remove the wild smell, Nat took a thick branch and lifted the pelt from the water. She carried it over and hung it over the railing of the porch to dry. She dumped the wash pot and refilled it with fresh water, and watched plumes of smoke rising into the chilled air.

Nat and Gyp returned to the cabin, added wood to the fireplace in the main room and in the bedroom. She felt weary and stretched before laying down on the bed for a short nap while she waited for Marissa. Gyp jumped up to lie at her feet. Within minutes, Nat had drifted off to sleep and she rested peacefully with Gyp warming her feet.

A low growl from Gyp alerted Nat to the presence of a visitor, cutting her nap short. She was not expecting company. She sat up in the bed, slipped on her boots, and reached for her rifle before heading to the door.

Nat opened the front door and recognized the Marshall riding into her yard. She closed the door behind her and propped her rifle on the doorframe. "Good day, Marshall."

"Nice to see you again, Miss St.Croix." His eyes were surveying the property and, when they landed on the large pile of firewood, he smiled. "You've been very busy."

"I was in desperate need of firewood before the snow starts falling in earnest. What can I do for you?"

He stepped down off his horse and looked even larger than their previous meeting. He approached the front porch. "May I have a drink of water?"

"Yes, you may. Have a seat and I'll draw a bucket." She picked up the bucket and walked past him as he stepped onto the porch. When she returned, she drew the dipper through the cold water and handed it to him.

"Thanks." He took a long drink and handed her the dipper. "Nothing like fresh, cold water."

"No there isn't, but I doubt if you rode out here for a drink."

"You're correct. I wanted to ride out personally, to let you know you've been cleared of any suspicion for killing the miner in town." He locked his cold grey eyes on her. "An eyewitness came forth to testify he saw the dead man and his traveling companion in an argument shortly after they stumbled out of the saloon. He watched them as the argument grew and then saw the flash of a knife. His companion slashed his throat and robbed him of his purse before dragging him to the bay."

"I had no doubt of my innocence, but I appreciate you coming out to inform me. Is his killer still in town?"

"No, I imagine he's well south of here by now, but I've alerted other lawmen to be on the lookout for him. I hope you understand the suspicion was just a part of the investigation."

"I can understand that. I think our run-in was a horrible coincidence, especially since he was killed by a knife, and I was new in town. I'm glad you were able to clear my name though." She smiled.

"I didn't expect you to have been guilty, but I had to follow all the leads."

"Yes, you had to be thorough."

"Well, thank you for the cold drink of water." He stood and looked up at the sky. "The weather's changing quickly now isn't it?"

"I think we'll be getting snow again soon," she answered.

"Stay safe out here." He stepped off the porch.

"I plan to do my best." She watched him swing into the saddle. "Stay warm and dry."

"Yes, ma'am." He grinned and tipped his hat, before turning his horse back to town.

Nat returned to her nap, slipping into a deep sleep and drifted down into the world of dreams. Nat dreamt of the previous night with Marissa and the pleasure they had shared. In her mind, the sounds and tastes of their lovemaking remained vivid and she moaned softly in her sleep. Gyp moved up beside her master and Nat's hand moved down to softly stroke the young dog's fur.

Chapter Six

Marissa returned just after lunch and noticed the freshly washed bear hide stretched across the porch railing to dry, and she winced remembering the pain Nat endured over the death of her father. She walked to the door and knocked softly.

Marissa listened carefully for an answer and when none came, she pushed the door open and stepped into the warmth of Nat's cabin. She walked farther inside and saw Nat and Gyp in the bedroom asleep with Nat's fingers wrapped deeply in Gyp's soft fur. She stepped on a loose floorboard and the sound of the creak made Gyp raise her head. Gyp jumped from the bed to greet her, licking her hand with a soft warm tongue.

"Hello, Gyp." Marissa knelt to pet the young dog.

"Welcome home," a rich voice called from the bedroom.

Marissa looked up to find Nat smiling at her. "Thank you." Marissa stood and walked into the bedroom.

Nat's eyes sparkled with the desire that was still fresh from her dreams. She watched the soft sway of Marissa's hips as she approached, remembering the way those hips felt grinding into her. She felt a hot rush flow through her veins. She got out of the bed and welcomed Marissa with an embrace.

Their lips met and her hands moved down Marissa's back to cup her buttocks, pulling her tightly into her. Their bodies melted together and Marissa softly moaned in her mouth.

Nat's hunger for Marissa was uncontrollable and her hands removed the thin shawl from her shoulders. She ended the kiss and watched Marissa's eyes widen as her fingers slowly started to unfasten the small buttons down the front of her dress. The fabric fell open across Marissa's breasts and Nat's heart raced. She lowered the dress from Marissa's shoulders, leaving her standing in her thin undergarments, and her fingers traced slowly down Marissa's neck.

Her fingers trembled with excitement as they rested on the laces of Marissa's corset and her heart raced with delight when the fabric spread open revealing Marissa's full breasts. Nat cupped them in her large hands, her thumbs stroking Marissa's nipples, feeling them grow erect under her touch.

Nat knelt in front of Marissa and her tongue flicked across the nipple she held cupped in her left hand. Marissa's eyes closed and her head tilted back in surrender. Nat filled her mouth with the soft flesh of Marissa's breast as her hands caressed down her lover's hips, slowly lowering her cotton bloomers. Naked and completely exposed to Nat's control, Marissa stepped out of the bloomers and softly kicked them aside. Nat's hands encircled her and cupped Marissa's buttocks kneading them as she gently sucked her breast.

Her hands stroked down the back of Marissa's thighs and down past her knees before circling around to the front of her. She caressed her way up the insides of Marissa's thighs until she could feel the heat radiating from her. Her fingers glanced across damp curls and she could feel Marissa tremble with excitement. Her mouth moved to Marissa's other breast while her fingers lightly teased soaked lips, her thumb stroking across her clit making Marissa shiver.

Nat stood and took Marissa in her arms covering her mouth with a heated kiss, her tongue swirling wildly in Marissa's mouth. She reached behind Marissa and lifted her, placing her legs around her waist and carefully walking to the bed. She lowered their bodies onto the bed, her full weight pressing into Marissa when she slowly began to roll her hips. She knew that the rough seam of her dungarees grinding into Marissa's center would make her explode with pleasure with each stroke of her body.

Marissa watched the look of wonder on Nat's face while she continued to caress her breasts. Nat's hands, strong and used for hard work, felt like velvet when they caressed her skin and Marissa felt the fire of desire spreading between her thighs. She did not care what Nat did provided that the euphoric feelings she was having continued to flow through her.

Marissa, gasping for air, broke the kiss. "Oh yes, Nat, please don't stop now."

Nat apparently had no intention of stopping and Marissa could feel Nat's hips thrusting furiously into her—the bed rocked wildly against the wall. She saw Nat look into her eyes before lowering her right hand between their bodies and pressing three fingers deep inside her, thrusting them in and out with each movement of her hips.

Marissa's cries of passion swelled into echoes in the room and Nat's voice joined hers as they climaxed together and collapsed in a pile on the tangled sheets. Nat lay gasping for air and Marissa rolled onto her side laying her head on Nat's shoulder.

"That was incredible," she whispered into Nat's ear. "Thank you, my love."

Nat raised her head and turned to look at her. "I have never felt like this with anyone before."

"Neither have I."

Marissa's reply surprised Nat and she wanted to ask about her husband, but didn't want to ruin the perfection of the moment by dredging up the past. She lay her head back on the pillow and remained silent.

After several minutes of silence, Marissa climbed on top of Nat and straddled her waist. "I rushed home thinking we were going hunting, but this was much more enjoyable."

"We are still going hunting. I bought you some warmer clothes and I thought I would help you change." She let a mischievous smile curl her lips.

"What happened? Did you get a little distracted?" Marissa asked.

"The sight of your bare skin gets me so excited, I just can't contain myself." Nat reached up and softly caressed Marissa's left breast.

"I do like your excitement." Marissa moaned feeling her nipples begin growing hard again.

"I can see that."

"We still have plenty of daylight left to hunt." Marissa rocked her hips against Nat.

"Yes we do." Nat reached up and covered Marissa's other breast with her hand, gently squeezing the soft flesh.

"Oh yes, Nat," Marissa crooned as Nat's fingers slowly twisted her aching nipples.

"You like that, don't you?"

"Oh yes, please don't stop what you're doing."

"Only for a minute." Nat pulled Marissa up to straddle her head. "Hold onto the headboard," Nat instructed.

Marissa reached for the rounded post across the headboard and held on tight when Nat's finger's parted her soaked lips and her tongue slipped inside her. Nat's hands returned to Marissa's nipples and resumed teasing them as her tongue swirled inside Marissa's wetness.

"Oh, my God," Marissa cried.

Nat's tongue dove deep inside her, licking her walls as she twisted and stretched her throbbing nipples. Marissa instinctively spread her thighs open wider giving Nat's tongue complete access. Nat ground her face into Marissa's body, her teeth roughly rubbing across her swollen bud and driving her tongue in and out of Marissa.

"Yes, yes, yes," Marissa chanted.

Nat's face was coated with Marissa's juices and she removed her tongue and took Marissa's clit in her mouth before entering her with two fingers. Sinking deep past her knuckles, she reached the spot that she knew was Marissa's final reserve, and Nat listened as she screamed out her pleasure repeatedly while Nat sucked her clit wildly.

Marissa raised her hips and moved down beside Nat on the bed. She hungrily licked her juices from Nat's face as her fingers unfastened Nat's belt and the buttons of her dungarees. Nat raised her hips from the bed and pushed the pants down, and Marissa's hand disappeared between her thighs.

Nat's fingers found Marissa still soaked and she entered her again with two fingers and moved with the same rhythm as her lover. Nat strained, thrusting her hips off the bed driving Marissa's fingers deep inside her and they came together, one soul twisting in the winds of pleasure.

Nat held Marissa in her arms for nearly an hour as they rested quietly together, not sleeping, but remaining silent in the wake of their passion. Nat looked out the window and saw the snow coming down in large flakes.

"Do you still want to hunt today?" she asked.

"I am so content to just lie here in your arms."

"There will be plenty of time for that later. That won't feed us during the long cold winter ahead."

Marissa smiled. "As long as you are here to share it with me, I could care less about food."

"That is very sweet of you to say, but that won't help us survive the cold."

"I know you are right, but you sure are warm and comfortable." Marissa rolled off the bed.

Nat stood and buttoned up her dungarees. "Your new clothes are on the chair."

Marissa walked to the chair and opened the small package to reveal the wool shirt and dungarees Nat had bought for her. She located her corset and bloomers, slipping them on before she pulled the shirt over her head and stepped into the dungarees. "You did very well with the fit." Marissa turned to show Nat.

"Yes, it appears I did." Nat smiled. "You look very nice."

"Thank you. Are you ready to go hunting now?" she asked.

"I will be in just a moment." Nat took Marissa in her arms for a long, slow kiss.

"Now we can hunt." She took her hand and they left the bedroom.

Nat took her range coat down from the hook by the door and slipped it over her shoulders, then handed Marissa her new coat. Once more, Nat had chosen well and the coat would provide great warmth for her lover. Next, she walked over to the mantel and pulled down the two rifles resting there, handing one to Marissa. "Have you ever shot one of these?"

"A few times, yes," Marissa answered.

"Great, let's go then."

†

The snow was beginning to accumulate on the ground, and their steps made a soft crunching sound as they walked behind the cabin and into the woods.

"Our buck will probably be moving around to stay warm. If we are lucky, we will cross his path and be able to track him."

She watched Gyp move ahead, her muzzle to the ground searching for scent. Several times, she would trot off the path they had taken only to return moments later ahead of them.

Nearly an hour had passed without any sign of movement in the woods. The snow had grown heavier, limbs burdened with its weight began to snap or hang low to the ground. It had grown colder as well and their breath blew like smoke out of their mouths and noses as they traversed the wooded hillside.

Nat was about to suggest they turn back for the day when she saw Gyp's ears perk to a sound just ahead. "Easy girl," Nat whispered. The excited dog and two women crept forward quietly.

They reached a small clearing that looked down over a small creek and standing there taking a drink was the buck Nat had thought they would find. He was large. His rack spread nearly thirty inches and he would easily weigh three hundred pounds.

"Do you want to take him?"

Marissa looked at her with what looked like fear in her eyes. Her trepidation was evident. It was obvious that she was doubtful about being able to kill such a majestic creature.

Nat had to remind herself that not everyone was a natural born hunter and it might take several hunts for Marissa to become comfortable with killing for food. Until then, Nat would provide for them and teach Marissa all she knew about hunting.

"I'll take this one."

With Marissa watching, Nat raised the rifle to her shoulder and took aim. She waited until the buck raised his head smelling the air. It was too late for him to catch their scent. Her finger pulled back against the trigger and a single shot rang out. The buck fell to the ground, the shot echoing down the valley and Gyp racing forward.

Nat had hit him squarely in the heart, dropping him immediately and killing him instantly. Her shot had struck a fatal blow and prevented any suffering he would have felt. They walked down to the creek and Nat turned to Marissa.

"This part gets a little messy." She took a long knife from her boot. "You might want to look away," she warned.

"I'll be fine." Marissa watched Nat kneel down beside the buck.

"Thank you for giving your life to us, my brother, to keep us fed during the winter to come." Nat spoke softly before drawing the knife across the buck's throat to drain the blood from him.

Next, Nat plunged the knife deep into the buck's chest and made a cut the length of his entire underside to eviscerate the animal and prepare him for transport back to the cabin. She took two lengths of rope from her small pack, and tied the buck's hooves together in front and back while she sent Marissa in search of a long branch they could use.

At first they struggled with the weight of the buck, but after several minutes they were traveling comfortably back through the forest to the cabin. They lowered the buck next to a tree, and Nat disappeared into the barn, returning with a length of rope which she used to hoist the buck above the ground.

"Would you mind going down to your smokehouse and starting the fire I have laid there?"

"Not at all, Nat." Marissa took the rifles inside and then disappeared down the path to her house with Gyp closely in tow.

Nat quickly removed the buck's pelt and draped it across one of the porch railings. She then began sectioning out the buck in quarters, carving out the ribs and loin meat. She carefully laid the meat on the stump she had used to chop firewood as she finished butchering the carcass. She placed the buck's head to the side. He would make a beautiful display that she would treat and mount for sale in town. Nat hated to waste any part of an animal and would put as much of it to good use as possible.

Marissa was returning to the cabin and Nat asked her to bring her the large box of salt from the cupboard. When she returned, Nat asked, "Do you want to watch how I do this?"

"Yes, I would."

"Take the rib sections and I'll carry the quarters."

They carried the meat down to the smokehouse and laid it across a small table. "Would you get us a bucket of water?" Nat asked.

Marissa disappeared and came back moments later with a bucket of water. She watched Nat rinse off a large hindquarter and then sprinkle the meat with a generous portion of the salt. Then Nat tied the quarter to the rafter above the fire and reached for another. Marissa had already rinsed it and Nat watched her coat the meat with the preserving salt. They strung the ribs on meat hooks to suspend them over the fire and soon they had hung all the meat for smoking except the loin. Nat took her knife and cut five large steaks before treating the rest of the meat and hanging it.

"Supper." She picked up the steaks and rinsed them in the water.

Marissa returned the bucket to the porch and followed Nat and Gyp back to her cabin. Nat laid the meat on a small table and went outside to wash up from the hunt.

When she returned, Nat smiled. "You did well today. That deer meat will last for several months and will help us survive if the winter gets too harsh to travel into town."

"You made everything look so easy. I'm not sure I'll make much of a hunter," Marissa admitted.

"That's no problem. Hunting is all I know and I can keep us in meat all winter long if needed." She smiled. "There's no need for you to kill."

Marissa blushed, but she knew Nat was correct in her assessment. She would go hungry before she would pull the trigger on an animal, and Nat knew this and accepted it politely.

"As long as you keep making biscuits, we will make a great team." Nat smiled and reached over to cover Marissa's hand with hers.

"You have a deal, my friend." Marissa returned her smile, relieved that Nat was not disappointed in her.

Nat pulled off her work shirt and rinsed it in the bucket she used for washing clothes and hung it by the fire to dry. Marissa admired Nat's taut upper body as she moved about the cabin in her undershirt.

Nat turned away from a task and caught Marissa watching her. "What are you thinking?"

"I was admiring how handsome you are, Nat."

"Thank you." Nat blushed and she moved to the fireplace to check on dinner.

"Is there anything you can't do?" Marissa asked.

"Cook biscuits that taste as good as yours and make decent gravy." Gyp let out a small bark, appearing to confirm her statement. "See, even Gyp knows my weaknesses."

Marissa laughed, and when she did, her blue eyes sparkled even brighter. Nat felt her knees go weak whenever she saw that look in Marissa's eyes. A rush of heat passed through Nat and she picked up the water bucket, heading outside for water and some cooler air. When she opened the door, she stopped dead in her tracks.

"You have got to come see this."

Marissa and Gyp leapt to their feet and walked to the door. Nat stepped aside so they could see that the ground was covered with several inches of pure white snow.

"Beautiful," Marissa said, standing beside Nat.

"Almost too beautiful to walk on, but I am thirsty." Nat stepped off the porch.

Following Nat, Gyp ran past Marissa and flew off the porch into the blanket of snow. Nat bent down and grabbed a handful of snow and pressed it into a ball before tossing it to Gyp. Gyp jumped to catch the ball which disintegrated in her mouth as soon as she caught it. Gyp shook her head and cocked it at her master, looking dumbfounded when the ball melted in her mouth.

"It's called snow, Gyp." Nat laughed and lifted the pump handle to draw some fresh water.

Gyp raced her back to the porch where Marissa was waiting for them. "Beautiful, but cold too." She led them back inside.

Marissa took the bucket from Nat and dipped them each a glass of water and set a bowl for Gyp.

"Will you stay here with me tonight?" Nat asked.

"Only if you promise to keep me warm."

Nat pulled her into her lap. "I think I can do that."

"I'm sure you can." Marissa leaned into Nat for a kiss. "I'm getting warm already."

"There is much more of that to keep you warm all night long," Nat promised.

"I'm off tomorrow, so I'll look forward to being kept warm all night long," Marissa whispered into Nat's ear, her tongue trailing down Nat's neck.

They kissed and caressed each other until dinner was ready. Then they shared a hearty meal, with plenty of leftovers for the next day. When Nat could eat no more she pushed the plate away and sat back in her chair.

"I'm about to explode. That was one fine meal."

"We make a good team."

"Yes we do."

Nat stood to start clearing the table and Marissa stopped her. "I'll get these. Why don't you relax?"

"I'll go down to the smokehouse and check the wood while you pick up the table. Then we are all done for the night and can both relax."

"That is a good idea." Marissa watched Nat and Gyp leave the cabin.

Marissa rushed to clean the dishes and then turned out the lamps except for one which she turned down low. She tossed another log in the fireplace in the bedroom and lit the lamp by the bedside before she stripped off her clothes and climbed between the cold sheets.

✝

Nat and Gyp walked the path down to the smokehouse where Nat placed several logs on the fire and checked the security of the meat. Content that everything was progressing well, Nat locked the smokehouse door and she and Gyp walked back to the cabin.

The room was dim when she walked inside and hung her coat by the door. She turned off the oil to the lamp and the room pitched into darkness. She could see the soft glow of another lamp coming from the bedroom and followed it like a moth to a flame.

Marissa was lying in the bed waiting for her return. "Welcome back," she purred from the nice warm bed.

Nat smiled at her and reached behind her head to pull the undershirt off. She then sat down on the bed, unlaced her boots and removed them along with her socks. Nat stood to unfasten her pants and turned to see Marissa watching her closely.

Marissa had not had the opportunity to watch Nat undress and she smiled as Nat's hands slowly lowered the dungarees and tossed them aside. Admiring Nat's long, lean body in the soft glow of the oil lamp, she was disappointed when Nat reached over and turned off the oil.

Marissa felt the covers rise and then felt Nat's weight as she entered the bed. Nat pressed next to her and she welcomed Nat into her warm arms with a passionate kiss. Marissa pulled Nat on top of her and wrapped her legs around Nat's waist, holding her close warming her body. The full moon was shining through the bedroom window illuminating her beauty and Nat looked down into Marissa's face. Her dark eyes shone with excitement and she heard Marissa speak.

"Love me tonight, Nat."

Nat covered her mouth with a kiss and loved her slowly and tenderly, then later with wild abandon. She loved her deep into the night and finally collapsed, exhausted in Marissa's arms, for a night of dreamless sleep.

Chapter Seven

The next morning, Nat woke to the smell of frying bacon. When she reached for her, Marissa's spot in the bed had turned cold and Nat realized she was not in the bed. She stretched and then quietly crept from the covers and slipped on some clothes. The air in the bedroom had grown cool with the dying of the fire and Nat placed more logs on the embers and stirred them until a small flame licked up the sides of the newly placed wood.

She walked into the kitchen and hugged Marissa from behind.

"Good morning." Her hands slid down Marissa's arms and turned her.

"I hope you are hungry. I felt like cooking a full breakfast this morning. Gyp has kept me company in your absence and I think she has worked up an appetite walking between the kitchen and bedroom to check on you."

Nat leaned down and stroked the dog's head. "She is a very faithful companion. I don't know what I would have done without her these last few months."

"Have a seat at the table and I'll bring you some coffee."

"Thanks."

Marissa placed a cup of steaming liquid in front of her.

After they finished eating, Nat stretched. "That was really good."

Gyp let out a soft woof, adding to her praise.

"I'm very glad you two enjoy my cooking."

"What plans do you have for your day off?"

"I have some laundry to do and I thought I might bake a pie if I could talk you into going to town and buying some apples."

"For your apple pie, I would walk a hundred miles. Are there other supplies we need?"

"We have some meat left over from dinner last night, so we can heat that. I'll also bring down some beans I canned this summer, so I guess we are good for now."

"I'll help you get the fire and wash pot ready before Gyp and I walk into town."

Marissa stood and was about to start clearing the table, when Nat took her arm and pulled her into her lap. She encircled Marissa with her arms and leaned down to softly kiss her lips. "Thank you for such a wonderful meal."

"You are most welcome." Marissa's cheeks flushed with color. "For a kiss like that, I'll cook for you every day."

"You don't have to cook to get a kiss from me." She kissed Marissa again, her tongue parting her lips to tenderly probe her mouth. Nat's hand slid up Marissa's leg beneath her skirt. Nat could feel Marissa quivering as she softly stroked her thigh. Marissa placed her hand on top of hers.

"If you keep that up, I won't get my wash done, and you won't get a pie tonight," she warned.

Nat looked into Marissa's eyes and she saw her desire sparkling. "I won't perish without pie and I'm sure we can find another clean outfit for you to wear." She lifted Marissa in her arms and carried her back to bed. "Besides, it is still early in the day."

Later, Nat turned to Marissa. "Do you still want to wash today?"

"Want to no, need to yes."

"I'll carry the water, if you'll get the fire started beneath your wash pot."

"Fair enough. When you get back from town, I want these clothes you are wearing so I can wash them, too."

"Yes ma'am," Nat grinned, moving from the bed to get dressed.

They walked outside to find that most of last night's snow had melted, and walking to Marissa's house, they held hands. Nat stepped inside the smokehouse to find the wood nearly depleted and she placed more wood on the smoldering embers. The wash pot was already hung over the fire pit, so Nat picked up the bucket and moved over to the well to begin pumping water while watching Marissa lay a small fire.

Marissa placed a small bundle of dried grass under the center of the wood and disappeared inside her home. She returned a few moments later with a small shovel filled with embers from her fireplace, which she dumped onto the dried grass. They watched the grass burst into flames and ignite the dried wood.

Nat carried four more buckets of water to fill the pot halfway and then returned the bucket to the porch.

"I will be back soon." She stopped to kiss Marissa softly.

"Hurry back," Marissa called, walking toward the house to get her clothing.

"Let's go, Gyp."

†

Gyp ran ahead of Nat with her nose near the ground, searching for the scent of any wildlife in the area. Nat watched her trail a scent twenty yards ahead and smiled at the small dog. She continued to walk as Gyp disappeared from the road into the dense woods. She emerged again five minutes later and trotted back to Nat.

"Did you have a nice run?" Nat asked Gyp who was pacing beside her master.

A few minutes later, they reached town and Nat walked directly to Smithy's shop.

"Hello, Nat," the large man called to her. "How are you today?"

"I'm well, Smithy, and you?"

"Very well, thank you. Is there something I can do for you today?"

"I took a very large buck yesterday with an impressive rack. I wondered if you were interested in purchasing it."

"These greenhorns pounce all over buck heads to mount in their smoking rooms, so bring it in and I will take it off your hands." He smiled at Nat. "What about the hide?"

"I need to have some new breeches made from that."

"There is an Indian woman right on the outskirts of town who makes wonderful deerskin breeches," Smithy shared with her.

"I'll have to look her up then. I'll bring the buck head in tomorrow," she promised before leaving the store.

"See you tomorrow then," Smithy called back.

Nat picked out a dozen apples and bought a pound of cane sugar as well. She browsed around the store and selected a lavender scented candle and some fragrant shampoo. With her small package tucked beneath her arm, she and Gyp left the store. Instead of turning right to go home, Nat took a left and walked to the edge of town to find a small shack. Sitting on the porch, tanning a length of buckskin, was a beautiful Indian woman. She didn't hear Nat approach, which gave her the opportunity to survey the woman as she worked. Although small, her arm muscles rippled as she worked on the hide. Her dark hair, laced with gray, glowed in the morning light. Nat slowed her approach and waited for the woman to look up and smile. When she did, her smile reached all the way to her dark brown eyes.

"Good morning," Nat said. The woman looked up.

She returned Nat's warm smile. "Good morning, my sister."

"Smithy told me you make the best buckskin breeches. I have a hide and a need for a new pair."

"Bring the hide to me tomorrow and I'll measure you then."

"How much do you charge for the breeches?"

The woman eyed the bag of apples Nat was carrying. "The remainder of your hide and a bag of those apples." the woman answered with a smile.

"I'll see you tomorrow then. By the way, my name is Nat."

"And mine is Maggie."

The woman had very little in the way of possessions. Nat had snuck a peek inside the small building and there was very little stored in the woman's food pantry. A bag of apples was a very cheap price for a pair of breeches so Nat planned to bring a few extras to exchange for the pants. She and Marissa had plenty of venison, so Nat would bring a slab of the smoked meat and maybe a small bag of flour.

†

Gyp raced ahead to Marissa's house and was sitting on the porch with her when Nat walked into the yard.

"Well now, aren't you two the perfect pair?" Nat asked.

"We were wondering if you were going to finally show up. Gyp has been here at least five minutes."

"Four legs are twice as fast as two," Nat reminded her.

"Very funny." Marissa grinned.

"I was thinking as I walked."

"Thinking of what?" Marissa asked.

"I have always wanted to see the ocean. Nathan and I were supposed to go this year." She frowned while sharing the sad memory.

"You are so fairly close to it now. A good three day's ride and you'd be there."

"Would you mind looking after things while I'm gone?" Nat asked.

"Like what?"

"Keeping the fire going in the smokehouse and feeding the animals, except Hardy and Gyp who will be going with me." Nat reached down to stroke Gyp's fur.

"I think I can handle that for a few days. When are you planning to leave?"

"You go back to work the day after tomorrow, correct?"

"Yes."

"I'll leave then, if that's fine with you."

"I'll hate to see you go, but I know that you'll be coming back soon."

"I would think no more than eight days." She took out her knife and started peeling the apples. "I assume you want these peeled?"

"Yes, please. Let me get a bowl and you can core and slice them too."

"That's the least I can do for fresh apple pie. Here, I brought you something, too." Nat handed Marissa the package.

Marissa opened it to find the scented candle and the fragrant soap. "We can use these later tonight."

"I wasn't sure if you needed sugar for the pie so I bought some just in case."

"I think I still have some, but it never hurts to have more. I'll be right back." Marissa disappeared into the house. She returned with a bowl and sat beside Nat as she peeled and sliced the fruit. When Nat had finished, Marissa picked up the peelings and headed for the yard.

"Where are you going with those?"

"I was going to toss them into the fire."

"Good idea, but make it the one inside, it will make the house smell so sweetly."

"I hadn't thought of that."

"I think I'll go tend to the animals while you put the apples on to cook."

"Stop by your house and pick up some clean clothes, and something else to put on now so I can get those washed."

"Yes ma'am." Nat walked to her barn, with Gyp close on her heels.

She tended the animals and then looked at the pelt she had stretched out on the barn wall. She removed the tacks, carried the pelt to her wash pot, still full of water, and dumped some of the ashes on top of the pelt. She used a piece of wood to stir the ashes coating the pelt. She would allow it to soak and then scrape the remaining fur from the pelt before drying it over the porch railing.

The afternoon sun still burned brightly down on her shoulders, warming her as she toiled with her chores. She fed the animals and checked her tack to ensure it was in good shape for her journey. Her buckskins and warm shirts were clean, and would be welcome on her trip. She would camp out under the stars or if the nights turned too cool, she would seek shelter. Nat was excited to know that very soon she would make another of her dreams come true.

Returning to the wash pot, she saw that the ash mixture had worked well and it took little effort to remove the remaining fur. She rinsed the pelt, hung it across the porch railing, and then returned inside her cabin.

Inside her house, she went into her bedroom to pack her bedroll. She would travel light, but have adequate gear to keep her warm during the cold nights. Her years in the woods with her father had taught her so much and Nat followed her instincts naturally due to his training.

Nat walked outside to draw a bucket of water and poured it into a large bowl. She stripped out of her clothing and used the water to bathe. After she was as clean as possible, Nat slipped into a flannel nightshirt and some buckskin slippers. She chose a clean pair of dungarees and work shirt to change into after her bath, and with Gyp following her closely, she returned to Marissa's cabin.

Chapter Eight

Nat woke up starving when she smelled Marissa cooking breakfast in the kitchen. Marissa had placed her nightshirt on the end of the bed and she slipped it over her head before going to the kitchen.

"Good morning, Marissa." She hugged her lover from behind.

"Good morning, my love." Marissa turned in Nat's arms and kissed her sweetly. "Are you hungry?"

"I'm starving." Nat squeezed Marissa.

"Have a seat at the table and breakfast will be ready soon."

Nat took a seat, eyeing the apple pie when Marissa turned around. "Don't even think about spoiling your breakfast," she warned.

"Yes, ma'am."

Gyp had waited on Marissa, and when she saw Nat begin to eat, Gyp stood and began eating.

"She is so well disciplined," Marissa said, watching the dog closely.

"Not discipline. Gyp has good manners."

They ate their fill of breakfast and Nat looked at Marissa. "What are you doing today?"

"I thought I would put a roast on for dinner, with some canned vegetables from the garden."

"Will you need to be here to watch over it?"

"No, I think the fire is low enough that it will cook slowly without burning. What do you have in mind?"

"I need to take the pelt into town and make payment on some new breeches. I also need to drop the buck head off to Smithy. Would you care to join Gyp and me?"

"I would love to." Marissa stood to clear the table. Nat reached for her and pulled Marissa into her lap studying her face closely before tracing the fine lines at the corner of Marissa's eyes with a slow fingertip. The smile on her face grew wide. Nat could see Marissa's eyes shine with excitement as she examined her face intently.

"Do you like what you see?" Marissa asked.

"No, I love what I see. May I show you how much?"

"We have an errand to run first, but then you will have all afternoon," Marissa promised.

"I'll hold you to that."

"I certainly hope so. I'll clean up and put the roast on while you get dressed and clean up the kitchen. Then we'll be off to see a woman about some breeches."

Nat returned her smile as Marissa left her arms, leaving her feeling so empty. "I love you, Marissa."

"I know, and I love you too."

Nat and Gyp waited for her out on the porch. When Marissa appeared from inside the house, Nat reached for her hand, picked up the small bag of supplies, and they walked to Nat's cabin.

Nat handed Marissa the small sack and walked around the cabin to pick up the buck head that she would sell to Smithy. She returned to Marissa, taking her hand as they started into town.

†

Marissa and Gyp waited outside while Nat went to bargain with Smithy. He was impressed with the size and perfect condition of the buck's head and paid Nat handsomely for the prize.

"I wouldn't be surprised if this sold today," Smithy said. "Be sure to keep me in mind if you do more hunting."

"I will." Nat tucked the gold coins in her pocket and stepped outside to join Marissa and Gyp.

Nat took the sack from Marissa. "Is there anything you need while we are in town?"

"I will buy some coffee."

"Take this then." Nat fished a gold coin from her pocket.

"I have money, Nat."

"I know you do, but I've been the one drinking all your coffee."

"That's a small price to pay for all that you have done for me."

"I'd say it was a pretty even deal, so let me buy this time."

Marissa took the offered coin and slipped it into the pocket of her coat before they walked to the general store. She bought coffee while Nat picked out a dozen yellow apples.

"More apples?"

"They're part of my deal for new breeches."

They paid for their items and then walked to the small house on the edge of town.

†

The Indian woman was sitting on her porch. She looked up and smiled when they approached.

"Good day." Nat stepped onto the porch.

"Welcome back, my friend. Come inside and I will size you."

Nat and Marissa followed the woman into the small house while Gyp waited outside.

"You may have a seat there," the woman told Marissa, pointing to a chair. She then took a length of rawhide in her hands as Nat set the sack on the table.

"You have long legs to be so small in the hips," the woman remarked while measuring Nat's inseam.

"I do a lot of walking so they get me where I need to go." Nat winked to the smiling woman.

"There." She stepped back after she finished measuring Nat. "Let's take a look at your pelt."

Nat took the deerskin from the sack and handed it to the woman.

She smiled at Nat. "You treated this piece well. I can easily get two pairs out of this."

"That's even better. Just let me know what else you need for the second pair."

Nat took the apples, venison, and other staples from the bag she had brought for payment and laid them out on the table.

The woman smiled at the smoked meat that Nat placed on the table. "Your payment is more than enough for two pairs of breeches. When do you need them?"

"I am going to the ocean as my father and I had planned, so there is no hurry."

The old woman's eyes lit up at the mention of the ocean. "Will you do something for me?"

"Certainly, what is it?"

The woman walked from the small room and returned a moment later with a waterproofed skin. "In the sands of the beach, close to the shore, you should be able to find clams. I would appreciate if you could bring me some stored in salt water when you return." She handed Nat the skin.

"You will have to tell me what they look like. I've never been to the ocean before."

The woman picked up a piece of charcoal and drew a crude shape on the table. "They look like this and will be buried in the sand where the waves wash over. When the tide is low, you will easily see the bubbles in the sand from their breathing and will know where to dig." She smiled at

Nat. "I will make you two some excellent chowder if you can bring them."

Nat picked up her sack and took the skin from the woman. "I'll do my best and will see you at the end of the week."

"Thank you, my friend." The woman walked them out the door. "Be safe in your travels." They walked off the porch to join Gyp.

"Thank you, I will." Nat waved goodbye.

†

They returned to Marissa's cabin and stored their supplies. "I need to go to my cabin to prepare for my trip. I'll be back soon."

"Is there anything I can help with?"

"No, I will take care of a few things and return shortly."

Nat and Gyp walked outside into the cooling air. When they got to her cabin, she lit the fire she had laid under the wash pot and added more water to the large pot. Then they walked down toward the smokehouse. She added more wood to the fire and turned the meat lying across wooden strips. She portioned out a pound of the dried jerky to take with her on the trip to the ocean.

She packed her bedroll, tucked it under her arm before she left her cabin, and walked back toward Marissa's cabin. She noticed that Marissa was running low on split wood and decided she would split more and carry it onto the porch before she left.

Marissa was placing the pie in the hearth to warm when Nat and Gyp returned from their errands.

"Are you hungry now or would you like to bathe before we eat?"

Nat placed the jerky on the table and wrapped it in cloth. "I can wait a time to eat. I want to split some wood for you and get you stocked up before I leave tomorrow."

"I will carry and stack while you split then."

"You have a deal." She removed her jacket and placed it on a hook by the door. She picked up the axe and walked to the splitting block where she began to rhythmically split the wood. Nat moved fluidly splitting it into small sections. When a small pile had formed, Marissa began carrying wood inside and then added to the stack just outside her front door.

Nat was working up a lather, chopping the wood, and removed her work shirt. Once she had split enough wood to last Marissa for a week or more, she picked up her shirt and hung it over the porch rail before storing the axe. Then she helped Marissa carry the remainder of the wood onto the porch.

"I'll begin carrying in water from the well if you are ready." Nat walked onto the porch to pick up two buckets.

"That should give the water on the fire time to heat up. I'll help you and we can bathe together if you wish."

"I would like that very much." Nat smiled at the blushing Marissa, and walked to the well, followed closely by Marissa and Gyp.

They filled the buckets and took turns carrying them into the house until the tub was one third filled with fresh well-water. Then they began taking hot water from the wash pot, and after several more trips, a steaming bath awaited them.

"You go inside and strip out of your clothes so I can wash them," Marissa instructed. Then she placed their soiled clothing in the pot to boil clean and pumped several more buckets of water for the tub before going inside.

Nat had grown cold in her nakedness and had stepped into the bath. "Sorry, I couldn't wait any longer."

"That's fine; I didn't want you to get chilled." Marissa pulled the dress over her head.

Nat watched Marissa undress, marveling at her gentle curves and soft skin. When Marissa lowered her undergarments, the cool air on her skin made her nipples harden. Nat smiled when Marissa looked up to see her watching.

"You are so beautiful." Nat's eyes followed Marissa while she walked to the tub and stepped into the steamy water.

"Thank you." She blushed. "It pleases me to know you think that."

"You are the most beautiful woman I have ever met, and I am happy that we have become friends."

"You are much more than a friend to me," Marissa answered, surprising Nat.

"What am I then?" Nat asked coyly.

"You are my protector, my provider, and most importantly, my lover," Marissa stated boldly.

Nat smiled and reached her hand out to Marissa. Marissa took her offered hand and leaned forward to meet Nat's lips. Nat kissed her lips softly, then covered Marissa's face with light kisses as her fingertips traced the outlines of her cheekbones and jaw line. Marissa rested against Nat's left arm and lifted her face, welcoming more of Nat's kisses. Nat felt her shiver as her tongue circled Marissa's lips until her lover parted them and their tongues danced sensually.

Nat felt herself tingling with the desire running through her as they kissed. Her hand cupped Marissa's left breast, her thumb stroking lightly across her aroused nipple. She broke the kiss and kissed down to Marissa's ear.

"I want to make love to you," she whispered, and felt Marissa quiver in response.

Nat took the bar of fragrant soap in her hand and soaked a cloth in the water before rubbing it across the soap. She lathered the cloth and started at Marissa's neck, and slowly washing down each arm and across her chest. "Stand for me please."

Marissa stood and took the soap from Nat's hand to bathe her womanly parts as Nat bathed her sides and legs and turned so Nat could bathe her back. She then took the cloth from her before sitting back into the water to rinse. Marissa rinsed the cloth, lathered it again with the fragrant soap, and bathed Nat with loving strokes. Marissa bit her lower lip as her hands glided over Nat's chest and down her firm, muscular body.

Nat rinsed and stepped from the tub. She raised her hand to Marissa. "Are you ready, my love?"

Marissa stood and climbed from the tub and allowed Nat to wrap her in a large towel and a warm embrace before she moved to dry her body.

Nat reached for a nightshirt to pull over her head.

"Don't bother with that. I need to feel your skin next to mine." She took Nat's hand and they walked to the bedroom.

Nat placed more wood on the fire as Marissa stretched onto the bed. Nat extinguished the flame of the oil lamp before lowering herself into Marissa's welcoming arms.

Nat kissed Marissa until she was breathless with desire. Their lower bodies entwined as their movements gently rocked the bed. Nat's mouth kissed down Marissa's neck and enclosed her right breast as she gasped for air.

"That feels so good, Nat." Marissa placed her hand between Nat's legs to find her soaked.

Nat moaned against the skin of Marissa's breast, feeling Marissa's fingers penetrate her, sinking deeply into her body. Nat moved her hand between Marissa's legs and entered her while her teeth grazed an erect nipple. She mimicked the movement of Marissa's fingers, moving slow and deep, the sounds of their pleasure filling the room.

Nat shuddered, calling out, "Marissa."

Marissa felt Nat's release, and when she called her name that was all Marissa needed to reach her own climax and she filled Nat's hand with a rush of juices.

Nat kissed Marissa and moved to lie beside her on the bed. Marissa reached down and pulled the covers over their bodies, and then curled up in Nat's arms.

Chapter Nine

The next morning Nat woke early, crept quietly from the bed, and dressed in her travel clothing before walking to the barn to saddle Hardy. The morning was crisp since the sun was slow to crest above the horizon and the excitement of her trip stirred Nat. Hardy met her in the stall. He seemed to sense an adventure and an opportunity to stretch his well-rested legs.

Nat tied her bedroll to the back of her saddle, walked Hardy to Marissa's cabin, and tied him to the hitching post. "We will be off soon," she spoke to the large horse, patting his neck while he nuzzled her. Gyp trotted beside her as she walked back onto the porch and went inside.

Marissa had gotten out of the bed, and was starting breakfast when Nat returned.

"Good morning."

"Good morning. I hope you weren't planning to sneak off without saying goodbye."

"No, ma'am, I wouldn't do that. I know you have to be in town early this morning and I wanted to leave when you did." Nat took Marissa in her arms. "I would never leave you without a goodbye."

Marissa kissed Nat's lips softly. "I would hope not," she said with a pout.

"Besides, we can't leave with empty stomachs."

"I have packed yesterday's biscuits and bacon for you and will make some flapjacks this morning if you would like."

"That would be great." Nat moved to get a jar of syrup down from the shelf.

Marissa, watching Nat prepare for her trip, stirred the batter for the flapjacks. Dressed in her breeches and travel shirt, Nat looked just like she had the first time Marissa had seen her at the hotel. "You look just as handsome as the first time I saw you."

"I hope I smell better though." Nat chuckled.

"Without a doubt."

Nat packed the jerky and biscuits Marissa had prepared for her into a sack with a drawstring, and took it along with the skin the Indian woman had given her, out to Hardy. From the window, Marissa watched Nat place the items inside the saddlebags and slip the rifle into the carrier on Hardy's left shoulder.

When Nat and Gyp walked back inside, Marissa placed their food on the table and Gyp's bowl on the floor. "Breakfast is ready."

She and Nat sat down at the table and began to eat their breakfast. "I will miss you."

"I will miss you too, but we will be back soon," Nat promised.

"I have grown so used to you being here. The cabin will feel so empty."

Nat was at a loss for words. She would only be gone for eight days. She wondered how Marissa would feel when she left in the spring to head back into the woods. She wouldn't worry about that now since she would have the long winter months to decide what she would do come the spring.

"Do you want me to leave Gyp with you for some company?" Nat asked.

Gyp looked up at the sound of her name.

"I would not deprive Gyp of the adventure with you," Marissa said.

Gyp went back to eating.

"It would seem strange without her."

"I'll be fine. I'll just have to keep myself busy."

"Time will pass quickly and we will be back soon," Nat promised.

"I know but I fear the hours will drag by."

When they finished eating, they rinsed their dishes and stood facing one another. Nat could see tears pooling in Marissa's eyes. She brushed the hair from around Marissa's face with her hands. "I'll be back soon." She leaned down, and then kissed her tenderly.

Marissa returned her kiss and hugged Nat tightly. "Enjoy your trip and hurry home to me."

"I will." Nat smiled then turned away from Marissa. She stopped at the door and took her hat, placing it atop her head and slipped her arms through her range coat before she turned back to Marissa. "I love you."

"I love you too."

Nat and Gyp walked out the door and Marissa placed her arms in the coat Nat had bought her and walked onto the porch. Nat looked at Marissa who was wrapping her arms around her waist with a mournful look on her face.

"I'm already missing you, my friend," Marissa said.

"I'll be back before you know it." Nat mounted Hardy and turned to wave goodbye before riding away.

✝

For hours, Nat followed the road south just as Marissa had instructed. The sun passed over her head and she could smell the fragrance of evergreens as she traveled further from town. They followed the trail until Nat decided to stop for the day. She turned from the trail and followed it a short distance to a southern tip of the Sound. She marveled at the expanse of the Sound, its waves crashing down upon the rocks and cliffs that separated earth from water.

Nat guided Hardy down a small path and across the soft sand with Gyp trotting ahead of them and chasing birds. Nat's eyes spotted a cave that should be high enough to protect them from the rising waters while providing protection from cold winds or rain should it begin to fall. She dismounted Hardy and led him up a narrow path until they reached the cave. She tied his reins to a small branch growing out of the rocks and went in search of dry wood before the night brought darkness. Nat gathered driftwood from the beach while Gyp chased the receding water and then turned to rush back to Nat as the next wave beat against the shore. The cave was deep and would provide the shelter she and her companions needed.

Nat took the saddle from Hardy's shoulders and carried it inside the cave. She removed his bridle, placing it on the branch where she had tied it earlier. Hardy would not wander far from her in his search of grass and Nat knew a whistle would bring him running to her.

She arranged her campsite and laid the fire in a small pit just inside the lip of the cave. She placed her food bag up off the floor of the cave, took a slice of jerky, and walked down to the water. She tore off a strip of the jerky and tossed it to Gyp while making her way down to the beach. The water was cold to Nat's touch and when she lifted her fingers to her lips, she tasted the saltiness of the water. She moved beyond the reach of the waves and sat with Gyp to watch the sun retire for the day, spreading its beautiful colors across the dark blue water.

"It is beautiful, isn't it, Gyp?" Nat placed her hand on the dog's back.

Gyp barked lightly in what Nat thought was agreement as they watched the sunset together.

Nat noticed a bubbling in the sand a few feet away from her and stood to walk over to it. She used her hand to scoop away the sand and found a clam nestled below the surface, just as Maggie had told her it would be. She picked up the small shell and inspected it closely.

"Can't be a whole lot of meat in there," she told Gyp. "It must take a lot of these to make a decent soup."

Another bubble appeared and Nat saw Gyp pounce and use her paws to dig away the sand. Nat laughed and walked over to pick up the shell Gyp had uncovered.

"Yours is bigger." Nat took the shell in her hand. She walked back to retrieve the skin the Indian woman had given her and dropped the two shells into it and filled it partially with water. She and Gyp hunted clams until the moon began to rise and then they walked back up to the cave. Nat lit the campfire after tying the clam bag to a branch. Nat doubted there were any bears in this area, but she would not risk her food to any other predators that might live nearby.

Nat took a bacon-filled biscuit from the bag, and handed it to Gyp and then took another for herself. Hardy had wandered back to the campsite and Nat placed a feedbag over his head before settling in for the evening. As the moon glowed across the rippling water, the three companions shared their meal at the cave.

Nat enjoyed the heat of the small fire. When the sun had set, the warm day had quickly disappeared and she was glad for the extra warmth. Leaning back against a rock outcropping and using her saddle for a pillow, she gazed up at the night sky. The night was cloudless and the stars spread across the sky like a shimmering blanket. Nat picked out the constellations she recognized from her father's teaching and marveled how beautifully they lit up the night sky. She couldn't help but wonder if Marissa was watching the same beautiful sky back at home.

Marissa had seen the night sky, but she was busy shuffling around completing her chores, and she did not take the opportunity to sit and enjoy the evening the way Nat was. She carried the last of the split wood she would need for the night inside and closed the door behind her, shutting out the night's beauty. She had lived alone in the cabin for three years, but it had never felt as empty as it did now.

Sitting around the fire staring up at the sky made Nat think back to the many such times she and her father had shared while trapping in the deep woods. She remembered one night when they camped while crossing over a wide prairie. They had gazed up at the sky and watched a shower of shooting stars until their necks became sore from the awkward position.

"I miss you, Father." Nat tossed another piece of wood onto the fire. Often, she would find herself thinking about her father and her hand would go to the bear-claw necklace she wore around her neck. She still felt the pain of his loss and wondered if the pain would ever dissipate completely.

The sound of the waves crashing upon the shore began to lull Nat to sleep and when she felt herself begin to nod, she picked up her saddle and walked inside the cave. She unrolled her bedroll and fell asleep watching the shadows of the fire flicker on the cave walls. Gyp curled up next to her, softly snoring as Nat drifted into dreams.

Hardy stood at the opening of the cave dozing. Deep into the early morning hours, Gyp woke to his soft huffing sounds and she stood and stretched beside Nat. Gyp walked outside to relieve her bladder, then trotted back inside to stick her cold, wet nose to Nat's chin to wake her.

At first, Nat just pushed Gyp away, but the dog was persistent and returned to lick her face until Nat stirred from her sleep.

"What has gotten into you, Gyp?" Nat asked petting her neck.

Gyp let out a soft "woof," walked to the mouth of the cave, turned back to Nat, and gave a short bark.

"Okay, I get it, you want me up, so just hold on a second," Nat grumbled searching for her boots.

Nat shook each boot before slipping them on and stood, stretching. It had been a while since she had slept on the hard ground and she winced, feeling her stiff back. "I am getting spoiled sleeping in a soft bed every night," Nat groaned.

When she walked to the mouth of the cave, Nat stopped in her tracks when she looked to the sky. No wonder Gyp had wanted her awake. Neither of them had ever seen anything quite so incredible as this sky. The Northern Lights were filling the early morning skies with swirls of brilliant green and Nat stood in awe at the most beautiful sight she had ever seen.

"Oh, my word, that is so beautiful."

Nat placed fresh wood on the fire and hung her coffee pot to make coffee while she and Gyp sat next to the fire admiring the beauty of the morning sky. When the coffee was ready, she poured herself a cup and sat with her arm around Gyp. They watched the Northern Lights fade when the sun began to creep to the horizon. The brilliant greens were replaced by orange and yellow rays as the sun rose to start the day.

Nat began to have second thoughts about traveling to the ocean. It had been her dream with Nathan, and without him, it wasn't as important. This spot seemed like a little slice of heaven to her and the more she pondered and idea, the bigger it grew. It was not quite a full days ride from town, had the clams Maggie asked to find, and was enclosed by forest she was certain held plenty game for her to hunt and trap.

Nat took the last two biscuits from the food sack and she and Gyp had breakfast. Nat wanted to do some exploring that morning, so after she and Gyp finished eating, she took the rifle from her saddle, and they started down the beach.

✝

Nat didn't think she would need a rifle for protection, but she took it just in case she ran into trouble. She knew there would be no bears still awake this late in the season, but she was prepared for any other predators in the area. She had no idea what form of wildlife would live in this environment, so Nat kept a vigilant eye open as they walked down the shoreline.

Gyp ran ahead of her, chasing the waves rushing ashore, running away from the approaching cold water, and going after it as the water receded. Nat laughed at her antics as they walked toward a small rock-lined pool. The outgoing tide had left a bounty of odd looking creatures stranded in the shallow water.

"We are going to have a nice dinner," Nat told Gyp, surveying the variety of creatures floundering in the pool.

Nat found a long stick and used her knife to carve a point on one end to form a spear point. She impaled a large fish, driving the point through its brain and killing it instantly. She stuck the other end into the soft sand and removed her boots. She rolled her breeches up her calf and waded in the shallow pool filled with cold water. Gyp sat on a rock watching her. Nat corralled what she recognized as a shrimp and snapped its head off, and then another, until she had several dozen to accompany the fish. They would feast well tonight. She placed the shrimp by her spear and left it behind with her boots as she and Gyp walked farther down the beach.

Nat slipped the barrel of her rifle down the back of her shirt as she and Gyp collected an armful of driftwood to use in the campfire. They returned to pick up the spear and shrimp for their dinner, and then walked back toward camp. Nat stacked the firewood next to the pit, took the large fish from her spear, and carried it down to the water's edge to clean it in preparation for cooking. She washed the blood from her hands and the carcass in the cold salty water and rinsed the sand from the shrimp.

Gyp trotted along behind her walking back up to the camp. Nat made a spit from the pieces of driftwood she had collected and laid a fire beneath it. She used her flint to ignite the dry grass and watched the flames began to lick up against the fresh wood. She then placed the fish on the spit and turned to Gyp. "We are going to need more wood."

They collected three armloads of wood and placed it around the fire pit. Nat turned the fish on the spit and then she and Gyp walked back to the water's edge. They sat just beyond the limit of the advancing water and listened to the relaxing sound of the waves rushing to shore. Gyp lay next to Nat, her head resting on her thigh as Nat's hand stroked through her thick winter coat. "This is beautiful isn't it, my friend?"

Gyp raised her head when she heard a strange noise, and she and Nat strained to see across the water. A hundred yards beyond the shore, they watched a large black and white beast rise to the surface and blow water from its body. As they watched, several more of the strange creatures surfaced, expelling air and water from their bodies. Amazed by the sheer size of the creatures that surfaced and dove again beneath the water, they waited. The creatures remained underwater for several minutes after each breath. They watched until the creatures disappeared from their sight and Nat stood, stretching her stiff muscles. "Let's go check on dinner." Gyp jumped to her feet and trotted beside her master.

The smell of the roasting fish met them halfway to the cave and Nat knelt to coat the fish with seasonings before turning it on the spit. Curiosity seized Nat as she stood and looked into the shadows of the cave. She picked a burning limb from the fire and walked farther into the cave. It was deeper than she had originally assumed, and as she walked, she began to see strange drawings on the cave walls. She brought the fire closer and saw images of the creature she had seen earlier painted into the rock of the cave walls. She continued on her search and turned into a broad opening.

The last visitor had left a small stack of wood in a fire pit and Nat used her flame to ignite the dry wood. As she had expected, hunters had used the cave as a refuge. The evidence was a large pile of bones illuminated by the fire. Large rib bones, were propped against the wall, but it didn't appear that anyone had used the cave in many years.

"These must be from the creatures we saw today," she told Gyp, who seemed to be eyeing the bones curiously. "The hunters must have slain one of the creatures and brought the carcass here for harvesting." She looked at the jawbones of the creature and marveled at the large tipped teeth that graced its ridges. She picked up a tooth that had fallen free from the bone and ran her fingers over its edges.

"Jagged and sharp as you would expect of such a large predator," she remarked while examining it closely. She tucked the tooth into her shirt and moved to explore the rest of the cave.

Nat's eyes searched the walls covered with artwork of creatures she had never seen in the deep woods. Large fishes and tusked creatures filled the walls. Nat walked around the cave, studying each image carefully. "Amazing." She looked in awe while making the circuit around the cave.

She watched the flames from the fire dance upon the walls bringing the creatures shimmering to life. "We shall move in here tonight," she told Gyp. They walked back toward the mouth of the cave. The fish was cooking well and Nat peeled the hard shells from the shrimps' bodies and placed them on a skewer, which she held above the flames, until the pink flesh roasted to a bright red. Satisfied that the strange meat was cooked, Nat removed them from the skewer and placed them on her plate to allow them to cool before she and Gyp would feast on them.

She and Gyp watched the sun sink past the horizon, its last rays casting long shadows across the water. Nat, wanting to taste the shrimp, offered one of them to Gyp watching him eat it slowly.

"They are kind of bland aren't they?" she said after biting into the meat. "I bet they would taste much better basted with some honey butter. Maybe we should take some home for Marissa to cook. I bet she knows just how to prepare them."

Her words reminded her of just how much she missed her lover. The southern tip of the Sound had turned out to be a beautiful surprise, but Nat was missing the comfort of Marissa's arms. She decided it was no longer important to travel on to the ocean, she'd found the paradise she'd been searching for right here. "Would you mind if we went home early?" Gyp looked back at her, wiggling her entire body. "No, I don't guess you would. You love her as much as I do, I think."

Nat took the fish from above the fire, peeled some of the flakey meat to place in Gyp's bowl, and placed a healthy portion on her plate. Hardy walked up to them and Nat stood to place some feed in his bag and slipped it over his head.

When she returned, she tasted the fish and moaned softly. "This tastes much better," Nat placed the bowl in front of Gyp. The seasonings had roasted into the meat and it flaked apart lightly as Nat picked it off the bones with her fork. Gyp finished her portion and licked her lips and Nat chuckled before adding another portion to the dog's bowl.

They ate the entire fish before walking down to the water to rinse out their dishes. The moon began to rise, and Nat and Gyp dug clams until the sack was half-full before walking back to the cave. "Tomorrow we will check the pools for more shrimp and then head for home." She moved her bedroll deeper into the cave and put more wood on the fire before stretching out with Gyp tucked closely into her side. She fell asleep with her left hand buried in Gyp's fur and dreamed of the creatures that danced upon the cave walls.

Chapter Ten

Nat woke up the next morning and put a pot of coffee on after stoking the fire. The Northern Lights were starting to fade when Gyp stretched before lying down by the fire. There was an extra crispness in the air this morning and Nat felt certain they would encounter rain before they made it home.

She lifted the sack and carried it down to the rock pools in search of shrimp with Gyp on her heels. Nat removed her boots and waded into the pool where she found a bounty of several dozen shrimp that she placed in the sack. She added more water and then tightened the drawstring on the sack. She sat down on a rock waiting for her feet to dry then put her socks on and slipped back into her boots. They walked back to the cave where Nat hung the sack and took out several slices of the thin jerky for breakfast.

"I sure could go for one of Marissa's breakfasts right now." She bit down on the chewy meat.

Gyp held the strip between her paws, chewing the meat until it was soft enough to swallow. Nat sipped her coffee as the sun crept into the morning sky and then she doused the fire with the rest of the coffee. The hot embers hissed and steamed, filling the air with smoke. Nat took the remainder of the wood into the cave and laid it next to the fire pit as the previous visitor had done. She rolled up her bedroll and fastened it to the back of her saddle, which she carried out and placed on Hardy's back. She cinched up the girth and placed the bridle on her faithful steed, preparing to leave for home. Nat slid the rifle back into the holder and hooked the strings of the food sack and the waterproofed sack over her saddle horn.

Nat placed her foot in the stirrup and mounted Hardy. "Let's go home, my friends." Her heel nudged Hardy into movement.

They traveled the path until midmorning, when Nat pulled Hardy to a stop and dismounted. She led him over to a small stream and allowed him to drink his fill of the cold water. She and Gyp shared more of the jerky. Nat knelt, filled her hands with the cold water, and quenched her thirst with Gyp lapping up water beside her.

After a short break, she mounted Hardy and pulled her hat down over her eyes to block the light rain that had begun to fall. Gyp ran ahead of them, chasing wild scents, and she would disappear into the dense woods and reappear ahead of them down the path, waiting for them to catch up. Nat observed an abundance of wild life as she trudged along, and she would have taken a large buck if she had brought Quincy the mule to carry the carcass. *You will only grow bigger.* She smiled watching him bound across the path in front of them.

The plodding of Hardy's hooves and the creak of her leather saddle, made Nat sleepy and she felt her head begin to nod. A sharp yelp from Gyp made her head jerk up and her hand instinctively moved to the butt of the rifle. She watched a rabbit bolt from the underbrush and flee quickly down the path with Gyp closely on its heels. Another ten yards and Gyp would have caught the rabbit. But it veered hard right and disappeared down a hole in the ground. Gyp skidded to a halt and used her front paws to dig at the hole.

"That rabbit is long gone, Gyp." Gyp stopped digging and trotted back onto the path.

When they arrived at the cabin, dismounted and grabbed a water bucket, dropping two dozen of the shrimp into it and covered them with the salty water. She left the bucket on the counter and returned to take up the sack and mount Hardy for the ride into town. Nat planned to drop the sack off to Maggie and then meet Marissa at the hotel to walk her home.

†

Nat rode Hardy to Maggie's small house on the edge of town. The Indian woman was sitting on her porch, peeling one of the apples Nat had brought her. Maggie's gray-streaked hair gave her an appearance of being older than Nat had originally assumed. Maybe in her forties, Maggie worked circles around women half her age.

"You are back sooner than expected," she told Nat when she dismounted.

"I decided against the full trip to the ocean, but I did find a location that one day I could call home." She took the sack from her saddle horn and walked to the porch. "I have a surprise for you."

The woman watched with anticipation as Nat opened the drawstring on the sack and placed her hand inside fishing around until her fingers came across one of the shrimp. She pulled it out of the sack and the woman cried out in surprise.

"Shrimp. I haven't seen those in ages." Her eyes shined brightly at the sight.

"There are a dozen or so in there with your clams."

"Wonderful." Maggie hugged Nat's neck before taking the sack she offered.

"What is the best way to cook those?" Nat asked. "I tried grilling them on the camp fire, but they were very bland."

"Remove the head and outer shell and then dip them in a whipped egg, then some seasoned flour, and fry them in some light grease," the woman instructed.

"Sounds easy enough."

"When they turn a golden brown, take them from the grease, and let them cool."

"I will try that tonight."

"If you and Marissa will come by tomorrow night, we will have some fresh clam chowder," the woman said with a warm smile.

"You have a deal," Nat promised and turned to walk back to Hardy.

"Wait just a minute."

Nat stopped and turned back to the woman.

"I have something for you." She took the sack inside and reappeared moments later with two pair of breeches tied up with a string.

"You're done already?"

"When you get to be my age, you don't sleep as well as you did when you were young." She handed Nat the package. "Try those on later and let me know if any changes are needed."

"Thank you, my friend." Nat reached for Hardy's reins and they walked to the hotel.

†

The sun was starting to set and Nat knew it wouldn't be long before Marissa finished her shift. She left Hardy tied to a hitching post, told Gyp to stay, and entered the hotel. When she stepped inside Marissa looked up and her smile lit the entire room.

Marissa rushed over and hugged her tightly. "You are home early."

"I missed you," Nat admitted with a smile. "How much longer until you are done here?" she asked.

"Just a few more minutes."

"We'll wait for you on the porch and walk you home then."

"I'll be right there." Marissa turned to walk back into the kitchen.

Nat walked back onto the porch and sat in a chair with Gyp beside her waiting for Marissa.

Marissa finished the last of the dishes and then joined Nat for the walk home. "I am so glad to see you." They walked from town and she reached for Nat's hand.

"I decided against the trip all the way to the ocean when I found a spot of pure heaven at the southern tip of the Sound. We saw some unique creatures, but we decided we missed your cooking and warm bed," Nat admitted.

"Are you saying I'm spoiling you?"

"Yes, that is it exactly." Nat grinned. "Tonight I have a treat for you, though. I am going to cook dinner for you."

"Oh goody, what are we having?"

"I am frying shrimp for you," Nat stated proudly.

"I haven't had fresh shrimp in years."

"Tonight you will. I caught them early this morning. As soon as I take care of Hardy I'll be over to cook for you," Nat said when they reached her cabin.

"I look forward to that." Marissa stood facing Nat.

Nat leaned down and kissed Marissa softly. "I'll see you soon."

✝

Marissa walked on to her cabin as Nat led Hardy into the small barn and removed the saddle from him. She wiped down his coat and filled his feed bin before leaving the barn. She took her bedroll and rifle back inside her cabin and then walked to Marissa's place.

Nat took her coat off and hung it behind the door. "Good you have the frying pan heating." Nat peeled and removed the heads from the shrimp while Marissa watched her closely. "Can you pour some flour in a bowl for me?" she asked.

"Yes, I will."

Nat took a small grate and placed it above the coals in the fireplace. She also put a large portion of lard in the heated frying pan and placed it on the grate to heat up. Next, she took two eggs, and cracked them, emptied them into a bowl, and used a fork to scramble them. She shook salt and pepper into the flour and shook the mixture, blending it together. Marissa watched Nat pick up a shrimp, dunk it into the egg, and then coated it with the flour. Nat repeated the process with a dozen of the shrimp and then carried the plate holding them over to the fireplace and placing them in the bubbling grease.

She returned the plate to the counter and breaded the remaining shrimp as the first batch began to cook. Nat took a clean plate and a long metal fork and sat on the hearth, watching the shrimp cook. Marissa, in the meantime, took the shrimp shells out in the bucket, dumped them in the fire, and rinsed out the bucket.

Nat turned the shrimp in the grease and smiled when she saw them beginning to turn a golden brown. Marissa placed plates and forks on the table and poured glasses of cool water for them while Nat cooked.

The first batch was cooked and Nat took them from the grease. She placed them on a plate to cool before cooking the next batch.

Marissa was watching her carefully. "You handle that frying pan well." She smiled at Nat.

"I can cook, it's just that I am limited to what I can cook. Most of my experience has come in the woods, where we eat what we have killed."

"Well those smell wonderful and I can't wait to taste them. How was your trip?"

"It was good to be on an adventure, but seeing the ocean was a dream I shared with my father and with him not present, it just didn't feel right. We traveled less than a day south and camped at a spot along the southern tip of the Sound that was as close to heaven as I've ever seen. Gyp woke me the first night, to get up and see the Northern Lights."

"Good girl, Gyp." Gyp lifted her head.

"They were a beautiful swirling green and we watched them until the sun rose. Later that morning, we found a small rock pool that was teaming with creatures stranded by the receding tide."

"That sounds interesting."

"I was amazed by how plentiful the food was, just swimming there in the pool, waiting to be harvested. I was surprised that no one had settled close with such a plentiful food supply."

"I'm sure someone will settle there in the coming years as the towns continue to swell," Marissa said. "I have heard that the winter storms on the coast can be wet bitter, and brutally cold, which may discourage settlers from moving in."

"We were lucky when we found a nice cave to take shelter in." She looked at Gyp, lying between them. "We saw some strange creatures in the water, didn't we, girl."

"How were they strange?" Marissa asked.

"They were huge black and white, fish-like creatures, but every few minutes they would come to the surface and blow water out of their bodies through a hole on the top of its head."

"Those are called whales. It sounds like Orcas if they were black and white. The natives hunt the gray ones for their meat and for the blubber that the animals store to help them maintain their warmth in the frozen waters up north."

"In the back of the cave we found paintings of the creatures and others I have never seen before." Nat turned the shrimp in the pan. "There was also a skeleton of one of those whales and I brought this back with me." She pulled the tooth from inside her shirt. "This was one of many inside the jaws of those creatures," she explained.

Marissa had never seen a whale, but had heard many tales of the giant creatures. She took the tooth in her hand and examined it closely. "This must be from an Orca. A tooth this sharp could only come from a predator," she observed.

"That is what I thought when I saw the size of the creatures." She took another batch of shrimp out and dropped the last few in the seasoned grease. "Why don't we start with these while the last of them cook?"

Marissa followed Nat to the table and watched her cut several shrimp into bite sized pieces for Gyp and placed them in her bowl. Then she took several of the shrimp and placed them on her plate. She bit into the crunchy morsel and smiled at Gyp. "These are much better fried than roasted."

Marissa took a bite. "These are small, but tasty."

"I roasted some over the campfire last night and they were terrible."

"Well, you didn't have the luxuries of home, so there wasn't much else you could do but roast them."

"That's true, but the fish I cooked was excellent, so we filled our bellies with that." She placed Gyp's bowl on the floor.

"She will eat anything you do, won't she?" Marissa asked.

"So far, but I think I was pressing my luck with those shrimp."

"She seems to be doing just fine with these," Marissa said.

Nat stood and walked to the fire to turn the shrimp still cooking. She was very pleased with how well they had turned out and Marissa seemed to be enjoying them.

"We have been invited to town tomorrow night for clam chowder." Nat turned and walked back to the table. "Maggie was surprised when I brought her some of these shrimp and gave me the secret to cooking them."

"You did an excellent job and I will look forward to the chowder. I have never had it, but I have heard of it from travelers."

"I think the next time I decide to take a trip, I will take Quincy with me. I could have taken a nice buck on the journey home, but wouldn't have been able to transport the carcass. I bet some of those fish would taste great smoked, too."

"Maybe next time I'll travel with you."

"I would like that," Nat said with a warm smile. She walked to the fire, took the remainder of the shrimp from the grease, and placed the pan on the hearth to cool.

She and Marissa ate their fill and then Nat allowed the remaining shrimp to cool, and dropped them into Gyp's bowl. Gyp stood and ate the rest of the food and then let out a soft burp.

Marissa and Nat laughed at the dog who cocked her head to the side.

"My feelings exactly." Nat patted her full stomach.

Marissa cleaned the dishes while Nat took the frying pan outside and poured the grease over the wood in the fire pit. Unlike bacon grease that she saved to season other foods, the grease from the shrimp smelled too pungent and Nat doubted it would be good for seasoning. She then took the pan to the well and rinsed it thoroughly.

Marissa was wiping down the table when Nat returned inside the house. "It is a bit cool, but it's beautiful out tonight." Would you like to sit outside with me for a while?"

"Just let me get my coat," Marissa replied.

Nat and Marissa sat on the front porch steps and looked up into the beautiful night sky. Nat wrapped her arm around Marissa and held her close, sharing her warmth with her. She pointed out the different constellations and told Marissa the stories her father had shared with her as a child.

"You really miss living outdoors, don't you?" Marissa asked.

"It is so beautiful, but I have to admit, after sleeping in a bed, the ground was a lot less comfortable." Nat followed up her statement with a long yawn.

"Comfortable maybe, but I was lonesome without you."

"So you missed me, too?"

"You could say that."

Nat felt her shiver beneath her arm. "Why don't we go warm up that bed?"

"That is fine with me." Marissa stood, smiled, and took Nat's hand.

"Let's go, Gyp." Gyp came bounding up the steps, racing for the door. "Are we set for firewood in the bedroom?"

"Yes, I stocked up before I left this morning."

Nat blew out the lantern in the kitchen and then followed Marissa into the bedroom. She placed several pieces of wood on the fire and then began to undress. Marissa offered her a nightshirt, but Nat shook her head. "Tonight I want to feel your skin next to mine."

Marissa stripped down and climbed between the sheets where she waited for Nat.

Nat joined her in the bed and pressed close to Marissa. "I missed you so much."

"I missed you, too."

"Will you roll over onto your side and let me hold you tonight?" Nat asked.

Marissa was disappointed that Nat was ready for sleep but understood her weariness from traveling. "Of course I will." She rolled over and turned her back to Nat.

Nat snuggled in close and placed her hand between Marissa's warm breasts. She fell asleep breathing in the fragrance of Marissa's skin.

Chapter Eleven

Nat woke the next morning with Marissa's head lying on her shoulder and her fingers toying with the bear claw around Nat's neck. "Good morning. Have you been awake long?"

"No." Marissa looked into her eyes. "Tell me about your father."

"Nathan and Nanya were my parents," Nat started. "My mother was full-blooded Mohican and died many years ago from influenza, so Nathan pretty much raised me on his own."

"Have you spent all of your life in the woods?"

"Mostly, with the exception of a few months each year, when we would take shelter for the winter months. Before the war broke out, we would winter with my mother's tribe. Once the war started, Nathan felt it would be best if we traveled west."

"You have never had any formal education yet you read and write?"

"Father was a well-educated man, and at night, he would teach me reading, writing, math, and history." Nat smiled with the memory of her father. "During the day he taught me everything he knew about tracking, trapping, and harvesting the valuable furs that were so plentiful along the border with Canada."

Nat fell silent for a few minutes. Sadness hanging around her like a mist. "I don't have many memories of Nanya." Nat's voice was sad. "I do remember, though, how beautiful she was and how my father looked at her."

"How was that?" Marissa asked.

Nat smiled. "The way you are looking at me now, with love and adoration."

Marissa blushed. "I understand the way he must have felt about your mother."

Nat rolled onto her side, facing Marissa, her eyes searching Marissa's face and fingers caressing her cheek. "I love you too," Nat whispered before kissing Marissa's lips.

They spent the morning making love under the warm covers, oblivious to the falling snow that was blanketing their world. When they finally crept from the bed, Gyp raced to the front door, ready to go out to relieve her bladder. Nat opened the door and sighed. "Would you look at this?"

Marissa walked to her side and looked out the door at the yard covered in at least two inches of snow. "Isn't it beautiful?"

"Very much so." They watched Gyp romp playfully in the snow. "I think Gyp likes it too." Nat couldn't help smiling.

"Don't forget we are supposed to go into town for clam chowder tonight."

"I'm looking forward to it. I think I have worked up an appetite this morning," she said with a grin.

"There should be some leftover bacon and biscuits if you would like a light meal. I can cook you some eggs too."

"You have my mouth watering."

"When we're finished, we will take a bath to be fresh when we go into town."

"You don't like the smell of the wild on me?"

"It is not as appealing as your fresh and clean smell after a bath."

"I guess I better go light the fire on the wash pot then."

"There is already cold water in the tub, so at least we won't have to carry more in. Three eggs for you and two for Gyp?" she asked.

"That should be plenty." Nat moved out the door and off the porch, taking several pieces of dry wood, and she used dry grass to stoke the fire. She watched the flames begin to lick up the side of the wash pot.

After scooping up a handful of snow and forming a snowball, Nat took aim on an unsuspecting Gyp. She hurled the mass at Gyp and struck her in the hindquarter. Gyp let out a sharp yelp of surprise and turned to look at Nat. Nat laughed and then shouted, "Caught you sleeping, didn't I?"

Nat was still chuckling and shaking her head while starting for the porch. Gyp ran up behind her and caught Nat by the ankle, causing her to trip and lose her balance, falling none too gracefully on her butt in the cold snow. Gyp looked at Nat and made a dash for the house. Nat saw her run and roared with laughter.

Marissa turned just as Nat entered the house, still wiping snow from her backside. "What are you two up to?"

"Just playing."

"Gyp ran into the house like her feet were on fire."

"She ran in for protection," Nat said with a chuckle.

"Were you picking on her?"

"I was, but she got the better of me."

"Good girl, Gyp."

"Hey, don't encourage her."

Marissa placed Nat's eggs on her plate and then cooked two for Gyp. Then she joined them at breakfast and ate a biscuit and some bacon while watching Gyp devour the meal. "This cold weather is good for her appetite."

"Was there something wrong with it before?" Nat asked.

"Maybe she has just gotten used to my cooking." Marissa grinned.

"Well, it is better than what we eat in the woods," Nat admitted.

"Maybe I need to fatten you both up some this winter then."

"Gyp maybe, but I need to be able to fit in my clothes."

"Not to worry, after all my good food, you haven't gained an ounce."

"That could be because you work it off of me," Nat replied with a mischievous grin.

Marissa blushed. "I think I'll start carrying some water in."

Nat finished her meal and took a bucket to assist Marissa in carrying water to fill the tub.

"Undress and let me have those clothes to drop in the wash pot," Marissa instructed.

"Yes ma'am." Nat undressed and held out her clothing.

Marissa took the clothes. "Get started on your bath and I'll join you shortly."

Nat climbed into the bathtub and began by washing her hair. It had grown well beyond her shoulders and Nat considered asking Marissa to cut it shorter for her as she bathed. When Marissa walked into the room, carrying fresh clothes for Nat, and began to undress, Nat forgot all about the length of her hair.

When they had bathed and dressed, Nat suggested they walk into town and stop by the store to purchase a pound of coffee.

"We still have coffee."

"It is not for us," Nat replied. "We should take it and maybe some sugar as a gift for the meal we are about to eat."

"Good idea."

"You know it is a shame, but I don't even know the woman's full name."

"It is Maggie Lightfoot."

"That is a nice strong name."

"She has been living there at the edge of town ever since I can remember."

"Besides her stitchery, what other services does she use to provide for her needs?"

"She gets quite a bit of business from the trappers, but she also does some baking and canning of vegetables she grows for the hotel."

"So let's add a pound of flour also."

"You really have a soft spot for this woman, don't you?"

"She charged me a fifth of the price she should have for those breeches. I would have had to pay much more for them anywhere else."

"Toss in a couple of spools of thread, too, then," Marissa added. "She collects scraps of fabric from old clothing and makes some of the warmest down quilts in the area."

"Any more and we will probably hurt her feelings."

"We will stop there then," Marissa replied, finishing dressing.

Nat pulled on her boots then reached for her range coat, sliding her arms through the warm garment. She handed Marissa the one she had bought for her and then wrapped a warm scarf around her neck. "Stay warm." She opened the door and they entered a light snowfall.

†

They made their purchases at the store and walked the short distance to Maggie's house. Nat knocked lightly on the door and they waited.

Maggie opened the door and smiled. "Come on in," she said, and the three of them entered. Gyp shook the flakes from her coat before going inside and making a beeline for the fireplace.

"Welcome my friends. Let me take your coats."

Maggie placed their coats on hooks behind the door to dry. She looked at the package in Nat's hands then back up to the two women's faces.

"We brought a few small gifts." Nat handed the package to Maggie.

"That was not necessary." Maggie took the package and placed it on the table to open it up. She smiled when she saw the coffee, sugar, flour, and thread. "Thank you."

"Thank you for the dinner invitation."

"You made that possible by bringing back the clams. Are you hungry?"

Nat looked at Marissa. "I'm always hungry," she said with a sheepish grin.

"You work very hard, so you work up a good appetite. That is very good for you." She took her coffee pot and poured water and some of the ground coffee into it and placed it on the fire. "We'll have coffee with dessert," she said with a smile. "Have a seat and I'll bring the meal."

"Is there anything I can help with?" Marissa asked.

"You can fill four bowls with the chowder while I get the fry bread," Maggie answered.

Marissa filled three of the bowls to the rim, and in the fourth she left some room. She took the water pitcher and poured a small amount of water in it to cool the chowder.

Maggie had torn up a piece of the fry bread. "Here, drop this in there as well to help it cool."

Marissa took the bread and dropped it into the steamy soup and then used a spoon to stir the mixture. Gyp was sitting and watching while licking her lips in what could only be anticipation.

"Better wait a few minutes yet," Nat said, taking a seat at the table. She looked at the creamy chowder and sniffed—it smelled wonderful.

"It is very hot, so be careful you don't burn your mouth," Maggie warned.

Nat lifted a spoonful and blew softly on it to help it cool. When she placed the mixture in her mouth, she moaned with appreciation. "This is very tasty."

"I hope you like it," Maggie smiled. "I used the clams that you brought back, and added diced potatoes and some corn."

"This is really good," Marissa praised.

Maggie dunked a piece of the bread into her chowder and took a bite of it after tasting a spoonful of the chowder.

Nat ate two bowls of the soup and three slices of the fry bread heartily.

"Save room for some apple pie," Maggie reminded them.

Nat placed her spoon in the bowl and grinned at Maggie. "I forgot you mentioned dessert, but that chowder was so delicious."

"I'm glad you enjoyed it."

"I'll definitely be bringing back more clams the next time I go on a journey."

"They are a great deal of work for such small portions of meat, but the meat is very rich and will give you energy," Maggie said.

"Nat used your instructions for cooking the shrimp last night and they were very tasty too," Marissa reported.

"I had the last of mine for lunch today. They were a very pleasant surprise."

"I still can't get over the bounty of life trapped in the rock pools," Nat said, remembering how simple it was to catch the shrimp.

"Maybe I could join you on your next trip and help harvest some of them," Maggie said. "Did you see shelled creatures with long feelers, and claws for hands?" Maggie asked.

"Yes, there were a few, but I had no idea what they were."

"Those are called crabs," Maggie said. "They have a very sweet, tender meat that, when boiled and dipped in melted butter, is like tasting heaven."

"That description makes me want to ride out and get some now."

"They more than likely have taken to deeper, warmer waters for the winter, but they will be plentiful again in the spring." She smiled at Nat. "We could probably sell all that we can carry back alive to the hotel."

"I think Joseph would jump at that opportunity," Marissa added, "but I'll be sure to ask just the same."

"You have a mule don't you?"

"Yes, a very stubborn one."

"I have a small wagon out back, and for a small price, we could buy a couple of those large pickle barrels and bring back quite a haul," Maggie said.

"I'll check on the barrels tomorrow. When the winter breaks, we'll go to the southern tip and bring back what we can."

"I'll look forward to that." Maggie grinned.

Maggie got up then and served pie and coffee. After they finished dessert, she sent them home with two large jars of the chowder.

As they stepped out onto the small porch, Nat noticed the very small pile of chopped wood Maggie had. *I need to chop some more for her,* she thought. The snow had begun to fall lightly, as she took Marissa's hand and they walked home.

✝

That was the first of the many light snows that would besiege them that winter. Nat and Gyp would walk into town with Marissa on the days she had to work, and Nat frequently found herself spending her days with Smithy, assisting him in evaluating the late season furs that trappers taking refuge from the bitter winter storms brought in from the northern border. She enjoyed spending time with the big man, and in some ways, he reminded her of Nathan with his gentle ways. He was ferocious when it came to trading but always treated his customers generously and professionally.

During that winter, Smithy taught Nat a great deal about what furs and products sold best in the market. As he had explained to her when she first returned to town, any type of bear products sold for excellent money. While he was not encouraging her to hunt for bear, he did say he could move any bear item she might bring in next year.

Along with bear items another big market item was mounted heads. "Buck heads and ram heads are also much sought-after items," he had told her after one customer had left the store. "The man that just left is the owner of the saloon and livery, and will buy any decent mounted piece to hang in the saloon. He loves to spin wild tales of his hunting adventures to inflate his sense of manliness." Smithy chuckled. "To be honest, I don't know if the man would even know how to load a weapon."

"What do you know about whales?" Nat asked.

"They are huge creatures that the Makah hunt as their main source of food and heating oil," Smithy answered. "Why do you ask?"

"When I camped at the southern tip of the Sound, I found the remains of what I believe to be one of those creatures in a cave."

"If you journey back there, bring back some of those rib bones." He smiled at Nat. "I bet some of these greenhorns would buy them, they seem to buy anything wild."

"I do hope to go back that way once this weather breaks. I saw a huge buck on my way home that I plan to go get."

Smithy chuckled. "You're always on the hunt, aren't you?"

"I guess I am," Nat said with a grin.

"Have you decided on what you will do this spring?" Smithy asked.

"No, not yet."

"You'll have a job here if you want it."

"Thanks, Smithy. I'm not sure what I'll do."

"I know you'll make the right decision when the time comes."

Nat left his store to meet Marissa for the walk home.

†

Every few weeks, Nat would wake early, hitch Quincy to a small sling, and bring in a pile of chopped wood for Maggie's porch. She was home by the time Marissa had breakfast on the table. Nat never saw Maggie during her deliveries, but Maggie would be there, behind the curtains watching Nat stack the wood close to the door.

One morning when it was time for Nat to make a delivery, she found a package wrapped in string with her name on it. She stacked the wood and picked up the package before she started home. She cared for Quincy and walked into the kitchen as Marissa was placing biscuits on the table.

"What do you have there?" Marissa asked.

"A gift from Maggie, apparently. I found it sitting on the porch this morning when I dropped off the wood."

"Open it," Marissa urged.

Nat untied the string and peeled back the paper. Maggie had sewn a quilt, the most beautiful Nat had ever seen.

"That is beautiful," Marissa said.

Nat lifted the quilt and opened it to reveal the bold pattern Maggie had sewn for her.

"We will need that on the bed if the temperature keeps dropping like it has."

"Have you been getting cold during the night?" Nat asked.

"A little, yes."

"I have the remedy for that. Take this and place it on the bed and I will be right back."

Marissa took the quilt, spread it across her bed, and then waited for Nat's return.

Nat walked back to her cabin and went to the bedroom. For the last several weeks, she had been working on the bearskin and had finally managed to clean all of the wild smell from it. If she placed the skin over the new quilt, she thought Marissa would not be cold again at night. She took the pelt in her arms and carried it back to Marissa's cabin. Once inside she walked to the bed and spread it on top of the quilt. "Now you won't get cold again."

That night after they entered the bed, Nat pulled the covers, quilt, and bearskin over their bodies and they slept the night away, wrapped in the toasty warmth of one another.

Chapter Twelve

Nat sat on the front porch while taking a break from splitting wood. The afternoon was fading quickly and Marissa would be home soon. She sat with one booted foot on the porch railing and watched the dripping of water from the roofline. Winter was almost over, and the frost that remained on the roof was beginning to melt. Nat sat mesmerized by the falling droplets and thinking about the future.

Earlier in the day she had delivered the pickle barrels to Maggie's home, and placed them securely on the small cart they would use to go to the southern tip of the Sound. She had also fashioned a small bench seat for Maggie to sit on while they traveled. If the weather continued to warm over the next few days, they would leave later in the week. She and Maggie had prepared for the trip by including proper pots and pans to do real cooking in the cave where they would shelter during the trip.

Nat also made a stop at the general store to purchase additional dungarees and warmer clothes for Marissa to travel in. There would be no comfort in dresses on this trip.

Gyp bounded off the front porch and ran to the road to greet Marissa who was returning home.

"Hello, Gyp." She knelt to stroke the dog's head.

Gyp walked with her until she came into view of the cabin and saw Nat sitting on the porch waiting for her to arrive. Marissa carried a small bucket filled with chicken and biscuits she had prepared for their dinner.

"Hello, my love," Nat said when Marissa stepped onto the porch.

"Hello, Nat, I hope you've had a good day."

"I have at that. I spent the morning with Maggie preparing for our trip."

"Is there anything I need to do?" Marissa asked.

"Other than trying on your new outfit? No, I think we are set."

"What new outfit?"

"I bought you some proper traveling clothes."

Marissa, followed by Nat, walked into the cabin and put the bucket down before opening the package sitting on the table. After Nat sat at the table, she held the dungarees next to her while taking out a long-sleeved undershirt along with a thick work shirt to wear on top. "Let's see how well you did on the sizes." Marissa disappeared into the bedroom to change.

Nat had actually done very well on selecting the correct sizes. Marissa slipped on the dungarees and then the undershirt, tucking it into the dungarees. She then slipped the work shirt over the undershirt. Other than the sleeves being a little long, it fit her quite well. She put her leather boots back on and went to model the outfit for Nat.

"What do you think?" She stepped back into the room and made a slow circle for Nat.

"I think you look like a proper out-of-doors woman now. The fit looks good and should be ample to keep you warm during our journey."

"It feels so odd to not be wearing a dress."

"Have you never owned dungarees before?"

"Not until you bought my first pair."

"I have prepared our bedrolls for the trip also," Nat said.

"I'm so excited, I can barely wait."

"We will leave soon, my love."

✝

For the next two days Nat made the final preparations for their trip. She took Quincy into town to have his hooves filed and she hooked him up to the small cart and pulled it home. Nat intended to take a small load of split wood to use in the cave, which would burn longer and hotter than the dried driftwood. She would load the wood the morning that they departed.

She also took Hardy and Buck into town to see the blacksmith for new shoes. While she waited for her animals, Nat went to the general store to buy several pounds of salt and a new box of cartridges for her rifle. They would camp at the small river on the return trip home while Nat hunted for the large buck she had seen. If successful in her hunt, she and Maggie would split the meat and coat it with heavy salt until they arrived home. Then they would smoke the fresh meat. She and Marissa still had a bounty of meat in the smoke house, so Nat intended the majority of the venison for Maggie. She would also take the pelt and the head to sell to Smithy, along with several of the whale ribs if they were still present in the cave.

It would be a fun trip for them as well as a profitable one, if their plans worked out.

Marissa was overwhelmed with excitement the night before they were due to depart. She baked biscuits and a fresh pie to take with them on the trip. Marissa bustled around the kitchen worried she would not sleep that night. When she curled up in Nat's arms later that evening, she slept soundly throughout the night.

✝

Nat woke before the sun rose and dressed in her breeches and travel clothes. She slipped quietly from the house and hitched Quincy to the cart, filling the back of it with the split wood she intended to take with them. She also loaded the axe and a small rake into the back of the cart.

She went inside to wake Marissa. She sat down on the side of the bed and leaned down to kiss Marissa. "It is time to wake, my love," she softly whispered.

Marissa stretched and turned toward Nat smiling. "Good morning, love."

"It is time to be up and moving about. I have Quincy hitched and will take him into town to load Maggie's supplies and bring her here."

"I'll be ready when you return, my love. I'll cook some breakfast to take with us and then douse both fireplaces."

"I'll saddle the horses when I return and we'll be ready to depart." She leaned down to kiss Marissa. "I love you."

"I love you too." Marissa threw her arms around Nat's neck and hugged her close.

Gyp and Nat walked Quincy into town. Maggie had her bundles ready and they loaded them into the cart. "All set?" Nat asked.

"I think I have everything we need," Maggie answered.

"Let's be off then."

Maggie walked beside Nat and Quincy, choosing to walk the short distance. She led Quincy the last way to Marissa's while Nat stopped off to saddle Hardy and Buck for the trip. Maggie and Marissa were sitting on the porch eating a bacon-filled biscuit when Nat led the two horses into the yard.

Nat ate a biscuit with them and then walked back inside the cabin to get the rifle and her range coat, which she tied across her bedroll. She handed Marissa her coat and Marissa tied it across her bedroll. The sun had risen and was shining down on them as they prepared to leave.

Nat helped Marissa into the saddle and then mounted Hardy. Maggie walked beside Quincy preferring to stretch her city legs for most of the morning. They made good time, and by the time the sun was overhead, they stopped at the small river.

"We will camp here on the return home since this is where I plan to take that buck."

"I saw his tracks a small way back and he is huge," Maggie said.

"He will provide enough meat to feed you through next winter." Nat grinned.

Maggie smiled back at her. "How much farther?" she asked.

"We will arrive by midday, but we should water the animals here and fill our flasks as fresh water is rare once we go down to the Sound."

After the animals were watered and flasks filled, the travelers continued on their journey. In another hour of travel, Nat could begin to smell the stronger scent of salt on the breeze and she knew that they were coming close.

"Can you smell the salt in the air?" she asked Marissa who was riding beside her.

"Faintly, yes," Marissa answered. "Will we be there soon?"

"Very soon."

As they approached the final hilltop, Nat could hear the roar of the water and she knew they had arrived. "Here we are." They crested the hill and looked down onto the beach.

†

Nat dismounted Hardy and handed her reins to Marissa, then took Quincy's halter and led him down to the beach and up the narrow path to the cave. Maggie and Marissa followed closely behind.

"Let's set up camp and then we can go explore those pools," Nat suggested to her friends.

Nat carried the wood into the back of the cave while Maggie lit a fire before she and Marissa carried their supplies inside. Nat unsaddled the horses, and placed the saddles deep in the cave. She watched Hardy and Buck run down to the water's edge. Nat then unhitched Quincy, propping the arms of the cart on a large boulder to keep it upright. She then watched Quincy joining his larger friends, rushing to them in his fastest speed—a slow trot.

She followed the three animals movement down to the water's edge, and then moved inside to see how the camp was coming. Marissa was looking at the painted walls with great curiosity as Maggie interpreted the meaning of each painting for her. Nat smiled and quickly found herself enthralled by Maggie's commentary.

"This one," she pointed at a drawing with a stick, "tells the tale of the hunt for this creature, a whale as we know it now. Hunters paddled out in their small boats with spears, and from the paintings, I'd say several of them failed to return to shore. They tell of a long battle with the whale, and the celebration they had when they finally pulled him to shore."

"What's this?" Marissa asked.

"The black-painted faces are the hunters who did not survive the battle."

"So four of them perished?"

"According to this story, yes, pulled under the sea for their eternal rest, as this one shows." She pointed to a drawing of the four black faced hunters floating on the water.

"That's an amazing story. Why do you think they left those behind?"

The whalebones were still tucked away in the shadows when they reached the rear corner of the cave.

"I would guess that with the loss of their brothers, they didn't have space to carry more than the meat and blubber they sought."

"I'm glad we're hunting smaller creatures. Are we ready to walk down to the pools?" Nat asked.

Both Maggie and Marissa nodded and followed Nat to the mouth of the cave. Nat stopped to take the rifle from her saddle and then led her friends to the rock pools.

She watched Maggie and Marissa walking around the pools pointing out various types of creatures, but also taking inventory. "I have counted twenty-five crabs," Marissa said excitedly.

"Wait here and I will bring one of the barrels and we can begin the harvest," Nat said.

Maggie had already removed her boots and was rolling up the legs of her breeches as Nat made her comment. Marissa followed suit, and within minutes, Nat returned with a barrel.

Marissa watched Maggie grabbing a crab, steering clear of the powerful claws that could inflict a painful wound if they were not careful. Nat removed her boots and joined in the harvest of the creatures until they had taken all of them from the pools.

Nat had also brought her spear back from the cave. "Would you like fresh fish tonight for dinner?" she asked.

"I saw two large ones in that pool that should do quite well," Maggie pointed to a larger rock pool.

Nat used her spear to impale the fish and then carried them back to where Maggie and Marissa were waiting for her.

"If you will take the fish and rifle, I will carry the barrel back to the cave. Then we will use a bucket to add water to the barrel."

Nat lifted the heavy barrel and walked quickly toward the cave, stopping halfway to catch her breath.

"Can I help?" Marissa asked.

"You could have if I had thought to fashion some sort of handles on the barrel. I'm almost there." Nat lifted the barrel again. When they reached the cave, Nat sat on a nearby rock to catch her wind.

"I will clean these for dinner if you will begin carrying water," Maggie told Marissa. Nat began to stand. "You rest for now."

"You heard the lady." Marissa grinned, picking up the bucket and starting toward the water with Gyp on her heels.

Maggie carried the fish down to the water's edge to clean, preparing them for roasting. When she returned to the cave, she walked past Nat and placed the fish on the spit above the fire to begin cooking.

Marissa dumped five buckets of water into the barrel to cover the crabs and then sat beside Nat.

"I have a surprise for you," Maggie said. "Bring your bucket and your rake and follow me."

Nat picked up the rake and Marissa took the bucket, following Maggie down to the beach. She took the rake from Nat and began raking when she saw bubbles forming in the wet sand. Nat and Marissa picked up the clams and dropped them into the bucket.

"I brought the cream broth for some chowder. All we need is fresh clams. I'll put it on to cook if you will help me prepare these."

"Just show me how."

"First, we have to boil them to get them to open properly." Nat watched as Maggie placed a small pot of water over the fire. They dropped the clams inside and waited until the shells began to pop open.

Maggie took Nat's knife from her boot, and showed her how to use the tip to cut the small morsel of meat from the shell.

"Just drop them in the pot as you shell them and they will cook into the broth," Maggie said with a grin. She then took containers of seasoning and shook them across the fish, and sprinkled more into the pot of cooking chowder. "We shall feast tonight."

Nat sat with her hand running through Gyp's fur, talking with Maggie and Marissa while they waited for dinner to cook. "I think we had a good harvest for a first day."

"Yes, we did," Maggie agreed. "It will be interesting to see what tomorrow brings, to see if the rock pools refill with creatures."

"I may journey past the rock pools tomorrow to see what else exists. If you think you and Marissa can handle the harvest."

"I think we will do just fine," Marissa said. "I will take the bucket and bring it back here as we fill it. Taking a full barrel is just too much strain."

"I agree," Maggie said. "You stretch your legs and we will care for the harvest."

✝

Gyp was laying on the cave floor when her ears perked and she rose to her feet before running to the mouth of the cave alerting the women.

"I wonder what she heard." Nat, closely followed by Marissa and Maggie, stood to follow her companion. When she reached the mouth of the cave, Nat looked out across the water and saw what Gyp was looking at. "Whales," she pointed to the water.

They all walked down to the edge of the water and watched as the creatures reached the water's surface and expelled air and water from their bodies before taking their next breaths. They watched until they swam beyond sight as the night began to bloom.

When they returned to the cave, Maggie and Marissa took out bowls, plates, and spoons from their packs and prepared to serve dinner. Maggie dipped out chowder and set it out to cool before serving up portions of the flakey fish. She crumbled pieces of fish into Gyp's bowl of chowder.

"It has to cool first, Gyp," Maggie warned.

Marissa poured coffee for each of them as they gathered around the fire to share their first meal.

"Thank you for this wondrous bounty," Maggie spoke to no one in particular.

They nibbled on the cooling fish waiting for the chowder to cool enough to eat. Between the four of them, they finished the fish and a bowl of chowder each. Gyp had an extra portion of fish while the women had a slice of Marissa's pie.

"That was a wonderful meal," Nat said to Maggie and Marissa. She placed more wood on the fire, and as the skies darkened outside, the shadows danced on the walls of the cave. "I am going to tend to the animals."

"Do you want some help?" Marissa asked.

"Sure," Nat replied. "Why don't we rinse these dishes, too, while we are at it." She picked up the dishes.

"I'll get those; you two care for the animals." Maggie took the stack of dishes from Nat and headed to the water.

Nat stood at the mouth of the cave and whistled. Then she and Marissa filled three feedbags for the two horses and mule. They watched the other two animals follow Hardy up to the mouth of the cave. Nat and Marissa slipped the bags over their heads and the animals fed on the tender oats and molasses mixture.

Maggie came back and took the dishes into the cave, while Nat and Marissa stayed with the animals until they finished feeding. Then, removing the feedbags and storing them for the evening, Nat then took Marissa in her arms to watch the moon begin to rise over the glass-like water.

"I'm very proud to have you here with me," Nat whispered in her ear.

"I'm proud to be here with you, it gives me a glimpse, however small, of what your world is like."

Marissa turned to face Nat. "I watched your face as we traveled today and you seemed so at peace under the open sky."

"It is the only home I've ever known, until now. I've spent more nights under a blanket of stars, than I have with a roof over my head."

"It must be beautiful to look up into the sky and see all those stars smiling down on you," Marissa said.

"It is beautiful, but it can become very lonely too. Sometimes I wish Gyp could talk, just so I could hear another voice. The silence can be very overwhelming."

"I can only imagine."

"It's starting to cool down. Are you ready to move inside?" Nat asked.

"Did our eggs make the trip?" Nat asked Maggie as they entered the cave.

"Yes, you packed them well. Would you like some for breakfast?" she asked.

"Only if it will leave enough for us to have shrimp for dinner tomorrow night."

"I think you must really like those," Marissa said.

"Oh, I do. Fried though, not roasted."

"Very well, we shall have fried shrimp tomorrow." Maggie pulled a blanket around her shoulders.

Nat placed more wood on the fire and removed her boots to crawl into her bedroll. "Goodnight, my friends."

"Goodnight," Maggie and Marissa said.

Nat turned onto her side and snuggled into Marissa to share warmth and she watched Gyp walk over and curl up next to Maggie. Maggie's hand reached out and buried in Gyp's soft fur.

✝

Nat woke once feeling a chill and got up to add wood to the fire. The next time she woke, Maggie was awake. Maggie had started the coffee and when she saw Nat awake, she poured another cup. Nat quietly stood and slipped her boots on before joining Maggie around the fire.

"Thanks," she replied taking the cup from Maggie. "How did you sleep?"

"I missed my warm bed," Maggie said with a smile, "but I wouldn't have missed this trip for anything."

Nat looked over at Marissa, who was still sleeping peacefully.

"Let her sleep for a while yet," Maggie told her. "Yesterday's travel took its toll on her."

"I noticed it did not take long for her to fall asleep."

"She is not used to all the fresh air like you are."

"I just hope she doesn't regret coming along."

"That woman would follow you anywhere." Maggie gave her a warm smile.

"You think so?"

"I know so." Maggie grinned. "For some reason she adores you."

Nat blushed slightly.

"You're a good woman, Nat, and you two deserve happiness together."

"Thanks, Maggie. I do love her so."

"Have you decided if you will return to the woods this spring?"

"I haven't decided either way yet. It's not an easy decision."

Marissa stirred and sat up. "Why didn't you wake me?"

"Because, you were sleeping so soundly we thought we would get a jump on the coffee before you woke." Nat grinned.

"Should I start breakfast?" Maggie asked.

"I could eat a bear," Marissa said.

"Are you that hungry?" Nat asked.

"You worked me hard yesterday." Marissa stretched. "I have a feeling today will be busy, too."

"Do we still have biscuits left?" Maggie asked.

"About a dozen with a little bacon," Marissa said.

"Scrambled or fried eggs then?"

"Why don't you just scramble them all with some of that bacon?" Nat suggested.

"You are so clever," Marissa said. "I will get our plates and the biscuits."

Marissa handed Maggie the bacon, watched her scramble the eggs and crumble the bacon in them.

"That smells good." Nat smiled at Maggie who was starting to serve up the eggs.

They ate the meal and cleaned the dishes as the sun continued to rise. Nat picked up the bucket and the rifle. "Are we ready?"

They walked to the rock pools and were pleased to find that more creatures had arrived overnight. Nat left them to begin the harvest as she and Gyp walked further down the beach. They passed several more rock pools gorged with creatures. They would harvest these crabs before heading back to the river tomorrow.

As they walked, Nat began seeing strange tracks in the wet sand, like none she had ever seen. She followed the tracks, and when she passed a large boulder, she saw what was creating the trail. Gyp saw the creature, too, and circled it with great curiosity. Nat had seen a turtle before, albeit none as big as this one. It was easily four feet long and she guessed it weighed at least three hundred pounds. She moved closer to touch the hard shell and the creature turned its large head to look at her.

"You are a beauty," she spoke to the large animal. Nat saw movement down the beach and walked toward it cautiously. "Easy Gyp." A low growl started deep in her throat. Nat ducked behind a large boulder and called Gyp to her. She peered over the boulder and watched a pair of wolves feed on some type of tusked animal. *Such a strange place.* Nat watched the predators go back to their meal. "I think it is time for us to head back."

She and Gyp walked back to the rock pool to find Marissa and Maggie harvesting the last of the crabs. "You two have got to see something we found."

They passed the other rock pools teeming with crabs and continued to follow Nat, surprised that something else had excited her so. When they passed the first of the large boulders, they saw what enchanted Nat.

"Have you ever seen a turtle this big before?" she asked.

"It is a turtle from the sea, and if I had to guess, I would say this one is very old," Maggie said. "She has probably come ashore to find a safe place to lay her eggs."

"She is amazing," Marissa marveled, slowly circling the large creature.

"Farther ahead, there is a carcass of a large tusked animal that two wolves are feasting on," Nat said.

"That sounds like a walrus," Maggie replied.

"It is something I have never seen before. There are such strange but wondrous creatures in the wild," Marissa said, her eyes shining brightly with excitement.

"Do you think the wolves have passed on?" Maggie asked.

"If not, I can send them on their way." Nat lifted the rifle.

"Those tusks are very valuable," Maggie said, piquing Nat's interest.

"Follow me. Gyp, stay close."

The wolves had passed on when they arrived, but Nat kept a wary eye on the beach ahead.

"That is a walrus," Maggie said. "It has been dead a few days. It must have been injured or ill to beach itself this way," she added.

Nat looked at Maggie. "How do you harvest those?" She pointed at the long tusks.

"Take your knife and cut around where they join the skin. Then we pull and pull hard."

Nat used her knife to cut away the skin from the exposed edge of the tusk. "Help me, Marissa." Maggie took the tusk in her hands. It took them several tries, but finally the tusk broke free from the animal's skull. They repeated the process with the other tusk and Nat walked to the water's edge to clean her knife.

"Smithy will have a field day with those." Maggie grinned. "They use the tusks to customize pistol grips and knife handles, and in some places to fashion jewelry. It takes great patience and a very good knife to carve the hard tusks though."

Marissa and Maggie each carried a tusk making their way back to the cave. They stopped by the rock pool and counted another dozen crabs that Nat and Marissa would harvest while Maggie collected shrimp for their dinner. They placed the tusks in the small cart and took the bucket back to the rock pool. Nat made four trips back to the barrel carrying crabs before they finished. She then added more water to both barrels to cover the wriggling creatures. Maggie had gathered a flask full of shrimp and was cleaning them at the water's edge when Marissa and Nat returned to the camp.

Marissa walked down to the water to assist Maggie with cleaning the shrimp while Nat went inside the cave. She carried out six of the largest rib bones from the whale carcass and added them to the cart.

"If we have much more luck, poor Quincy won't be able to move this cart. As it is, I may have to carry the ribs and tusks and other supplies up the hill before we load him down."

"We can carry everything but the barrels," Maggie replied, "and I will walk home."

"There is no need for that. Once he gets on solid, flat land, Quincy can pull a mountain," she stated proudly.

"We still have a buck to add, too," Maggie reminded her with a grin.

"Oh, I haven't forgotten about him, but I won't spend long tracking him. I can always come back for him later, if need be."

"The crabs will be fine as long as they are packed in the salt water," Maggie stated, "So take what time you need."

Nat saw her animals walking toward them on the beach and placed their feedbags over their heads, adding a little extra for Quincy.

They spent the remainder of the afternoon on the beach resting from their adventures, and when the sun started to fade, Maggie stood and walked to the cave to start their meal.

"I will go help Maggie," Marissa said. "Don't be too much longer out here."

"We won't be far behind you, my love."

Nat picked up a small piece of driftwood and tossed it down the beach for Gyp to retrieve, and they played their game of catch for twenty minutes before moving down the beach. As they walked back toward the cave, Gyp stopped in her tracks and looked at the cliffs above the beach. Nat looked and then heard the howl of wolves, speculating that they were probably the feeding pair they had seen earlier on the beach. She looked and saw that Quincy, Buck, and Hardy were safely at the mouth of the cave. They should stay inside tonight. Nat could not afford to lose one of her animals to a pack of wolves. She would light a fire at the mouth of the cave and she would sleep there with the animals, just in case they received unwelcome visitors that night.

When she reached the mouth of the cave, she tethered the animals together and went inside to gather some firewood to start an outer fire.

"What is going on?" Marissa asked.

"We may have company tonight, so I'll sleep out front with the animals to protect them."

"Protect them from the wolves?" Maggie asked.

"Yes, did you hear them too?"

"Yes, just a few minutes ago and fairly close." Maggie frowned.

"They should not be a problem, but I'll sleep out with the animals just to make sure," Nat said. "We will be gone from here early in the morning and they can have their territory back."

Maggie and Marissa were cooking the shrimp and they were beginning to smell good. "You two have my mouth watering. Those smell good."

"We should be finished in just a few minutes, but if you want to start breaking some up for Gyp, that would be fine," Maggie said.

Nat took several of the cooked shrimp that had cooled, for Gyp, and placed them in her bowl. Maggie handed her a jar of warmed chowder saying, "Here, pour some of this over them for her."

Nat looked at Gyp. "You are getting so spoiled."

Gyp barked sharply.

"And so rebellious, too." Nat laughed as she set the bowl on the cave floor for Gyp. "Go ahead."

Gyp stepped forward and ate the meal, lapping up every drop of the chowder from the walls of the bowl. Nat poured more of the rich chowder in the bowl and Gyp ate it as she sat by her master who had also begun to eat her own meal.

When they had cleaned up the meal and the moon had risen, Nat said, "We should get an early night tonight, so we can be up early in the morning."

"Would you like for me to join you outside?" Marissa asked with a hopeful smile.

"No, sweetheart, you stay inside the cave with Maggie where it is warmer." Nat recognized her disappointment.

Marissa watched Nat moving her bedroll out to the mouth of the cave and then looked at Maggie. Maggie smiled and nodded at Marissa who picked up her bedroll and followed Nat.

"What are you doing?" Nat asked.

"I'm joining you, my love. If I get cold, I know you'll warm me up." She smiled softly.

"Very well, have it your way."

The lonesome call of a wolf broke the night air as Nat sat against a rock. Marissa came and sat with her and they cuddled and listened until the calls grew further apart and in the distance. The pack was moving away from the beach.

"Do you think it is safe now to sleep?"

"I think so. The animals will alert us if they return."

"Good." Marissa led Nat to their bedrolls. Marissa snuggled down into her covers and then reached for Nat, taking her face in her hands. She kissed her sweetly and pulled her close to share warmth and they slipped off to sleep.

Chapter Thirteen

Nat woke the next morning to the soft crunch of footsteps. Maggie had awakened earlier and was busy carrying the supplies up to the top of the trail to lessen Quincy's burden. By the time Nat had wiped the sleep from her eyes, Maggie had carried the last of the crates with their supplies up the hill.

"Good morning," she whispered. "The coffee is on the back fire."

"Thanks," Nat whispered back.

She gently shook Marissa awake and stood to get them coffee. She poured sand from her boots and slipped them on her cold feet before walking into the cave. Nat returned moments later with cups of coffee and stirred the embers in the fire to give them warmth as their bodies woke.

Marissa had rolled up their bedrolls tightly. She gladly accepted the coffee from Nat and used it to warm her hands.

"Thank you." She took the cup from Nat. "You have been busy," she said to Maggie.

"I woke up early and thought I would make good use of my time," Maggie said with a grin. "I also dug some clams to take back with us. I hope you aren't sick of chowder yet."

"I could eat that almost every night." Nat grinned.

"I will make some tomorrow when we arrive home while you and Marissa do our bartering."

"With fry bread, too?" Nat asked.

"Yes, I will make fry bread." Maggie smiled.

They drank another cup of coffee together and then went about the task of breaking camp. Marissa doused the fires, Nat saddled the horses, and Maggie hitched Quincy to the small cart. Only the barrels of crabs and clams remained on the cart, so he would be able to pull the cart through the soft sand up the hill. There they would add the rest of the supplies and goods Maggie had already carried.

Marissa led the horses, while Maggie guided Quincy and Nat pushed the cart from behind. As it turned out, Quincy did not need the extra help, but it got them up the hill more quickly.

Maggie and Marissa loaded the rest of the supplies and then Nat lifted Marissa into the saddle.

"I will walk for a while." Maggie took Quincy's halter and started him toward the trail.

Nat smiled and mounted Hardy. Gyp was walking beside Maggie and they left the beach shortly after sunrise. Nat turned in her saddle and looked back at the water one more time before riding away.

They made good time getting back to the river. Nat unhitched Quincy from the cart and watched him move down to the water to drink deeply. She joined the small animal for a long drink and then turned back to Maggie and Marissa.

"If you two will set up camp and care for the animals, Gyp and I'll begin the hunt." Nat pulled the rifle from its sling.

"We can do that," Marissa said.

"I'll see you sometime later then." Nat turned and left.

Marissa watched until Nat and Gyp disappeared into the woods and then turned back to the animals. She removed the saddles from Buck and Hardy while Maggie laid a campfire. She went to the river, dipped out a bucket of fresh water, and carried it to the campsite. When they had finished, she and Maggie sat back and enjoyed the relaxing sound of the river flowing across the rocks. The trickling of the moving water was the only sound that filled the air until Maggie pointed to the sky and they saw a majestic eagle soaring toward the coast. The large bird called out when it spotted something moving on the ground, then flew out of eyesight.

Maggie opened a small sack, pulled out pieces of soft buckskin and began sewing the pieces together.

"What are you making?" Marissa asked.

"I am making Nat some new boots, but it is a secret."

"I won't say a word."

Maggie showed her the leather and the hard sole she was sewing the buckskin onto and Marissa watched Maggie's hands move quickly. "Do you braid?" Maggie asked.

"Yes, I do."

"Would you like to make the boot strings for these?"

"I'd like that, yes."

Maggie pulled six long strands of buckskin from the sack. "Three to a string and make them as tight as you can."

Marissa went to work braiding the long strands under Maggie's watchful eye. When she finished one, Maggie inspected it and praised her good work. "That is perfect."

Marissa reached for the other three strands when they heard a gunshot.

"Nat has found something," Maggie said.

✝

As she and Gyp walked through the woods in search of hoof prints to track the buck, they heard a turkey gobbling in the distance. Nat and Gyp followed the sound and approaching, Nat began mimicking the sound made by the large bird. She crouched low, next to a tree, and waited as the turkey approached the sound of her call. Gyp sat patiently by her side, waiting. Gyp was the first to see the large colorful bird enter a clearing just ahead of them, and looking excited, she shook.

Nat lifted the rifle and with one clean shot, she took the bird's head off dropping it instantly. It wasn't the buck she had hoped for, but there was plenty of daylight left to track him. She walked to the clearing and picked up the bird. She would carry it back to Maggie, who could pluck it and prepare it for roasting over the campfire, while she and Gyp crept back into the woods.

Nat emerged from the woods carrying the large bird and wearing a smile.

Maggie smartly put her goods back into the bag several minutes after they heard the gunfire. When she next looked, she saw Nat approach with Gyp running from the woods ahead of her master.

"You got us a turkey." Maggie stood, watching Nat approach.

"I thought he would make a good dinner and then some. I'll go back in search of the buck, if you'll prepare the bird for dinner."

"No problem. Turkey feathers make for good warmth, too." She took the bird from Nat and headed for the river.

"I'll be back later." Nat smiled at Marissa. Then she and Gyp returned to the woods.

✝

They walked the banks of the river for nearly an hour before they came to an outcropping of rocks next to the river. Nat had not seen any evidence of the large buck, so she and Gyp climbed on top of the pile of rocks. From this point, she could see quite a distance, and would be able to see any wildlife well before their approach to the river to drink before nightfall.

Nat settled into a comfortable position and waited. She watched smaller animals; rabbits and a red fox made their way cautiously to the river to drink before disappearing into the dense forest. Nat was stroking Gyp's head when they heard a larger animal moving toward the water.

Gyp's ears perked to attention as they watched a small buck move to the water, drink, and then bound across the river to disappear once more. Nat relaxed back against a rock and they continued to wait. They watched more small critters come to drink, and Nat had just about given up on seeing the large buck, when Gyp lifted her head and looked off to the right.

Walking toward them in all his beauty was the buck, his large rack making noise in the brush as he approached. They watched him clear the brush and move into the open near the river. Nat raised her rifle and when the buck lifted his head from drinking, she squeezed the trigger and a slug pierced his heart dropping him to his knees.

Nat climbed down the rocks and walked toward the river. She took a length of rope from her pack, and tied one end around the buck's hind legs and tossed the other end over a branch of a nearby tree. She expertly severed the bucks head to allow the blood to flow freely.

When finished, she walked to the water to rinse her knife and slipped it back into the sheath in her boot. She picked up the head and her rifle. "Let's go back for Quincy," she told Gyp.

They followed the river back to the campsite and Maggie jumped to her feet when she heard them approach. "Got him. Nat wore a huge smile. "I need Quincy to bring him back."

Nat placed the buck's head on the cart and turned to see Marissa staring at it. "Are you okay, sweetheart?" she asked.

"Can you turn that around so I don't have to look at those eyes all night?" Marissa requested.

Nat grinned. "Sure thing." She turned the head away from Marissa's sight.

Maggie, leading Quincy over to her, smiled at Nat. "Do you need some help?"

"Sure, I can always use help."

"Let me turn the turkey and I'll be ready."

"Go ahead, I'll tend to the bird," Marissa stated.

"We'll be back soon." Nat walked Quincy to the woods.

"She has a difficult time with the hunt, doesn't she?" Maggie asked.

"If it deals with blood, she tends to get a little squeamish."

"That is not an easy thing to deal with if you weren't raised in the wild."

"I noticed," Nat said with a grin. "She seems fine with the meat, once it is cut, but she has difficulty with a whole carcass."

"Should we go ahead and skin and quarter the buck then?"

"That would probably be a good idea and we can hang the quarters away from camp until we get ready to head home tomorrow," Nat agreed.

They worked quickly when they reached the buck, skinning him and then cutting him into four quarters and two loin portions. They tied the meat onto Quincy's back on top of the skin and walked back to camp. They stopped a few yards from camp and used the rope to hang the meat high up off the ground out of reach of any predators that might catch the scent of fresh blood. When they returned to camp, Maggie hung the skin over the edge of the cart, away from Marissa's view.

"Dinner is beginning to smell very good." Nat sat beside Marissa.

"We had a few potatoes left, too, that I thought we could fry to go with the turkey," Marissa said. "I have already cut them up and will fry them once the meat is close to being done."

Maggie was busy at the cart and Nat walked over to see what she was doing. Maggie had harvested the liver and heart from the buck and was salting them down to preserve them. She then tucked them away in a small sack next to the barrels.

Nat returned to the fire, and a few minutes later, Maggie walked over to join them. "We have a little butter left which should make the skin a nice golden brown," she told them, rubbing the butter across the bird's cooking skin with the blade of her knife.

Gyp sat next to Nat and licked her lips.

They turned the bird on the fire frequently for the next hour. "Why don't you cut off one of the legs and let it cool for our girl," Maggie suggested. "Then we can pull the meat from the bone and put it in her bowl."

Nat cut off a leg and laid it on a plate to cool. She then walked over to the animals and slipped the feedbags over their heads as Marissa began to fry the potatoes.

The turkey roasted to a beautiful golden brown, and Nat used her knife to cut thick slices of the juicy meat for their meal. After eating, they snuggled in for a cool night's rest without the protection of the cave walls. Nat hugged Marissa close, struggling to rest on the cold ground.

The following morning, they drank coffee, and then Nat and Maggie broke camp.

"Are we ready to head for home?" Nat asked.

"I'm ready to sleep in my warm, comfortable bed," Marissa admitted with a sheepish grin.

Nat and Maggie shared a knowing smile. "Tonight you will, my love," Nat promised.

They had traveled about an hour when Gyp emitted a low growl deep in her throat and all progress came to a stop. Nat watched in disbelief as a small grizzly stepped from the clearing fifty yards ahead of them.

"Stay very still everyone," she warned. "He has caught the scent of the buck's carcass and I imagine he is extremely hungry after his winter sleep." Nat took her rifle from the sling slowly.

"We cannot outrun him, so the decision is his. He is thinking about food only at this point and deciding if he is willing to confront three humans for an easy meal."

Nat looked at Marissa and saw the terror growing in her eyes. "Just relax, if he starts this way, I will drop him in his tracks."

Maggie held tight to Quincy's lead to keep him from bolting.

Nat watched the bear cautiously, thinking back to her father's death. This bear was not as large as the one that had mauled Nathan, but he was large enough to do plenty of damage if allowed.

"Marissa, slowly pull back on your reins to back Buck toward the cart," Nat said when the bear turned to face them fully. Nat carefully dismounted and handed her reins to Maggie. "Stay, Gyp." Gyp sat obediently beside Maggie, her small body quivering.

Nat stepped away from Hardy and watched the bear slowly approach, swinging his head from side to side, growling. If it hoped to scare them off it didn't work. He began to gallop toward them and when he had traveled twenty yards, he skidded to a stop and stood up on his hind legs bellowing a furious call. Nat knew that would be her best shot and raised her rifle, taking careful aim and squeezing the trigger. She watched the bullet enter the bear's chest just above his heart. A good shot, but not enough to drop the bear. He stumbled back down to his feet, but continued his approach. Nat stepped forward to advance on the bear and when he stood up erect again, she took another shot, which struck him squarely in the heart.

Nat slowly approached the bear and knelt beside him. Marissa watched in horror as the bear's left paw struck out and grazed the right side of Nat's face, drawing blood immediately. Nat jumped to her feet, aimed her rifle, and fired a shot directly into his brain.

Marissa jumped from the saddle and ran to Nat. Nat had a three inch gash down her right temple. "I'm okay." She saw Marissa's face turned white at the sight of all the blood.

Maggie submerged a handkerchief in the salty water in one of the barrels and rushed to Nat's side. She pressed the wet cloth against the wound and when the salt hit open flesh, Nat flinched in pain.

"I know it stings, but it will help the wound to heal." Maggie kept pressure on the wound until the bleeding stopped. "You go sit on the cart, and Marissa and I'll prepare the bear for travel. Then we will finish the ride home."

Nat obediently followed Maggie's instructions and walked to sit on the edge of the cart, with Gyp closely in tow.

"You are going to have to help me," Maggie told Marissa, who nodded in response.

Nat watched Maggie take a length of rope and with Marissa's help, they dragged the bear from the path close to a tree. Maggie then tied the rope to the bear's hind legs, and using Hardy's strength, they hoisted the bear off the ground to bleed and gut him in preparation for the travel home. Maggie severed the head to make the carcass bleed out more quickly and placed it on the cart close to Nat.

"This isn't your first grizzly, is it?" Maggie asked.

Nat's hand went to her neck. "No, I killed the one that mauled my father to death."

"Then this has brought back painful memories." Maggie watched Nat stroke the bear claw hanging around her neck. "You kill, only when necessary, to feed and protect the people you love, which is right." Maggie's arm slipped across Nat's shoulder. "You gave the bear the opportunity to turn away, and when his instinct to eat kicked in, your instinct to protect took over, just as your father trained you."

Nat looked up at Maggie with tears in her eyes. She knew Maggie spoke the truth. As she had done with the bear that took her father's life, Nat would take a claw from this bear and add it to the necklace she wore as a memory of her father. Unfortunately, she would also carry a scar from the wound as a reminder of the encounter.

"Are you ready to go get that wound looked at?" Maggie asked.

Nat nodded and stood from the cart. Maggie led Quincy to where the bear was hanging in the tree and lowered him onto the cart. Nat helped Marissa back onto her horse and then mounted Hardy.

"We'll head for town and you go see the doctor while Marissa and I drop the crabs off at the hotel," Maggie said. "I'll take care of the bear and buck while Marissa takes you home for the night," Maggie instructed. "You can care for the horses, correct, Marissa?"

"Yes, I have seen Nat do it often," Marissa answered.

"Good. When we finish in town, take her home, and put her straight to bed. She will probably insist on helping, but stand firm and make her rest."

"You are worse than a mother," Nat teased.

"Someone needs to watch over you," Maggie let out a soft chuckle.

Nat knew Maggie was correct. The side of her face had already begun to swell and become painful. The doctor would sew the wound closed after cleaning it, which would not be pleasant. "Yes ma'am." Nat tried to relax back in her saddle and hold the compress against her face.

They traveled for another two hours before they passed the cabins on their way into town. It was just after midday when they arrived and Nat went in search of the town doctor. Marissa and Maggie pulled the cart in front of the hotel. Smithy had witnessed their approach and walked out to meet them as they were hitching Buck and Quincy outside the hotel.

"Nice haul you have there, but where's Nat?"

"She is over at the doctor's office. She took a swipe from a bear who tried to take the buck from her," Marissa added.

"Dear child, is she okay?"

Maggie chuckled. "She is no mere child, Smithy, you of all people should know that, and yes, she will be fine."

His eyes wandered toward the doctor's office. "Do you two need help here?"

"No, you go ahead and check on Nat," Maggie said.

Marissa shot a smile to Maggie.

✝

Nat sat down on the doctor's treatment table and removed the poultice Maggie had made.

"What on earth happened?" the Doctor asked.

"I had a little run-in with a bear."

"I certainly hope he paid for this nasty little swipe he took at you," the doctor said, examining the wound. "This will leave a nasty scar."

"His head will be hanging over someone's mantelpiece soon," Nat replied, with a grin that made her flinch with pain.

Smithy walked in at that moment. "Dear God, Nat, are you okay?" he asked his eyes darting to the swollen, bloody side of her face.

"I'll be fine, Smithy, I had no choice, he started to charge us, so I had to take him down."

"The hell with the bear, are you okay?"

"I will be, once doc here finishes with me."

"I won't lie to you, this is going to hurt." He looked at Smithy. "Will you bring me that bottle of whiskey?" he asked, pointing to the bottle in the cabinet.

Smithy walked over, took the bottle from the cabinet, and pulled the cork from its neck before handing it to the doctor.

"Thanks." He poured some of the alcohol onto a clean cloth. "You may want to take a nice long drink." He handed Nat the bottle.

Nat lifted the bottle to her lips and took a long drink of the whiskey, flinching at the strong taste. She welcomed the dullness to her mind while the doctor cleaned her wound as gently as he could. He applied ten stitches to close the wound on her face. He handed her the bottle for another drink.

"Does she have someone to help her home?"

"Yes, I'll see to it." Smithy paid her bill.

"Very well, let her know to return to me in two weeks and I'll remove the stitches." He helped Nat to her feet and Smithy guided her back out to Hardy and helped her mount. The way she swayed in the saddle worried Smithy. "This is not going to work."

He carefully led Hardy to the hotel where Maggie and Marissa were just completing their transaction with the owner. "We need to use the wagon to get Nat home." He gently took her off Hardy, and carried her to the wagon and sat her up. "I will accompany you to get her home, and then I will help Maggie with the buck and bear when we have Nat safely tucked in bed.

"Thank you for your help, Smithy," Marissa said.

"No problem at all. Why don't you ride back here with Nat and I will take the horses."

Marissa climbed in beside Nat and held her close as they turned for home. Smithy took the horses to Nat's barn and cared for them as Marissa and Maggie got Nat into Marissa's cabin.

"I will see to the meat and be back as quickly as I can." Maggie left Marissa to undress Nat and tuck her into the bed.

"Thank you, Maggie, and tell Smithy thanks again, too, please," Marissa requested.

"I'll see you soon," Maggie promised, and with a soft smile, she left the cabin.

Marissa returned to the bedroom and began undressing Nat. When she removed the work shirt from her shoulders, Nat opened her glazed eyes.

"I love you," she whispered.

"I love you, too." Marissa lowered a nightshirt over Nat. "Rest now, my love." She kissed Nat and laid her back on the bed. She pulled the warm covers over her and looked at Gyp. "I know you are worried, so for tonight, you can sleep on the bed." She patted the bed.

Gyp jumped onto the end of the bed and laid her head on Nat's thigh.

Marissa lay wood in the fireplaces and started fires to warm the chilly house. She placed the coffee pot in the kitchen fireplace as she toiled, putting away their supplies from the trip. She prepared a batch of biscuits and went to the springhouse to fetch the bacon.

†

Smithy walked with Maggie back to town and helped her unload the two carcasses. "Would you like help skinning this monster?" he asked.

"I'll start on him if you will hang the deer meat in the smoke house and get the fire started for me," Maggie requested.

"No problem." Smithy went to work.

Maggie pulled out a sharp skinning knife and began removing the pelt. She was halfway done with one side when Smithy returned.

"He is big even though not fully grown yet," he stated.

"He was well over six feet when he reared. Nat was fearless as she took him down."

"Nathan would have been proud." Smithy began cutting away the pelt.

"Yes, he taught her well." Maggie smiled up at Smithy.

Maggie cut away the large paws, took a claw from one of the front paws, and tucked it in her shirt. "To add to her necklace," she told Smithy who nodded in agreement.

They finished skinning the bear and Smithy helped Maggie nail both pelts onto a wall to allow them to dry. "Looks like you all will have a very profitable trip."

"Enough to keep Nat from going into the woods if she chooses," Maggie said. "I really don't see that happening though."

"It's too ingrained in her blood. Hunting, trapping, and living off what she kills is her life."

"That is very true," Maggie agreed. "Do you want to take these heads and claws with you tonight?"

"I can and that will be one less worry for Nat," he replied. "She knows I'll treat her fairly."

"More than fairly, usually," Maggie added with a grin.

"If she wakes tonight, tell her to see me if she needs anything," Smithy told Maggie while they walked to the center of town.

"I will. I'll stay with them tonight and drop by tomorrow with a report," she promised.

"Thanks," Smithy told her and watched Maggie lead Quincy out of town.

Chapter Fourteen

Maggie knocked softly on the door and stepped inside when Marissa opened it. "How is she doing?"

"Resting quietly so far."

"Good, you'll need to watch her for fever tonight, in case an infection has set in," Maggie warned. "I'll stay tonight if that is all right?"

"That would be great. Would you like some coffee or something to eat?"

"Coffee would be good."

Maggie took the claw from her pocket and pulled an awl from her bag. She took the cup of coffee from Marissa and took a sip of the steamy liquid. "Would you like to finish the boot laces?"

"Did you bring them?" Marissa asked.

Maggie smiled and handed her the strips of leather and watched Marissa start to braid. Then she took the awl in her hand and began to bore a hole in the bear claw. When she finished drilling the hole, she stood and placed the claw on the mantel. She opened her bag and began working on the boots. She had one part of the leggings attached to the sole and was reinforcing the sections where she would bore the holes for the bootlaces. If she were lucky, she would have the boots finished in just a few days.

Marissa watched the ease of Maggie's hands as she worked the soft leather. "How did you learn so many talents?"

"Like Nat, my family lived off the fruit of the land for many years when I was a child, and we learned to use everything we harvested," she explained. "We did not have money for new clothing, so we used the hides of animals we took for food, to sew our clothes and to make our footwear."

"Were you ever married?" Marissa asked.

"I was in love once. He went out on a hunting party one day and never returned. A warring tribe ambushed the party he was with, and he fell during the battle."

"I am so sorry, Maggie."

"It was a great love and one that will last me to the next world," she said with a comforting smile. "You were married before, correct?"

"Yes, for a few years before he died in the war."

"So, you know what it is like then to miss someone you loved."

"Yes, I do. I was completely lost in my solitude until Nat showed up and taught me what it was like to feel again."

Maggie remained silent, thinking of the pain Marissa would soon be experiencing if Nat chose to go back to the woods until next winter. She knew the two women had formed a special bond in the short months they had known each other, but they were from different worlds. Nat was like a wild animal, roaming free in the dense forests and plains, while Marissa enjoyed the comforts and conveniences of town. Neither of them would thrive in the other's environment for very long, and Maggie worried what would happen when the call to return to the wild tugged at Nat's heart.

Marissa finished the second boot string and stood to stretch. "I'm going to check on Nat," she announced, leaving Maggie alone.

Maggie continued sewing as Marissa walked quietly into the bedroom. Nat was still resting peacefully, tucked under the warm covers. The moonlight covered her face and Marissa could see the dark purple bruise that had formed on the right side.

Marissa heard her stomach growl and remembered that they had not eaten all day. She had baked fresh biscuits and had bacon ready to cook. She would fry the bacon, and if the smell did not wake Nat, she would wake her long enough to get some food into her and then send her back to bed.

"I don't know about you, but I'm hungry," she told Maggie. "I'm going to cook some bacon and eggs to go with the biscuits I cooked earlier."

"Would you like some help?"

"No, you keep working on those boots," Marissa smiled. "If Nat doesn't wake up from the smell of the bacon, I'll wake her long enough to get some food into her."

"That's a good idea," Maggie agreed.

Gyp trotted into the kitchen, alerting the two women that Nat was awake.

"I'll check her." Maggie tucked her sewing away in her bag.

Maggie walked into the bedroom and found that Nat was struggling to sit up in bed. "Here, let me help you."

"I smelled bacon cooking and thought I was dreaming, but then I remembered that we were home and I was hungry."

"How are you feeling?"

"Like I have been run over by a herd of buffalo and I haven't eaten in weeks."

"It wasn't buffalo, but you haven't eaten all day." Maggie sat next to Nat on the bed. "Marissa is preparing a late dinner for us. She has made fresh biscuits and plans to cook some eggs too."

"That sounds wonderful."

"Are you ready to walk into the kitchen?" Maggie asked.

"Yes."

"Take it slow, there's no need to rush."

"Yes, Mama."

"I would be proud to be your mama." Maggie helped Nat stand.

"Am I spinning or is it the room?" Nat asked with a grin.

"Your head is a little off right now. Can you walk or would you prefer to eat in bed?"

"I can walk." Nat took a few steps forward with Maggie by her side.

Nat walked into the kitchen area and sat down at the table. "That smells good," she said to Marissa.

"That's a good sign. You haven't lost your appetite. Would you like some eggs?"

"Do we still have some honey?"

"Yes, we do." Marissa plucked a jar from a cabinet and placed it on the table in front of Nat.

"I think I will stick to honey and butter mixed together and some bacon then." Nat poured some honey into a small bowl and dropped a spoonful of butter on top. She slowly stirred the mixture watching Marissa cook.

"Would you like some eggs, Maggie?"

"Yes, Marissa, I'll join you in some eggs and I think Gyp will, too." Maggie watched Gyp lick her lips.

Marissa finished cooking the bacon and placed it on the table. "How are we eating eggs tonight, ladies?"

"Scrambled please," Maggie answered.

Marissa scrambled six eggs and portioned them out between her, Maggie, and Gyp. "Last chance," she told Nat.

"I'm good, thanks."

"Are you feeling all right?" Marissa asked. "It's not like you to pass on food."

"Yes, dear, now that I'm up I'm just not real hungry," Nat replied.

"Let's eat then." Marissa took a seat beside Nat and placed Gyp's bowl on the floor between them.

Nat ate two biscuits and drank a glass of water. She was in obvious pain while trying to keep her head upright. Soon after she finished eating, she said, "I'm going to lie back down."

Marissa stood and helped Nat back into the bedroom. She tucked the covers up to her chin and kissed her forehead. "You are a bit warm."

Marissa put another blanket on the bed. "Is there anything you need?"

"Just you here beside me," Nat answered with a painful smile.

"I will come to bed soon."

Marissa walked back into the kitchen area and found Maggie washing up the dishes.

"You don't need to do that."

"You cooked, so I clean," Maggie replied with a smile. "If you are ready for bed, go ahead and I'll stay up a little longer."

"Let me get you a pillow and a blanket." Marissa moved toward a small closet.

"I sleep very little these days."

"I'll see you in the morning then," Marissa said.

"Good night, my friend."

"Good night, Maggie."

Marissa walked into the bedroom. Gyp had jumped up on the bed and had her head resting on Nat's thigh as her hand stroked through her thick fur. Marissa changed into a thick nightshirt and carefully climbed beneath the covers next to Nat. She cuddled and laid her head on Nat's shoulder.

"Welcome back, my love." Nat's arm encircled Marissa.

"It feels so good to have you back in a bed," Marissa teased.

"You didn't care much for sleeping on the cold ground, did you?"

"That is not the life for me," Marissa answered honestly. "I don't know how you do it."

"You get used to it after a while."

"I don't know if I would ever get used to it."

"There is no need. You have this big comfortable bed to sleep in every night." Nat's hand stroked down Marissa's arm before it fell still.

"But I won't have you in it for much longer, will I?" Marissa shook her head realizing what she said.

"I don't know yet."

"I'm sorry. I didn't mean to pressure you on your decision and now is not the time for us to have this talk."

"You are right, talking right now is painful."

"Sleep now, my dear, and we'll talk later."

Marissa remained tucked under Nat's arm until Nat drifted off to sleep. She was exhausted from the restless night she had experienced the night before and fell quickly off to sleep.

Maggie sat up for several more hours, working on Nat's boots. She could see the longing in Nat's eyes when she was outside and instinctively knew she would be heading into the woods soon. She wanted to send her friend off with new boots in appreciation for all that Nat had done for her. When she could no longer focus her eyes, Maggie took the thick blanket and pillow and curled up in front of the fireplace for a few hours' sleep.

When the sun began to rise, Maggie woke, and after folding the blanket, she put on a pot of coffee while waiting for Nat and Marissa to wake. She crept into the bedroom to check on Nat and found her brow covered with sweat. Her fever had broken sometime during the night and her skin was soaked. That was a good sign and Maggie hoped that Nat would feel much better when she woke.

Gyp followed Maggie from the bedroom and went to the front door. Maggie pulled her coat over her shoulders, and opened the door to allow Gyp outside. They stepped out into a crisp, clear morning and Maggie heard a familiar noise. She looked to the skies where a flock of geese was flying overhead, heading back north from their warmer winter grounds. The season was changing rapidly; green sprouts of grass were poking through the soil as she and Gyp walked around the yard.

When they returned to the cabin, Nat and Marissa were up and sitting at the table drinking coffee. "Good morning." She hung her coat behind the door.

"Did you get any sleep at all?" Marissa asked.

"Yes, I slept well for several hours," Maggie answered. "How are you feeling, Nat?"

"I'm soaked from breaking a fever, but my head feels like it is back to normal size at least."

"Are you up to a hot, soaking bath?" Marissa asked.

"Maybe in a little bit."

"I'm going to finish my coffee and walk back into town. Is there anything you need?"

"Not that I can think of, Maggie," Nat answered.

"I'll work on the pelts for a little while and then come back out to check on you later," she promised. "Do you think you can eat some chowder and fry bread for an early dinner?"

"That sounds very good."

"I'll bring a pot of chowder and make the fry bread fresh when I return."

Maggie walked over to the fireplace and took the bear claw from the mantel. "Would you like me to add this for you?"

"Yes, please." Nat slipped the strip of buckskin over her head.

They watched Maggie untie the knot and thread the buckskin through the hole she had bored through the bear claw the previous night. Maggie stood and with a smile tied the buckskin around Nat's neck again.

"All set," she said. "Will you do me a favor?"

"Of course, what is it?"

"Don't add to your necklace for a long time." Maggie grinned.

"Trust me. I have no desire to add to it at all. Hunting bear is not my choice of activities."

"That is refreshing to hear." Marissa frowned. "You scared me to death."

"I had no choice. That bear was hungry enough to take on three people and only a bullet was going to stop him from attacking us. I would have much preferred he kept on going."

"I know, honey, but seeing all that blood running down your face was terrifying."

"It looked much worse than what it actually is."

"Another inch or two and he would have taken out an eye," Marissa claimed.

"But he didn't, and I am sewn up, so all is well."

Maggie thought it was time to leave and stood to go. "I'll see you two later," she said and picked up her bag.

"Thanks for all your help, Maggie," Nat said.

Gyp stood and walked Maggie to the door. "Do you want to go with me today?" Maggie asked. "Would it be okay if she went with me?"

"I think Gyp would like that. I know she gets tired of being cooped up inside."

"Would you like me to light the wash pot fire as I go by?"

"Yes, thank you," Marissa said.

Maggie took a small piece of wood with a burning flame and walked from the cabin. She stopped at the fire and lit the dry wood positioned under the wash pot before continuing on to town.

Chapter Fifteen

Once Maggie left, Marissa looked at Nat. "Do you want to lie back down until I have your bath ready?" Marissa asked.

"Yes, I think I will, if you don't mind."

"Not at all. Come, let's get you back to bed."

Nat slept for an hour while the water heated for her bath. Marissa picked up around the house and brought more wood inside for the fireplace. The weather was growing warmer and soon she would only need a fire for cooking. She went to the smokehouse and picked out venison chops to cook for the midday meal, along with some canned vegetables and fresh cornbread. While the water in the wash pot heated, she began carrying in buckets of water to mix with the well water left in the bathtub. She lit some fragrant candles and walked to the bedroom to wake Nat.

Marissa sat on the edge of the bed and placed a soft hand on Nat's shoulder. "Your bath is ready, darling."

At the sound of Marissa's voice and the touch of her hand Nat's eyes fluttered open. "Are you ready to soak for a while?" Marissa asked.

"I think that would feel nice."

"Let's get you in the tub then and I will put some wash on. When I finish, I'll come in and give you a bath."

Nat smiled at the thought of Marissa's hands on her. "I do love it when you spoil me so."

"I love spoiling you, too."

Nat sat up on the bed. "My head is spinning."

"Take it slow. There is no need to hurry."

Nat swung her feet around to sit on the edge of the bed beside Marissa. "I think I'm ready."

Marissa stood and guided Nat to her feet. She walked beside her into the room where she had the bathtub partitioned off. "Let's get that nightshirt off you." She lifted the shirt over Nat's head.

The right side of Nat's face had turned an angry purple from the trauma and Marissa was careful not to touch the area. She took Nat's hand and helped her gingerly climb into the tub. "Just lay back and relax. I'll be right back."

Nat lowered herself into the steaming water, stretched her legs, rested her head on the back edge of the tub, and closed her eyes. "This feels heavenly against my sore body, and it smells so good in here."

Marissa took their dirty clothes to the wash pot and dropped them into the boiling water. She used a stirring stick to push the clothing under the water and tossed a handful of soap chips into the pot. She would bathe Nat, get her into a clean nightshirt, and then return to hang the clothing out to dry on the porch railing.

Marissa looked up to see Smithy walking into the yard.

"Good morning."

"Good morning, Smithy, it is good to see you."

"I wanted to walk out and check on Nat. How's she doing?"

"She is doing well. Right now, she is soaking in a hot bath."

"That will help her rest easy."

"I hope so. If you want to have a seat on the porch, you can stay and visit with her."

"No, that is all right, just tell her I came by to see her. I'll drop by later this week."

"I sure will. Thank you for dropping by."

"Is there anything either of you needs?"

"No, I think we're in good shape."

"I'll see you later this week then."

"Thanks, Smithy."

She watched him disappear down the road and then walked back inside. Nat was almost asleep in the tub when Marissa walked into the room.

"You look nice and relaxed."

"This bath feels so good."

"Smithy came by to check on you and said he would be back later in the week." Marissa took a cloth and began to lather it.

"That was nice of him."

"He thinks very highly of you."

"He's a good man."

Marissa bathed Nat and then washed her hair, careful to not touch the right side of her face. "Does your head still hurt?"

"Not as bad as last night, but it is still sensitive to touch. How bad does it look?"

"You are still swollen and your skin is bruised a dark purple, but that will fade soon." She smiled at Nat. "You are all done. Are you ready to get out or would you like to soak more?"

"My skin is beginning to prune up, so I think it is time I get out."

"Let me go get a clean nightshirt and I'll be right back."

"Marissa dear?"

"Yes, Nat, what is it?"

"I need clothes not a nightshirt, my love. The longer I lay in that bed the weaker I'll become."

"But you still need rest," Marissa claimed.

"I will rest, sitting out on the front porch. I need fresh air."

"All right. I'll get clothes for you then."

"Thank you."

Marissa went to the bedroom and collected clothing for Nat. When she returned to the bathing area, Nat was standing in the tub drying her upper body.

"Let me help you from the tub."

Nat climbed from the tub and finished drying. She dressed slowly in the dungarees and work shirt Marissa had brought.

"Do you want your boots and socks?"

"No, I think it is warm enough outside without them."

"I need to finish the wash, so you can sit on the porch and watch, if you would like."

"That is a good plan. That way you can keep a close eye on me," Nat grinned painfully. "Just let me get my knife."

"You go sit and I will bring it to you."

Nat walked onto the porch and picked up a small block of wood, then sat down in a rocking chair. She had found the piece when she was chopping wood and had decided she would whittle something from it.

Marissa came out and handed Nat the knife. "What are you going to make?"

"I don't know yet." Nat turned the wood in her hands looking curiously at the block.

Marissa walked to the wash pot and resumed stirring the clothing.

Nat took the knife from the sheath before setting the block of wood on the floor. She picked up a honing stone and began sharpening her knife. She stroked the blade softly across the stone until she was satisfied with the sharpness of the blade.

Nat placed the stone back on the floor and looked up to see a flock of geese heading north to Canada, honking loudly to one another and exchanging places in the characteristic V-formation they flew. Their calls pulled at Nat's heart. She missed the sounds of the wild, especially at night, when owls would call to their mates and wolves would howl in the distance, their cries long and lonely.

She watched until the geese disappeared from sight and then picked up the block of wood. The wood was ash, not too hard or too soft for carving, and it would have a very nice grain to work with. Nat began by rounding off the edges of the block while she concentrated on what creature hid inside the wood.

Marissa used the stirring stick to pluck each item of clothing from the wash pot and carry it to the porch railing where she would hang them to dry. When she finished with the wash, she carried an armload of wood into the house before returning to sit beside Nat.

"I was thinking I would cook some venison chops, green beans, squash, and cornbread for dinner," Marissa said.

"That sounds delicious."

"I'm going to walk into town for corn meal, if you'll be all right by yourself."

"I'll be just fine, and I promise not to move from this spot unless I need to answer the call of nature."

"Very well, I will be back soon. Is there anything you need?"

"Yes, as a matter of fact there is."

"What can I get you?"

"A kiss, before you leave." Nat looked up at Marissa.

"That's an easy request to fill," Marissa said. She leaned down and her lips softly brushed across hers. "I love you."

"I love you, too. You know what else?"

"What?"

"You don't have to worry about me, my other babysitter is about to arrive."

Marissa stood to see Gyp and Maggie enter the yard. She watched Gyp run onto the porch and go directly to Nat.

"Welcome home, my friend." Nat patted Gyp's head. "Hello, Maggie."

"Good afternoon, my friends. How are you feeling?"

"Much better, thank you."

"It's good to see you up and about."

"It's good to be outside for a while." Nat smiled sweetly at Marissa.

"I need to walk into town. Will you join us for dinner tonight and help me keep an eye on these two?"

"That would be fine. If you will pick up some apples, I will make us a pie for dinner."

"Now we're talking," Nat said.

"I'll be back shortly then." Marissa left the porch and aimed for town.

"I'm sorry I forgot to start the chowder for dinner."

"That's not a problem, we can have that tomorrow."

Maggie sat down beside her watching the knife as Nat resumed her whittling. "Do you know what it is yet?"

"Not yet, but I am sure it will come to me."

"I finished tanning the buck and bear hides and they are in the process of drying out."

"I'm sorry I wasn't there to help you."

"Smithy helped me tack them up and the rest is just time consuming. Do you have any plans for the bear hide?"

"I'm sure Smithy would love to have it to sell, but I think I may use it differently."

"He was thrilled with the heads and claws."

"I'm sure. He can be like a kid at Christmas sometimes," Nat said with a warm smile.

"He told me he stopped by earlier, but you were taking a bath."

"Yes, he caught me soaking."

"I'm sure that felt good to your muscles."

"I was so relaxed, I almost fell asleep."

"A day or two of rest won't hurt you one bit, you know."

"I know, Maggie, but I'm beginning to feel so restless."

"Is it your heart pulling you back toward the woods?"

"It probably is. I saw a flock of geese headed north this morning, which means I'm already late and my feet are itching terribly."

"You know you'll have to go, don't you?"

"Yes, I don't think I can handle much more of this sedentary life."

"Will Marissa join you?"

"No, Maggie, she is as uncomfortable in the woods as I am under a roof. I can't ask her to give up her life here."

"You know, there may be a compromise for all of this?"

"I'm listening."

"I know that Smithy has a job waiting for you, and we could make trips to the water for crabs and clams to supplement your income. It would be a lot less stressful on you, but would still allow you time in the wild. "

"That is something to consider. I think I'll have to go and make a huge decision. I'll have to decide whether my love for the wild is stronger than my love for Marissa."

"I don't envy you that decision."

"I don't look forward to it either, but I don't see that I have any choice. If I don't at least attempt to return, I think I'll regret it forever. "

"Yes, you're right about that."

Nat had continued to whittle as they talked, her hands moving with a will of their own. She was surprised when she looked carefully at the chunk of wood in her hands and saw the form of a rearing bear emerging.

"I think that is only fitting, given the recent circumstances," Maggie said when she saw the bear taking shape.

Nat chuckled. "You're probably right about that too."

Gyp jumped to her feet and ran to the edge of the yard to meet Marissa who was returning from town.

"That was a quick trip. Welcome back," Nat said.

"Thanks."

"Would you like to peel these for Maggie?" Marissa asked, handing Nat the bag of apples.

"I'll get those, if you'll loan me a knife," Maggie offered.

"I'll bring a knife and a bowl for the apples."

Marissa returned and handed Maggie a knife and a bowl. "Do you want me to make a crust for you?"

"No, I'll roll one out once I put the apples on to cook."

"So you can pull up a seat and join us," Nat said.

Marissa pulled up a crate and sat down, watching Maggie and Nat busy with their knives. "Those apples smell so sweet." She watched Maggie's hands expertly coring and slicing the peeled apples.

"This summer, we can begin scouring the woods for wild berries," Maggie said. "The blackberries and raspberries in this area make great pies and jellies."

"A blackberry pie sounds good. It has been years since I have had any," Nat said.

"I'll be sure to remedy that," Marissa smiled.

Maggie finished with the apples. She looked at Marissa. "If you have a small pot, I'll put these on to cook over the wash pot fire."

"Yes, I'll be right back."

When Marissa returned with a pot, Maggie took it from her and dropped the apples inside. Then she walked to the pump, covered the apples with water, and then hung the pot over the open fire. "If you will show me where your supplies are, I'll prepare the crust."

Maggie and Marissa went inside, leaving Nat and Gyp alone on the porch.

Gyp looked out toward the woods, following the sound of a small creature, probably a rabbit.

"You miss it too, don't you?" Nat asked her companion.

Gyp looked at Nat, her eyes sparkling.

"Soon, my friend, very soon."

Chapter Sixteen

For the next week, Nat worked around Marissa's cabin, cutting wood and making sure Marissa had enough meat to last for several months. She returned to town to have the stitches removed by the doctor.

"You're going to have a scar, but as time passes it should reduce in size."

"Thanks, Doc," Nat said, and paid him for his services.

When she left the doctor's office, Nat went to see Smithy. He paid her handsomely for the bear and buck heads. "I still have the bear claws up on auction and I think you will be pleased with the final price."

"Thanks for all that you have done for me, Smithy."

"I should thank you for bringing me such good business. Have you given consideration to my offer of a job?"

"I have indeed, my friend. I feel I must go back into the woods, at least for now, and see how things go without Nathan."

"I can understand that," he answered with a warm smile. "The position will be yours whenever you are ready."

"Thanks, Smithy."

"Do you know yet when you will be heading out?"

"In two days, I think. I'm already so far behind."

"Does Marissa know yet?"

"No, and it is not a conversation I'm looking forward to."

"That is one I don't envy you, my friend."

"Maggie brought up another solution."

"What would that be?"

"That I work here with you, and then she and I travel down to the water and harvest crabs and other sea life."

"That isn't a bad idea at all. There's also a bit of hunting and trapping that you could do in that area."

"It is definitely something to think about. I need to go meet Marissa for lunch, but I'll stop in before I leave for the woods."

"Good, I'll see you then."

†

Nat left the store and walked to the hotel to meet Marissa. They had agreed to meet for a fried chicken lunch, and Nat ate a good portion of the meal.

"I'm glad to see your appetite picking up again."

"Did it ever slack off?" Nat asked with a grin.

"Yes, you haven't eaten heartily until today since our trip."

"This fried chicken is just too good to stop eating."

"I'll cook extra and bring it home tomorrow for your trip."

"What trip?"

"I can see it in your eyes, Nat, I know you are going to the woods soon."

"I need to go and see if that's what I need to do."

"I know," Marissa answered, with tears in her eyes. "That won't mean I'll miss you any less."

"I'll go in two days then. I can't afford to wait much longer."

"What can I do to help you prepare?"

"Cook chicken and biscuits for me to take," Nat said with a smile. "I'll stop by the general store to buy supplies when I leave here."

Nat left the hotel and walked to Maggie's house. "Hello, Nat," Maggie called from her familiar spot on the front porch. "How are you feeling today?"

Gyp walked up and placed her head in Maggie's lap, making Nat smile.

"Very well, thank you. I got the stitches out today, so maybe my face will stop itching."

Maggie grinned. "You are leaving aren't you?"

"Yes, I'll leave in two days. Are you set for wood and supplies?"

"I'm in good shape, thanks to you. I even have some money built up in case I fall upon hard times."

"That is very good news. You might want to keep an eye on those pickle barrels at the store and pick up a few more for us."

Maggie smiled. "That sounds promising."

"Regardless if I stay in the woods, we will still go to the water in the fall to make a few harvests."

"I'll be glad to see you return. Would it be all right to drop by tomorrow to say goodbye?"

"Of course, you're welcome to visit anytime, Maggie."

"I'll see you sometime after lunch tomorrow then."

"I look forward to it, my friend." Nat stepped off the porch to walk to the general store.

Nat ordered her supplies and requested delivery later that day. When she finished, she and Gyp made the slow walk home. She stopped off at her cabin. Next time, she would not bother renting the cabin. She had spent very few nights here, and if she and Marissa were to continue, there was no need to rent the cabin. She began packing up her belongings in preparation for her trip and carried her packs to the front room. Gyp followed behind her closely, moving through the house and watching her pack.

When the wagon from the general store arrived later that afternoon, Nat took the supplies into the cabin and prepared the last of the packs. She would bundle up her clothing later that evening, leaving all of the next day to spend with Marissa, and Maggie when she visited. She walked out to the barn to check on the animals.

Hardy rushed to her and nuzzled into Nat. "Are you ready to travel?" she asked the large horse.

Quincy and Buck also came trotting into the barn. "Hello, boys." She patted each of them on the head. "It's almost that time." Nat had thought briefly of leaving Buck behind with Marissa and then changed her mind. Marissa always walked to town and Buck could lessen Quincy's load, making it easier on the smaller pack mule.

She fed the animals a hearty portion of grain and tossed the last of the winter hay into the bin. "Eat well, boys."

Nat made a stop at the smoke house to survey the supplies. She would take several pounds of the jerky for her trip. She walked to the house to find Marissa in the kitchen, warming dinner for them by the fireplace.

"Hello, darling," Nat said when Marissa turned to face her.

Nat could see tears pooling in Marissa's eyes while walking toward her. She encircled her with her strong arms. "I'll be back. I promise. I just can't say when."

"I know, but I have become so used to coming home to you every day."

"I'll be right here with you every day." Nat tapped lightly on Marissa's chest above her heart. "It's not easy for me to leave you, but I must go to find out where I'm destined to be," Nat explained.

Marissa nodded, but it did not stop the flow of tears running down her face. Nat hugged her close and felt sobs wracking her body.

"I'll miss you terribly and worry about you while you're gone."

"I'll miss you, too. There's no need to worry. I have Gyp and the boys to watch over me. "

Nat held Marissa until her tears subsided and then sat down with her at the table. "I have checked supplies and you are in good shape. I also gave you access to my bank account, if you are in need of anything while I'm away."

"You didn't need to do that, Nat." Marissa wiped her tears away.

"It gives me comfort to know you won't go without something if you need it."

Marissa smiled at Nat. "I love you so."

"I love you too."

"Are you all packed?"

"For the most part, yes. I'll bundle up my clothing tonight or tomorrow morning, and then we'll have all day together."

"That will be nice."

"Maggie will come by sometime after lunch to say goodbye, but other than that, I'm all yours."

"So we don't need to jump up out of bed in the morning."

"No, there is no hurry, so we can sleep in if we want."

"Good, because I plan on keeping you up tonight," Marissa replied with a coy smile.

"I guess I had better eat a good dinner then."

"Are you ready to eat now?"

"I'm hungry, but it'll wait, if you are not hungry yet."

"I'll put the food on the table if you'll get us a bucket of fresh water."

They shared a simple meal of leftovers and cleaned the dishes together. "It's such a beautiful night, would you like to sit on the porch for a while?" Nat asked.

"That would be very nice."

Nat took her hand, leading her out to the porch. She sat down on the steps, leaned back against the porch rail post, and sat Marissa between her legs. She pulled her back onto her chest with her arms circling Marissa's waist. They enjoyed the comfort of their closeness until the moon was high in the sky and then walked inside to go to bed.

†

They didn't bother with nightshirts after stripping off their clothes and crawling beneath the covers. Nat moved on top of Marissa and looked down into her sparkling eyes as Marissa's hands circled her waist.

"I feel like I'm in heaven when I'm with you," Marissa said.

"You do have a heavenly body," Nat replied with a grin.

Marissa lifted her hand to Nat's face and her fingertips caressed the length of the fresh scar. "On anyone else, this would be just an ugly scar, but on you it adds to your rugged charm." Marissa lightly touched her skin.

"I'm glad you don't mind it. Doc told me it would be with me for a while yet."

"I love every inch of you, my darling."

Nat leaned down and pressed her lips softly against Marissa's eyelids and down her cheek to her lips. The tip of her tongue traced across her lips, memorizing the sweetness that lay there waiting for her. Marissa parted her lips and welcomed Nat's tongue into her mouth, and their kiss turned into a sensual dance. Their hands explored each other, making love slowly, deep into the night.

Later, they lay relaxing in one another's arms and Nat whispered, "I will love you forever."

Nat felt the touch of warm tears on her chest as Marissa cried softly in her arms. She wiped the tears away from Marissa's cheek with soft fingers. "I would be worried if I didn't know that those are happy tears," she whispered softly.

"Yes, Nat, I'm so happy with you."

"We will be happy for years to come, I promise." Nat stroked Marissa's hair. "Relax now," she said softly.

Nat held her until they fell asleep, and when they woke the following morning, their bodies were still entwined in a lover's embrace.

Nat woke first and watched Marissa sleep peacefully on her arm. She was so beautiful and Nat struggled with her heart. She did not want to leave Marissa, but she was compelled to return to the woods. Only time would tell which was the right place for her. She snuggled closer to Marissa and closed her eyes to fall asleep once more.

Chapter Seventeen

Nat and Marissa slept until mid-morning, until the call of nature woke Marissa and she climbed from the bed to walk out to the privy. Nat was awake and smiling at her when she returned.

"Good morning, my love," she said when Marissa sat on the edge of the bed.

"Yes, it is barely still morning." Marissa grinned. "I bet you are starving."

"How did you know that? Did my stomach growling wake you?"

"That was your stomach? I thought it was thunder rumbling in the distance."

"Yes, ma'am, I am starving. What's for breakfast?"

"How about sugar-cured ham, flapjacks, and syrup?"

"Oh yes, darling, that sounds wonderful."

"Let's wash up and get dressed then and I'll cook."

"I'll start a pot of coffee," Nat said.

Marissa poured cool water into the washbasin and they washed their hands and faces before dressing for the day.

"What can I do to help?"

"Nothing, darling. You can go ahead and get your clothes together and get that out of the way while I cook."

Nat kept out clean socks, a work shirt, and one of the new pair of buckskin breeches Maggie had made for her and packed the remainder of her clothing. Nat tied the bundle up neatly and set it beside the bed.

Marissa had warmed the ham slices and was pouring the batter into a frying pan to cook the first of her large flapjacks.

Nat walked back into the kitchen. "That smells good."

"It won't be long before breakfast is ready."

"I'll get some fresh water."

Nat went out the front door and bent to pick up the water bucket. Her eyes came to rest on the block of wood she had been whittling on all week. Today she would finish it and give it to Marissa before she left.

Marissa placed the first of the flapjacks on Nat's plate. "Cut some off for Gyp while I cook the next batch, please."

Nat cut a large piece of the flapjack into smaller pieces and tore a slice of ham into smaller strips. "Do you want syrup too?"

Gyp licked her lips in response and Nat poured a small amount of the sweet liquid across the food.

"You are spoiled rotten." Nat put Gyp's bowl down on the floor.

"Just like her master."

"So it's your fault then."

"I'll take ownership of that. Eat, before it gets cold. I'll have another ready in just a few minutes."

Nat and Gyp began to eat their meal. "This ham is really good."

"I'm glad you like it. I'm going to cook some for you to take with you tomorrow."

"Thanks, Marissa. I sure am going to miss your cooking."

"Back to camp fire grub for you."

"Don't remind me that I have to eat my own cooking. Enjoy it, Gyp, we are back to camp stew and fry bread soon."

Marissa put another flapjack on Nat's plate and cooked one for herself. She sat down beside Nat and poured syrup over the flapjack. "These are pretty good. You can take cornmeal and cook these for yourself, you know."

"I bought five pounds yesterday, but they won't taste near as good as yours."

Marissa smiled at Nat's compliment. "You'll just have to hurry back then."

Nat took a bite of the ham and smiled at Marissa. "That I will," she promised after she swallowed.

After breakfast, Nat and Gyp walked onto the porch while Marissa cleaned the kitchen. Nat sat in the rocker and picked up the carving she had begun. The top portion of the bear had been finished, so Nat went to work on the bottom half of the wood block, slowly whittling until the bear's thick legs began to form.

Marissa joined them on the porch, sat next to Nat, and peeked over her shoulder. "That is coming along nicely." Marissa propped her feet upon the porch railing and enjoyed the sun on her skin as they sat together.

Gyp napped at their feet until Maggie approached, and she bolted from the porch to meet her. Nat walked inside to grab a chair for Maggie to join them on the porch. When she finally came into sight, Nat said, "Good day, Maggie."

"A beautiful day indeed." Maggie stepped onto the porch carrying a small crate. "How are you three doing today?"

"Just wonderfully, thank you, Maggie," Marissa replied.

"I brought some things for you." Maggie sat the small crate on the porch floor.

"Thank you, Maggie."

Maggie reached in and pulled out the new pair of buckskin boots. "Marissa helped me with these." She handed the boots to Nat.

Nat looked at Marissa and then at Maggie. "These are beautiful."

"Maggie, all I did was braid the leather for the boot strings."

"That's still helping," Nat, reminded her.

Nat took her boots off and slipped the new ones on her feet. "A perfect fit." She demonstrated by dancing around the porch. "They are comfortable, too."

Maggie smiled proudly and reached back into the crate. "I thought I would send a few jars of chowder out with you, too. Instead of bringing them back empty, you can fill them if you find that honey tree again." Maggie smiled.

"Sounds like a fair trade to me."

Gyp sat in front of Maggie wiggling in anticipation. "I did not forget you." Maggie pulled out a large bone and handed it to Gyp. Gyp took the bone, moved to the edge of the porch, and began gnawing on the gift.

"I also made you a new blanket for your bedroll." Maggie handed Nat a colorful blanket.

"That will come in very handy on the cool nights." Nat reached down to hug Maggie tightly. "Thank you, my friend."

"Thank you for all that you have done for me," Maggie said.

"I do believe we have one more item to discuss. I want you to keep the bear pelt and use it to warm your bed next winter."

"But, that pelt is worth a lot of money."

"Okay, then sell it to Smithy. Either way, it is yours."

"It will warm my bed for many years to come." Maggie's eyes glistened with tears. "I'll be going now, but I wanted to give you my gifts and tell you goodbye. I hope to see you again soon. Take good care, my friend," she said to Gyp before standing and hugging Nat tightly.

"I'll miss you, Maggie. Gyp will too."

"Come home to us soon then."

"I will," Nat promised.

They watched Maggie pick up her crate and walk across the yard to return home. She stopped once at the edge of the yard and turned to wave at them.

"I think she will miss you almost as much as I will."

"She has been a good friend to us. These boots are beautiful. You did a good job on the boot strings, too."

"Maggie put a lot of love and time into sewing them for you. She really appreciates all you have done for her."

"I know. That's what makes it so easy to hunt or chop wood for her."

Nat settled back into the rocking chair as Gyp trotted back onto the porch. She picked up her knife and the bear carving and, after another hour, she put the finishing touches on the base of the carving. "Not bad for a first try," she said to Marissa. "I want you to have this."

"It's beautiful, Nat." Marissa's fingers moved over the smooth wood. "I can't believe this is your first piece. You made it look so easy."

"You just have to open your heart to the creature hiding in the wood and let him come to life." She picked up the honing stone, sharpened her knife, and then slipped it into the boot sheath Maggie had sewn into the boot. She smiled at the fact that Maggie had remembered that detail.

As the sun started to fade, Marissa turned to Nat. "Would you like to share a bath tonight?"

"I would love that."

"We have cornbread and chops left for dinner if that's okay with you."

"Sounds wonderful. Would you like me to start the fire?"

"Yes, please, and I will pack up the ham and biscuits for your trip. I already have the chicken wrapped up for you."

"Thank you." She kissed Marissa and walked out to start the fire under the wash pot. Marissa went inside to wrap up the food.

Nat was kneeling down beside the wash pot when she felt Gyp brush up against her thigh. Gyp looked up at her with what looked like sadness in her eyes. "I know you like it here, too, don't you, my friend?"

Gyp responded by licking Nat's hand. "We will be coming back here."

The longer she stayed, the harder it would be for Nat to leave and it was already difficult for her to separate from Marissa. Never in her wildest dreams had she thought four months ago that she would meet and fall in love with someone like Marissa. Her life was changing quickly and thoughts of the future scared Nat, even though she would not admit this to anyone besides herself. If she left the woods, would she make enough money to compensate for not trapping, or would she need to change her standard of living? Nat chuckled softly at her thoughts. Her standard of living had much improved with Marissa. She had a roof over her head every night, a home-cooked meal, and a beautiful woman to wrap her arms around each night when she went to sleep. Nathan would probably think she was crazy to leave that behind, but Nat had to know.

With a deep sigh, Nat stood and walked back into the cabin. Marissa had lit candles in the bathing area and had set out fresh towels for them to use. Marissa had made them a cup of coffee and was sitting at the kitchen table when Nat entered. They ate the meal Marissa had prepared and talked quietly.

Marissa looked up at Nat. "Will you return here at the end of the fall?"

"I'll definitely be coming back here. The latest would be at the end of fall."

"My heart already misses you."

Nat smiled warmly at Marissa, but had no words of comfort for her. She could not tell her exactly when she would return and would not fill her with false hope.

"I can't believe how quickly this day has passed." Marissa stood to walk out to check the water temperature.

When Marissa entered carrying a bucket of steaming water, Nat joined her in carrying the water in for their bath. After several trips each, they had plenty of water and stripped out of their clothing to enjoy a steamy bath.

Nat climbed in first and then Marissa followed and rested her head on Nat's shoulder. "This feels really good."

"I will miss our bath times. Not too many opportunities for hot bath water in the woods."

"How do you bathe?"

"Usually in cold streams, or lakes."

"I can understand why a hearty meal and a bath are so appealing to you then."

"I typically don't get to lay my head back and hold a beautiful woman in my arms when I bathe in the wild."

"It makes me happy to know that you think I'm beautiful."

"You are beautiful, and thoughts of you will keep me warm on the long chilly nights."

"That is so sweet of you to say."

"You have given me so many fond memories to take with me, Marissa." Nat nuzzled into her lover's neck.

"If you keep talking like that you will have me crying again."

"I'm sorry, but it's the truth."

Marissa sighed. "I know exactly how you feel." She turned in Nat's arms to face her and leaned in for a kiss. "I'll miss your sweet kisses, too."

"I promise to make up for lost time when I return."

"You had better give me plenty tonight then, to hold me for a while."

"That is no problem." Nat held Marissa in her arms and kissed her softly.

They kissed until they were breathless with passion and Marissa locked eyes with Nat. "It's time you take me to bed."

They climbed from the bathtub and dried their bodies. Nat took Marissa by the hand and led her to the bedroom. They lay down beside one another and continued to kiss as their hands caressed and explored each other's body.

Nat rolled Marissa onto her back and touched between her legs to find her drenched with excitement. She locked eyes with Marissa and watched them glaze over with passion when she entered her with two long fingers and gently caressed her delicate body. Nat's mouth moved down across Marissa's breasts, tantalizing her nipples with an expert tongue. Marissa arched her back, tempting Nat to take more of her sensitive flesh into her mouth, but Nat continued to tease Marissa into a frenzy of desire. The juices of her passion spilled into Nat's palm as Marissa climaxed with a violent shudder, calling out Nat's name and pulling her head firmly onto her breast.

Nat could feel Marissa's inner muscles quivering around her fingers as her climax faded, and she slowed the movement of her fingers, nuzzling her breasts and massaging Marissa's swollen clit with her thumb.

"You are driving me mad with desire." Marissa arched her back and filled Nat's mouth with her breast.

Nat teased her breast until she felt Marissa vibrate with pleasure and then lowered her mouth to take Marissa's throbbing clit deep into her mouth, sucking it gently in and out of her mouth. Marissa gushed with a flow of pleasure and Nat's tongue fervently lapped up her sweetness. The taste of Marissa's passion filled Nat's senses and she allowed Marissa to roll her onto her back.

Marissa burned with excitement as she lowered her face into Nat's wetness for a long, deep, sensual kiss, her fingers twisting Nat's aching nipples.

"Turn toward me," Nat instructed between groans and Marissa climbed to her knees, turning her body to Nat's reach. Nat penetrated her with three fingers and thrust deeply inside Marissa's velvety wetness, mimicking the movement of the tongue inside her.

Marissa's deep moans of pleasure vibrated inside Nat and she erupted onto Marissa's face, soaking her with her juices as Marissa bucked wildly onto Nat's thrusting fingers.

Nat lifted Marissa's head to cover her clit as Marissa continued her wild ride, and her excitement flowed through her mouth, greedily sucking Nat's clit until they both were overwhelmed with passion and collapsed breathing hard onto the bed.

Marissa's head rested on Nat's chest waiting for their bodies to calm. "You make me feel so incredible, Nat," she whispered against Nat's skin.

"That feeling is mutual." Nat softly stroked Marissa's hair.

Silence hung between them as they embraced and, when Nat heard the soft purring of Marissa sleeping, she carefully pulled the linens up to cover their bodies.

Chapter Eighteen

Nat woke the following morning to the smell of bacon cooking. She climbed from the bed and pulled a nightshirt on before walking to the kitchen to find Marissa toiling away.

Marissa looked up and smiled when Nat approached. "I had to send you off with a full stomach."

"It smells wonderful. How long have you been awake?"

"For almost an hour."

"Long enough to cook fresh biscuits and bacon." Nat grinned.

"I have eggs, too. I was just waiting for you to wake. Fried or scrambled?"

"Fried, ma'am, if you please."

"Did you sleep well?"

"Like a rock, and you?"

Marissa blushed slightly. "So well, I fell asleep on you."

"That's all right. Last night was beautiful."

"Yes, it was." Marissa cracked a half a dozen eggs into the frying pan. "Will you break up a biscuit and put some bacon for Gyp in her bowl while I finish the eggs?"

"Yes, ma'am. Are you hungry, Gyp?"

Gyp sat at Nat's feet and her entire body wiggled.

Marissa smiled at Gyp as she dropped two fried eggs into her bowl and then served the remainder onto her plate and Nat's.

Nat mashed up her fried eggs and took a bite of bacon while dipping half a biscuit into the yellow mixture to sop up the yoke. "Are you sure I can't hide you away in one of my packs?"

"No, my love, even with all your skills, I would not do well living like you do."

"I know, but I couldn't help but ask one last time."

"I have to leave for work soon. Will you stop by after you are packed?"

"I couldn't leave town without saying goodbye."

"I would have to hunt you down if you did."

"Now that could be fun."

"I love you, Nat, don't ever forget that."

"I love you too, Marissa, and will come back to you."

Marissa stood and carried her plate to the counter to hide the tears in her eyes. "You two better eat all this food so I don't have to store it."

"I don't think that is going to be a problem. We both love your cooking."

"I'll go get dressed and will be back shortly."

Waiting for her return, Nat and Gyp finished off the breakfast.

"How long do you think you'll be?" Marissa asked when she returned to the kitchen.

"No more than an hour. I just need to pack the animals and saddle Hardy for the trip."

Marissa embraced Nat and kissed her passionately. "I'll see you soon then, my love." She turned to rush from the cabin to go to the hotel.

Nat rinsed off her plate and Gyp's bowl and then turned to her companion. "Are you ready to get started?"

Gyp jumped to her feet and rushed to the door.

"Not quite that fast." Nat picked up her old boots, carefully slipped the jars of chowder down inside them for protection, and then added a pack of the food Marissa had wrapped to add cushioning to the glass jars. She then tied the boots together using a thin strip of rawhide and hung them over the bundle of clothing.

Nat walked to the bedroom to dress in the new breeches Maggie had sewn for her, a new work shirt, and her new boots. Everything fit well and she felt good when she walked from the bedroom.

After picking up the small pack, she walked to her cabin to add the final pack to her growing pile. She then went out to the barn to saddle Hardy and prepare Buck and Quincy to carry the packs. Leading all three animals to the hitching post, she tied their leads securely.

Walking back inside, Nat picked up the largest packs before carrying them outside and strapping them onto the harness across Buck's shoulders. Returning to the cabin, she collected the remaining three packs, and took them outside to tie them onto Quincy's back. One last walk through the cabin to make sure she was not leaving anything behind had Nat letting out a soft sigh. She closed the door behind her and led the animals down to Marissa's cabin.

Nat walked inside to pick up her bedroll, and range coat, which she tied onto the back of her saddle. She went back outside and placed her rifle into the sheath tied to her saddle. Nat was just about to mount Hardy when she had an idea. She turned and walked back into the cabin and walked to the bedroom. She carefully took the bear claw necklace from around her neck and placed it on Marissa's pillow. The scar on her face would remind her of the bear she had killed, and the cabin would remind Nat of her father. She was leaving her most personal possession behind for Marissa and she hoped she would understand the commitment Nat was making to her.

Pleased with the thought, Nat turned and walked from the cabin. She placed a foot in the stirrup and mounted Hardy. She reached down, took the lead for Buck, and they started toward town. Quincy, tethered behind Buck, trotted behind the large horse. Gyp took the lead and walked quickly in front of Nat and Hardy.

Nat turned in her saddle before they left the yard and took one long last look at her new home.

✝

Nat rode first to Smithy's store and found Maggie and Smithy sitting on the front porch waiting for her. She smiled brightly when she saw the two of them. "Good morning, my friends," she said as she dismounted and stepped onto the porch.

"No chance of talking you out of going, is there?" Maggie asked.

"No, but I will be back."

Smithy stood and handed her a small cloth wrapped bundle. "I wanted to give you this before you left." He held out his hand and looked down at Nat.

Nat took the bundle and opened it. Inside was a beautiful hand-carved knife handle attached to a gleaming new blade. "This is beautiful, Smithy," she raved.

"The handle is made from a piece of the whale bones you brought back. It was Maggie's idea and she helped me with the carvings."

"You both did a wonderful job," Nat replied, with tears forming.

Maggie had also stitched a heavy sheath to place the knife on Nat's belt and she smiled when Nat unfastened her belt and hung the knife and sheath there.

"All set now." She hugged each of them tightly. "Thanks for such a wonderful gift."

"Hurry back to us," Smithy said.

"I will." Nat took Hardy's reins and led him to the hotel to say a final goodbye to Marissa.

She dropped the reins over the hitching post and was about to step onto the porch when Marissa ran into her arms. Nat embraced her and could feel Marissa trembling. "Come home to me soon."

"I will."

"Damn, you look handsome in those new clothes," Marissa said, and Nat returned her compliment with a painful smile.

Nat turned away from Marissa before the tears began and mounted Hardy. Nat tucked her hair underneath her hat and smiled at Marissa. "I love you." She turned Hardy toward the road from town.

✝

Nat turned and waved at her friends before riding toward the trail that would take her deep into the woods. Her heart ached with the sound of Hardy's footsteps, each step taking her farther away from the woman she loved. She rode for several hours. The sun traveled across the sky and dark clouds were ushered in on a cool wind. Just after a short lunch break, the mist began to fall, and by midafternoon rain was pelting down upon them. Nat stopped to cover the packs with new ground tarps and slipped her arms inside her range coat. She mounted Hardy, pulled the brim of her hat down, and continued the journey to the cave where they would spend the night.

Nat knew she was about another hour's ride from the cave. She prayed that no one else had used it and depleted the pile of dry wood she had stored there several months earlier when she had left the woods. The rain seemed to have settled in and more than likely would last all night. There would be no chance of finding dry wood in this weather, and Nat knew she might be in for a long, uncomfortable, first night in the woods.

When the surrounding area began to look familiar, Nat was relieved and soon found the small trail that would lead back to the cave. There was no sign that anyone had traveled the path recently so Nat's hopes for dry wood soared. She dismounted Hardy at the mouth of the cave and led the animals inside away from the falling rain.

Nat walked to the back of the cave. She nearly jumped for joy when she saw the pile of wood just as she had left it. She took an armful to the fire pit and started a fire, then turned to tend to the animals. She unsaddled Hardy, took the rifle from its sheath, and leaned it against a boulder where it would be close at hand if needed. Then she removed the packs from Buck and Quincy and dried each of them the best she could with an old saddle blanket. Watching the rain come down in earnest just beyond the mouth of the cave, Nat hung the blanket and her coat to dry.

"Well, this certainly isn't the start I had hoped for." Nat removed her hat and shook the raindrops from it.

The fire grew quickly as she spread out her bedroll and then pulled a bundle of food from her spare boots. Nat and Gyp feasted on fried chicken and corn bread while their companions ate oats from their feedbags. After their meal, Nat sat with her back resting against her saddle with her hand buried in Gyp's fur, staring into the flames and listening to the falling rain.

†

Marissa had a miserable day and took off early from the hotel. When she walked into the cabin she immediately sensed how empty it felt without Nat and Gyp there waiting for her. Her heart sank as she pushed the door closed behind her, and she stoked the fire. She wondered how Nat and her traveling companions were faring as they holed up for the night.

Marissa ate a light meal, even though she did not feel much like eating, and then walked into the bedroom to change clothes. She lit the bedside lamp and her eyes sparkled when she saw Nat's gift lying on her pillow. She picked up the necklace and slipped it over her head, holding onto the bear claws that until recently rested against Nat's skin. Marissa sat down on the bed, picked up Nat's pillow, and held it to her face, searching for the familiar scent of her lover. Marissa cried herself to sleep that night, still clutching the pillow while her heart ached for Nat.

†

Nat felt her head nodding and stood to remove the feedbags from the animals. The rain was still coming down and she hoped it would let up before the morning came. Another day's ride would bring her to the cabin and she didn't look forward to a ride in the rain. She put several large logs on the fire and with Gyp curled up beside her lay down to sleep. "Good night, my love," she whispered to Marissa, closing her eyes and letting the sound of the rainfall lull her to sleep.

Nat woke the next morning to the sound of Hardy stomping his feet. The rain had stopped during the night and Nat thought he was anxious to get on the trail. Nat quickly replaced the packs on Buck and Quincy and then saddled Hardy.

"I know I'm eager to get going too." She took a ham biscuit out and tossed it to Gyp. She took two others out and mounted Hardy. She would eat her breakfast on the trail to save a little more daylight. As it was, it would be near nightfall by the time they reached the cabin.

With the rain gone, Nat listened to a chorus of birds and animals singing or calling to their mates in the woods. Her spirits lifted, listening to the soft creak of leather from her saddle and the gentle jingling of the metal traps packed on Buck.

The trail turned into small hills after she made a momentary stop to water the animals and eat another of Marissa's ham biscuits. Soon, Nat knew, she would cross a small river and then be just a few miles from the cabin. Her spirits lifted even higher when she heard the cry of an eagle soring overhead. Not far from the cabin was an outcropping of rocks that had been home to a family of eagles for several years. Even Hardy's steps seemed quicker. From all the times she and her father went to the cabin, Hardy instinctively knew exactly where they were heading. She could feel what she thought was excitement quivering in his muscles as they grew closer.

Nat noticed the sun starting to fade. "It won't be long now, boys, before you are grazing on some sweet clover."

Even Gyp seemed excited, though she had been such a young pup the last time she was at the cabin. She ran ahead of Nat and would rush back to hurry them on. Nat had not given any thought to anyone else being in the cabin, so as they got closer she looked for signs of recent travel. There were no signs that would indicate anyone had taken over the cabin, but still she cautiously rode into the small front yard.

There was no fire burning in the fireplace or in the outdoor fire pit. Nat's eyes drifted to the end of the cabin where she had buried her father and was grateful to see that his grave was undisturbed. The small cross she had placed at the head of the rock mound was still securely in place. She smiled and dismounted Hardy. She would have to work quickly to get unpacked and tend to the animals before darkness overtook them.

She carried the first of the large packs inside and lit the wood she had left in the fireplace. If anyone had followed her last visit, he had been kind enough to lay a fire. Nat carried in the remainder of the packs and then took the saddle from Hardy's back. She led the animals into a small fenced corral and closed a gate behind them. The fence would not be a deterrent if any of them wanted out, but Nat knew that they would not wander far from the cabin and a loud whistle would bring them trotting back.

As she walked back to the cabin, Nat stopped at her father's grave. "Hello, Father. I cannot begin to tell you how much I miss you. My life has changed so much since you died, and I have never been more confused in my life. I hope some time out here with you will help me sort through who it is I have become and where my life shall lead me."

Nat bent down and ran her fingers over the rough wood of the cross. "I love you, Father."

Nat walked into the cabin and began to sort through her packs and set up house in the small room. The cots she and her father had slept on were still in place, much to her delight. She spread her bedroll out across one and began to unpack her food supplies.

She located the small grate that fit into the fireplace and took the lid off a jar of the chowder to warm over the fire. She and Gyp would finish off the chicken and corn bread while the chowder would give them something hot in their bellies. Nat then picked up the bucket and made her way down the path to the small creek for fresh water. It had grown dark, but Nat had traveled the path so many times she knew exactly where to go. She dipped out a bucket of cold water and walked back to the cabin with Gyp close on her heels.

Tomorrow she would survey the streams and surrounding areas to determine if the beaver and other wild game seemed to be plentiful. Nat had hoped that she could reap her bounty here without having to travel any farther away from Marissa.

Nat and Gyp ate their meal, and after cleaning up their dishes, decided to call it an early night. The day on the trail had been long and they were both tired from their travels. Nat pulled the empty cot next to hers and laid a saddle blanket out for Gyp. She placed more wood on the fire to keep it burning through the night. Nat took off her boots and the belt holding her new knife, and laid them on the cot beside Gyp. She stretched out onto the cot and stared up at the shadows dancing across the ceiling until the call of dreams enticed her to drift off to sleep.

Gyp woke Nat the next morning by licking her face. Nat nuzzled Gyp's neck. "Do you need to go out?" she asked, and Gyp raced for the door. "I'll take that as a yes." Nat opened the door for Gyp and saw the verdant, green, plant life that ringed the cabin glistening brightly beneath the early morning dew. Nat watched Gyp race around, nose to the ground, smelling the many scents of animals that had passed through the yard, stepped into her boots, and placed her knife on her belt.

Nat turned and walked back inside and foraged through the wrapped bundles to find three ham biscuits left. Gyp came trotting back inside. "This is it, girl, one for you and two for me. After these, it is back to my cooking."

Gyp took the biscuit from her hand gently and sat down to eat. Nat bit into the biscuit and her mouth watered at the taste of the ham. It made her long for Marissa even more. "Maybe we should find us a wild boar so we can have ham."

She had become so used to speaking with humans over the past four months that it seemed strange to hear her own voice with no one there to answer. Gyp was a great companion, but Nat wished during moments like this that she could speak. "Okay, maybe it isn't such a good idea that you speak." Nat patted Gyp's head. "You would probably keep me up all night talking."

Nat ate half of the last biscuit and gave the remainder to Gyp. She drank a cup of water and looked at Gyp. "Are you ready to get to work?"

Gyp ran out the door and waited at the top of the steps while Nat bent down to pick up her rifle. "Let's go," she called and started down a path. The cabin was ideal for a trapper. Three of its sides were close to three separate small creeks, which joined a mile away to form the river where Nat's father had died. Nat walked down to the first creek and looked for signs of beaver dams. There were plenty of saplings hewn by the beaver's sharp teeth, and Nat walked a hundred yards more to find several dams that looked fresh. She traveled to the other two creeks and found the same evidence. On her way back to the cabin, she listened for a familiar hum.

She heard what she was looking for and turned to Gyp. "You stay here." Gyp dropped on her haunches and sat obediently. Nat walked farther into the woods. "I was hoping you were still here." She carefully approached a large split tree. She cautiously peeked inside and saw a mass of honeybees swarming as they worked. "I'll be back for you later."

"We are going to have us some honey, Gyp." Gyp danced to her feet. It was still early morning, so Nat took a half a dozen traps and walked to where her father died. The spot where she had burned the bear carcass was filled in with new grass with just a faint hint of evidence of the scorched ground. Nat worked for an hour, setting the traps, and then walked back to the cabin. "Let's go down by the creek and see what we can shoot for dinner tonight."

Gyp followed Nat down to the water's edge and they sat patiently watching small animals come to drink. Nat's thoughts drifted to memories of Marissa as she leaned against a small tree. Gyp licked her hand to bring her back to reality just as a large rabbit sat up on its hind legs staring at them.

"Rabbit stew it is." Nat lifted her rifle and killed the rabbit.

Gyp bounded off ahead of her and sniffed around the dead rabbit.

"With some potatoes and carrots that should taste just fine."

Gyp sat patiently on the porch, watching Nat skin the rabbit and prepare it for the stew pot. The rabbit was still lean from winter, but it would provide ample meat for their stew for a few days. Nat put the meat into the stew pot and hung the pelt to dry.

She cut up a few of the potatoes and carrots from her stores and left them soaking in water. There was still plenty of daylight left so she and Gyp went in search of more firewood. Nat picked up the axe and her rifle. She used a narrow strip of buckskin to fashion a strap to the rifle so she could carry it over her shoulder, leaving her hands free to carry an armload of wood. She had seen a few trees behind the cabin that had fallen during the winter snows that she would chop first for their fireplace.

Nat chopped for nearly an hour, separating the fallen trees into sections she could carry back to the cabin. She stacked the small logs beside the cabin door and returned to split and carry the larger sections of the trunks. As the sun started to fade, Nat took the axe and returned to the cabin, smiling at the sizeable stack of wood she was able to bring in. She placed the axe and her rifle inside and walked to the creek for a fresh bucket of water. She poured water into Gyp's bowl and into her cup before resting from the labor. She added another few cups to the cooking stew and dropped the vegetables in with the meat.

She mixed up a batch of cornmeal and placed a skillet into the fireplace to bake. It would be awhile before dinner was ready, so Nat looked at Gyp. "Should we go steal some honey?" she asked.

Gyp heard the word *go* and bounded to the door. Nat picked up the glass jar she had emptied the night before. It still held a small amount of water. She made a long torch, using a tree limb with an oily cloth wrapped around the end, and lit it before she and Gyp walked to the honey tree. "You will have to stay back. I don't want you stung by angry bees."

Gyp sat patiently watching her master approach the tree. Nat poured a small amount of the water on the torch to make the oily cloth smoke. She then lifted the torch into the heart of the tree and ducked when an angry swarm of honeybees flew from the hive. Nat quickly poured the water from the jar and dunked it into the sticky, sweet honey, careful to break off a small portion of the comb to place inside the jar. When the jar was full, Nat moved quickly away from the tree, and she and Gyp rushed back to the house. She extinguished the torch and rested it beside the cabin to wait for their next raid.

Nat took the jar inside and wiped away the coating of the sweet honey and lifted the jar to her lips. "Mm, this is sweet." She watched Gyp wiggle with anticipation. Nat ran her fingers through the sweet liquid and offered her fingers to Gyp, who licked them with great appreciation of the tasty treat. Nat placed the metal lid on the jar and set it in the middle of the table.

Nat walked onto the porch and picked up an alder branch that she had found earlier that day. She returned inside the cabin, took a chair over to the fireplace to sit, and began skinning the light bark from the limb. She carefully shaved the limb and stopped every few minutes to drop the shavings into the fire. She would make this into a walking stick for Maggie. She sat back and enjoyed the smell of the cooking food. Each night, before she retired for the evening, she would add another carving onto the stick, she promised herself. It would make a beautiful gift for Maggie and would help her pass the time during the long nights ahead.

When Nat had skinned the bark, she carefully held the stick over the heat of the fireplace. As the wood heated, it turned a darker shade that would make Nat's carving's stand out more prominently on the wood. By the time she had finished staining the stick, the cornbread had risen, and the stew was ready for dinner. Nat carefully propped the stick next to the fireplace and dished out hearty portions of the stew. She placed the frying pan on the table and cut the cornbread into four large slices. She removed Gyp's cornbread to cool, and then crumbled it on top of the stew, before settling in to her own meal.

"It's not too bad, huh, Gyp?" Nat asked.

Gyp was busily devouring the meal and did not even look up at the sound of her name. "Must not be too bad."

Nat cleaned the dishes and took the stew from the fire before preparing to retire for the evening. They would have cornbread and honey for breakfast the next morning, and Nat would bake biscuits for leftover stew the following evening.

Tired, but satisfied with the day's accomplishments, Nat took off her boots and lay down on the cot. Gyp jumped onto the cot beside her and curled up next to Nat. "Good night, Marissa," Nat whispered. Gyp whimpered lightly, as if sensing Nat's loneliness, and Nat reached over to run her fingers through Gyp's fur.

"Everything is going to be all right, Gyp," she promised softly to herself and her companion.

Chapter Nineteen

Nat spent the next few weeks trapping and treating the pelts she was able to harvest. Each night she would sit by the fire, whittling away the time, carving on the walking stick. Her longing for Marissa did not fade. As the days grew longer, Nat found herself thinking of home.

Nat spent a good deal of time talking to Nathan's grave while she worked on her pelts. She knew her father could not answer her directly, but being near to him made Nat think like Nathan. Her heart grew unbearably lonesome, and her decision was clear. Nathan loved the wild, even more deeply after her mother had died, but he had taught her that no matter what, Nat should follow her heart. Nat had no doubt that she loved the life that Nathan had taught her, and it was a life she knew well, but without him or Marissa, it wasn't the life she yearned for anymore.

The more she thought about Maggie's suggestion, to harvest seafood and do some trapping near home while working for Smithy, the more excited she was about going home. She had several good weeks and she was sure the quality of the pelts was exceptional. Smithy would give a fair price for them, especially this early in the season.

On a sunny morning, a month after she had left home, Nat collected her traps and prepared for the trip home. She would leave the following morning and spend the day setting up her packs and topping off her supply of honey. She had not killed the wild boar she had hoped for, but there would be plenty of time to hunt once she returned home. Even better, she and Marissa could raise their own pig for slaughter if they added a small pen.

That evening, Nat packed up the last of her cooking utensils. She would eat leftover biscuits and jerky on her trip home. It wasn't a hearty meal, but Nat knew she would soon more than make up for it with Marissa's home cooking.

Gyp, too, seemed excited about traveling. She danced around Nat's heels as she walked to and from the woods, restocking the cabin's firewood. She doubted she would return to the cabin for a long time, but she wanted the next person to stumble across it to be properly welcomed.

They ate the last portion of a pheasant with cornbread. When done, she sat by the fire and picked up the walking stick. During her weeks in the forest, Nat had carved numerous animals deep into the smooth wood, and she was pleased with the final product. She would honor Maggie with the gift and hoped she would use it often in their future journeys together.

When dawn arrived the following morning, Nat had to wake Gyp who was still softly snoring on her cot. "It is time to start for home, lazy bones." Nat pulled her boots on.

Nat packed the animals, and after feeding Gyp a strip of jerky, she placed one in her mouth and mounted Hardy. She tore off bites of the dried meat and sucked on it to allow it to soften enough for her to chew as she rode through the morning. Nat had not seen another human since leaving town so she was surprised to catch the smell of a campfire. She kept her hand close to her rifle and approached a small clearing.

Nat saw a young couple, barely out of their teens, milling around the campfire. Startled by her approach, the young man jumped to his feet.

"Hello, there," Nat shouted as she rode closer.

"Hello," he answered eyeing her warily.

"What brings you two out to these parts?" she asked. Nat nudged Hardy closer to the fire.

"Me and my wife, Susan, are trying our hand at trapping," the strapping young man stated proudly.

"Are you having much luck?" Nat asked.

"Not near as well as you apparently," he answered, pointing to the heap of pelts on Quincy's back. "My name is Jim Calder." He cautiously offered his hand to Nat.

"Nat St. Croix." She shook his hand. "Would you mind a suggestion?"

"No, not at all," he answered. "Why don't you join us for some coffee?"

Nat stepped down from Hardy and tied him to a small tree. She took the cup of coffee Susan offered and joined them by the fire.

"I just left a cabin about four hours ride from here. To have a roof over your head would provide you better protection from the elements, and it is an area filled with plentiful game."

"Why are you leaving it then?"

"My heart just isn't into the life anymore since my father passed. That will be his grave at the end of the cabin, and I ask that you tend to it respectfully if you choose to use the cabin."

"I'm sorry you lost your father," Susan told her.

"Thank you. It was at the end of last year's season, so he has been gone awhile."

"A roof over our heads would be nice, Jim."

Nat smiled at the young woman and looked at her husband. "The cabin sits between three creeks that join a mile away to form a nice-sized river. All four spots are great for trapping and the game is plentiful to keep you well fed."

"We thank you for the information and will take advantage of that. What was your father's name?"

"It was Nathan and he taught me everything I know about trapping and living in the woods." She finished her coffee and handed the cup back to Susan. "Thank you for the coffee. If you will follow this trail for half a day, you will come to a small trail that bears to the right. Follow it, and it will lead you to the cabin. A fire is already laid in the fireplace."

"Thank you so much," Jim replied, and shook her hand with enthusiasm.

"You're welcome and good luck. Oh, and for something sweet, you will find a honey tree if you take the trail off to the left of the cabin and there's a smoke stick resting at the end of the porch."

"That sounds good to me," Susan smiled. "Thanks again and have a safe trip home."

Nat walked over and mounted Hardy. With a wave and a smile, she left the clearing, hoping to make the cave by nightfall.

Riding away from the clearing, Nat could hear the couple scurrying about, gathering their supplies. She smiled knowing that the couple who so desperately needed help would use the cabin.

Nat reached the cave just as dusk began to settle in. She removed the packs from the animals and allowed them to graze freely while she started a campfire. She selected portions of jerky for herself and for Gyp, and then sat listening to the stirring night.

The animals returned to the mouth of the cave after grazing and watched over Nat who curled into her bedroll and slept soundly that night.

The next morning the sun's light crested the horizon and Hardy began stomping his feet shifting his weight. *Who needs a rooster when I have Hardy?* Nat climbed from her bedroll and rolled it tightly before tying it onto her saddle. She slipped into her boots and pulled her hat over her brow. "Let's pack up and head for home."

She packed the animals and climbed up onto Hardy's back. The day promised to be warm and Nat would be grateful for a stop at a river along the way to bathe. She did not want to return to Marissa with the musk of a month's sweat on her. As they plodded down the path her thoughts were of Marissa and home. *If there is no one close, I'll strip down, bathe quickly in the cold waters, and put on fresh clothing.*

Soon, very soon, she would be back in her love's arms. Her smile grew with each step and when they reached the river, she cheerfully tolerated the frigid water to bathe and wash her hair. She would still wear a faint musk that only a long, hot bath would soak from her skin, but she was at least tolerable to smell.

As the sun began to set, Nat could smell the smoke from Marissa's fireplace. They rode into the yard and Gyp raced ahead to scratch at the front door.

✝

Marissa was just sitting down to enjoy a meal of fried chicken and biscuits when she heard the scratching. When the noise appeared for the second time, Marissa stood and walked to the entrance. She opened the door and Gyp rushed to her side.

"Welcome back, Gyp." Marissa bent down to pet her and looked up to see Nat stepping down from Hardy's back. She smiled brightly and rushed to Nat's arms. "Welcome home, my love."

"Thank you."

A sweltering-hot kiss from Marissa prevented any further comment. She held Nat tightly in her arms kissing for several minutes.

"I'm so happy to see you."

"I can see that," Nat teased. "It is good to be home."

"Let me help you with the animals and I will get you something to eat."

"I'll unload the animals if you will start the wash pot fire. I'm in desperate need of a hot bath."

"You have a good point." Marissa wriggled her nose.

Nat lifted the packs from the animals and left them on the front porch. "I'll deal with unpacking and take the pelts to Smithy tomorrow. Tonight, I want nothing more than to be with you and fall asleep in your arms."

"I like the sound of that."

"I'll take the animals to the barn and feed them grain and make sure they have water. I'll be back before you know it." Nat left, walking past the heating water in the wash pot.

Marissa was preparing the bathing area for Nat when she returned.

"I was just sitting down for dinner. Would you like to share my chicken, or would you like something else?"

"There is not enough chicken for both of us, so you eat that while I cook some flapjacks."

"Better yet, you snack on the chicken and I will prepare flapjacks, along with eggs if you want them." Marissa handed Nat a chicken leg.

"We are starving. We've lived off jerky for a few days now, so anything hot would be good."

Marissa cooked Nat and Gyp two thick flapjacks each, and then she scrambled a dozen eggs. She sat with them and shared the eggs and the last of the chicken. When the meal was over, Nat started bringing in hot water for her bath while Marissa cleaned the dishes.

Nat was undressing when Marissa joined her in the bathing area. "You have lost weight," she remarked with a look of concern.

"My cooking tastes nothing like yours."

Marissa kissed her again and then looked into her eyes, her fingertips tracing the fading scar down her face. "You really are home."

"Yes, my love, I am."

Nat finished undressing and climbed into the steaming, hot water. "This feels so good," she groaned.

Marissa knelt beside Nat to wash her hair, and then bathed her as Nat relaxed in the soaking bath.

"I'm beginning to feel human again." Nat looked at Marissa with what could only be described as adoring eyes when she stepped from the bathtub.

"You certainly smell better." Marissa wrapped Nat in a thick towel.

After drying Nat, Marissa reached around her head and slipped the necklace off, placing it over Nat's head. She looked at the bear claws resting on Nat's skin. "Now you are truly home."

Chapter Twenty

Nat's decision to leave the trapper's life along the Canadian border earlier that summer had been easy. Being with Marissa was where she wanted to always be. She initiated a backup plan for the woods by secretly convincing her friend and surrogate father, Smithy, to oversee the building of a new homestead for herself and Marissa near the Sound. There she could continue to trap and harvest the bounty of seafood from the Sound to supply the growing population of the town. She and Gyp had found the location when she pursued her dream of seeing the ocean. Nat had fallen in love with the beauty of the spot and had dreamed of creating a home there.

The money from the seafood, and the nest egg she had accumulated from selling her pelts, allowed Nat to fund the building of the log home she would soon be revealing to Marissa. The home also had a second room. She hoped to offer this to Maggie if she was interested in joining them at the coast.

Months after her return, the winds of a late summer gale howled around the walls of the new cabin as Nat worked inside the newly built bedroom. Nat was adding the final touches to the bed she had built for herself and her lover, Marissa.

Nat used a hand auger to drill holes in the thick planks of lumber she had fastened to the head, foot, and side rails of the bed. Then she weaved a sturdy rope into the frame. She would later place a feather mattress on top of it that her friend, Maggie Lightfoot, was making for her. If all went as planned, Maggie would bring the mattress in two days, with the delivery of the rest of her supplies from the general store in town. Then Nat would be prepared to give Marissa the surprise of her life.

She had dreamed of the plans for the bed on the lonesome nights she had spent in the woods while trapping. When the rope foundation was finished, she went to her pack for the last few items she needed to finish the project. During her final trapping run, Nat had found a solid ash limb that she carried back to the trapper's cabin and cut into four sections. She spent her nights sitting by the fire carving each of the sections into post nobs for the bed she envisioned building for Marissa.

The first carving was of a bear standing full height. After she pulled the carving from the protective cloth, her hand moved instinctively to her neck and the grizzly claw necklace in memory of her father, Nathan. The next two carvings were of a wolf and an eagle, both animals that mated for life. Nat had chosen them to symbolize the love she and Marissa had for one another. She had been the lone wolf, surviving and living from what Mother Nature provided for her, until she met Marissa, her eagle and free spirit, who taught her how to love. The final carving had surprised her when her knife revealed the form of a bison. Nat had seen the majestic creatures moving in large herds as a child with her father when they crossed the plains on their journey west. The carving of the bison would symbolize the strength and the courage they needed to form their new home together.

Nat used the auger to drill a single hole in the top of each of the four bedposts and then used paraffin to seal the base of the carvings in each of the posts. When the task was complete, Nat admired her work, circling the bed, her fingers gliding over the posts.

"This will do quite well," she spoke aloud.

Gyp, laying on the hearth of the fireplace and watching her master with loving eyes, barked in what sounded like approval.

"I'm glad you approve, Gyp." Nat chuckled as she sat next to her companion.

Nat leaned against the wall breathing in the cedar fragrance and admiring the new home. Her fingers instinctively buried themselves in Gyp's coat. "Just a few more chores to do and we will be ready," she said.

She had been at the site for three weeks under the ruse of preparing to set traps for the fall. It wasn't a complete ruse, for she had scouted out several locations and laid her traps, but the majority of her time she spent preparing their home. The cabin was finished along with a small outbuilding for the animals and a smokehouse. She stocked the smokehouse with venison from her hunting trips, and dozens of fish to provide meat for the coming winter. Nat had been pleased to find game in the area plentiful and had plans of putting in a late fall garden.

Nat had spent several days cutting, splitting, and stacking firewood for the cold winter ahead. She had also arranged for Smithy to purchase a draft horse and larger wagon. They would use the equipment to deliver the seafood and other items to town, and then fill it with needed supplies for their trip home. When she traveled back to town in a few days she would take delivery and fill the wagon with hay and feed for the animals as well as any other household supplies they needed.

Gyp whined softly and Nat went to open the door to let her outside. She had noticed that Gyp was spending more time outside just after nightfall, but she always returned when Nat whistled for her. "I'm beginning to wonder if you have a male friend out there." She held the door open and Gyp looked up to her with soft brown eyes before trotting into the falling darkness. Nat chuckled and returned inside with an armload of firewood.

She added wood to the fireplace and went about the task of preparing a simple meal. She would fry some venison chops and onions to accompany the last of her biscuits. She placed her frying pan on the fireplace rack and went outside to retrieve a bucket of fresh water. Nat was about to turn back to the house from the water pump when she heard playful yips from the edge of the woods. Maybe her suspicions were true and Gyp had found a companion. The thought brought a smile to her face as she carried the water into the cabin.

Nat prepared the meal and had cut a portion of the meat for Gyp with a biscuit and some warmed gravy. Gyp had not scratched at the door to request entrance, so Nat opened the back door and whistled. Several seconds later, she could hear Gyp rapidly approaching the cabin across the open field. When Gyp came into view, the mournful sound of a howl filled the air from behind Gyp.

"Someone seems sad you have left." Gyp bounded onto the back porch. Nat stood a moment longer, gazing into the darkness, and smiled when she saw the silver glint of fur in the bright moonlight. Then she turned and followed her companion inside.

Gyp rushed to the table eager for the meal. After Nat had cleaned their dishes, Gyp snuggled against Nat's feet for a nap while Nat added several items to her list of supplies. Rolling her shoulders and stretching she yawned before settling onto the pallet she had laid in front of the fire. Nat removed her boots, laid down pulling a blanket over her shoulders, and then waited for Gyp to curl up in front of her.

"Tomorrow we will go for a ride." Her hand rested on Gyp's side. The crackling of the wood and the warmth of the fire were the last memories Nat had before drifting into dreams of Marissa.

The next morning, Nat fished around the kitchen for supplies and made biscuits with the last of her flour. "If the goods don't arrive soon, I'm afraid we will go without biscuits," she told Gyp who looked at her curiously. "Do you need to go out?"

Gyp barked quietly and Nat chuckled, walking to the door. "Don't be long. I'm going to get the biscuits cooking and then get Hardy saddled and ready to go." She closed the door behind Gyp and rolled out the biscuits, placing them in the skillet to bake over the fire, then walked out the back of the cabin to the small outbuilding built for the stock.

Hardy looked eager for a ride and stood patiently as she saddled him for the trip to the woods. Quincy, her overly stubborn, but sure-footed mule, stomped his feet, seemingly agitated at the thought of being left behind on an adventure. "Don't worry, Quincy, you're coming along too." She took a long lead from the wall and attached it to his halter. She led both animals to the back of the cabin and tied them to the hitching post. "I won't be long," she promised and started for the door.

Gyp bounded onto the porch and met her at the entrance. "You always come running when you smell food cooking," she teased before opening the door.

Nat pulled out a smaller frying pan and tossed in the last slices of cured ham to warm over the fire. She wanted to explore the woods behind her home during the morning and then hook the small wagon to Quincy before returning to the beachside cave to collect the remaining whalebones. Some she would take back to Smithy, and the smaller ones she would keep at the cabin to try her hand at carving. The knife Maggie had made for her as a going away gift had an excellent blade, and Nat found she enjoyed whittling to pass her time alone.

While she waited for the biscuits to finish baking, she put together a small pack to take with her and filled a canteen with fresh water. Nat also checked her rifle, making sure it was loaded and ready for action if needed.

Stepping out on the front porch, she looked out at the calm water. "I think it's time for some shrimp," she told Gyp who was standing beside her. "Does that sound good to you, girl?"

Gyp licked her lips in answer.

"Well then, let's go eat a biscuit and get this day started."

Nat crumbled a steaming biscuit into Gyp's bowl, tore strips of the ham, and then covered it with some gravy. "You need to let this cool first." Gyp sat in front of the bowl and watched Nat prepare ham biscuits and wrap them in cloth before placing them in the pack.

"In case we get hungry later." She took a bite from her biscuit. "Eat up, girl." Gyp hungrily attacked the food.

Nat carried the pack and hung the loop over her saddle horn. She slipped her rifle into the sheath and untied Quincy. Taking Hardy's reins, she swung into the saddle. "Let's go see what we can find."

✝

Marissa entered the dining room of the restaurant to find Smithy had taken a seat. The crowd was thin for the early morning, so she carried a cup of coffee to him and took a seat. "Good morning, it's good to see you."

"Likewise, how have you been?"

"I'm good. Work's been pretty steady, which helps the time pass more quickly before Nat comes home."

"You miss her terribly, don't you? I know I'm not much of a substitute, but I'm sick of my own cooking, so I thought I'd stop by to see you. Do you know when she's coming back our way?"

"Early next week if all goes well. She mentioned buying a draft horse and larger wagon to help out with transporting the seafood and supplies."

Smithy chuckled and smiled at her. "Rusty is chomping at the bit to meet his new owner. He was delivered with the new wagon yesterday and is about to eat me out of house and home. I hope Nat knows what she's getting into with him."

"I'm sure she has taken that into consideration."

The sound of heavy boots coming down the stairs caught their attention and they turned to see three rugged looking men approaching the counter to pay their bill.

"Have you noticed the increase in traffic through town the last few weeks?" she asked.

"Yes, I have. Gold seekers headed to British Columbia in search of their fortunes. Most of them won't survive the year up there."

"I bet it's difficult up there in the best of times."

"Add a glint of the shiny stuff and you not only have to worry about surviving what Mother Nature throws at you, but you have to prevent someone slitting your throat to steal your hard-earned bounty."

"I think I'll stay right here." Marissa stood when the men turned to approach the dining room. "What can I cook you for breakfast, Smithy?"

"Take care of them so they can get back on the trail, and I'll wait to eat for a bit."

Marissa waited for the men to take a seat before she approached. "What can I get you men this morning?"

"Well, hey there, pretty lady. What do you suggest?"

She poured them cups of coffee. "Some flapjacks and ham steak would stick with you if y'all are heading out on the trail today."

The youngest of the men looked up at her and smiled, his eyes bright with excitement. "Yes, ma'am, we're headed to British Columbia," he stated proudly.

"Mining for gold?"

"We are hoping so."

"Flapjacks and ham steaks will be fine all around," the other man answered.

"I'll get right on it for you."

Smithy, sipping his coffee watched the interaction. *I sure wouldn't want to be heading where they are going, especially this time of year.* He listened to the chatter of the men and determined they were a father and two sons. He couldn't help but smile at the eagerness of the youngest man who chattered excitedly while they waited on their meal.

When Marissa emerged from the kitchen carrying three large platters of ham steaks and flapjacks, he could see the anticipation on their faces. "I'll bring butter and syrup out. Is there anything else I can get you?"

"Do you have fresh biscuits, ma'am?" the father asked.

"Yes, I do."

"Could you prepare a dozen for the trail with some of this ham?"

"Certainly." Marissa smiled.

She brought the coffee pot with her to top off their cups when she delivered the condiments. Marissa looked over at Smithy and he nodded before she walked over to refill his cup.

"Those flapjacks and ham looked good. I think that's what I'll have, too."

"Coming up."

Marissa worked on the ham biscuits while Smithy's flapjacks cooked. She placed them carefully inside a cloth bag and tied the bag closed. She also had cornbread left over from the previous day and she added it to the bag she prepared for the men. She would bake fresh bread later, so the cornbread would go to waste if not eaten today.

She took Smithy's flapjacks from the griddle, placed them next to a thick slab of ham, and carried the plate out to him.

"Enjoy." Marissa set the plate in front of him.

Smithy picked up pats of butter and tucked them between the cakes before smothering them in the rich maple syrup.

"I'll be back to check on you," she told him before returning to her other guests. "Is there anything else I can get you?"

"Just the bill and the biscuits, ma'am," the father replied.

"I'll be right back then." Marissa walked back into the kitchen to pick up the bill and the sack of food she had prepared for them and returned to the table. She placed the bag in front of the young man and looked at the father. "I had leftover cornbread I was going to have to throw out today. I hope you don't mind."

He smiled up at her brightly. "Not at all, thank you, ma'am. This may be the last good cooking we have for a while."

Marissa nodded and handed the grateful man his bill. "You can pay at the front desk. Good luck and safe travels," she told them before clearing the dishes from the table.

"Thank you, ma'am." The father left the table and picked up their bags once the bill was paid.

Marissa watched them leave the building and wondered if she would ever see any of them again. When the door closed behind them, she turned back to the kitchen with an armload of dishes.

✝

Nat's former forays into the forest for firewood had begun to carve out a trail. When she reached the boundary of her explorations, she urged Hardy forward. Gyp trotted ahead of them, her nose to the ground, scenting the wildlife of the area. Hardy's ears perked at sounds in the brush, and Nat kept her eyes and ears open as they rode deeper into the unknown. Trees were marked with deep gouges she assumed were from a bear, but the scratches were not recently made. She would still be alert for more recent signs of a bear.

They came across a game trail that Nat decided to follow. Her eyes roamed both sides of the trail as Hardy plodded along and she pulled him to a stop when she spotted something curious. She dismounted and walked toward the object that had caught her eye. She smiled broadly when a large rack of moose antlers appeared before her eyes. There was no sign of a carcass, so she assumed the animal had shed his antlers during the annual molting. The rack was quite impressive and she pulled the vines that had grown around them free and held them in front of her. "These will sell nicely once cleaned a bit," she told Gyp, who was eyeing the antlers.

Nat carried the antlers to Quincy and strapped them across his back. She then returned to where she had found the antlers and began scouring the area. Soon she found several more sets of antlers from moose, elk, and deer. After settling them onto Quincy's pack, she mounted Hardy and moved forward.

She rode for several more minutes and then Nat's ears picked up the sound of trickling water. They followed the game trail until it opened into a large meadow and a freshwater lake. Across the lake, she spotted movement and saw a large bull moose, grazing on the lush aquatic plant life around the edge of the lake. Gyp had also scented his presence and was growling softly.

"Easy girl, we will come back for him another day." She guided Hardy around to the opposite end of the lake. Her eyes spotted several more sets of antlers and she knew she would need Quincy's cart to harvest them. She was about to turn away to return down the path when she heard a familiar sound.

Buzzing.

She dismounted and tied the horse and mule to a tree and followed the sound until she came to a huge tree. The buzzing sound grew louder and her eyes fell on a honey hive larger than she had ever seen. Thousands of buzzing bees toiled across a large comb dripping with a tasty treat.

"We have found our honey hole," she told Gyp. For a moment longer, she stood watching the movement of the bees.

Instead of returning the way they had arrived, Nat decided to follow the game trail that followed the edge of the lake before turning back to the forest. She would follow it and then pick her way back to the cabin from there. Nat hoped to find one or more creeks that fed the lake because these would be prime locations for setting her traps.

The sun had risen overhead while she was under the cover of forest, so she stopped at the lake's edge and dismounted. She drank from her canteen while Hardy, Quincy, and Gyp drank from the cool, clean water of the lake. Taking the biscuits from the pack, she tossed one to Gyp and munched on the other, her eyes studying the lake. Ducks and geese floated across the surface and there were several game tracks leading down to the water.

"This appears to be a watering hole for a variety of animals," she spoke aloud. They would never go hungry with the bounty from the sea and the fresh game that appeared to be abundant in the area. She smiled, pleased with the location, and mounted Hardy.

As she entered the canopy of forest leading away from the lake, she noted the rising of small hills and rocky crags. Her sharp eye spotted a large nest atop a crag and she surmised it belonged to a pair of eagles.

She hadn't spotted them yet, but she had heard their cries in the distance as she chopped firewood nearly a week ago.

Nat continued along the ridge until she smelled the smoke of her fire and knew she was getting close to home. Gyp seemed to know it too. When the trees opened to the field behind the cabin, the dog sprinted across to the cabin and drank from her bowl.

Nat pulled the animals to a stop and tied them at the hitching post before unloading the antlers from Quincy's back. She placed the antlers across the back porch, her smile spreading with the growing pile. Then she led the animals over to the outbuilding, unsaddled Hardy, and removed the pack frame from Quincy before hitching him to the small wagon. Dropping hay into the bin, Nat returned to the cabin and slipped inside.

She busied herself attaching an oily rag to a stick and then packed her flint set and several empty glass jars into her pack. She walked back to the outbuilding, placed the pack in the back of the wagon, and took her rifle from her saddle. She took the rope attached to Quincy's halter and began leading him back into the forest. She decided she would harvest some honey first and then return for as many of the antler sets as she could fit into the wagon.

†

The trip back to the honey tree passed quickly and Nat called Gyp into the wagon. "You have to stay here where it's safe, my friend."

She wrapped a cloth around her mouth, picked up her jars and the oily stick. She approached the tree quietly then placed her jars on the ground before using her flint to light the oily rag. The initial flame flared and then died down to a smoky torch. Nat moved as quickly as she dared carrying her jars to the opening in the tree. The bees fled in droves from the smoke and Nat worked quickly to fill her jars with the golden dark honey and put a slab of comb in each. Jars filled, she moved quickly away from the tree just as the bees began to return.

She hurried back to the wagon and left the jars sitting on the seat before walking to the edge of the lake to dowse the torch. When she returned to the wagon, she removed the honey from around the lip of the jars with her fingers, tasting the sweetness before attaching the lids. Gyp whined from her seat until Nat offered her fingers for the dog to lick the remaining honey. She held up a jar of the golden sweetness and smiled. The Mason jars were not cheap, but Nat decided she would purchase as many as she could the next time she traveled to town. Raw, wild honey was not common, and she was certain she could barter with the owner of the general store to obtain her jars and other supplies.

Nat stowed the jars and torch before taking Quincy's lead and walking down to the lake. "Better get a drink now." She dropped down to a knee and cupped the clean, cool water in her hands. She drank her fill and turned to the animals. "Let's get to work." They began moving away from the lake.

The afternoon sun was burning brightly when she finished unloading the antlers and started walking down to the shore with Quincy. Gyp dashed ahead of them, running down the beach and chasing the waves as they flowed smoothly toward the shore and then rushed back to the Sound.

She led Quincy past the cave to the pools that frequently filled with shrimp and fish. As she had hoped, several dozen shrimp floated in the chilly water. Nat took her bucket and harvested the creatures for a delicious meal later in the day. The sun still shone brightly on the beach and Nat shed her work shirt before making several trips to the wagon carrying the whalebones. When she had loaded the wagon with all Quincy could pull, she took his lead and headed up the hill.

She added the whalebones to the pile of antlers on the back porch before she took Quincy back to the outbuilding and fed him an extra ration of feed for his hard work. Nat stored the wagon, and carrying her rifle, started back to the cabin. She took a seat on the steps and leaned back against the railing to admire her growing pile of bones and antlers. Pleased with the day's harvest she rested, her hand buried in Gyp's soft fur until the sun finally settled beneath the horizon.

When the symphony of night creatures began, Nat stood, stretched, and walked inside to start cooking their dinner. She shelled and prepared the shrimp for cooking while the lard heated over the fire. With the flour gone, Nat used corn meal and was surprised at the crispy coating it made for the shrimp. She placed several of the shrimp in her bowl for Gyp and waited until they cooled to set her bowl on the floor. Nat took her meal to the front porch, enjoying the cool breeze from the water and seeing the moon rise above the Sound.

She didn't expect Maggie and the wagon of supplies until late morning, so Nat planned to get an early start to check her traps before they arrived. She entered the house, leaving the door open to allow Gyp to reenter when she returned from her nightly romp in the woods, and cleaned the dishes from their meal.

Nat was sitting at the table sawing a small antler into button rounds when Gyp finally returned and stretched out next to her. Maggie would use a small awl to drill holes in the antlers to make buttons for the clothing she fashioned and then sold. She hoped to have several dozen ready for Maggie when she arrived. When the night air cooled, Nat stood and stretched before closing the door and preparing to sleep.

Ready for bed, Nat kicked off her boots and climbed onto the pallet in front of the fire. She would be delighted when Maggie arrived tomorrow. She was bringing the feather mattress for the bed and Nat could sleep on a mattress again. Her thoughts turned to Marissa and she smiled thinking of her lover adding wood to the fire. *I wonder if she is as lonesome as I am and if the bearskin is keeping her warm?* Gyp chose that moment to snuggle in next to her and within minutes, they were both fast asleep.

✝

Gyp's warm tongue licking her face woke Nat the next morning, and she was surprised she had slept later than planned. She still had plenty of time to complete the rounds of her traps before Maggie and the wagon arrived from town. Pulling on her boots, she strapped her knife to her belt, picked up her rifle, and left the cabin.

Quincy stomped his feet as she fastened the wagon to his harness and they left the homestead. She found her traps filled with beaver and she skinned the carcasses, filleting the meat and placing it into a pan. Beaver meat was not her favorite, but it made decent jerky, and Gyp didn't mind supplementing her diet with the chewy offering. Nat tossed her what was left of a carcass and Gyp eagerly crunched the boney remains while Nat finished working. The pelts were good quality and Nat would deliver them to Smithy in a few weeks, with another batch she had curing. The pelts from the deer she had harvested she would keep for Maggie, who would fashion them into pants and shirts that would keep them warm during the cold and wet winter to come. Satisfied with what she found, she headed back home.

Nat had just finished stretching the pelts to cure when she heard the sound of wagon wheels approaching. She rushed down to the edge of the trail to meet Maggie and John, the deliveryman from the general store.

"Good morning," she called when they finally came into view.

"Hey, Nat," John replied. "You sure you really want to live way out here? I thought for a while Maggie was taking me on a wild goose chase."

"Oh, stop that." Maggie slapped his shoulder. "I told you it would take most of the morning to reach Nat."

John chuckled. "Yes, you did."

"How are you, Nat?" Maggie asked.

"Doing good, and you?"

"Glad to finally be here." Maggie chuckled and jumped down from the wagon to solid ground. "Let's go see the place."

"Follow us." Nat looked at John and began walking up the trail with her arm draped around Maggie's shoulder. "It's good to see you, my friend."

"Are you a bit lonesome out here?"

"Gyp's good company, but she still doesn't talk much."

When they rounded the corner and the cabin came into view, Maggie stopped in her tracks. "This is beautiful."

"I'm very pleased with it," Nat said before they started walking again. "Pull around back so we can unload the supplies," she requested of John.

"My, you have been busy," Maggie told her when she saw the stacks of firewood and the pile of antlers on the back porch.

"I guess we won't have to worry about you going hungry out here." John pulled the wagon to a stop and jumped down from the seat.

"I have the best of both worlds here. We can have food from the Sound and food from the forest."

"Will you have time for a bite of lunch before you head back, John?" Maggie asked.

"I will make time. This place is beautiful."

"Are you ready for some clam chowder and fry bread?" she asked Nat.

Nat chuckled. "I have a bucket of fresh shelled clams just waiting for you in the kitchen."

"Good. You two unload the wagon and I'll cook lunch."

"That sounds good to me," John said. "I've heard about your chowder, but I've never tasted it before."

"You have a treat ahead of you then," Nat told him. "Let's get to it." She took a bag of flour off the wagon and carried it into the kitchen. "You're going to need this. I'm fresh out," she said, placing it on the counter.

Once the staples were unloaded, John helped Nat carry in the heavy feather mattress and placed it on the bed. "This bed is beautiful. Did you make it yourself?"

"All the way down to the post carvings," Nat stated proudly.

"This is a real work of art," he remarked, admiring the bed.

Maggie heard them talking in the bedroom and walked in to join them. "You did well." She moved closer to admire the carvings and smiled. "These are beautiful."

"I carved them while I was out trapping."

They admired the bed for a short while, and Nat told John how she made it. "Let's unload the stock supplies and then we can relax until lunch."

"It will be ready soon," Maggie promised and walked back to the kitchen.

John led the horse over to the barn and they made short work of unloading the hay and feed for the animals. "You know, you should consider adding some chickens for fresh eggs," he said.

"I thought about that, but wasn't sure I could keep them alive in the winter," Nat replied.

"If you built their roost beside the smokehouse, the heat escaping would help to keep them warm. If that doesn't work you can fry them up or smoke them and start fresh in the spring."

"That is an idea, and I sure do miss fresh eggs for breakfast." Nat placed a bale of hay on the stack.

"You could make a hen house easily, and a bit of wire would protect them from foxes or any other predator that would raid an unprotected hen house."

"You've really got me thinking now, John," she replied.

"I've got one and could get you all set up if you'll buy the supplies," he offered. "I could come back out later this week if you wanted."

"Do you also have chickens for sale?" she asked.

"I do in fact," he added with a smile. "I'll even throw in a pesky rooster to boot and you can raise more on your own."

"You have me sold on the idea. How much do you need to get it going?"

"A gold piece should do nicely."

"That sounds reasonable."

When they returned to the cabin, John settled on the front porch while Nat disappeared for several minutes and came back with a gold piece for John. "He's going to set me up with a hen house," she told Maggie.

"As much as you love eggs, that's a good idea. Come on in and I'll serve lunch."

"That's a lovely view you have." John stood and stretched. "I'm still not convinced I could live this far from civilization though." He ducked to enter the cabin.

"Well, I grew up in the woods, so this is more natural for me than living in town. Besides it's only a half day's ride to town."

Maggie had bowls of chowder served and waiting on the kitchen table with a plate full of fry bread.

"This looks and smells delicious," John said, taking a seat.

"Bring your wife up with you when you come to build the hen house and I will teach her how to cook it if you like it. It's not difficult and I'm sure Nat could keep you supplied with clams when she makes deliveries to town."

John took a spoonful of the chowder and grinned at Maggie. "You have a deal. This is delicious."

Two bowls later, John had to excuse himself. "If I don't leave now I'll be driving in the dark. I'll definitely be back in two days," he added.

"Deal then." Nat shook his hand. "Drive safe and I'll see you soon."

Nat and Maggie watched until John and the wagon disappeared, and then stepped into the cabin. "Now that he's gone, I want to show you something." Nat led Maggie to the second bedroom.

"This is a good-sized room," Maggie said. "What are your plans for it?"

"I was hoping it could be your room, if you want to join us out here," Nat replied.

Maggie's eyes grew wide. "Really? I can come live here?"

"I had it built hoping you would."

Maggie rushed over to her and grabbed her in a crushing hug. "I'd love to. I can still do my sewing and help you with the harvests."

"Good, that's settled. How is Marissa?"

"Missing you terribly, I'm afraid. She still doesn't have a clue about this, does she?"

"No, I think we've managed to keep the cabin a secret. I hope to bring her out when I go to town for the horse and wagon. We can also bring your things out then, too, if you'd like."

"Yes, that will be good. I was afraid I'd be lost without you in town."

Nat smiled at the honesty of Maggie's comment. "I have something else I want to discuss with you, if you'll come outside."

They walked outside and Nat pointed to a level area of ground. "Do we want to put in a garden?"

"I would love that, and if you will help me plow it, I'll do the rest of the work," Maggie said. "I've always wanted to have a big garden spot."

"I know and I'd appreciate your fresh vegetables," Nat replied. "I've a few other ideas I'd like to discuss with you."

"Go ahead then."

Nat led her around to the front yard. "I have been thinking about an easier way to harvest the seafood. If we buried a post here and one on the shore, bought a long length of rope and some pulleys, we could harvest from the beach and then send buckets up here to more solid ground."

"That makes sense. Even a larger draft horse would have a difficult time pulling a wagon through that sand. We could load the barrels into the wagon here," Nat pointed to the yard. "Then when they're full, we can hitch up the horse and drive to town."

Maggie smiled. "I can see you are excited and it's clear that you've been thinking a lot lately."

"I like it. I really do," Nat said.

"It's a great idea," Maggie said. "I've been meaning to ask you about all those antlers on the back porch. Have you killed that much wildlife?"

"You aren't going to believe this," Nat said before walking onto the porch and sitting down. "The forest is filled with antlers shed by moose, deer, and elk. I've found a beautiful lake, a meadow, and a honey tree."

"This place must surely be heaven." Maggie's eyes were aglow with excitement.

"On top of the seafood, I thought we could gather the antlers and honey to barter with in town. There's evidence of moose, elk, deer, and other game within walking distance." She smiled at Maggie. "You can use the deer hides to fashion your breeches and shirts. The deer antlers will keep you supplied with buttons. I've already started cutting some for you."

"Is there anything you haven't thought of?" Maggie asked.

"I hope I have everything covered." Nat smiled and lifted a shoulder. "I've had a lot of thinking time lately."

Gyp bounded onto the porch and placed her head in Maggie's lap. "I've missed you, too, my friend," Maggie told the happy dog.

"I think even our young friend here has found a companion," Nat told her.

"Oh, really?"

"She disappears every night after supper and I usually have to call her back inside. I haven't seen him yet, but I catch glimpses of a silver coat in the moonlight sometimes, after she has run inside."

"Is it a wolf or wild dog?" Maggie asked.

"I don't know yet. My guess would be wolf."

Maggie took Gyp's face in her hands. "Have you got a male friend hiding out there waiting for you?"

Gyp shook as Maggie talked to her. Nat chuckled and then looked up at a sound coming from the beach. She looked out across the water to see a whale surface and blow water from its spout.

"Yes, I can get used to this," Maggie said with a bright smile.

Chapter Twenty-one

Nat woke the next morning to the smell of breakfast cooking. She stretched, enjoying the night spent in her new bed. Maggie had done an excellent job on the down mattress, making it difficult for Nat to escape the comfort of the mattress.

Slipping into her work pants and boots, she walked to the kitchen to find Maggie at work. "You've got something smelling good."

"I raided your smokehouse and brought in some sausage. I thought I'd make biscuits and gravy."

"You definitely have my stomach's attention. Is there anything I can do?"

"Draw a bucket of water and I'll put on a pot of coffee."

Nat walked out back to the pump and drew up the bucket of cold, clean water. The morning air was brisk and she could smell the salt on the breeze. Gyp came rushing across the yard just when Nat was about to lift the bucket and go inside.

"Good morning, my friend." Gyp bounded onto the porch.

Gyp followed Nat back into the house and sat at Maggie's feet, licking her lips. "It won't be much longer." Maggie chuckled. "What do you have planned for us this morning, Nat?"

"We have two days before John will be back to build the hen house, so I thought we might start working on your garden spot."

Maggie smiled. "We can put a fall garden in if we hurry."

"That was the plan," Nat answered. "If you'll stake out the size, I'll get Quincy rigged with the plow John delivered and we can get started."

"When we go to town next week, I'll get the seeds we need from the store. I'm so excited to have room for a garden."

Nat poured them a cup of coffee. "One thing's for sure, we won't starve out here."

"Are you worried about the winter?"

"I'm trying not to be. Even if we get snowed in, and can't travel to town, we will have plenty of food and stores to survive. If we run low on meat, there's plenty of game to bring down something fresh. Then there

173

is always the Sound. We might get cabin fever, but I'm trying to make sure we have enough antlers and hides to keep us busy."

"We can get steel knife blades made by the blacksmith in town, and spend time this winter honing the edges and fastening whalebone or antlers as handles. I would think they would be great sellers for Smithy."

"That's one I hadn't thought of." Nat grinned.

They shared a hearty breakfast with Gyp and finished off the coffee before Nat left to get Quincy rigged for the plow. Maggie cleaned the kitchen from breakfast and then walked around outside the cabin until she found four large rocks she used to plot the boundary of the garden spot. The location was perfect. The plot was relatively level and would be close enough to the planned hen house to make it easy to use the bird droppings as fertilizer to enrich the virgin soil.

Nat led Quincy to the hitching post and removed her outer shirt before returning to the barn for the plow. She moved the mule into place and attached the plow to the harness before preparing to break ground. "Let's go, Quincy." She tapped the reins to his neck to move him forward while she forced the plow blade into the solid ground.

Maggie picked up a hoe and began chopping the large blocks of soil churned by the plow blade and removed rocks, making a pile at the end of the plot. Nat and Quincy worked hard to carve out the first few rows of the garden before Maggie made them take a break. Nat's undershirt was soaked with perspiration and Quincy was breathing hard.

"That's some solid soil." Nat took a cup of water from Maggie.

"It's never been turned. The first time will be hard, but the soil is rich and will provide well for us in the future." She took a bucket of the cool fresh water to Quincy, who drank his fill. Maggie scratched behind his ears. "You will earn a special treat tonight, my little friend."

"What are you planning for him?"

"I'm going to mix some molasses into his feed to provide a treat, and it will also replenish his strength," Maggie replied.

Nat smiled. "I just had an idea come to me." She turned to face the house. "The bathtub is right here. If we can think of a way to drain the bathwater through the flooring, into a trough or barrel, we can use it to water the garden."

"Let me think on that." Maggie grinned.

Nat dipped another cup of water. "What about us? What do you want to eat tonight?"

"One of those." Maggie pointed up to the sky as a group of geese flew overhead. "You said they were plentiful at the lake, didn't you?"

"Yes, among other wild birds."

"If you will shoot one, I'll bake it for dinner."

"You have yourself a deal. I think we can stop for today at lunch and go hunting. To be honest, I'm not sure how much more Quincy and I will be able to do today."

"There's no rush, so stop when you need. We have time left before the planting season is over."

"A few more rows then." Nat wiped her brow and walked back to Quincy.

An hour later, her energy spent, Nat sat on the back porch.

"I'll care for Quincy while you catch your breath." Maggie unhooked the plow and led the tired mule back to the barn.

Nat slowly sipped on the cool water, the sweat drying on her skin. Maggie emerged from the barn and walked inside the cabin. She returned carrying two meat-filled biscuits and handed one to Nat.

"We got a lot done this morning." She pointed at the freshly turned soil in the plot.

"Yes, we did, but I have to be honest…that last big rock kicked my tail." Nat looked at the small boulder it had taken her and Maggie to carry away from the plot.

"I'll make you a deal. You go kill us a bird for dinner and I'll heat your water for a bath. You can relax while I cook dinner."

Nat smiled brightly. "You have a deal, my friend." She turned to find Gyp. "Let's go get a bird." She walked inside to retrieve her rifle, and then slipped her shirt over her shoulders leaving it open in front. "We'll see you soon."

"Keep your eyes open for some wild onions, too." Maggie watched Nat step off the porch. "I'll start the wash tub fire while you're gone. It will make it easier to remove the feathers and I can wash those clothes you have on while you bathe."

Nat stopped at the barn to pick up a feed sack then continued to walk to the lake. Around the edge of the lake, she found the wild onions Maggie wanted which she stuffed in the sack. Gyp was stalking the shore and Nat could hear honking in the distance. Nat had the advantage of height and could see above the tall reeds which hid the birds from Gyp's view. She crept as close as she dared, took aim at the bird closest to shore, and fired a shot. The rest of the flock took flight, sailing to the opposite end of the lake.

"Time to get wet." Nat placed her rifle on the ground, rolled up her pants, and removed her boots and socks. The goose floated ten feet from shore. Nat stepped into the cool water and prayed the lake would stay shallow until she could reach the goose. She took one final step close enough to reach the goose and sank up to her waist. Nat had bathed in colder water, but knowing Maggie was preparing a hot bath for her gave her incentive to grab the goose and wade back to the shore. She dried her feet with the socks and slipped her feet back inside her boots.

Picking up the goose, her sack, and the rifle, Nat turned toward home and the bath she prayed would be ready for her. After the morning she had spent plowing, she could definitely use a long, hot soak.

Maggie was sitting on the porch waiting for her return and Nat smiled when she and Gyp emerged from the woods.

"Welcome back," Maggie said with a smile.

"Mission accomplished." Nat held up the goose and sack of onions.

"Drop them here and get out of those clothes. I'll grab the last pot of water and you can relax while I get the bird on to cook."

"I won't argue with that." Nat placed the goose over the railing and set the onions on the floor. "Don't get any ideas," she told Gyp, and followed Maggie inside the cabin.

Nat lowered her tired body into the steamy water with a deep sigh. The water went instantly to work, relaxing her muscles. It had been many months since she had expended so much energy. Even her hardest day trapping had not been as exhausting as several hours behind a plow. Nat was glad that once the initial plowing was over, the ground had been broken, and the rocks removed, any future plowing would be much easier.

Maggie went to work cleaning the goose, preparing it for cooking. Once she had the bird ready, she placed it in the Dutch oven and hung it over the fire. She returned to the back porch and hung the sack filled with the goose feathers from a nail inside the small barn. She would let them dry for a few days, then boil them to remove the dried blood and odor before storing them for a future project.

She snuck quietly into Nat's room to take the dirty clothes from the floor. She had already replaced the water in the wash pot and tossed the sweaty clothes in to soak. When she walked back into Nat's room to lay out clean clothes, she heard Nat's voice.

"How long will it take the goose to cook?"

"Several hours. Why? Are you hungry now?"

Nat chuckled. "No, I can wait for a while yet. I found something you might be interested in down by the lake."

"What did you find now?"

"Blackberry briars loaded with ripe berries."

"I haven't had those in ages," Maggie commented.

"I thought we might walk back to pick some for a cobbler."

"I thought you were going to rest."

Maggie could hear Nat climbing out of the tub.

"I can rest while you make us a cobbler." Nat entered the room with a thick towel wrapped around her waist. "Go to the kitchen if you will and look in the small storeroom. On the bottom shelf are a couple of empty flour sacks. Grab those to put our berries in while I get dressed."

Maggie left the room while Nat dried and dressed in fresh clothes. Maggie saw her slipping clean socks on her feet when she returned. She saw the holes in Nat's socks and laughed. "You need to give me those socks to repair." She was pointing at the holes.

"I can do that." Nat grinned and stepped into her boots.

Nat met Maggie on the porch and showed her to the path she was slowly wearing through the woods. It was much faster to take the direct line to the lake versus taking the long way around by following the game trail.

"We could go that way," she said to Maggie, pointing out the game trail, "but this way is quicker."

Twenty minutes later, the lake came into view and Maggie smiled. "This is beautiful."

"Cold and clear. Good drinking water, too."

Nat guided them to the blackberries she had spotted earlier and they began the harvest. She couldn't resist eating a few of the juicy berries. "These are tasty," she moaned.

Maggie had also sampled the goods, and she turned to smile at Nat, with berry juice smeared across her lips. "Yes, they are." She grinned. "There is enough to pick for making jelly too."

"Now you're talking," Nat replied. "I'll have to get some extra jars for that."

"I have plenty that I have saved," Maggie told her. "We'll get an extra bag of sugar and some paraffin when we go to town."

Back at the cabin, Maggie took the bag of berries from Nat. "You go relax. I'll get a cobbler started and we'll have a great dessert tonight."

Nat was tired, too tired to argue with Maggie, so she picked up a block of wood, her knife, and walked out onto the front porch. Gyp followed her and curled in a ball, napping in the warmth of the sun bathing the porch.

Nat's hands went to work shaving the rough edges of the wood as her mind relaxed. She was so intent on her project she did not hear Maggie approach.

"Seems like we aren't the only ones who got tired today," Maggie said, nodding toward Gyp.

Nat looked over at Gyp, now soundly asleep in the patch of sunshine. "She hasn't seemed her usual energetic self for the last few days."

Maggie sat next to where Gyp was lying and leaned back against the porch railing. Her hand softly stroked the sleeping Gyp.

Nat's attention returned to her carving for several minutes until Maggie's voice broke the silence.

"You are going to be a grandma."

Nat looked up from the wood. "What did you say?"

"I said you're going to be a grandma. Gyp is pregnant."

Nat stared at Maggie for several long seconds. "How do you know?"

Maggie smiled up at her, eyes shining with excitement. "I can feel her young moving inside her."

Nat placed her knife and the wood aside and sat down beside Maggie.

Maggie took her hand and placed it low on Gyp's side. "I can feel three."

Nat's face lit up with a smile when she felt movement beneath her hand. "Gyp's going to be a mama."

Gyp raised her head when Nat said her name. "You're going to be a mama, my friend," Nat said stroking the dog's head. "When do you think she will have the pups?"

"Hard to tell, her milk hasn't come in, so it will be a few days yet."

"We will have to make a nice bed for you and your babies," Nat continued stroking Gyp's head.

"I bet there will be wood left over from building the hen house that you can use," Maggie said. "We can use those feed bags you have stored in the barn for bedding that can be washed after she whelps. If you can get us a few more geese to put in the smokehouse, I can use the down for a proper bed once they arrive."

"I can do that." Nat grinned. "We're going to have babies."

"Yes, we are." Maggie smiled and slowly climbed to her feet. "I'm going to check on dinner. Would you care for something to drink?"

"That would be nice." Nat smiled when Gyp crept closer and placed her head in Nat's lap.

Maggie reappeared carrying a cup of water. "The goose is coming along, but it will be a while yet for the cobbler."

"You've got it smelling good," Nat replied. "We need to boost her meat intake to help her prepare, don't we?"

"That would probably help. Adding some corn meal to her food will also help her bring in her milk."

"After we finish plowing tomorrow, I'll check my traps. There will probably be several beaver caught and Gyp loves beaver meat. I can hunt some rabbits too."

"Rabbit pelts would make a nice soft bed cover."

Nat chuckled at the hint. "It will keep them out of our garden too."

"That it will." Maggie nodded and took a seat. "I will use the rocks you have uncovered to stack in a small fence around the plot. It won't keep much out, but at least they'll have to work a little harder to get to our greens."

Nat prepared a large portion of the juicy goose mixed with corn meal for Gyp, and then filled her plate. "I don't think I'm going to be able to stay up long enough for dessert," she admitted after they finished eating.

"I'll stay up until it's finished baking and we will have it for tomorrow. I wanted to start drilling holes in some of the antler rounds you have cut, so that will keep me busy."

"I'll say goodnight then." Nat turned away and retired to her bedroom.

✝

Nat woke refreshed and ready to finish plowing the garden spot. She dressed and found Maggie in the kitchen preparing breakfast. "I'm going to get Quincy ready," she said as she snuck a slice of bacon from the plate.

"We have some eggs left if you'd like some."

"Do we have biscuits left?"

"There is a fresh pan cooling," Maggie answered.

"Fried then, please, ma'am." Nat walked to the back door.

Gyp trotted along behind her. "You need to start taking it easy, Mama."

Gyp let out a sharp woof in answer and followed Nat out the door to the barn.

The sun, slowly climbing the horizon, was barely peeking through the trees as they walked to the barn. The air was crisp and cool, the scent of salt riding the breeze that blew softly, causing a chill to rise on Nat's uncovered arms. She knew the pleasant morning would soon give way to midmorning heat, and she'd be dripping with sweat from toiling in the garden. "At least I'll have a full belly," she told Gyp, opening the gate to Quincy's stall.

She placed the rigging over the mule's head and led him from the stall.

"We will finish this today." Nat scratched him behind the ears. "Maggie will mix you another treat for your hard work." Nat tied Quincy's lead at the hitching post and walked around to the partially plowed plot. They had accomplished a great deal of work the day before, and she hoped in a few hours to have the hardest part done. Maggie had not hollered for her to come to breakfast, so she picked up a hoe and began removing rocks that were already visible in the ground. She had a dozen uncovered and added to the pile when Maggie stepped out on the porch.

"Are you two ready to eat?"

"We were born ready," Nat answered with a grin. She leaned the hoe against the side of the cabin and removed her gloves. "Let's go, Gyp," Nat called, waiting for her companion to catch up with her.

Nat and Gyp finished off their meals quickly.

"Do you want some cobbler?"

"Want, yes, but if I eat any more right now I won't get anything done today. I think I'll wait until we break for lunch."

"I'm using some of the goose to make a pie for lunch."

"Goose pie? I've never had that."

"I think you'll like the rich gravy it's cooked in."

"You haven't failed me yet."

"I'll pick up in here if you want to get back to work before it starts to really heat up."

Nat walked out onto the porch and took her work shirt off, hanging it over the railing before stepping down beside Quincy. "Time to get to work, my boy." She led him over to the plow. She had half a row plowed before Maggie came out and picked up the hoe.

"This looks like really good soil." Maggie hacked at a rock still buried in the ground.

"I can taste those vegetables now." Nat turned Quincy to start a new row.

Halfway through, Maggie called for a break and brought them cups of cold water and a bucket for Quincy. "How much longer do you think it will take?"

"The next section seems to be getting softer. The plow seems to be cutting deeper without as much effort, so maybe an hour."

"I was thinking I would go down to the shore while you check your traps and harvest some clams."

"For John?" Nat asked.

"Yes, I thought I'd go ahead and collect some to teach his wife how to cook the chowder. She and I can gather some for them to take home. I thought I'd see what the pools might have for our dinner. Any idea of what you'd like?"

"I'll keep my fingers crossed that there may be a few crabs in the pool, but if not, shrimp or fish will work too."

Nat saw Maggie smiling at her. "What?"

"You are very easy to cook for."

"You make it easy. The food is always good, and there's plenty of it."

"You work hard, so you need plenty to eat to keep your strength."

The last row turned easily and when Nat reached the end of the row, Maggie was pulling out the last of the large rocks. "I'm going to take care of Quincy, and I'll be back to help you finish."

"Take care of him and then go check your traps. I can finish here."

Nat nodded and unhooked Quincy from the plow and led him back to the barn. She removed the rigging, hung it on the wall, and filled his food and water troughs. "You did well today," she praised him as she used an old blanket to wipe him down. Nat dropped an extra flake of hay in his bin. She walked back to the cabin and went inside for her rifle and pack as Maggie was walking onto the porch.

"Would you mind keeping Gyp with you? I don't want her to overexert herself."

"Of course she can stay with me."

"I'll be back soon." Nat stepped off the porch. When Gyp stood to follow her, she turned back. "You stay with Maggie."

Gyp cocked her head and remained on the porch.

"Keep your eyes out for rabbits," Maggie hollered to remind her.

"Yes, ma'am," Nat called out, and disappeared from view.

†

The forest was alive with sounds and smells as she walked to the first creek where she had set traps. She kept her eyes and ears alert for sounds of small game, but other than an overly friendly skunk, there was very little movement. Her traps were full, and when she turned back

181

toward the cabin, she had a dozen new pelts to prepare. She had asked the men building the cabin to leave a stump at her waist level, which she used for a skinning table. After another long day, she'd have a dozen more nice pelts to trade and Gyp would have plenty of fresh beaver meat to enjoy.

She was nearly home when a large rabbit bolted out of the woods on the path ahead of her. Nat watched it stand on its back legs to look at her then dash off into the woods. "I'll be back for you another day," she promised, and trudged on home.

Maggie was sitting on the front porch, shelling the cooked clams when Nat returned. "We will be eating crab tonight," she said with a smile. "Come, let's have some lunch and I can help you with those pelts."

"I'll be right there." Nat walked to the stump and placed the beavers on top.

The goose pie turned out to be delicious. Baked in a biscuit crust with a thick gravy, the meat took on a different taste altogether. Nat had two large portions and Gyp licked her bowl clean before Maggie placed another large scoop in front of her.

"This is really tasty. I bet you could use other fowl, too, couldn't you?"

"Turkey, duck, or chicken would taste just as good," Maggie assured her. "Are you ready for cobbler?"

"Yes, I am." Nat gave her a huge grin.

Maggie filled a large bowl with the sugary cobbler and placed it in front of her.

Nat took a large bite and moaned her pleasure. "This is good." She scooped up another bite.

"Keep your eyes open for other berries while you are in the woods. I would think there may be others around the lake somewhere."

"I haven't made it all the way around the lake yet, so you may be right."

They were processing the last two beavers when they heard a loud honking and looked up to see a flock of geese flying overhead toward the lake. "Do you think it is warm enough here for the geese and ducks to remain at the lake year round?" she asked Maggie.

"That seems to be a good possibility."

Gyp was lying a few feet away, gnawing on a carcass, crunching the bones between her strong jaws.

"She seems to be enjoying herself," Maggie stated. "How does she like her beaver cooked?"

"I usually turn it into jerky for her, but I think we could boil it for her or fry it up to make some gravy."

"Fried then, she needs the fat in her diet right now. Have you seen her mate lately?"

"I get a glimpse of him now and then. From the prints I've seen, he's a good size."

"It will be interesting to see what happens once the pups are born."

"Do you think he will become more visible?"

"To see and be with his offspring, I'd bet on it," Maggie answered.

Nat had never heard of a domesticated wolf, but she would do her best to make him a part of their family. She was daydreaming of playing with Gyp's puppies, when another flock of geese flew overhead.

"What are you planning to do with the rest of the carcasses?"

"I was going to bury them, why?"

"I think we need to take them down to the beach. The blood and scraps of meat will draw more creatures into the pools."

Nat chuckled and shook her head. "You never cease to amaze me, Maggie Lightfoot. Let me rinse the rest of this meat and place it in the smokehouse. Then we will walk down to the shore."

"Let me amaze you some more." Maggie picked up the bucket of beaver remains. "I was thinking you could use the auger to drill a hole in the floor under the tub drain and we could make a trough under the flooring that drains out to a deeper trough. Then we could dip out the water as needed and the trough can even trap rain water or snow melt in the winter."

"I can carve out a plug for the floor drain to keep the cold and critters from coming inside when not in use."

"We can use the axe and hatchet to hollow out the logs to make our troughs," Maggie said.

"I guess we need to pick out some trees then."

They reached the beach.

"That shouldn't be hard." Maggie stopped to remove her boots and roll up her pant legs to prepare to wade to the pool. The tide was going out, but there was still a foot or so of water surrounding the pools.

"Do you need some help?"

"No, I've got this." Maggie took the bucket from Nat.

Nat and Gyp took a seat on a nearby dune and watched Maggie plant the carcasses inside the pools. She rinsed the bucket and joined them on the dune. "You picked a great spot to live."

"I think so, too. Do you think Marissa will like it here?"

"As long as she doesn't have to sleep on the ground, she'll be fine." Maggie chuckled.

Nat remembered the times Marissa had joined them on their trips to harvest the water's bounty. Marissa had enjoyed the trip except for sleeping on the cold ground for several nights. "Good thing she has a nice soft bed to sleep on then." Nat grinned.

"I think we can keep her busy," Maggie said.

"We don't seem to lack for things to do."

"No, we don't, and I doubt that will change until winter."

The two friends sat in a comfortable silence for a while, pondering their private thoughts. As the sun began to fade, Nat stood and stretched. "Should we go back up the trail before it gets dark?" Nat held out her hand for Maggie.

"Probably so." Maggie allowed Nat to help her up from the soft sand.

"I'll start the water to boil the crabs while you tend to the animals," she said when they reached the cabin.

✝

Gyp followed her to the barn and sat at the entrance. Nat went inside to tend to the horses and Quincy. Maggie had left a jar of molasses near the feed bin, so she mixed some of the thick syrup into his food as a treat. He had his stubborn moments, but when he put his mind to working, Quincy was hard to beat. She poured the grain into his bin and scratched behind his ears before leaving his stall. Hardy and Buck were eager to see her bringing grain for them. "We will ride to town soon, boys," she told them.

She planned to hook Quincy to the small wagon to carry Maggie and Gyp to town, along with a load of pelts and antlers. She would also take Buck to town and have the blacksmith fit them all with new shoes and trim their hooves. Marissa could ride on the new wagon bench when they returned to the cabin with Maggie's goods and the additional supplies they would need at the cabin. Nat mentally made a list of the items they would need, including several bags of chicken scratch to feed her new chickens. She smiled at the thought of having fresh eggs. When Nat left the barn, Gyp was nowhere in sight. Nat figured her mate was somewhere close and they were visiting. She would whistle for her when it was time to eat if she hadn't returned before then.

"Is there anything I can do to help?" Nat asked when she walked into the cabin.

"No, I've got everything under control, so relax for a while."

Nat picked up her knife and the block of wood she had started carving and went to the front porch. The deep blue water was calm as she settled into a chair, propping her feet on the porch railing. Her knife had whittled away the rough edges and an animal form began to emerge. She was surprised to find the image of a bull moose evolving from the block of wood. The blade bit into the wood, coaxing out the rack of antlers. Carving the last detail on the rack, she felt her smile growing on her face.

From the doorway Maggie watched Nat's hands chisel out the figure. *Nat has many talents and her skill with a carving knife is improving.* She saw the smile growing on her friend's face. "Are you at a stopping point?"

Nat startled at the sound of Maggie's voice. "I need to teach you how to stomp your feet, so I hear you approaching," she teased.

Maggie chuckled. "I'll start shuffling when I get close, so you don't slip and cut yourself. Dinner's ready, if you are."

Nat dropped her feet back to the floor and held up the carving. "What do you think?"

Maggie eyed the figure closely. "He's a handsome bull," she replied. "Is that what you thought it would be when you first started?"

"I never think of what animal it will be. It just appears in the wood."

"Amazing," Maggie remarked. "Come, let's eat before it gets cold." She motioned for Nat to come inside the cabin.

Nat was becoming an expert at harvesting the sweet meat of the crab from the crunchy shells, and she savored each bite of the meal. Maggie had melted a small slab of butter which enhanced the sweetness of the meat. She also heated the rest of the goose for Gyp, who was suspiciously absent.

"I wonder where our girl is." Nat stood from the table to go whistle for Gyp. She hadn't made it to the door, when Gyp came hustling in. "Here you are. You were about to miss dinner."

Gyp rushed to her bowl and greedily attacked the food.

"Someone worked up a healthy appetite." Maggie removed a fresh crab from the pot for Nat.

Nat's eyes lit up as Maggie approached with a second crab. "Have I told you today how much I love living here?"

"I could get used to eating like this, too," Maggie answered with a chuckle. "It would cost a fortune to eat like this in town."

"The crabs won't be close much longer, will they?"

"Unfortunately not. They will be heading to deeper waters all too soon. We will be lucky to have them through the fall."

Nat remained silent for a few minutes while she cracked the shell and removed the meat. "We could use one of our old barrels to harvest what we can. If we keep them in fresh salt water, they should keep for a while yet, shouldn't they?"

"I would think so. I will harvest as many as I can tomorrow if you will carry the water up the hill while we wait for John."

"You have a deal. I'll put a barrel on the back porch while you cook some breakfast, and then we can get started."

"Will ham biscuits hold you until we have lunch?"

"They should."

Maggie served the last of the cobbler. "We need to get more berries soon, too."

"That can be our first task when we get back from town next week. After setting up your room, that is," Nat said.

"That shouldn't take long at all. As soon as we make it to town, I'll start packing. How long do you plan on staying?"

"Long enough to take delivery of the new horse and wagon, purchase supplies, and convince Marissa to come out for a few days."

"That will be exciting, to see her reaction." Maggie smiled as she cleaned off the table.

"I'm just praying she'll like it well enough to stay."

"Do you think there's a chance she won't?"

"Maggie, I sure hope not, but if she chooses to stay in town, then I'll see her when we make trips to trade."

"I don't see that happening," Maggie said.

Gyp settled in beside the bed and Nat reached down to scratch her ears. "We have a busy day ahead of us tomorrow." She stroked Gyp's head. "Get some sleep, mama." Nat blew out the candle, sending the room into darkness.

†

Marissa laid out a clean dress for work and prepared for bed. The cabin was unusually quiet, making her miss Nat and Gyp even more. Just two more days and they would be home from the trip and she could snuggle into Nat's warmth again. She knew how much Nat sacrificed to be with her. She was giving up the only life she had ever known just to be near her, and Marissa prayed her love would be enough to keep Nat satisfied.

Only time would tell. She pulled the covers over her tired body to dream of the first time she met Nat.

Chapter Twenty-two

John must have left before sunrise, since he and his wife, Mary arrived midmorning, just as Nat and Maggie were finishing their harvest of the crabs. Nat had filled a barrel half-full of salt water, and Maggie had captured eighteen crabs for future meals.

John pulled his wagon to a stop in the back yard and ran around to help Mary down from the wagon. "Good morning," he said with a wide smile.

"Welcome back," Nat replied. "Did he sleep at all last night?" she asked Mary.

"Barely," Mary answered. "He is so excited to be here."

"We're glad to have you both."

"I was telling Mary about your offer to teach her how to make that lovely chowder," he told Maggie.

"Once she catches her breath, we will go down to the shore to dig the clams and then get started in the kitchen."

Nat looked at the back of the wagon. "Looks like you've been busy."

"I thought I would build as much as I could in advance to make today go easier," he stated. "I've got a lot of the hen house built already."

"I see that," she grinned.

"I brought a dozen chicks, a dozen laying hens, and a rooster for you," he said, unloading the cages holding the birds. "I thought we could let them out to roam while I build their home."

"That sounds good to me." Gyp smelled the cages with curiosity. "Those are not for eating," Nat warned her.

Gyp sat on her haunches, watching the birds emerge from the cages, eager to give chase, but only watched as they began pecking the ground looking for seeds and insects.

"What do we need to do first?"

"I'll start digging the holes to set the poles if you want to carry them over to me."

"That sounds easy enough," she replied, taking a long post from the bed of the wagon and tossing it over her shoulder.

Maggie looked at Mary. "Are you ready to dig some clams?"

Mary nodded and took one of the buckets and a rake from Maggie, and the two women disappeared around the cabin.

†

Maggie led the way down to the beach near the pools and showed Mary how to use the rake to find the clams. Mary caught on quickly, and with the two of them working together, they filled the buckets.

"Hang on for just a second." Maggie removed her boots and walked out to the wading pools to see what the tides had brought. "Do you and John like shrimp?"

"Oh, yes," Mary answered.

"Good, we will have some shrimp to go with our chowder." Maggie plucked several dozen shrimp from the pool.

John and Nat had made good progress building the fence for the chickens by the time the two women returned from the shore. Nat looked up to see them approach, their buckets filled to the brim.

"Welcome back." Nat wiped the sweat from her brow.

"Come take a break and get something to drink," Maggie instructed.

John looked up at Nat. "Sounds good to me and we can take a peek into those buckets."

"I have a feeling we are going to have a feast later today." Nat fastened the last section of wire to the fence and joined him at the opening. "Looks good." She slapped John on the back.

John stepped onto the porch, took a cup of cold water from Maggie, and then looked at the buckets full of clams and shrimp. "You gathered all of this that quickly?"

Mary nodded. "Yes, with very little effort. The shrimp were in a small pool and the clams were buried under the sand on the beach."

John looked back to Nat. "The wildlife is plentiful, too. Are you ready for a neighbor?"

Nat surprised by his comment, quickly regained her composure. "Yes, the wildlife is plentiful and there is ample room. I'm really surprised no one else has chosen to settle out here."

"We should give it some thought," John told Mary, his excitement written all over his face.

Nat could tell that Mary wasn't as excited about the prospect of living so far from civilization.

"Yes, we should," she answered, but with less conviction.

"I thought we might fry these shrimp to go with the chowder and fry bread," Maggie told them.

"That's a good idea," Nat agreed. "We probably have a couple more hours before we finish."

"That will give us plenty of time to prepare. Are you ready, Mary?"

"Yes, thank you," she answered, and picked up her bucket to follow Maggie inside.

The smells wafting from the inside of the cabin were inspiration for Nat and John to work harder. They installed the coops and ramp, and put the finishing touches on the hen house.

"Are you ready to bring your chickens home to roost?"

Nat smiled brightly. "Yes, I am."

John walked back to the wagon and opened a burlap sack of scratch and filled a container with the cracked-corn mixture. "Here chick, chick." John shook the container to grab the hens' attention.

Nat watched, amazed at how the chickens followed John inside the fence. He rewarded their compliance by scattering the scratch around the ground inside the fence. She counted as every one of the hens and chicks marched into their new home.

"We have one more task to do before we call it done," he said. "We need a bale of hay to line the coops for the hens."

"I'll be right back." Nat left the pen and rushed to the barn. The curious rooster, that John called Rufus, followed her to the barn and then back to the hen house, but refused to enter. She dropped the bale of hay and turned back to him.

"Do I need to be concerned about him?" she asked John.

John chuckled as he looked at Rufus. "A rooster is not allowed in the hen house. He will wander about outside the fence, but won't enter. I brought a crate we will set up for him beside the smokehouse with some of this hay."

"Should I worry about predators attacking him?"

"If they do, they won't make the mistake but once. Rufus, like all roosters, have very sharp talons and beaks to protect himself and his hens. I don't think you need to worry. He's especially ornery."

"How long before we can expect eggs?"

"It will take a few weeks for the hens to settle into their new home, but after that, you will have plenty. Just remember to let them sit on some to keep you supplied with chicks. When a hen stops laying she's ready to go in your cook pot, but the ones I brought you are young and should produce for a good while yet."

"That sounds good."

"One more benefit," he nodded to the freshly plowed garden plot, "they'll keep the bugs out of your garden and fertilize it too."

"Maggie will be glad to hear that." Nat chuckled. "Let's get cleaned up and ready to eat."

John started picking up the scraps of wood to carry back to the wagon.

"Would you mind if I kept those? I want to make a bed for Gyp since she's going to be a mama soon."

"Should we build one now?"

"That would be great."

John was tapping in the final nail for Gyp's bed when Maggie stepped out on the porch.

"Are you two ready to clean up for some lunch?"

"We've worked up an appetite," Nat answered.

"Well, we cooked up a storm in here, so come eat."

"I can't argue with that." John carried the bed onto the back porch, and then returned his hammer and nails to his toolbox.

"You sure have something smelling good." Nat entered the kitchen.

"Mary has done everything herself," Maggie stated proudly.

"With you telling me how to do everything step by step," Mary said, with a blush to her cheeks.

"All that matters to me is that it tastes good." John took the seat beside Nat.

"That will be no problem then." Maggie and Mary served bowls of the steaming chowder along with a platter of fry bread and fried shrimp.

John took a spoonful of the chowder into his mouth and smiled. "This is fantastic, Mary."

"I can't believe how easy it was to make. The hardest part was shelling the clams after they boiled, but that got easier after the first dozen or so."

Nat bit into one of the shrimp. "You did a good job on these, too."

"Maggie is a good teacher."

"That she is," Nat agreed. "If she can teach me, she can teach anyone."

Nat and Maggie watched John and Mary drive away. "Tomorrow we will go to town, get new shoes for the animals, and arrange to take delivery of the draft horse and wagon. You can go home to begin packing. As soon as I can get Marissa awake and moving, we will come to town and load up the rest of the supplies." Nat looked at her with excitement shining in her eyes. "We can put some lighter items in Quincy's wagon and the rest in the new wagon."

"I'll go to the general store and order the seeds and supplies we will need for the garden." They went back inside the cabin.

Nat walked to a shelf and pulled down a list and pencil. "I've started a list of supplies, but add to it whatever else you will need," she said, laying the list on the table.

Gyp trotted inside and laid at Nat's feet. "I think you should ride on the wagon next to Maggie, my friend." Nat reached down and stroked her head.

"That's probably best. What are you planning to take for Smithy?"

"The pelts that are finished curing and some of the moose racks."

"Do you plan to take any seafood for the restaurant?"

Nat thought for a second. "Probably not on this trip. If Marissa decides to stay, I'm sure I'll have to take her back in a few days to work out her notice at the hotel and to pack her supplies. I'll get an order for what they want then and take it when we return."

"I will stay back on that trip if you don't mind. I can do the planting and care for the animals while you're gone."

"When I return, we can harvest the berries. You can make your jelly while I set up the rigging down at the beach and begin to harvest more seafood."

"We won't lack for things to do."

"Not for a long time yet. I still need to cut a tree so we can make the watering trough, too."

"Like I said, we won't lack for things to do." Maggie grinned.

Nat ran a hand over her face.

"Do you want dinner or was lunch filling enough for you?"

"I think I'm good. If I get hungry, I'll have a ham biscuit later."

"Will the chickens be okay while we are gone?"

"Yes, I'll scatter scratch for them in the morning before we leave. They will be safe behind the fence until we return."

Maggie busied herself cleaning the kitchen as Nat sat in front of the fireplace, working on her carving. When she finished the moose, she placed it next to the fire to allow the heat to cure the wood, bringing out a subtle color that resembled the coloring of a moose.

"That turned out nicely," Maggie said, settling down beside Nat and Gyp.

"Yes, I think so, too," she answered with a smile. "It's a good way to pass time and do some thinking."

"What have you been thinking about?"

"Just life in general," Nat sighed. "Gyp having puppies, whether Marissa will be satisfied here or not, how we will survive the winter."

"Have faith that everything will work out as it should," Maggie said. "You have planned well and worked hard to make this happen."

Nat smiled at her friend. "You know, today when John mentioned moving out here, I was disappointed with the prospect of having a neighbor. I know it will be an eventuality, but for now I hope it stays just us."

Maggie chuckled. "I don't think you have to worry about that. Did you see the look on Mary's face when John mentioned moving here? She was horrified, so I don't think we'll have neighbors anytime soon."

Nat stood and stretched. "I think I'll turn in for the night. I'll see you in the morning."

"Sleep well. I'll have coffee and some biscuits ready when you wake."

"Thanks, my friend." Nat hugged Maggie close. "You coming to bed?" she asked Gyp.

Gyp stood and stretched before trotting behind Nat to the bedroom.

✝

Marissa sat at the kitchen table finishing her meal. If her timing was correct, Nat would be returning tomorrow. She was excited to see her lover, and to hear what Nat had been up to for the weeks she had been gone. Marissa also remembered that she had promised to return to the shore with her for a few days.

She wasn't looking forward to sleeping on the cold, hard ground, but at least Nat would be there to keep her warm. With that thought still on her mind, Marissa cleared the kitchen and walked to the bedroom to sleep. *Just one more night alone, and then I'll have Nat. At least for a few nights.*

The rumble of thunder echoed in the night, waking Marissa. She prayed that the storm would bypass them, giving Nat and Maggie good weather for traveling.

✝

Nat woke to the sound of Rufus crowing just outside her window. The noise startled her until she realized it was Rufus, the rambunctious rooster, welcoming in the new day. "That will take some getting used to," she said kicking the covers off.

Rufus crowed again as she climbed from the bed to begin dressing.

The leaves still dripped with the last remnants of the gentle rain that had fallen most of the night. While Nat went to the barn to prepare the animals for travel, Maggie fed Gyp and then made ham biscuits.

Nat saddled Hardy, clipped a lead on Buck's halter, and hooked Quincy to the small wagon. She walked the animals to the cabin and secured them at the hitching post, and walked inside.

Maggie handed her a steaming cup of coffee and placed biscuits in front of her. "I'll feed the chickens while you load the wagon." Maggie took a bite of biscuit.

"That would be great." Eager to be on their way, Nat wasted little time chewing, downing the biscuits and coffee eagerly.

"Go, and I'll join you in a minute after I tend to the fireplace and grab a small bag. Is there anything you need from in here?"

"Just my rifle and I'll take that on my way out. It's a bit damp outside, so you might want to take a light coat until the sun warms the air a bit."

"We have a few biscuits left if you want me to pack them."

"That will be fine. I'll fill my canteen so we can have fresh water."

Nat left the cabin, loaded several dozen pelts and four sets of the large moose racks, while Maggie closed down the house, and fed the chickens. She tied Buck's rope to the back of the wagon and looked down at Gyp.

"You have to ride this trip with Maggie," she told her friend. She bent down and carefully lifted Gyp onto the wagon bench. "Do I need to lift you up too?" she teased Maggie.

"No, I think I can still climb that high." She punched Nat's shoulder.

"Are we ready then?"

"Yes, I think we are."

Nat mounted Hardy and they left the cabin to ride into town. Gyp settled in beside Maggie as the wagon rolled across the wet ground. The rain had soaked in quickly, the ground thirsty for nourishment, and the air smelling fresh and clean.

Nat and Hardy settled into a comfortable pace beside Quincy who seemed eager to be on the road.

"Will you let me treat you to lunch at the hotel when we get to town?" Nat asked.

"Why don't you let me take Quincy on to Smithy's? I'll eat a biscuit, and that will hold me over until I can cook something at home while I'm packing."

"Very well. Tell Smithy I'll be by to see him later."

They stopped at the small river to water the animals and give them a short rest break. Nat looked up at a cloudless sky. "It looks like we will have a clear sky the rest of the trip."

"It has been a beautiful morning."

"I hope we will have a couple more months like this before the days begin to cool down."

"I think we will."

Nat lifted Gyp back onto the bench. "She's getting heavy."

"We will have puppies soon. I just hope she waits until we get back to the cabin."

"I didn't think about that." Nat couldn't help the concern she knew must be etched on her face.

"Don't worry. Even if she whelps while we are in town, she'll be fine. I put the bed in the back of the wagon just in case."

Nat let her shoulders relax in relief. "I'm glad you were thinking."

"Your mind is full of other things." Maggie grinned.

Nat chuckled, but could not deny Maggie's comment. "Will you drop our list off at the general store, and tell John we'll bring the wagon by to be loaded tomorrow?"

"Of course I will." Maggie climbed into the wagon and urged Quincy forward.

With each passing mile, Nat felt her excitement growing. It had only been a few weeks since she had left, but it seemed forever since she had held Marissa in her arms. Her heart raced as they crested a hill and Marissa's cabin came into view.

As they reached the edge of town, Nat looked over to Maggie. "I'll come by your place once I'm finished with Smithy."

"Do you want me to drop Buck and Quincy off at the blacksmith's?"

"Yes, if you would, and let him know I'll be bringing Hardy in as well."

"No problem. Tell Marissa hello for me." They separated and Nat turned toward the hotel.

†

Nat's heart hammered in her chest as she pulled Hardy up to the hitching post and dismounted, tying him to the post. Her boots thumped on the wooden sidewalk as she approached the hotel and stepped inside. She walked the few short steps to the dining room to see Marissa waiting on a group of men.

When Marissa turned around and saw Nat, she stopped in her tracks, smiled, and then rushed over to embrace her lover. "Welcome back, stranger."

"Hello." Nat returned Marissa's hug. It felt wonderful to have Marissa back in her arms, and she was eager for their bodies to be entwined as they made love. Dreams of her soft skin, her scent, and taste had filled Nat's nights since they parted. Soon those dreams would become real.

"Are you hungry?"

Nat grinned, giving Marissa a devious smile. "For food and you," she whispered.

Marissa's face turned scarlet. "Well, let's start with lunch."

"What do you recommend?" Nat was still smiling as she sat at a table.

"I have just the thing for you." Marissa winked and walked into the kitchen. She returned with a glass of water for Nat, then took the pitcher to refill the men's glasses before returning to the kitchen. When she emerged the next time, she carried a large platter of fried chicken, mashed potatoes and gravy, with corn bread on the side. "Will this work?"

"That will work just fine." Nat grinned, feeling her mouth watering at the sight of the food.

"Let me finish with these men and I'll join you for a few minutes."

Nat nodded, bit a large bite of the chicken, and she moaned.

Marissa delivered the bill to the men. Once the men left the dining room, she carried their empty plates into the kitchen before joining Nat at the table. "It's so good to see you."

"Did you miss me?"

"Of course I did. I can't wait to hear what you have been doing these last few weeks."

"I have exciting news to share with you. We are going to be grandmothers."

"What do you mean?"

"Gyp is pregnant and will be having puppies any day now."

"How did that happen?"

"Do I really need to explain that to you?"

"No. I mean who's the father?"

"A rather handsome silver wolf she's taken up with."

"That is good news. Gyp will make a good mama. Where is she by the way?"

"She's with Maggie who is dropping some pelts and horn racks off to Smithy. When I leave here, I'll go see Smithy, and then go to Maggie's until it's time for you to head home. Will you ask your boss what kind of seafood he wants delivered later this week?"

"Yes, I will. I know he's anxious to get more soon. We've had a big influx of travelers the last few weeks."

"I noticed the men at the table. What's going on?"

"Men, young and old, are heading to British Columbia to find their fortune in gold."

"I hear that can be brutal," Nat said, before taking another bite of chicken. "I'd rather work hard here than take that kind of gamble."

"I'm glad to hear that. I don't think I could handle all that snow and ice."

"That makes two of us. I sure have missed your cooking."

"I hope that's not all you've missed."

"Not at all." Nat grinned. "I'll show you that tonight."

Marissa wiped at a spot on the table but it didn't hide her flushing cheeks. "I can't wait to be in your arms again. My bed and my heart have been so lonely without you."

Nat swallowed the final bite of food. "I've missed you terribly, too. Let me get on with my chores then. I'll be at Maggie's if you finish before I return."

"I'll see you soon then." After squeezing Nat's hand affectionately, Marissa picked up the silver piece to pay for Nat's meal.

✝

Nat saw Smithy admiring one of the large moose racks Maggie had dropped off, and walked over to him. She was smiling when he looked up.

"I may have to buy this pair for the store."

"As much as you've done for me, please accept them as a gift."

"I couldn't," Smithy said.

"You can and you will," Nat insisted.

"Those were some nice pelts you sent in. Do you see those continuing?"

"Yes, I think so. For a while at least."

"How many of these racks do you think you can bring in?"

"As many as you need. I have a few other racks, but I didn't want to flood your market right away."

"As usual, a smart business decision," Smithy replied. "Let me hang this set in the store and I guarantee I can sell as many as you can bring in."

"I will bring you another half dozen later in the week then. If you'll give me a total for the horse and wagon, I can settle up with you."

"Do you want to see him first?"

"Yes, that would be nice."

Nat stopped at the hitching post to collect Hardy and walked with Smithy toward the stables. The blacksmith was shoeing Quincy. "Can you do Hardy, too?" she asked.

"Sure thing. Rusty is in the back stall."

Nat tied Hardy's reins to a railing before eagerly walking to see the newest member of her family. The horse lifted his head over the top of the gate when they approached.

"He's a big boy." Nat reached out to stroke his face and open the stall gate. She stepped inside and ran her hand down his side. "Strong as an ox, too, I bet."

"He'll pull anything you hook to him," Smithy said. "I got a great deal on him, too."

Nat's hand glided down his left leg and she lifted his foot to find he was fitted with new metal shoes.

"He's all set. Just hook him up to the wagon outside and you're good to go," Smithy said.

"So, what's my total?"

"Let's wait to settle up until you return later this week. That will give me a few days to sell some of the racks and sort out the pelts. I'll probably end up owing you money."

"Very well then. I can wait."

"Have you told Marissa about the cabin yet?"

"No, I want it to be a complete surprise. As far as she knows, she'll be sleeping on the ground this week."

Smithy chuckled. "I know how she hates that. She's going to be very surprised."

"I hope so. Maggie is getting her belongings together for the move. We've already broken ground on a fall garden spot, and made plans for several other projects."

"She was very excited when she came by. She said Gyp was going to have pups, too."

"Yes. Very soon we think."

"If you will part with one, I'd sure like to have one of her pups."

Nat smiled. "I haven't thought about giving any of them away, but if I do you'll be on the top of the list."

They walked from the stables and parted ways. Smithy went back to his store while Nat went to the general store to check on her order. The owner assured her that they had everything on her list in stock, and he would be prepared to load her wagon by midmorning. With that done, Nat strolled to Maggie's cabin.

†

Gyp was lying in the sun on Maggie's front porch. She lifted her head when Nat approached. She stopped to stroke Gyp's head.

"Come on in," Maggie called from deep inside the cabin.

Nat stepped inside the cabin and saw that Maggie had been busy since she arrived home. Piles of clothing and bed linens were stacked neatly on the kitchen table, and wooden crates were filled with the contents of her pantry. Jars of vegetables and meats filled the crates, and three crates were full of empty jars of varying sizes.

Maggie entered the room. "Those should be enough to make our jelly with some left over for honey," she said.

"My mouth is watering already."

"You will have jelly biscuits next week. I promise."

"Is there anything I can help you with?"

"No, not really. There's not much room for the two of us in here, but there will be plenty to do tomorrow when I start loading."

"Quincy was being shod when I came by the stables so he'll be ready when you are."

"Go spend some time with Marissa and let me finish up here. I know you're eager to be with her."

"Yes, I am. I'll see you in the morning then."

"One last thing, have you given any thought to what you're going to tell Marissa when she sees Quincy pulling a wagon full of my goods?"

"No, not really." Nat bit her lip while running her hand through her hair. "Do you feel comfortable leaving ahead of us and driving Quincy back to the cabin?"

"I was thinking the same thing. Yes, I'll be okay. I'll take my rifle and Gyp if you don't mind. You can tell her I'm getting a head start on the harvest."

"That will work. I'll come in early tomorrow morning and help you get loaded. That way you can be on your way before she's up and moving around. I'll drive the new wagon to the store, and as soon as they finish loading it, we will be on our way."

†

Nat walked toward the hotel and found Marissa climbing down the steps. She looked up to see her lover and the smile she wore warmed Nat's heart.

"Where are Hardy and Gyp?"

"Hardy is being fitted with new shoes and Gyp is staying with Maggie tonight."

"So, I have you all to myself?"

"Yes, ma'am, you do. I thought a night alone, just the two of us was overdue." They started walking to the house.

Once they cleared the last of the buildings in town, Nat reached down and took Marissa's hand in hers. "I've missed you. I think about you every day, and at night my arms ache to hold you."

"It seems like months since I've seen you. I know you've only been gone a few weeks, but it has felt like forever."

"Soon, I hope, we won't ever have to be apart."

Marissa looked at her and cocked her head. "How do you propose we do that?"

"You will find out in due time," Nat smirked.

When they reached the house they went in and Marissa closed the door behind them. "What would you like for dinner?"

"Dinner is a long way off. Right now I want you." Nat took Marissa in her arms. Her lips brushed softly down from Marissa's forehead to her lips for a slow, sensual kiss, her hands caressing Marissa's back.

Marissa's heart fluttered in her chest as she broke the kiss before leading Nat into the bedroom.

Nat sat on the edge of the bed and pulled Marissa between her legs. Her hands gripped the hem of Marissa's blouse and lifted it over her head, tossing it onto a nearby chair. Her hands and eyes feasted on the soft skin hidden beneath the fabric, and her fingers deftly unfastened the corset ties leaving Marissa's torso naked. Nat felt her fingers tremble as they stroked soft skin, exploring each curve with restrained passion, reintroducing themselves to Marissa's body. "You are so beautiful," Nat whispered against her skin, her face nuzzling into soft cleavage.

200

A soft moan escaped Marissa when she buried her hands in Nat's hair. She had dreamt of this reunion, and her body was alive with sensation. Nat's lips burned a trail of desire as the tip of her tongue grazed a nipple, and Marissa felt her knees go weak. Her hands flew to Nat's strong shoulders for support. Nat's arms encircled her waist as she lowered her lover to the bed, and Marissa's eyes glowed with desire when Nat stood and undressed.

The smile on her face grew when Nat looked down on her. Her hair fanned out like a halo against the pillow, her breasts rising and falling with each breath she took. Her eyes filled with hunger as Nat slowly eased onto the bed, lying down between her legs. "I want every inch of you," Nat whispered lowering herself onto Marissa.

"I'm already yours," she answered with a breathless voice. She quivered with anticipation when Nat covered her mouth, her tongue sweeping across her lips, inviting Marissa's tongue to a sensual dance. She obliged, opening her lips, a soft moan releasing as Nat's hips pressed into her center. Her nails dragged slowly along Nat's spine, causing a moan that vibrated deep in her mouth.

The heat of their passion ignited and their hips undulated, the room filling with the sounds of their lovemaking. Nat placed soft kisses on Marissa's skin, her mouth slowly trailing down to suck a breast while her hand caressed the other. Her breathing labored as Nat teased her nipples into pointed peaks, her body trembling with an approaching climax. "Oh yes, my love." She shook with uncontrollable pleasure seconds later.

Nat smiled up at her and her mouth moved lower, placing kisses across Marissa's skin. Her fingers expertly lowered the last remnant of clothing that was preventing them from being skin to skin.

Marissa thrummed with excitement at Nat's warm breath before her tongue pierced her core.

The scent and taste of Marissa's desire filled Nat's senses as her tongue traveled along the layers of her opening, lapping at the salty juices of her pleasure. Marissa's moans urged her deeper, her tongue probing her interior while her fingers teased the sensitive mound of her growing clitoris.

Marissa's hips thrust to meet each stroke of Nat's tongue, her heartbeat pounding in her ears, fighting unsuccessfully to restrain a second climax. The force of her release contracted the muscles of her thighs that were locked around Nat's head, holding her in place as Nat feasted on her lover.

Nat felt Marissa's thighs release and she fell back to the bed, fighting to catch her breath. She moved onto the bed beside Marissa and held her lover while the last pulses of pleasure coursed through her spent body.

When her speech returned, Marissa turned in Nat's arms. "That was even better than I dreamed."

"I've yearned for weeks to be with you again."

"I hope you enjoyed it as much as I did."

"I'm certain I did," Nat grinned.

Marissa placed her head on Nat's arm. Her fingers reached up to trace the scars along Nat's temple from the swipe she had taken from a bear. "I've really missed you—us," she admitted.

Nat bit her tongue, holding back a desire to tell Marissa about the cabin and her plans for them being together year round. She desperately wanted to surprise her lover, but the temptation to spill the beans was growing. "We will just have to cherish the time we have together."

"I do cherish you." Marissa stretched upward to kiss Nat.

In the silence that followed, Nat's stomach came alive, growling loudly.

"Are you hungry?"

"My stomach thinks so. I can wait to eat."

"I thought I would fry some venison chops, unless you want something else."

"That will be good for me. I thought I spotted a fresh pie on our way through the kitchen."

Chuckling, Marissa said, "You never miss a pie, do you?"

"Not one of yours," she answered. "I think a slice now would hold me over until dinner. Would you like one?"

"I could eat the whole thing right now."

"Stay right here then." Nat climbed from the bed. She pulled her work shirt on, then walked to the kitchen where she poured a cup of water, and picked up the pie and two forks before returning to the bedroom.

Marissa had recovered and moved to a sitting position, her back propped against the headboard. She smiled when Nat returned to the bedroom, carrying the whole pie.

Nat handed her the cup of water and a fork before climbing into the bed.

"What time do you plan on us leaving tomorrow?"

"The new wagon should be loaded by lunchtime."

"That was a wise decision. I'm sure Quincy won't miss pulling those barrels full of seafood."

"He will still have plenty work to do helping me with the pelts and other small loads. I've found several spots in the forest where the elk and moose have shed their antlers. I brought several for Smithy to sell on this trip with a promise of more to come."

"Those should sell quickly."

"That's what he thinks, too. When do you have to be back to the hotel?"

"I am yours for the next four days. Joseph was excited about getting more seafood next week. With all the travelers heading to the gold fields, business has increased. He's even thinking of hiring another woman for the kitchen."

"Business all over town seems to have increased. The general store was packed earlier today, and Smithy said he had been busy, too."

"Our little town is growing. Several new families have moved in, too."

They ate pie while talking, and Nat smiled when she looked at the pie to see they had eaten more than half. "This is so good, but if we keep going there won't be any left for dinner."

Marissa took another bite and shot Nat a wicked grin. "I'd rather have you for dessert."

"That won't be a problem, but I think we should have a bath too."

"Not a bad idea since we'll be sleeping in the cave the next few days. You don't smell like the woods. Have you been bathing in the Sound?"

"No, I've actually found a nice lake. The water's a bit chilly, but at least I get clean."

"Have you had a chance to explore the area?"

"Yes, it's a little piece of heaven. I've even found a honey tree."

"That's good to hear, my little bee charmer," she said with a smile. "I'm still amazed you can steal their honey without as much as one sting."

"I've done it all of my life."

"Well, bees aren't the only ones you charm. You've got me buzzing for you too."

"That's so honey sweet," Nat teased. "Are you ready to cook some food for your bee charmer?"

Marissa chuckled. "Why don't you start a fire under the wash pot to heat our bath water while I cook?"

Nat pulled on her pants, and boots then walked to the water basin to wash her face. Marissa's scent was all over her as she gently washed her face and hands, smiling at the lingering smell. "If you don't mind, I'm going to light the fire and walk to town to check on Gyp and Maggie."

"Just don't be all night."

"I won't. Gyp is getting close to whelping, so I want to make sure she's all right."

"Maggie loves her almost as much as you, but I understand your concern, grandma to be."

Nat took the pie plate from her hands and bent down to kiss her. "I'll be back soon."

†

After filling the pot with fresh water, Nat lit the fire, and walked to Maggie's house. When she stepped onto the porch, she could hear Maggie talking with Gyp, who was curled next to Maggie on the floor, her head in the woman's lap.

"You will make a good mama." She softly stroked Gyp's head.

The sight of her two best friends together was heartwarming, and Nat knew Marissa was right—Maggie did love Gyp. She watched them for several seconds before walking through the open door. "You two have made great progress," she said.

Maggie looked up to her with eyes sparkling with excitement. "We are all set for loading in the morning."

"Have you two eaten?"

"Yes, we finished off the last of the venison from my stores."

"Is Gyp doing all right?" Gyp lifted her head at the sound of her name and locked her dark caramel eyes with Nat's, her rear end wiggling in excitement. Nat knelt to scratch behind her ears.

"Yes, she's been a good girl, and has been resting while I puttered around here."

"We will be heading home tomorrow." Her hand rested on Gyp's belly. "Your little ones are getting quite active," she said with an excited grin.

"It won't be much longer now."

Nat stood and stretched.

"Are you enjoying your time with Marissa?"

Nat couldn't hide the blush that rose to her cheeks. "Yes, I am. I'm heating water for a bath while she's cooking supper. I thought I'd come check on you two while waiting."

"We both are doing fine and will be going to bed soon, so we can get up and be ready to load in the morning."

"I'll be here as quick as I can," Nat told Maggie. "Rest well my friends," she said, and left the house.

✝

Nat pumped a bucket of clean water and carried it into the house when she returned. Marissa was busy preparing dinner when she walked in with the bucket of water.

"I've already got some water in the tub, but you can add that bucket and sit with me until supper is ready. After we eat we can carry the hot water inside, and we will have our bath."

"It smells good in here." Nat poured the bucket into the partially filled tub. "Do I need to draw a bucket for supper?"

"Yes, please. if you would."

Nat walked back outside to the pump and looked up at the sky while she filled the bucket. The sun had quickly disappeared and the stars were beginning to awake in the night sky. A howl in the distance brought a smile to her face as she wondered if Gyp's mate had followed them to town. She waited for another howl then walked inside when no other call filled the night.

After the meal, they settled into the tub for a long soak. Marissa cuddled in Nat's arms as they relaxed in the steamy water. "This feels so good." She moaned and laid her head on Nat's shoulder.

"A great way to end the day." Nat nuzzled Marissa's hair.

"I am far from done with you, Miss St. Croix," Marissa purred.

Nat chuckled. "I do like the sound of that."

Several hours later, the exhausted lovers collapsed on the bed and cuddled together. Nat had worried that sleep would be difficult for her, due to being so excited about the coming day, but the exertion of their passion had her completely relaxed. Content and with smiles playing across their faces, they slept in the comfort of one another until the light of dawn peeked through the window, waking Nat.

Chapter Twenty-three

Nat slipped quietly from the bed and dressed. Marissa snuggled under the covers with a smile still playing across her face. Nat crept quietly from the room and out the front door. The morning air was crisp as she walked to the woodpile and filled her arms before returning to the house to stoke the morning fire to warm the cabin. She looked in on Marissa and marveled at the beautiful woman who had stolen her heart, and turned away to walk to town.

Maggie was emerging from the stables with Quincy in tow when Nat arrived in town. "Are you as excited as me to be going home?"

"Yes, I hardly slept at all last night," she admitted. "Thank you again for this opportunity, Nat."

"It wouldn't feel right without you there with us," she answered. "You are family to us."

"Stop, before you make an old woman cry." Maggie wrapped an arm around Nat's waist as they walked.

They loaded her bed onto the wagon first and tucked the rest neatly around it. The final two crates would not fit, so Nat carried them and tucked them away in the new wagon. When everything was secure, Nat lifted Gyp onto the bench and kissed the top of her head. "I'll see you later today. Take care of Maggie." Gyp's soft tongue lapped at the palm of Nat's hand. "Good girl," Nat said and stepped back to allow Maggie to climb into the wagon.

"Be careful on the road. Do you have your rifle?"

"Right here." Maggie reached behind the bench into the wagon bed.

"Hopefully we won't be more than a few hours behind you."

"Take whatever time you need. I'll get the fires going and start unloading my goods. What do you want for supper?"

Nat grinned. "I think we need to celebrate our homecoming with some crabs."

"I will make some fritters to go with them. Do you want shrimp, too?"

"I can always be convinced to eat shrimp," she answered.

"We better be on our way then." Maggie chuckled.

Nat walked with them as they left town, and when they reached Marissa's house they stopped briefly.

"We'll see you soon." Nat scratched behind Quincy's ears.

"I'll make him a special treat for his hard work today." Maggie clicked and gently slapped the reins on the horse's neck. "Let's go home, Quincy."

Nat smiled at Maggie's words. Even the normally placid Quincy seemed to have a lighter step as he lunged forward to start the small wagon in motion. Nat watched them until they disappeared from view and then returned inside the house.

†

Marissa was still sleeping soundly when Nat peeked into the bedroom, so she slipped out to the smokehouse. She was delighted to find rashers of bacon that would make an excellent companion to the last six eggs in the pantry. She added wood to the smokehouse fire and walked back into the kitchen to cook the bacon.

The aroma of bacon cooking woke Marissa. She stretched lazily in the bed, surprised to find muscles sore from the night's activities, but a smile crossed her face, remembering how much pleasure they had shared. She climbed from the bed and dressed in her bloomers and one of Nat's work shirts before walking to the kitchen.

"You're up early." Marissa went over to kiss Nat.

"I thought I might cook us some breakfast and let you sleep in a bit. I've been to town and saw Maggie and Gyp on their way."

Her face crunched in a frown. "Why so early? I haven't seen either of them yet?"

"Maggie went ahead to get started on the harvesting. We have a big order to fill, remember, but you'll see them later today."

"I know, but still."

"You were sleeping too peacefully to wake you."

Marissa poured a cup of coffee and strolled over to the fireplace where Nat was cooking. "I've got a pan of biscuits I baked yesterday. I can scramble some eggs with cheese unless you would prefer fried."

"Scrambled sounds great. I've missed your cooking," Nat replied. "You've gotten me spoiled."

"You deserve to be spoiled."

Nat grinned. "You have the next four days to spoil me."

"I just hope they don't fly by quickly."

"Me too." Nat pulled bacon from the pan. "I noticed you still have a ham steak or two in the smokehouse. Would you mind frying those to go with some biscuits for our trip today while I go to town to get the supplies loaded?"

"That's no problem." Marissa whipped the eggs and mixed in slices of cheese. "Are you done with that frying pan?"

"Yes, ma'am, let me pour up this grease and you can have the pan."

After a quick meal, Nat stood and stretched. "I do love your cooking."

Nat kissed Marissa. "I'm heading to town. Be ready to leave when I get back, so we can make it to the shore before we lose the sunlight."

"Yes, dear." Marissa smacked her on the butt as she turned to leave. "I'll see you soon."

†

Nat walked to town for the second time that morning and went directly to the stables to pay the blacksmith, Charlie, for the shoeing and housing of her animals. Charlie, a short, barrel-chested man, looked up from hammering a shoe at the forge.

"Maggie's already paid you up." He walked with her to Rusty's stall.

"That sneaky little woman," she said with a chuckle.

He helped her hitch Rusty to the wagon and she turned back to him. "I'll be back for Hardy and Buck in a few minutes."

"Do you want me to saddle Hardy and bring them both to the store for you?"

"Yes, thanks, that would be good, Charlie." Nat smiled at him. "Did Maggie ask you about forging some knife blades for us?"

"Yes, she did. I'll have plenty ready for you by the time winter arrives."

"Thanks." She gave him another warm smile.

"I'll see you in a few minutes then," Charlie said, before returning inside the stables.

"No hurry, it's going to take a bit to load the supplies I need." Nat climbed into the wagon and drove Rusty to the store.

Nat stood on the front porch of the store, watching John and another man load the wagon with the supplies she had ordered. She looked up to see Smithy approaching with a smile.

"I've hung that rack up you gave me, and have already sold two of the others." Stepping up beside her, he grinned.

"That was quick."

"Just keep them coming in."

"You know, you should take a couple of days and come for a visit," Nat told him. "The place is gorgeous, and there's also a freshwater lake if you wanted to do some fishing."

"I may just do that. Things have been really busy, but that will probably taper off when the weather starts to change."

"You are welcome any time. I hope you know that."

"Thanks. When will you be back in town?"

"Marissa has to be back to work in four days from now, so the end of the week."

"Maybe we can catch up then, and talk over some business prospects."

"I'd like that. We could meet for lunch or you could come out for supper."

"Let's see how busy this week is, and I'll let you know when you return."

"You have a deal." Nat embraced Smithy warmly before he turned to go to his store.

"I think that's it," John said, loading the last of the supplies. "Could I ask a favor?"

"Sure, anything."

"Would you bring me a large batch of clams when you return?"

"You're hooked aren't you?"

"I just love that chowder."

"Yes, I'll bring you a large batch." Nat followed him inside to settle the bill. "I hope to bring some honey and blackberry jelly, too, if you'd be interested?"

"I'd love some. If you could bring some fresh berries in that would also be great," John said. "I'm sure they would sell fast."

"I'll see what I can do."

Nat walked back outside and tied Hardy and Buck to the back of the wagon. Climbing back up to the bench, she saw John watching her with a grin and waved before slapping the reins on Rusty's neck. "Let's go home, big boy."

✝

Marissa rushed outside when she heard them approach. She shielded her eyes with a hand, giving Rusty the once over. "He's huge." She giggled.

"Strong as an ox, too. He pulls this wagon like it's nothing." Nat beamed with pride.

Marissa glanced back at the bed of the wagon. "That's a lot of supplies. Will they fit in the back of the cave?"

"I'm pretty sure they will," Nat replied. "Are you ready?"

"Yes, come down, and you can carry the picnic basket for me."

Nat set the brake on the wagon and jumped down to the ground to follow her inside. She smiled at Marissa who had changed into dungarees and a work shirt for traveling. "You look very nice by the way."

"Thanks. I thought these would be more comfortable and practical for the trip."

"Yes, they will be." Nat picked up the basket and her rifle. She waited while Marissa closed up the house and then loaded the basket and her bag on the wagon. She helped Marissa onto the bench and then handed her the rifle while she climbed in.

"You can put that behind the bench if you would," Nat requested, and took up the reins. She waited for Marissa to settle before releasing the brake. "All set?"

"Yes."

"Let's go, big boy." She snapped the reins and Rusty pulled the wagon out of the yard.

The sun was burning brightly overhead and Nat saw that Marissa, riding beside her on the bench, was fighting sleep. They stopped at the river to water the animals and rest for a few minutes. The cool water and a short walk helped to revive Marissa and stretch her muscles. They ate several of the ham biscuits before continuing on their way.

"What all do you have on there?" Marissa motioned to the wagon.

"More barrels to use in harvesting, feed for the animals, jars for honey, cooking and other general supplies."

"That seems like an awful lot," Marissa said.

"It just looks big with the bales of hay and barrels."

"If you say so," she said as Nat helped her get back into the wagon.

Nat chuckled at Marissa's growing suspicion as she walked around to the other side of the wagon and climbed aboard.

Marissa looked over to see a smile of happiness on Nat's face. "You are really happy at the shore, aren't you?" she asked.

"Yes, I am. I never dreamed I could be happy being settled anywhere, but this place feels like home. I have the Sound and the forest in one perfect spot. All it's missing is you."

Nat knew they were close and steered Rusty on to the path to the cabin.

Marissa asked, "You want to live here, don't you?"

"Yes, I do, and I hope this will convince you to live here with me," Nat replied. They crested a hill and the cabin came into view. She pulled Rusty to a halt to allow Marissa a good view.

"Oh, my goodness, Nat, when did all of this happen?" she asked.

"I had it built for us while I was out trapping. I've been putting the finishing touches on it these last few weeks. Do you want to see more?"

"Of course I do, let's go," Marissa answered.

Gyp trotted out to greet them. "Hey, Gyp," Nat said to the dog walking beside the wagon.

"Maggie will also be living here." Her friend stepped out to the small wagon that she was unloading.

"That's wonderful news."

As they approached, Nat pointed out the various buildings. "The cabin, of course, a smokehouse with a hen house next to it, the barn for the animals, and at the end of the cabin will be our garden."

"This is beautiful," Marissa replied, her eyes alight with excitement.

"Welcome home," Maggie said.

Nat pulled Rusty to a stop. She jumped down and raced around to help Marissa to the ground. Gyp danced in circles around her, excited to see her.

"Hello, little mama." Marissa knelt to hug and pet Gyp.

Gyp licked her face, making her giggle.

"You've made good progress. Let me show Marissa around and then we can help."

"Take your time," Maggie answered.

Nat offered Marissa her hand. "Come with me." She lifted her to her feet. She led her in through the back door, pointing out Maggie's room, the bathing room, and finally their bedroom.

Tears slid down Marissa's cheeks when she walked inside the room, her fingers gliding over the footboard of the bed. "This is beautiful."

"I made it all myself, except for the mattress which Maggie made for us," she explained.

Marissa inspected each of the bedpost carvings and smiled at Nat. "This is all such a surprise."

"You can't begin to imagine how tough it was keeping this from you. I had to threaten Smithy and John to keep their silence until I could bring you here."

"They both knew about this and didn't tell me?"

"Only for fear of losing life or limb," Nat said. She reached for Marissa's hand to continue the tour. She showed her the kitchen, pantry, and then stepped out onto the front porch.

"What a beautiful view." Marissa sighed when Nat's arms wrapped around her from behind.

"Do you think you can live here?"

Marissa turned in her arms, her tears returning and she nodded. "Yes, I can. I'll need to give the hotel time to find a replacement, but yes, I want to live here with you."

"That makes my day." Nat hugged her tightly. "I had no idea what I was going to do if you said no."

"I'd be crazy. What will we do with my house?"

"I think we can find someone to rent it, or we could sell it, or keep it for our trips back to town. The options are wide open."

"Let me think those over," she said. "Let's go help Maggie and get the wagons unloaded."

With the three of them working together, the unloading was complete, and the animals attended to in three hours.

"I'll start on supper if you will put these supplies in the pantry," Maggie told Marissa.

"What would you like me to do?" Nat asked.

"I'd like you and Gyp to take a bucket down to the pools and see if you can catch us some shrimp. We've got plenty of crabs, but if you spy some, bring those to replace those we will eat tonight."

"We can do that," Nat said. "We'll be back shortly."

†

Nat left her two favorite women toiling in the kitchen as she and Gyp left the cabin. She picked up two buckets and they started down the path to the shore. When they reached the pools, Nat sat and removed her boots, rolling her pant legs up to her knees.

Gyp took the opportunity to lick her face. "I've missed you too, my friend," Nat said. "Soon, we will all be together again and we will be even more when your pups arrive."

Nat went to work quickly and filled her buckets with fresh shrimp and four more crabs. She slipped her boots back on her feet and they climbed the hill to the house. Nat carried the buckets into the kitchen.

"If you two have things under control here, I owe someone a rabbit dinner," she said.

"Go ahead and hunt. I'll get the fire ready to roast the rabbit for our girl," Maggie said.

Nat picked up her rifle and started down the path to the creek where she had seen the big rabbit. Gyp crept along silently by her side. They hadn't traveled far when Gyp froze in her tracks, her ears perked forward.

"I hear him." Nat knelt beside her. "Let's see if he will come into the open."

They waited patiently for several minutes before the rabbit made his way slowly from the brush and stepped tentatively onto the open path. Nat waited until he reared on his hind legs to check his surroundings before she leveled her aim and shot, taking the rabbit quickly from this world.

Gyp rushed ahead and sniffed the rabbit, prepared to take chase if the rabbit was still alive. Nat's shot had struck him in the head, so there was no need of a second shot. Nat picked him up by his hind legs and they started for home.

They heard the single gunshot at the cabin and Maggie grinned. "Gyp's got her rabbit dinner tonight," she said.

"Nat's a great hunter."

Maggie smiled. "Yes, she is. Her father taught her well."

Nat leaned her rifle against the cabin and took the rabbit to the skinning stump. She pulled the knife from her boot and expertly separated the pelt from the carcass after gutting the rabbit. Gyp sat beside her, licking her lips, waiting for a handout. Nat tossed to her the heart and liver while she stored the intestines in a bucket to bait the pools in the morning. She took the meaty carcass to the pump and rinsed it before carrying it inside to Maggie. "Will you put this on to roast so I can finish the pelt while there's light enough to see?"

"Of course I will." Maggie took the rabbit from her.

Nat finished scraping the pelt, removing any remaining fat and tissue, and then stretched it across one of her tanning boards. She took care in cleaning and drying her knife before replacing it in her sheath, and then washed her hands and arms before returning back into the cabin. It had been a long day and she felt weariness creep in as she entered the kitchen.

"We are doing well here if you want to take your carving and relax on the porch until dinner," Maggie suggested.

"Why do I think that's a polite way for you to say get out of your kitchen?"

Maggie smiled. "You've worked hard today. Let us prepare supper and we'll all celebrate together."

"I'm convinced." Nat stepped to the mantel to retrieve a new block of wood. She smiled at the moose she had finished and strode out to the porch.

Propping her feet on the railing Nat began to shave off the edges. Gyp stretched out next to her, snoring softly, until she heard a lonesome howl from the forest. "That sounds like your mate," she said. Gyp looked up at Nat, her deep caramel eyes seemingly pleading for permission. "Go ahead, just don't be out long." Gyp trotted from the porch.

The aromas wafting from the cabin made Nat's mouth water. She could hear the sizzling of the shrimp frying next to the fritters Maggie had prepared. The rabbit was roasting, the sound of popping filling the air as fat droplets dripped into the flames. She was imagining the taste of the shrimp when she heard footsteps approaching and looked up from the wood to see Marissa stepping out to the porch.

"Are you ready to eat?"

"Yes, ma'am, the smells coming from the kitchen have my mouth watering."

"Come and we'll start with the shrimp and fritters while the crabs cook."

She gladly followed her lover into the cabin and took a seat at the table. When seated, she smiled at them. "Our first meal together as a family in our new home."

Marissa took a bite of the shrimp and moaned. "These are fantastic," she said looking at Maggie.

"We've been testing out a few recipes," Maggie said with a chuckle.

"I think you should stick with this one," Nat said.

Maggie walked to the pot and pulled out the first round of crab to cool, then dropped the next in to cook. She added the melted butter to bowls for each of them and placed them on the table while Marissa refilled their cups with water.

Nat picked up the crab, twisting the claws free. She used a small hammer to crack the thick shells of the claws, and passed the hammer to Marissa. Nat peeled the meat from the claw and dipped it into the butter. She took a bite of the sweet meat as a drizzle of butter slid down her chin.

Marissa gladly reached over to wipe the salty liquid from her chin, popping the tip of her finger in her mouth with a moan. "I'm going to love eating here," she added with a grin.

"Wait until you taste the smoked fish," Maggie said.

"Nothing can compare to this crab," Marissa said.

"Well, we certainly won't go hungry here," Nat added.

Maggie nodded, "What do we need to start on tomorrow?"

Nat thought for several seconds. "First, I'd like to cut down the tree for our watering system. Maybe you and Marissa can take Gyp and go collect some blackberries."

"What's the watering system?" Marissa asked.

"We thought we could cut a tree into a long and a short section, which we would dig out like a canoe, to hold the water we drain from the bathtub through the floor. We won't waste water that way and it will make watering the garden easier and faster than pumping buckets of water."

"Do I need to even ask whose idea that was?"

Maggie quickly pointed at Nat.

"That's what I thought."

"Once I'm done dropping and trimming the tree, I'll use the saw to cut it into sections. Then I'd like to go ahead and rig up our pulley system for the harvesting."

"What pulley system?"

"We will bury a post in the front yard, and one on the beach and use the rope I bought to set up a pulley system to bring the buckets of seafood and saltwater up the hill."

Marissa grinned. "So, no tromping through that thick sand for us or the animals?"

"That's the plan. We can position the wagon in the front yard, put the barrels in the wagon, and use the pulley system to fill them. When we are ready to head back to town, we hook Rusty to the wagon and go."

"Efficient and brilliant," Maggie said. "Who knew this young trapper was so smart?"

Nat blushed. "I just try not to waste time or energy when we don't have to."

Maggie pulled the second round of crabs from the pot. "Will this be enough or do I need to cook more?"

"This will fill me," Nat said.

Marissa nodded. "Me too."

"Oh, I almost forgot to tell you, we got our first egg," Maggie said.

"I hope the hens will start producing regularly," Nat said.

"I'm pretty sure they will. We can let them out to range tomorrow after you have felled the tree."

"What are we doing with the blackberries?"

"Maggie will make jelly to sell and some to keep for this winter. The owner of the general store has asked for fresh berries, too, if we can bring him some. That reminds me, we need to take a large batch of clams for John and Mary." She grinned at Marissa. "Maggie taught her how to make the chowder for John and now he's hooked."

"That's good news," Maggie said. "I will dig them before you return to town."

Gyp came trotting inside and sat beside Maggie. Maggie had already chopped some of the cooked meat to cool for her and placed it in her bowl. "Are you ready to eat?"

Gyp let out a soft woof, and Maggie placed the bowl on the floor for her.

Nat watched Gyp attack the food. "I think after our young friend here finishes eating, we should clean up the kitchen and call it an early night. The next few days will be busy."

"You two go ahead. There's not much to clean and it won't take me but a few minutes."

"Are you sure?" Marissa asked.

"Yes," Maggie answered.

"Thank you both for such a terrific meal," Nat said.

"Thanks for making us a beautiful home," Marissa said.

Nat was asleep nearly as fast as her head hit the pillow. Drained, both physically and emotionally from the day's work, she slept peacefully, pleased with Marissa's decision to join them at the shore.

Chapter Twenty-four

The next morning when Rufus made his announcement, Marissa, shocked from a deep sleep, sat straight up in the bed. "What the hell was that?"

Nat chuckled. "Let me introduce you to Rufus, our very own rooster."

"Dear Lord, does he do that every morning?"

"Yes, ma'am, bright and early right outside our window," Nat answered.

Marissa flopped back onto the bed. "I may have to reconsider my decision to move."

"I'll cook him in the stew pot tonight, then."

"No, ma'am, you won't. I'll get used to it, eventually."

"If you say so, he probably would be too tough to eat anyhow."

"Speaking of eating, we have ham biscuits left, unless you want something hot," Marissa said.

"The biscuits are fine with me." Nat got out of bed and started dressing.

"No snuggling after that scare?" Marissa pouted.

"I think you'll survive. I'd like to get that tree cut before the sun starts bearing down."

"I'll be there in a minute." Marissa watched Nat walk from the room.

Maggie was already sitting at the table, drilling holes on the antler buttons, when Nat came into the kitchen. "Coffee's in the pot and the biscuits are on the table."

"Can I get you a refill?"

"I'm good. I've already finished several cups."

Nat poured two cups as Marissa came dragging into the kitchen.

"How did you sleep?" Maggie asked.

"Like a rock until that horrid noise a few minutes ago."

Maggie smiled, but said nothing.

Nat sat with Marissa and ate some of the ham biscuits.

"I have buckets and empty flour sacks ready for the berries," Maggie said.

"I'll be ready in just a few minutes." Marissa stood and rushed outside toward the privy.

Nat finished her coffee and ambled out onto the back porch with Maggie to wait for Marissa. She had just picked up her axe to check the edge of the blade when Gyp let out a low growl. Nat's eyes flew up in time to see a young man step into the clearing out of the light fog of the morning. "Step inside and have a gun ready," she told Maggie.

Maggie slipped back inside the cabin, picked up Nat's rifle, and stood just inside the back door.

"Easy, Gyp." Nat stepped toward the young man to greet him. She left ample space for Maggie to have a clear shot if needed.

"Good morning." Nat slowly approached him.

"Morning, ma'am. I smelled the smoke from your fire and I was hoping I could do some work in exchange for a meal. My name is Tom Wilson."

"What brings you to these woods?" Nat asked.

"Pure foolishness, if you listen to my Pa." He kicked a small rock with his boot. "I'm headed to British Columbia to strike it rich mining gold."

"You should probably heed your Pa's words then, young man. Where are you from?"

"California," he answered.

"How old are you?"

"Sixteen, ma'am."

"Not even old enough to grow a beard." Nat looked at the area the young man came from. "Are you traveling alone?"

"I am now. I was traveling with another boy from California, but he decided to go back home a few days ago when our food ran out."

"When was the last time you've eaten anything?"

"It's been about three days, ma'am. I had some nuts and berries I found along a trail."

"Are you armed?"

"Just my buck knife that's tucked in my boot, ma'am."

"For goodness sakes, call me Nat. You make me feel old."

"Who are you talking to?" Marissa opened the door to the privy and stepped outside. "Oh hello."

"Marissa, this is Tom Wilson. He wants to work for us for some food. What do you think?"

"Well, he does look hungry."

"Maggie, you can put the rifle down. Will you bring those biscuits out here?" She turned back to Tom. "Are you carrying a cup with you?"

"Yes, I am, m—Nat."

"Draw some water and come up on the porch."

Maggie stepped out of the cabin, carrying the rifle and a plate of ham biscuits. "It's okay. I think you can leave the rifle inside, Maggie."

Maggie put the rifle inside the back door and waited for the others to return to the porch.

Tom pumped a cup of water and his eyes lit up when he saw the plate of biscuits. It was obvious to Nat that the young man was famished. He stopped before reaching the steps. "Do you have work I can do for you?"

"Yes, as a matter of fact I do, but you need some food first."

Tom climbed the first step and took a seat on the top step after he took the plate from Maggie. "Thanks, ma'am."

Nat sat on the railing, her hand working a file sharpening her axe blade. She looked at Maggie and then at Marissa. "You two can go ahead. Tom and I will fell the tree once he has filled his belly."

"Are you sure?" Marissa asked.

"Yes, I am." Nat nodded at her lover. "Go, I'll be fine. Tom and I will see you when you return."

Maggie picked up the buckets and bags and stepped off the porch, still eyeing Tom suspiciously.

"Go with them, Gyp," Nat said, and Gyp followed Marissa off the porch. "Don't let Marissa eat all the berries before you get back."

"I'll try not to." Marissa grinned.

Tom had downed the first biscuit and picked up a second.

"Chew that one," Nat said.

Tom nodded taking a bite and chewing it before swallowing. "Do you need some firewood cut? I've got plenty experience doing that."

"This one's not for firewood," she said. "I'm going to cut a tree into sections and dig out the wood to make some troughs to use for watering the garden."

"I can do that for you, just tell me what you want." Tom swallowed another bite.

"Finish your biscuits and we'll get started." Nat looked up from honing the blade. She ran her thumb over the blade before picking up the hatchet to sharpen that blade as well.

"Those were good." Tom finished the last of the biscuits and handed Nat the plate.

"Drink some more water while I take this back inside." Nat walked into the cabin.

Tom had lowered his pack to the ground and pulled off his traveling jacket when she returned. Nat noticed he was thin as a rail as she handed him the axe. "Let's go."

They walked to the edge of the clearing to the tree she had chosen to use. "Drop this one and we will trim the branches. Then we can use a saw to get smooth ends."

Tom picked up the axe and began chopping the tree. Nat stepped back a safe distance and watched the blade cut from the top and the next stroke cut from the bottom. It was evident in the way he wielded the axe that young Tom had cut a tree or two in his young life. She was impressed by the accuracy and speed with which he chopped the tree.

When he had cut nearly through the trunk, he stopped and looked at Nat. "Is there any particular direction you'd like this to fall?"

"Bring it toward the cabin."

"Step back a few steps then." He walked around to the backside of the tree, dropped the axe to the ground, and used both hands to push the tree forward.

Nat heard a loud crack as the tree began falling, crashing loudly on the ground.

"Well done. Now let's trim these branches and toss them in the smokehouse once we're done here. Do you need a water break?"

"If you don't mind."

"Go ahead, you're the one doing all the hard work." Nat took the hatchet and started trimming the smaller branches, placing them in a pile.

Tom walked over to the pump, drank two cups of water, and was starting to walk back when Nat yelled to him. "Open the gate on that chicken pen on your way back, please."

He walked over to open the gate and the hens and chicks rushed out around him.

"They're looking for scratch," she said. "Have you ever fed chickens?"

"Yes, we have some on our farm."

"There's a bucket of scratch just inside the barn if you want to scatter some for me."

Tom walked to the barn to retrieve the bucket and scattered scratch around the ground for the chickens, then replaced the bucket and joined Nat. He took up the axe and started working on the larger branches.

Nat watched him work while she cut the branches. Tom certainly wasn't afraid to work, and an idea began to form as they worked together to clear the tree. While Tom worked on the last branch, Nat walked to the barn to retrieve the saw they would use to section the trunk. The first section would be roughly eight feet long, and would be the section running under the cabin to drain the tub. She measured out the section, marked it with the saw blade, then marked off another section of about fifteen feet that would run into the garden plot. The rest they could use as wood for the smokehouse.

She handed Tom the saw and instructed him to cut from the longer section first to take some of the weight off the tree. When he was nearly through the trunk, he stopped and they rolled the log so he could get a clean cut through the tree. Tom started sawing the next section as she chopped the top portion into firewood lengths. When he was ready to turn the log again, she stopped long enough to help him, and then she walked to the barn to place Quincy's rig on his back so he could pull the logs up to the garden area.

As she walked Quincy over to the tree, Tom looked up. "Do you want me to cut a smooth end on the bottom of the short section?"

"Yes, please." Nat tied the rope to the longest section and then wrapped it around the horn on Quincy's harness. She held onto his halter, urging him forward. The sturdy mule struggled briefly to get the log moving, but once he started, he pulled it all the way to the garden plot.

"Good boy." She released the log. "Just one more and you'll be done." She led Quincy back to the tree and attached the smaller log, which was heavier for him, but he moved it easily. When she turned back toward the tree, Tom was gathering the sections she had cut in his arms. She turned Quincy and walked him back to the barn.

"You can place those beside the smokehouse," she said when they passed in the clearing.

"Yes, ma'am."

Nat growled and just shook her head. She removed the rigging from Quincy and brushed the hair on his back while Tom carried the smaller logs and branches to the smokehouse. "Do you need a break?" she asked.

"Just long enough for some water."

"Me, too." Nat grinned.

They both drank several cups of cool water to quench their thirst while sitting on the steps of the cabin. "You did a good job on that tree."

"Thanks. I'm used to hard work."

"Do you really want to go to the north to hunt for gold?"

"I'm the youngest of four boys, so there was little chance of me being anything but a hired hand to my older brothers who will take over the farm once our father passes on," he said. "So, if I want anything of my own, I have to go and seek it. Gold mining sounds as good as anything, I reckon."

"There are probably thousands of other men thinking that same way, but the competition and the weather will be brutal up there. Not a safe environment for anyone to be, especially someone working alone."

Nat saw he was listening to her words carefully, and she understood that he felt his options were limited.

"What's next?"

"You see those poles over there?"

"Yes, I do. Where would you like them?"

"Pick one up and follow me."

Tom walked over to the two poles that were resting against the side of the barn and shouldered one of them. Nat handed him a bucket, before picking up a shovel, her toolbox, and a small length of board. "Ready?"

Tom nodded with an eager expression. He followed Nat down the trail to the beach and they passed the cave to the beach by the pools. When Nat stopped, he looked at her curiously. "Now what?"

"I want you to dig a hole to bury part of this pole in the ground."

Without further question, Tom dropped the pole in the soft sand, took the shovel from Nat, and started digging. When the hole was about four feet deep, she motioned for him to stop.

"Let's try that out," she said.

Tom laid the shovel on the ground and lifted the pole into the hole.

"That looks like it will be solid once the hole is filled in," she said.

Tom went to work filling the hole with the wet sand, packing it as tightly around the pole as he could. When he finished, he placed his hand on the pole and pushed on it. "It seems pretty solid to me."

Nat opened the toolbox and removed a hammer and three nails which she handed to Tom. She picked up the board and held it in position on the pole. "Nail that board onto the pole," she instructed.

Tom hammered the three nails into the board and handed Nat the hammer to return to the toolbox. "Now will you explain to me why we just planted a pole in the middle of the beach?"

Nat chuckled. "First, take off your boots and socks. You might also want to roll up your pants." She sat in the soft sand and did the same, noting that Tom watched her with curiosity, but complied with her requests.

"Come." Nat started toward the water.

"I can't swim," he said.

"Don't worry, you won't need to," she answered. "The Sound is a wonderful garden of seafood." She waded out toward the first pool. "With the passing of the tides, these pools fill with all kinds of wonderful things to eat. Have you ever had seafood, Tom?"

"Can't say as I have."

When they arrived at the pool, he saw it was full with a wide variety of creatures. Nat pointed out shrimp, several types of fish, and a crab that had wandered into the pool. "There is a town a half-day's ride north and east of here that has a hotel owner who loves to sell seafood to his customers. So, Maggie, Marissa, and I harvest them and deliver them to town, in large wooden barrels filled with salty water to keep them fresh."

"I see, but I still don't understand about the pole."

"I plan to plant another pole, up there." She pointed back up to the cabin. "I'll rig a rope and pulleys to transport the buckets of water and seafood up to solid ground. This sand makes it difficult on human and horse alike to carry anything heavy, so I've come up with this idea." She grinned at the young man. "If it works, it will save us a great deal of work."

She could see the idea come to life in Tom's head as he looked at the pole and then up the steep cliff on the beach. "I can see where that would work."

They walked back to the shore and she picked up the shovel and handed him the bucket.

"Now what?"

"Now we dig for lunch."

Tom shook his head and followed her to the shoreline. He watched her using the shovel to turn the wet sand and saw several shells buried in the sand.

"Clams. They will be made into a delicious soup, called chowder. Served with fry bread, it makes for an excellent meal." Nat dropped the clam into the bucket and saw Tom pick out several more. She continued turning the sand until their bucket was full.

They returned to the beach, dried their feet, and put their boots back on, then collected the tools, and the bucket of clams before walking back up to the cabin.

At the clearing, Nat could see that Maggie and Marissa had returned from the lake. Gyp rushed out to greet her. "Hey, girl." Nat reached down to scratch her head.

"She's a beautiful dog."

"A smart one, too," Nat answered.

Marissa and Maggie were rinsing the berries when they arrived at the porch. Nat took in their bounty. "It looks like the berries were plentiful."

"There are still plenty to be had, we just ran out of space," Marissa said. "I've never seen so many in one spot before."

"You two have been busy, too," Maggie said.

"We have. The tree is down, the beach pole is planted, and we brought a bucket of clams, hoping you would make some chowder and fry bread for lunch."

"That's an easy request. Why don't you and Tom boil and shell them for me, while we finish rinsing the berries?"

"Sounds like a fair trade to me. Grab your knife, Tom, and follow me."

After boiling the clams, Nat picked up an empty bowl and carried it around to the log they had cut earlier and sat down. She showed Tom how to use the tip of his knife to sever the meat from the shell.

"There's not much meat to them, is there?"

"That's why we need so many. These will go a long way though."

Maggie picked up the bowl of shelled clams. "These will do well."

Tom looked at the pile of empty shells. "What do we do with the shells?"

"We'll drop them in the outdoor pot. We can boil them again later, and then I want to use them to ring the cabin at the drip line to help prevent the soil from washing out under the logs. Boiling them should rid them of the fishy smell."

Tom was grinning. "How did you get so smart?"

"My family and I were fur traders, and we had to utilize everything we could to survive in the woods for months at a time."

"You are something else." He collected the shells and carried them over to the pot.

"Let me get to cooking." Maggie walked inside the cabin.

"What are you going to do next?" Marissa asked Nat.

"I'm going to take advantage of young muscles and plant the other pole for our pulley system." Nat grinned as Tom returned.

"What can I do to help?"

"Go to the barn. There's an extra-long length of rope, two heavy metal hooks, and the pulleys. Bring them here and when Tom is done planting, we can try out our system."

"I'm on my way."

Nat stood and handed Tom the shovel. "Let's get this done."

They walked into the front yard, and Nat lined up the next pole with the one buried at the beach while Tom retrieved the other pole.

"Dig here," she used the shovel to mark the spot.

Tom started to dig as Nat collected the board, nails, and hammer. Marissa arrived with the pulley equipment and placed them on the ground.

"What else can I do?" Marissa asked.

"Go to the fire pit and pick out a few chunks of charcoal, along with a section of the board over by the henhouse."

When Marissa returned with the items, Nat took a chunk of the charcoal and moved to the shorter log. "We need to mark out the area that needs to be removed for our troughs." She made a u-shaped mark at both ends of the log. "Use the board as a guide to draw lines down the log to connect these marks." Nat demonstrated the first line for her.

"Got it." Marissa replied and took the board and charcoal from her.

Tom was digging the hard ground with gusto and had reached a depth of three feet when Nat stopped him. "Let's try the pole."

Tom lowered the pole into the ground. "It's not as deep as the one on the beach."

"We needed the extra depth there for stability. The ground is solid here." She looked at one pole, then the other. "I think that'll do."

Tom packed the dirt into the hole and then secured the board, just like they had done at the beach.

Nat showed him how to fasten the hook and pulley to the crossbar on the pole. "Take the other hook and pulley and fasten it to the pole on the beach. When you're done, I'll toss one end of the rope down to you and you can thread it through the pulley and then toss the end of the rope back up to me."

"What can I use to give it weight to toss it back up?"

"Tie the end of the rope around the hammer."

Tom picked up his supplies and started for the beach.

Nat turned around to check on Marissa. She had finished one side of the log and was working on the other. Nat picked up a chunk of the charcoal and marked the u-shapes on the longer section, then walked to the barn for the axe and a hatchet. When she returned, she peered over the cliff to check on Tom. He was finishing hanging the pulley, so she picked up one end of the rope, threaded it through her pulley, and tied the end to the pole. She picked up the remaining coiled rope and tossed it to Tom on the beach.

Tom picked up the rope, threaded it through the pulley, and then tied it onto the claw of the hammer. He swung the rope back and forth gaining momentum and released the rope. The hammer fell ten feet short of the top. Tom swung the rope harder the next time, and when released, it soared over the edge and landed near the pole.

"Great shot," Nat yelled down to him and waved for him to return to the top.

Nat tied a knot in one section of the rope, slid it through a solid round top of a smaller hook, and tied another knot to keep it from slipping. Then she moved ten feet down the rope and repeated the process. They would hang the bucket on the hooks and then pull them up the cliff. Nat pulled the rope tight and tied the pieces together carefully trimming the excess rope. She was excited to try out the system, but as Tom walked back into the yard, Maggie stepped onto the porch.

"Lunch is ready. Tom, will you draw up a bucket of fresh water and bring it with you?"

"Yes, ma'am." He grabbed a bucket and trotted to the back yard.

Nat smiled when she looked at Marissa. The charcoal had blackened her hands and she had a streak across her cheek where she had wiped her face. "Time to get cleaned up for lunch," she said when Marissa looked up at her.

Marissa dropped the charcoal and followed Nat into the cabin. Nat washed her hands at the basin and handed Marissa the block of soap.

"You're going to need this to get that charcoal off your hands."

Tom carried the bucket of water in from the back and washed his hands when Marissa was finished.

Maggie poured cups of water for everyone and portioned out bowls of the chowder. A large plate of fry bread was already sitting on the table.

Tom's eyes grew wide when she placed a bowl in front of him and then served the others. "This smells terrific."

"Just be careful, it's still hot," Maggie warned.

He picked up a piece of the bread, dipped it into the chowder, and took a large bite. "This tastes good."

Maggie smiled at his compliment and began sipping her chowder. "It looks like you have accomplished a lot this morning."

"The extra pair of hands has made a big difference. Thank you for your help, Tom."

"It's been my pleasure. I've learned a lot from you this morning."

Nat smiled and took another bite.

"What would you like for supper?" Maggie asked.

"There's a nice-sized venison roast in the smokehouse. Why don't you put that on to cook with some of the onions, potatoes, and carrots? That and some fresh biscuits would be great."

"I'll get the biscuits ready for you after lunch," Marissa said.

"I'd like to hook Rusty to the wagon and pull it into the front yard. We can also load the barrels and then try out our pulley system."

"If you and Tom can handle that, I'd like to start on the jelly so it will be ready to go back into town when you leave," Maggie said.

"That reminds me, I have to collect some honey, too. We can harvest what we can from the pools today, and then Tom can help me with the honey."

"I'll get the biscuits ready to bake and get back to the logs. When I finish that, I can help Maggie with the berries," Marissa offered.

"It looks like we have the rest of today planned," Nat said.

Tom listened intently while he ate, and when he reached the bottom of the bowl, Maggie asked, "Would you care for another bowl?"

"Yes, ma'am, if I could please."

Maggie poured another bowl for him. "Anyone else?"

"I'll take a half." Nat handed her the bowl.

Nat and Tom loaded four barrels into the wagon and used Rusty to position it in the front yard. Tom took Rusty back to the barn and removed the rigging, then placed him in his stall.

Nat noticed that Gyp was not on the porch where she had been earlier. She stepped inside the cabin and asked, "Have either of you seen Gyp?"

Maggie smiled and answered. "She's in the bedroom in the bed you made for her. I think she may have puppies tonight."

"Really? This soon?" Nat asked.

"Don't be surprised."

Nat's face glowed with excitement as she left the room to check on Gyp, who was curled up in the bed and sleeping soundly. Nat crept quietly from the room and walked out to the front yard.

"Do you want to harvest while I'll pull the buckets up and empty them into the barrels?" Tom asked.

"That's fine. One barrel for crab, one for shrimp, and another for fish. We'll save the last for the clams."

Nat picked up four buckets and walked down to the shore. She kicked off her boots and socks, then rolled her pants to her knees. Carrying two buckets, she waded out to the first pool and filled both buckets half-full of water. She filled one of the buckets with shrimp and managed to trap three large fish that filled the other bucket. She carried them back to the pole and fastened the first bucket.

Tom took up the slack and she hung the second bucket. She watched the buckets edge slowly up the cliff, and then returned to the pool with the other buckets. There were no crabs in that pool, but Nat saw several in the shallows around the pool. She collected them in one of her buckets. Filling the other with more shrimp, she walked back onto the beach. Tom had returned the empty buckets, which she removed from the hooks. She hung the filled buckets on the pulley.

She waded out to the next pool, and smiled. There were eight large crab in this pool, which she scooped up for her buckets. For the next hour, she and Tom emptied buckets of seafood into the barrels, until the pools were bare. She picked up her boots and the empty buckets and walked back to the cabin.

Tom was at the pump rinsing the salt water from the buckets. He looked up at her and grinned. "We did well, didn't we?"

"Yes, we did." She placed her foot under the flow of water to rinse the salt from her skin. She sat on the steps and allowed her feet to dry before she pulled her socks and boots on.

Tom dipped them a cup of the cold water and handed one to Nat.

"How hard was it to pull the buckets up the cliff?"

"It wasn't too hard, but I think I'll be sore tomorrow."

"Speaking of tomorrow, would you like to stay here for a few days? I'll be taking Marissa back to town with the seafood in two days. You could ride in with us then."

His grin gave Nat her answer. He nodded bashfully. "Yes, I'd like that."

"Let's check on the others and then we'll go get some honey."

Marissa and Maggie were busy filling jars with jelly, and the cooking roast had the cabin smelling delicious.

"Marissa has a wonderful idea for breakfast in the morning," Maggie said.

Marissa smiled. "I thought I would use the pulp from the berries to make some blackberry flapjacks. How does that sound?"

"Is it breakfast yet?" Nat teased.

"No, but dinner is coming along well," Maggie said.

"Tom and I are going to the honey tree, so we'll be back soon."

Nat took a crate of jars from the pantry and handed them to Tom. They walked out into the yard and she stopped at the smokehouse for the smoke stick that she had fashioned to use with the bees. "Let's go steal some honey." She grinned.

Tom followed her willingly through the forest. Nat took the opportunity to talk to him in private. "Are you dead set on going to British Columbia?"

He shrugged his shoulders. "It sounded like a good idea at the time, but I'm beginning to have second thoughts."

"Would you be willing to hear a proposal?"

Tom grinned. "Of course I would. What do you have in mind?"

"In a few weeks, Marissa will be moving here on a permanent basis. She has a small cabin a half a day's ride from here, just south of town. I have a good friend who owns a traders warehouse who may be able to offer work to a young man willing to learn the trade," she explained.

Tom's eyes brightened with excitement as they walked.

"What I propose is that you rent Marissa's house and work for Smithy. If needed, you will also assist with the delivery of seafood to town and help in delivering supplies here?"

"Do you really think your friend would hire me?"

"You have a strong back, aren't afraid of hard work, and you have ambition to learn and improve your lot. I don't see why he wouldn't be interested."

"I would like that. Have you talked this over with Marissa?"

"No, not yet, but it would solve the issue of what to do with her house. We would still spend a night or two there when we came into town, but the house has plenty of room to accommodate three people."

"Can I come out here and work with you when I'm not busy in town?"

Nat chuckled. "Smithy will keep you plenty busy, but yes, you can come out here when you want."

"Good. I've learned so much from you in just one day." He grinned.

They had reached the area close to the honey tree and could hear the bees buzzing as they worked inside of the tree.

"How are you going to get the honey without getting stung to death? They already sound angry."

"I'm going to charm them."

Nat laid her torch on the ground, pulled out her flint set and within a minute had her greasy torch smoking. "Hand me two jars and follow me closely, but move slowly," she warned.

Tom handed her two of the empty jars and followed her to the tree, stopping several feet away as she approached with the torch. He was amazed as the bees flew from the tree and Nat was able to fill each jar with the golden honey.

She turned back to him. "Take these and bring me two more."

Tom exchanged the jars and carefully replaced the lids on the full jars. They successfully filled six jars before the bees began to return and Nat slowly backed away from the tree. He followed her to the edge of the lake where she dowsed the torch. They rinsed the excess honey from the sides of the jars. Tom licked the sweetness from his fingers.

"This honey is heavenly. How did you learn to charm them?"

"Just another of the skills I learned from my father."

They walked back to the cabin and Nat placed the honey on the front porch. She would take the jars to town for trading at the general store, along with the jelly and fresh berries. She walked inside to find Marissa and Maggie still filling jelly jars. "That looks good." She reviewed the jars they had filled. "How much longer do we have before dinner?"

"At least an hour," Maggie said.

"I think Tom and I will start on the logs then." She walked back to the garden spot.

"What next?" he asked.

"We start digging out these logs. Grab the buckets from the porch. We'll use the woodchips for kindling to start the fires, so drop them in the bucket. We'll transfer the chips to a burlap sack as they get filled."

"You don't waste anything do you?"

"Not if I don't have to." Nat grinned. "Once dried, these chips will start a fire much faster than green wood."

Tom returned with the buckets. "Do you want me to tackle the longer one?" he asked picking up the axe.

"That's fine with me." Nat picked up the hatchet, straddled the shorter of the logs, and began cutting out chunks from the traced out sections.

Tom watched her cut for several minutes then began work on the longer section. Soon they were hammering out a rhythm while hollowing out the logs. They stopped when they had enough chips to fill their buckets. "Gather these and I'll get a sack." Nat walked to the barn.

Maggie walked out on the back porch. "You two are making great progress on those logs. The roast has finished cooking so dinner is ready if you're hungry."

Nat looked at Tom. "I don't know about you, but I'm starved."

"We worked up a good appetite today."

"Let's go eat then." They carried their tools to the porch. "Might as well wash up out here." She pointed him to the pump.

They walked inside to find Maggie slicing the roast and Marissa placing a pan full of biscuits on the table.

"Would you like some fresh jelly?"

"That would be great," Nat answered. She picked up her cup, drank a deep drink of the cold water and poured another cup. The clicking of Gyp's claws made her turn and smile as her companion approached. "Hello there, my friend. Did you decide to join us for dinner?"

Gyp wagged her tail and then sat beside Nat, waiting patiently for Maggie to place her bowl on the floor.

"Just a few minutes and it will be cool, mama." Maggie carried a platter of sliced meat to the table. Maggie had chopped up bits of the meat, broken a biscuit into pieces, and smothered it with the gravy from the roast. Gyp licked her lips in anticipation of the meal to come.

"This looks wonderful." Nat spread butter over the vegetables and coated a biscuit with some of the fresh jelly. She took a bite of the biscuit and moaned loudly. "I'm not sure any of that jelly or berries will be making it to town. This tastes too good to share."

"We already have two dozen jars put back for us," Marissa informed her.

"That's a relief. It looks like there are still plenty of berries to be picked."

"We will work on those tomorrow and there should be one final growth before the end of the season." Maggie placed the bowl in front of Gyp.

"I guess you and I will finish off the seafood harvest and continue working on the troughs," Nat told Tom.

His mouth was stuffed with food, and all he could do was nod and grin at her. He took a drink of water. "That will be fine with me."

"I was talking with Tom when we went to the honey tree, and I want to run something by you." She looked at Marissa and Maggie. "Since you will be living here with Maggie and me, it leaves a decision on what to do with your home. Correct?"

"Yes, it does. I assume you have a solution."

"I think Smithy could use a strong young man to help at the store. I was thinking Tom could rent the house from you and work with Smithy. When we need his help next season to harvest seafood, he can ride out to help us and also assist with delivering the supplies we need."

"That's assuming I can afford a horse," Tom said.

"You can use my father's horse, Buck, if you take good care of him." She turned back to Marissa. "He's also in agreement that we stay at the house when we come to town for deliveries. He can keep the property up for you and provide us some help when needed."

"That sounds like a good plan," Marissa agreed.

"No need for you to go up to the gold fields, then." Maggie smiled at him.

"No, ma'am. I'd just about talked myself out of that anyway," he admitted with a sheepish grin.

"Welcome to the family then, Tom." Marissa smiled.

"Thanks," he said, and took another bite of food.

Nat picked up the next block of wood and walked out to the porch to do some carving while Maggie and Marissa cleaned up from dinner. Tom and Gyp followed her out to the porch and he leaned up against the wall, watching her whittle the wood.

"You said you have a hand auger, didn't you?"

"Yes, I do. Why do you ask?"

"I was thinking. You could hollow out a branch and attach one end to the drain and run the other end through the floor to drain into the troughs."

"That's a great idea. If you'll find a strong section of one of the branches we cut today, I'll go and get the auger."

"Deal."

Nat walked inside the cabin and returned with the auger just as Tom arrived with several lengths of wood.

"What do you think of this one?"

"Too thick, but the other looks like it might work. Have a go at it." She handed him the auger.

When the light faded, Nat returned inside the cabin with Tom. "We don't have a spare bed, but you can bunk down in front of the fireplace here and keep plenty warm."

"That's still much better than sleeping in the woods. Thanks."

"You're welcome." Nat walked back to her bedroom.

†

Nat woke from a dream and instinctively looked over the edge of the bed to check on Gyp only to find her absent. She crept quietly from her bed and went in search of Gyp. The shadows from the fireplace in the kitchen danced along the walls as she walked softly ahead. She ducked her head into Maggie's room to find her friend sleeping soundly, but no sign of Gyp. Nat stopped in her tracks when she reached the opening to the kitchen. Tom had curled into a ball in front of the fireplace hearth and Gyp had snuggled in next to him. It reminded her of the many nights in the woods when they had slept in that same position and it brought a smile to her face. He had fallen asleep while stroking her fur and his hand remained on her side, buried deep in her fur.

Nat turned and walked back to her bed to snuggle into Marissa's warmth.

Gyp returned to the comfort of her bed in the early morning and her whimpering woke Nat before the sun rose. She got up quickly to rush to Gyp's side to check on her. Marissa lit the lantern on the bedside table and handed it to her lover. With the illumination of the lamp, they observed the contraction of Gyp's muscles as the first puppy pushed toward the birth canal. Gyp's eyes locked onto Nat's, filled with pain. "Will you wake Maggie?"

"I'm here. I heard Gyp's cry, and came to check on her," Maggie said from the doorway. "The puppies are coming." There was a sparkle of excitement in her eyes.

Gyp whimpered making Nat cringe. "Is there anything you can do to ease the pain for her?"

"I can make her an herb broth, but that's the best I can do. She needs to be alert to help birth the puppies."

"Will you bring the soft rags we've been keeping for this time?" Maggie asked Marissa. "Stay with her while I prepare the broth. Use the rags to wipe down the pups when they arrive and then let Gyp lick them dry," she instructed, and left the room.

Tom arrived at the door still wiping the sleep from his eyes. "What's all the excitement this morning?"

"We are having puppies." Nat could feel her excitement along with fear while sitting next to Gyp.

"What can I do to help?" Tom asked.

"Add wood to the fires and bring in some fresh water." Nat turned her attention back to Gyp who was whimpering. "You're going to do just fine, little mama." She stroked her head.

Marissa rushed into the room, barely escaping a collision with Tom who was leaving to stoke the fires. "Here are the rags." She knelt beside Nat. "Don't worry she's going to do just fine."

"I know." Nat knew that they could all see the worry on her face.

"Look, our first born." The puppy emerged from Gyp and Nat moved to wrap the pup in a dry rag. Gyp watched her carefully.

The pup was a silver male, trembling in Nat's hand while she softly wiped the afterbirth from its tiny body. "A boy," she said to Gyp, laying the pup in front of her.

Gyp began to lick the pup's coat with her warm tongue. Her contractions continued and soon another pup arrived. The next had her blue coloring with patches of black. "And now a daughter." Nat's voice trembled with excitement.

Maggie returned carrying a small bowl filled with a warm broth. "See if she will drink this." She handed the bowl to Nat.

Nat picked up the male and handed the small bundle to Marissa. "Keep him warm." She then took the female and handed her to Maggie while she lifted the bowl to Gyp's mouth. "Drink, mama."

Gyp's tongue lapped at the warm broth until half of the bowl was gone.

"Good girl," Maggie said from her position on the bed.

Tom raced back into the room. Nearly breathless, he asked "How many?"

"Two so far, a male and a female," Nat answered.

The broth appeared to help and Gyp rested for a few minutes before the contractions resumed and the third pup arrived. A silver female. When no others arrived for several minutes everyone thought she was finished whelping. Gyp lapped up the remainder of the broth and rested.

"Will you fix our new mama some breakfast?" Nat asked Maggie. "Some of that gravy from yesterday would be good with eggs and some meat."

"I'll be back with breakfast in a few minutes."

Tom and Marissa cuddled with the pups while Nat stayed with Gyp. "You did good, mama," she whispered.

Gyp crawled forward to place her head in Nat's lap and looked up at her with eyes that looked pain-filled. Nat stroked her head and down her side. She jumped when she felt another contraction. "We are not done yet."

Several minutes later, another pup arrived and Marissa picked up the stillborn silver male in her hands. Panic filled her eyes when she looked at Nat. "He's not breathing and he's cold."

"Let me take care of him." Tom gave Marissa the three pups. "They need to nurse."

Tears streamed down Marissa's face as she handed the dead pup to Tom.

"Help them find a nipple," he said and left the room.

Gyp watched him leave and let out an exhausted whimper. "Time to feed your babies." Marissa guided each of the pups to a nipple and instinct took over and the pups nursed.

Maggie watched Tom leave the cabin and poked her head back into the bedroom and looked at Nat. Marissa was wiping the tears from her face.

"The last was stillborn," Nat said sadly.

Maggie nodded. "Breakfast is ready, but I'll let her nurse for a few minutes before I bring it in."

"Thanks." Nat stroked Gyp's head as they watched the puppies nurse.

Tom carried the pup and a shovel over to a large tree behind the cabin and carefully wrapped it in the soft rags. Placing it gently on the ground, he dug a small grave and placed the tiny bundle inside, covering it with the loose soil. Then he went to the garden spot, picked out a large rock, carried it to the tree, and placed the rock on top so no scavenger could disturb the grave. With a heavy heart and a deep sigh, he returned the shovel to the barn and walked back into the cabin.

He walked into the bedroom to witness the pups nursing and forced a smile to his face.

"Thank you for taking care of the pup," Nat whispered.

Tom, afraid his voice would give away the sadness he was feeling, nodded his acceptance.

The puppies nursed for several minutes then located one another to snuggle into a warm pile to nap. Maggie brought a bowl of food in for Gyp and placed it in front of her. Gyp looked at the food, then struggled to her feet and walked out the back of the cabin to relieve her bladder. From the door, Nat watched Gyp finish her business and walk directly to the tree where Tom had buried the puppy. She sniffed the ground and then lifted her muzzle to release a howl of mourning and sat next to the grave.

The sound tore at Nat's heart and tears flowed down her cheeks. Her vision blurred and she stepped out of the cabin walking to her companion. She dropped to her knees beside Gyp and buried her face in her fur. They mourned the loss of the pup together.

As Nat's tears subsided, Gyp turned to her and licked the tears from her face. Nat felt more tears rise to the surface and she hugged her companion close. "I'm sorry we lost one," she whispered.

Gyp licked her face again, then took Nat's hand in her mouth and gently led her back to the cabin.

They returned to the bedroom where her pups were sleeping soundly. Gyp ate a small portion of the food Maggie had prepared for her. She drank deeply from the cool water Tom had brought before snuggling around her pups.

"I think we should let them rest, and go eat some breakfast of our own," Maggie said. Tom and Marissa followed her from the room, leaving Nat kneeling beside Gyp.

"I'm very proud of you, my friend." She stroked Gyp's head. "I'll be back."

Maggie and Marissa began cooking a breakfast of hearty flapjacks, scrambled eggs, and ham steak. Tom busied himself carrying wood to stock the fireplaces, and Nat was at a loss for something to do. "Is there anything I can do to help?"

"I've used the rest of the eggs. Will you go out and see if the hens are laying yet?" Marissa handed her a basket.

"That I can do." Nat left the room and peeked in at Gyp sleeping with her puppies before walking to the hen house.

As they finished the meal, Marissa looked at Nat. "Is it okay for Maggie and I to go pick more berries today, or would you rather we stay close?"

"That will be fine. Tom and I will finish harvesting and work on the troughs today. I can keep a check on Gyp and the pups."

"I'll work the beach, if you want to stay up here," Tom volunteered.

"It shouldn't take us long," Nat added.

"We'll pick up here if you two want to get started," Maggie said.

Nat nodded and drained her water cup. She looked in on Gyp, who was nursing the pups, and then joined Tom on the front porch. "Get as many crabs as you can find, and then later we will dig some fresh clams."

"You got it, boss." Tom raced down the trail.

She watched him disappear and then appear again on the beach. Tom slipped out of his boots and rolled his pants to his knees. He picked up a bucket and waded into the water to the first pool.

Nat hooked empty buckets and lowered them to the beach with the pulley rig. When she turned back to the cabin, Marissa and Maggie were walking toward the woods. Marissa turned to see her watching and raised her hand to wave. Nat smiled and waved back. Then she began chipping the wood from the inside of the longest log they would use to irrigate the garden. When Tom whistled from the beach, she returned to the pulley to pull the first buckets full of crab up the cliff.

It took six more buckets to fill the last of the barrels. Tom fastened the last to the line and raced up the hill. "Do you still plan to take these to town tomorrow?"

"Yes, the sooner we get these to town the better."

"Marissa is going back, too, isn't she?"

"Just long enough to work out a notice and pack what she intends to bring here."

"Will you need Rusty and the wagon for a while?"

"Not until we need to harvest again in a few weeks. Why?"

"I was thinking. If you left them with me, I could help Marissa load her goods and bring her back here for you."

Nat smiled. "You know, that's not a bad idea at all."

"You've done so much for me, it's the least I can do."

"We can get you started with Smithy when we hit town. He will work you like a dog, but he's a good man."

"I trust that you would only look out for my best interests."

"He can teach you many useful skills, if you are willing to learn."

"I would really like that, and I promise to work hard and make you proud."

She smiled at him and slipped an arm around his shoulders. "You already do, my young friend. Now let's get to work."

After supper, they settled in for the evening. Nat sat on the floor with Tom and they watched the puppies feed and then curl up next to Gyp to sleep. Gyp had eaten a hearty meal and had slipped outside for a short period as darkness began to fall. Nat knew where she was going— to tell her mate of their offspring.

When she heard Gyp's claws on the wooden floor upon her return, Nat lowered the lantern light until she settled with her pups and then extinguished the light completely. "Good night, mama," she whispered.

Nat snuggled into Marissa's warmth and drifted in a sea of dreams.

Chapter Twenty-five

When Marissa woke the next morning, Nat was gone from the bed. She wondered where her lover was until she heard a soft laugh and rolled over to peek over the side of the bed. Nat was sitting on the floor nuzzling with one of the puppies.

"How long have you been awake?"

"An hour or so. The noisy pups woke me when they were trying to nurse." She lifted a silver pup to the edge of the bed. "This one has a healthy appetite."

Rufus, crowing loudly, chose that moment to announce the dawn, breaking the silence of the early morn.

"I swear he's going to end up in a stew pot," Nat growled. She placed the pup back on the teat he'd nursed earlier.

"Are you sure you want to go into town today?"

"Yes. Gyp will be fine with Maggie if that's what you worry about."

"Well, only if you're sure."

"I'm positive. The sooner we get you into town, the sooner you can return to me." Nat sat on the edge of the bed and kissed her softly.

They could hear the other two stirring in the front of the cabin. "I guess Rufus did his job. Come, let's start this day." She stood and offered Marissa her hand.

They dressed and joined the others in the kitchen.

"Tom and I will get the wagon loaded if you two will prepare breakfast," Nat said.

"Will ham and eggs be enough with leftover biscuits?" Maggie asked.

"That will be plenty. Do you mind watching over Gyp and the puppies until I get back?"

"Not at all. I thought I'd use some of the deer hide to sew you a new pair of breeches."

"Are you tired of this worn out pair?"

"Pretty soon you will be showing more than is necessary."

"On that note…Tom are you ready to start loading?"

"I'm right behind you."

238

†

Tom followed Nat out to the barn and helped her harness Rusty. Nat pointed to a large bundle of furs she planned to take to Smithy. "Those are beautiful," he said.

"Will you carry them to the wagon and position them near the front?"

"Sure thing," Tom lifted the bundle. "How long did it take you to trap these?"

"The trapping is still untouched here. I've managed these furs in just a few weeks."

He followed her out of the barn. "Maybe next spring you can teach me to trap."

"I'd like that." Nat led Rusty to the front of the cabin and attached the rigging to the wagon.

Tom went inside and brought the crates full of jelly and honey before returning for the bag of fresh berries. "I'd better place these toward the back if you expect them to make it into town." He popped a handful into his mouth.

"Let's go saddle the horses and get them ready for the trip," Nat said, shaking her head at his antics.

As she passed Quincy's stall the mule looked at her sadly. "You don't need to go on this trip, my friend." She placed a thick flake of hay in his bin, then dumped a bucket of feed, and filled his water. He looked sad as they took Buck and Hardy from their stalls. "There will be plenty for you to do when I get back." Nat scratched between his ears.

"You can just toss the tack for Buck in the back of the wagon. I assume you know how to drive."

"Yeah, I do." He grinned.

"Just tie his lead on the rear of the wagon then. I'll saddle Hardy and be right there. Hey, toss a half dozen of those antler racks on the wagon, too. Smithy enjoys it when I bring those."

"Surely you haven't killed all those animals in such a short time."

"No, I have a secret spot just full of shed antlers. Be sure to put one of the moose racks on there. Those seem to be his biggest sellers."

Tom nodded and left the barn with Buck in tow. She hated to see him go, but she knew Tom would take good care of him, and he needed more exercise than she could give him. Her father would have approved of letting Tom use him to better his life. She finished saddling Hardy and led him to the front of the cabin.

Tom had stowed his pack and Marissa's bag under the wagon seat and they were waiting for her to arrive. "Is there anything special I can bring you from town?" she asked Maggie.

"Some apples would be nice for a pie."

"Are you sure you will be okay by yourself?"

Maggie chuckled. "I was by myself a long time before we met. Besides, I will carry the pistol you gave me in case I run across a snake."

Tom was petting Gyp who was laying on the top step.

"You have to stay with Maggie and take good care of those pups," Nat told Gyp while stroking her head. "It seems really odd leaving without her," she admitted.

"She will keep me good company." Maggie stood beside her.

"That she will. Just don't spoil her too bad while I'm gone."

"*Pfftt*, like I could do any worse than you."

"Daylight's wasting." Nat held her hand out to Marissa, and then turned to Maggie. "I'll see you in a couple of days."

Maggie looked up to the pair sitting on the wagon bench. "How long will you be gone, Marissa?"

"Hopefully no more than two weeks, but I'll be back earlier if I can."

"And you, young man, I'm going to miss your high energy and hard work," she told Tom. "Hurry back to see us." She grinned.

"I'll be bringing Marissa back, so I'll see you soon."

Gyp whined when Nat mounted Hardy. "I'll be back soon."

Maggie and Gyp stood on the porch and watched as they disappeared from view, and then walked back inside.

✝

Nat was lost in her thoughts as Hardy plodded along as she rode ahead of the wagon. The jingling of Rusty's rig sounded like chimes as he followed Hardy's lead. She could hear Tom and Marissa keeping up a steady stream of conversation, but she could not tell what they were discussing.

"I couldn't help but notice the bear claws Nat wears around her neck. Did she kill the bear?" he asked.

Marissa smiled. She could tell that Tom already thought of Nat as his hero. "Two actually, the first was the beast that mauled and killed her father while they were trapping along the border. Nat's father was

240

checking a string of their traps when he was confronted by a large grizzly."

"That had to be terrifying."

"Nat heard the bear bellowing and then a shot from her father. She rushed to his aid to find him battling the bear with his knife after his shot failed to kill it. She took aim and dropped the huge bear with a bullet to his brain, but she was too late to save her father. He was losing blood much faster than she could stop it and he died in her arms."

"How old was she?"

"A little older than you are when her father died," Marissa answered. "She buried her father at the cabin they were using and then went back to skin the bear and remove his paws. She burned the carcass, refusing to taste the creature that had devastated her world."

"I can sympathize being alone in the woods. I rarely slept on my journey here."

"The bearskin on my bed is the one she took from the grizzly. She kept one of the claws for a necklace to remember her father, and sold the rest to Smithy. He offered her a tremendous price for the skin, but she refused to part with it as you would imagine."

"Nat's tougher than most men I've known in my life."

"Yes, she is." Marissa smiled in agreement.

"Where did the second claw come from?"

"On this very trail, so be armed when you travel back and forth. You can use my rifle. I have no use for it. Nat tried to teach me to hunt, but it's just not in me."

"Thanks."

"Anyhow, we were on our way into town and Nat had taken down a large buck along the way. The smell of blood attracted the bear, ravished after his winter hibernation. Nat hoped that the scent of humans would intimidate him, but his hunger outweighed his fear and he rushed her. She got off a kill shot, but he did not drop instantly, and came close enough to take a swipe at her. That's how she got the scar down the side of her face."

"I've never noticed it."

"Her hair covers it most of the time. She decided to give Maggie the pelt to warm her bed and she also enjoyed the meat."

Nat felt eyes on her and turned to find Tom watching her with what looked like amazement. She slowed to allow the wagon to catch up to her. "Is everything all right? Do you need a break?"

"No, we're good, just chatting about you," Marissa said. "Will we stop at the creek to water the animals?"

"Yes, we will."

"I have something I'd like to ask you," Tom said.

"Well, go ahead then."

"I know you've done a lot for me already, but would it be possible for me to have one of Gyp's puppies for a companion?"

"That's not up to me to decide. You'll have to ask Gyp. It appears that she likes you though, so I think your chances are good."

"Thanks."

"They do make good companions." She lifted her eyes to follow the track of a hawk soaring on the headwinds.

They stopped to water the horses and stretch for a few minutes. Nat dipped out a cup of the cold water for Marissa. "Are you excited to be headed back to town?"

"Only because it will allow us to be together sooner."

"Will you be bringing much from the cabin?"

"I'll leave the basics for Tom's use, so mostly clothing and personal belongings. One trip with the wagon should be plenty," she grinned.

"Will there be room left for a load of supplies?"

"We will make it work. What did you have in mind?"

"I've got a list I'll leave at the store. I'll go ahead and pay for the supplies. You and Tom can bring them back with you. I'll also make sure he's got some basic groceries and supplies for the animals before I leave. Are you okay staying with him for a few weeks?"

"Yes, he's a fine young man. Besides, he knows that you've killed two bears, so he's probably scared of making you mad."

"I was wondering what you two were talking about." Nat downed the rest of her water. "Are you ready to move on?"

Tom hitched Rusty back to the wagon.

"Yes, I'm good."

"Tom, did you get a drink?"

"Yes, I did thanks. I'm ready to move on if you are."

"Good, it won't be long now." Nat mounted Hardy and Tom helped Marissa back onto the wagon bench.

Nat crested the hill and saw the small cabin she had rented when she first came to town. It was close to Marissa's and soon they would pull up in front of the cabin where they had shared so much love. In a small way, she was sad that this portion of their lives was over, but then she thought of the exciting days the future held for them at the Sound.

She pulled Hardy to a stop at the hitching post and dismounted. "Do you want to drop your bags before we head into town? You can give Tom a quick tour and I'll put Buck in the stall."

"This is very nice." Tom stepped inside the cabin.

"It's been a good home to me for years. You will need to get busy cutting firewood for the winter soon. Nat usually does that, but she was busy surprising me with the new cabin so the supply is low."

"That's no problem. I still can't believe I get to live here."

It made Marissa happy to hear his excitement. "You can take the big room since I will only be here a few weeks at most."

"No, ma'am, that is your room, the second room is plenty big enough for me. I'll keep it clean and ready for when you and Nat come to town. I really don't mind."

"Fine then." Marissa placed her bag on the bed.

Nat was waiting for them when they emerged from the cabin. "What do you think?"

"It's going to be great living here." Tom helped Marissa back into the wagon and climbed in behind her.

Nat smiled and mounted Hardy. "Not much farther now. I think we shall have a steak at the hotel tonight."

"You won't get an argument from me," Marissa said.

Tom had a worried look on his face.

"It's my payment for your helping out the last few days. You've earned it and saved me hours of work."

"Thanks," he said, sounding truly grateful.

"Let's go get this wagon unloaded. When do you plan to talk to the owner?" she asked Marissa.

"I thought I'd talk to him while you unload the seafood. I can't see any need to delay the news."

"Perfect." Nat grinned and urged Hardy forward.

Tom guided Rusty to the back of the hotel after letting Marissa off in front, and he pulled to a stop. "Where do we put the seafood?"

"The owner has bought some troughs, so we just empty our barrels and we are good to go."

"I thought I heard you coming," a deep voice said, and Nat turned to see Smithy approaching.

"Just the man I need to see."

"Let me give you a hand with these barrels," Smithy said, and then spotted Tom.

"Smithy, this is Tom Wilson."

Smithy reached out his hand. "Nice to meet you, son. How did you end up with Nat?"

"It's a long story, one I hoped we can tell you about over a steak dinner tonight," Nat said.

"That sounds like a good idea," Smithy said. "C'mon, Tom let's put those muscles to work."

Nat watched the two men unload and empty the barrels. When the last barrel emptied, Tom turned to ask, "What did Marissa think of your surprise?"

"It was love at first sight. She's inside breaking the news to the owner now."

On cue, the back door opened and Marissa and the hotel owner, Joseph, joined them. "I should be mad at you," he told Nat. "She won't be an easy woman to replace, but at least I'll still be getting this great seafood from you," he told her with a grin. "Let me get a count going and I'll get your money."

"Just hang on to it. After we finish unloading the rest at Smithy's and get the animals cared for, we are coming back to town for a steak dinner. You can pay me the difference then."

"That works for me." He looked into the back of the wagon and saw the moose rack and his eyes grew wide. "Will you bring me a set of those? I'd buy them from Smithy, but he'd charge me an arm and a leg for them."

Smithy grinned at the remark.

"Well, they haven't made it to Smithy yet. Will you trade four steak dinners for a rack?"

"In a heartbeat," he answered.

"Tom, will you carry the rack in for the man?"

"Yes, ma'am," he said, and set to work.

"Hey, what about me?" Smithy cried.

"I will bring you more on our next trip."

"All right then." He grinned and turned to Tom. "You want to pull the wagon behind my store, and we'll unload the rest before she goes and barters it all away?"

"Yes, sir." Tom climbed onto the bench and slapped the reins against Rusty's back.

Nat and Marissa walked with Smithy to his store. "How has business been?"

"I can't keep a shovel or pick axe in stock with all these prospective miners coming through town. I get them sold before Charlie can make them."

"Has it slowed down any?" Marissa asked.

"Some, but we still get a half dozen or so a week coming through town."

"Tom was headed that way, but we'll talk more about that a bit later," Nat said. "Marissa and I have honey and jelly to deliver to the general store while you muscle men unload."

"Jelly?" he asked.

"Fresh blackberry jelly."

"Can I get a couple jars and some honey? I'll add it to your other wares."

"Are you afraid the store owner will rob you blind?"

"Yeah, something like that." He grinned.

"Is three of each enough?"

"That'll work. What do you have in that bag?"

"Fresh blackberries," Marissa answered. "You want those too?"

"I'd love them." He let out a deep chuckle. "I'll stop now or I'll owe you half interest in the store."

"I'm sure we could work something out." Nat gave him a wink.

Tom walked over to them. "When you're done unloading will you take the wagon back to the cabin and tend to Rusty and Hardy? Marissa and I will take these to the store, and I need to place some orders. We'll meet you back at the hotel for dinner?"

"Yes, ma'am." He grabbed the bundle of pelts and followed Smithy inside.

"Let's go do some bartering," she said to Marissa.

†

"Hello, ladies," Richard, the shopkeeper, called when they walked into the store. "What do you have there?"

"Wild honey and some blackberry jelly," Nat answered. "We had fresh berries, but Smithy saw them first."

"I will take all the fresh berries you can bring in, so next time don't let Smithy see them first."

"We'll see what we can do."

"What do you want for these?"

"There's a young man who will be renting Marissa's cabin once she moves to the shore with me. His name is Tom Wilson and he's a fine young man. I need to get some basic groceries and supplies for him, and get some hay and feed delivered for two horses."

"Make me a list of what you need and I'll have it delivered tomorrow. You want me to subtract your goods from the total?"

"Yes, and I'll need this list of supplies ready in two weeks when Marissa moves. She and Tom will pick them up and deliver them."

"Make that a week," Marissa said.

Nat looked at her. "A week, really? That's even better."

"Yes, the other cook is interested in more work."

"One week it is, then." Nat smiled and handed Richard the list. "I'll go ahead and pay you now, if you'll add it up."

"You make a new list and I'll start totaling this one."

"Do you have some apples?" she asked.

"I just got a couple of bags in today," he smiled.

"Good, I want them."

She and Marissa started working on a list of goods for Tom, adding feed and hay for the horses. Then they browsed the store while the shopkeeper reviewed the lists and did the math. "Is there anything you want?" she asked Marissa.

"No, I think I'm good right now."

"I need your help." Nat browsed through a selection of work shirts. "Maggie's shirts are getting pretty threadbare, and I'd like to get her a couple. What size and color do you think she'd like?"

Marissa smiled and walked over to her. "She likes colors, so I'd say the red and blue. I would think this to be a good fit for her." Marissa held up a shirt.

"Pick out two of each then, please, and add them to our order."

"It wouldn't hurt you to have a few more either."

"Pick out a few for me, too, then." Nat watched Marissa pick out a tan and green shirt for her. "Are you set for clothing?"

"I have plenty," Marissa answered.

"This will take a while to get everything together. Would you mind coming back in the morning?" Richard asked.

"No problem. We'll see you in the morning."

They left the store and Nat looked at Marissa. "Are you hungry?"

"Starving actually. My breakfast is long gone."

"Mine, too. Let's go eat."

They met Tom who was walking into town and they went to the hotel together. Smithy was already waiting for them in the dining room. "I'm glad you're here, the smell is killing me."

The server came out, took their order, and brought a plate of biscuits to get them started.

"Tom here was heading to the gold fields to find his fortune gold mining."

"You were traveling by yourself?"

"Well, not originally. I started out with several others, but they decided to turn back and go home. I traveled the last five days alone until I smelled the smoke from Nat's fireplace."

"He wandered in about half starved," Nat said. "He's been a huge help to me around the cabin and he isn't afraid of hard work. He's decided going to the gold fields is no longer what he wants to do. I'm wondering if you could use him around the store. He's a hard worker and learns quickly."

"Where will he be staying?"

"I'm going to rent Marissa's cabin."

Smithy looked at him sizing him up. "I've already seen how strong you are. If Nat stands by you, I'll give you a shot."

Tom shot out his hand. "Thank you, sir. I promise I won't let you down."

"You'll have to answer to her, if you do, and I wouldn't wish that on anyone."

"Yes, sir, I agree with you on that."

"I'll need to use him from time to time to help with the harvests. Will that be a problem?"

"No, I think I can handle business for a few days alone. Been doing it for years."

"I can start tomorrow."

"The day after will be fine." Smithy chuckled. "You need to get settled into your new home."

Tom grinned. "I'm excited to have my own home."

"How long will you be in town?" Smithy asked Nat.

"I'll get things set up tomorrow, and head back the day after."

"So soon?" He sounded disappointed.

"There's still a ton of work to do. Maybe once your new help gets settled in you can ride out for a visit."

"I'd like that," he answered with a smile. "I really would."

†

Once they finished the hearty steak dinner, the trio walked home with a promise to meet Smithy for lunch the next day. The sun had set and darkness was quickly falling around them when they arrived at the cabin. Tom busied himself starting the fire in the kitchen while Nat enjoyed the night sky view from the front porch with Marissa.

The air cooled quickly and when Marissa shivered, Nat asked, "Are you ready to go inside?"

"Yes, I think we better, it's starting to get cool."

They walked into the bedroom to a warm fire and dressed for bed. Nat extinguished the lantern and reached for Marissa. She snuggled next to Nat talking as the shadows from the fireplace danced upon the wall.

"I hope the next week passes quickly."

"Will you miss me?"

"I have waited months for us to finally be together—I guess I can survive another week."

"What would you have done, if I hadn't wanted to move to the shore?"

"I'd have been terribly disappointed. I'm so thankful you said yes."

"I'd be crazy to not want to live there. It's beautiful and I can wake up next to the woman I love every morning."

"That sounds really good, doesn't it?"

"Yes it does." Nat rolled Marissa onto her back and kissed her deeply. The heat built between them and they loved the night away, finally falling asleep wrapped in one another's arms.

Chapter Twenty-six

The next morning passed too quickly for Nat. Tom had already risen and was in the barn tending the horses when they entered the kitchen. They ate breakfast and Tom turned to Nat. "Would it be easier if we hitched Rusty to the wagon and picked up the supplies?"

"Yes, we can do that. Why don't you get him ready?"

"I'll be back quick then." Tom left the house.

Nat and Marissa walked beside the wagon to town. When they got there, Marissa headed for the hotel while Nat and Tom went to the general store. The shopkeeper, Richard, was arranging their supplies on the front walk when they arrived. He was a small man in stature, but his smile lit up the store when customers arrived.

"You decided to pick them up yourselves?"

"Yes, we did. Tom here needs a good workout this morning."

"I have most of your home goods out here, but you'll need to take the wagon out back for the horse supplies. I packaged your shirts and apples for travel."

"Thanks, I'll be taking those back with me tomorrow."

"Tell Maggie that I'm missing her pies."

"I will. If you'll start loading, I'll go pay and come back to help," she told Tom.

"Take your time. I've got this."

"Oh, to be young and energetic," Richard groaned as he pushed the frame of his spectacles up the bridge of his nose. "Do you want a job, young man?"

"Sorry, but Smithy's already snapped him up," Nat answered, and followed the man inside the store.

"I'll have the big order ready for the young man to pick up next week as promised." Richard walked behind the counter and pulled out a note pad. He turned the pad to her and explained the charges and the credits he had given her for the honey and jelly.

"Your honey has been a big hit, so keep it coming. I added two more cases of jars to the total, in hopes you'd fill them up and bring them on your next visit."

"That shouldn't be a problem. I'll be back in a few weeks. Will you be interested in fresh wild blueberries when they ripen?"

"I'll take all you can bring. Have you been smoking fish?"

"I've got a few."

"I'm pretty sure I could sell some smoked fish. Bring some with you next trip, if you have room, and we'll give it a try."

"What about venison? Would you trade me pound for pound for ham and bacon? I haven't run across a wild boar yet and I do love ham steaks."

"Yes, but I'll tell you what would be a good seller. That would be jerky. Several of the men headed to the gold fields have asked for it, but I don't have the equipment to make it."

"That sounds like an excellent task for Maggie." Nat paid for her purchases and walked outside to help Tom finish loading the supplies. When they pulled the wagon around back, he loaded the bags of grain and bales of hay for the horses.

"Let's take this home and get it settled. By then it will be time for lunch at the hotel."

†

Nat's mouth watered when they walked into the hotel and she smelled chicken frying in the kitchen. Marissa came out to greet them and announce fried chicken, mashed potatoes with gravy, and corn was the lunch of the day.

"I knew it," Nat said. "I can't wait to sink my teeth into your fried chicken. Tom, run over and get Smithy so we can get started."

"Have you gotten a lot done this morning?" Marissa asked.

"We have. All the supplies are in, and I've got several new items the shopkeeper wants me to bring him, so I'll be busier than planned when I get home."

"That will help the time pass quickly."

"Yes, it will," Nat agreed.

"Let me get busy. I'll bring your meals out when Smithy gets here." Marissa walked back into the kitchen.

Tom rushed into the dining room. "He'll be here in a minute."

Nat turned to Tom. "What do you think about going to work for Smithy?"

A huge smile covered his face. "I'm very excited about it. He can teach me so much about business, trapping, and survival."

"That he can." Nat spotted Smithy walking across the dusty road toward the hotel.

"Good morning," Smithy said joining them at the table. "Damn, it smells good in here."

"Yes, it does. Fried chicken dinners are on the way," she told him.

"I sure am going to miss her cooking. It's not fair that you have the two best cooks in town under your roof, you know."

"I'm just lucky like that," Nat answered. "Did Tom tell you she only has to work a one-week notice here? Will you be able to do without Tom for a couple of days to get her moved?"

"It'll be hard, but I think I can make it."

"I'll be sure to send a surprise back for you."

"That makes it sound even better."

Marissa arrived carrying the first of three large platters of food and a pitcher of cold water. "Here you go. Who wants to go first?"

"Tom seems to be drooling the most, so let him get us started," Nat answered.

There was no argument from Tom when she placed the platter of food in front of him. "I'll be right back with the rest."

"Well, go ahead and dig in. You worked hard this morning."

"Did you get everything you needed from the store?"

"We picked it up this morning and we've got Tom set for a few weeks at least. He'll need to cut some firewood, but other than that he'll be in good shape."

"I'll let him go a few days early next week so he can get wood brought in before it gets dark. We'll have a few long days of light left."

Marissa brought the remainder of the platters to the table just as two customers walked in. "I'll join you later if I can," she said, and went to wait on her customers.

"Thanks," Nat watched her for a moment, before her stomach called her attention to the food. "Did Tom tell you Gyp had her pups?"

"No, that's great news. How many?"

"Four, but one was stillborn. Three lived—a silver male and female, and a blue female like mama."

"I'm sorry to hear she lost one. How's she doing?"

"Wonderfully, I think, for her first litter. I'm very proud of her."

"Do you have any plans for the puppies once they are weaned?"

Nat grinned. "Tom here thinks he wants one, but I told him he'd have to ask Gyp."

"Do you think she'd let me have one, too?" he asked excitedly.

"I think she knows you'd give it a good home."

251

"I'd love to have the blue female, just like Gyp."

Nat looked at Tom. "Which would you like?"

He perked up from his meal. "The silver female," he grinned.

"I'll keep you posted on the weaning, but it'll be about two months."

"Just in time to get them house-trained before the weather changes," Smithy said.

"If they are anything like their mama, they will be easy to train."

"That's for sure. Gyp's the smartest dog I've ever met."

†

After lunch, Nat and Tom returned to the cabin to begin preparing the place for the encroaching winter. She and Tom scoured the surrounding woods and felled trees that he could later chop for firewood. Always aware of her surroundings, Nat spotted large hoof prints which led off toward the small creek behind the cabin.

"How are you with hunting?" she asked.

"I love to hunt," he answered. "Why?"

"I've spotted some fresh tracks that should belong to a rather large buck. There is some venison in the smokehouse, but not near enough to feed you through the winter. We've got enough trees felled, so why don't we go hunting?"

"That sounds good to me. The sun will be setting before long, and I bet he'll go to that creek for some water before it's full dark."

"I'd take that bet. Let's go get our rifles and see if we can get that buck."

Marissa had made it home when they returned to the cabin. "I brought leftovers home for dinner, if you two don't mind."

"Not at all, but we're going to see if we can bring down a buck for Tom so he'll have smoked meat for this winter. Would you care to go with us?"

"No. If you don't mind, I'll stay here and start planning for the move. I need to get an idea of what I'll take and what stays behind."

"That's good. We'll see you soon."

Nat took her rifle from above the hearth and handed Tom the gun that had once belonged to Marissa's husband, James. "Let's go and do this."

Tom smiled as she handed him the rifle, and he loaded the gun with the shells she gave him. They left the cabin and stopped by the barn to pick up a length of rope to take with them. As they headed back down the trail, deeper into the woods, Nat breathed in deeply, enjoying the fragrance of the woods. The scent of pine and evergreens filled the air and her eyes rose to the sky when she heard a hawk calling to its mate.

She had become accustomed to the smell of salt in the air over the past weeks, and as they moved deeper into the woods, the aroma of pure forest reminded her of her life with her father. So much had changed for her in the past year. A part of her missed the freedom of living in the woods as she trapped along the border, but her longing to be with Marissa and to finally have a solid roof over her head outweighed the longing. The cabin at the shore would provide both those needs. A home for them while still allowing her to hunt, trap, and harvest seafood from the Sound. It was the perfect solution. The best of both worlds, she was thinking, when she heard movement ahead of them. They had reached the small path that led to the creek and she placed her hand on Tom's arm to stop him in his tracks.

Fifty yards ahead of them, she spied a large buck picking his way through the woods toward the creek. As they had expected, he was heading for the water for a cool drink after a long day of foraging. They were downwind of the buck, so there was little fear of him catching their scent, but the buck would have excellent hearing. She spoke very softly to Tom. "Let him get as close to the creek as possible without moving out of range and then take him."

Tom nodded his understanding, and as quietly as possible, he pulled back the hammer on the rifle. A soft click filled the air, but went undetected. The buck's movements masked the sound, leaving him unaware they were stalking him.

Seconds ticked by slowly as Nat watched Tom's concentration. She could see his pulse beating rapidly in his neck as his excitement grew, watching the buck's approach. She glanced back at the buck who was five feet from the creek. She was forming the words to speak, when she heard the shot ring out. The smell of spent gunpowder filled her nose and she turned in time to see the buck stumble and fall to the ground.

"Great shot. Let's go get your buck."

Tom lowered the rifle and walked with her to the buck. It was a clean shot, and he had been dead when he hit the ground. Nat knelt beside the animal. "Thank you for giving your life to us, my brother, to keep us fed during the winter to come." Having thanked the animal for his sacrifice, Nat stood and said to Tom, "Tie his back legs with one end of the rope, and we'll pull him off the ground using this branch."

She watched and provided guidance where needed while he hoisted the carcass from the ground. It was evident that Tom had prepared a carcass before in the way he handled his knife, slashing the throat to drain the blood, and splitting the belly to eviscerate the buck. While he completed this task, Nat located a long tree branch for them to use in carrying the buck to the cabin.

"Tuck the heart and liver back inside the cavity once we lower him to the ground and tie his front hooves together. Then we will run the branch between his legs and carry him back to the cabin."

Tom followed her instructions perfectly and soon they were on the way back to the cabin. Once they arrived, she showed him where to hang the buck, and he began skinning the carcass as she went inside to check on Marissa.

Not finding Marissa in the front part of the house when she went inside, Nat looked in the bedroom. Marissa was sitting on the edge of the bed, her hands covering her eyes, weeping. Nat rushed to her side and knelt in front of her. "What's wrong, my love?"

Marissa seemed startled at the sound of Nat's voice and quickly wiped the tears from her eyes. "I'm sorry, I was just thinking about leaving this place. It's been a good home for me and I've got many memories here."

"Are you doubting your decision to move to the shore?"

Marissa grabbed Nat's hands and brought them to her lips. "Never, I look forward to starting a new life with you. I'm just being a bit melancholy."

"I guess that's to be expected." Nat pulled her to her feet and into a gentle embrace. She kissed her softly. "I understand if you need more time here. I'm not going anywhere."

"I can't get to you fast enough to suit me," Marissa said. "Where's Tom?"

"He's out in the yard, dressing the buck he killed."

"Are you going to help him?"

"Yes, but I needed to get some salt, and look in on you first."

"I'm fine, really," Marissa answered. "I'll start warming up dinner to be ready when you two finish."

"Thank you."

"Thanks for being patient with me."

"This is a big change for you. Take whatever time you need. There's no need to rush, when we have the rest of our lives together." Nat moved to the pantry to pick out a small bag of salt. "It shouldn't take us long to prepare the meat for smoking." She kissed Marissa again. "See you soon."

✝

Tom had removed the buck's head and was nearly finished skinning when Nat returned. "Smithy would love that head. He'll take the skin, too, unless you would rather Maggie make you some breeches from the hide."

"Maggie would do that?"

"She makes the best breeches in the area. She might get two pair out of that monster."

"I'd like that."

Together they butchered the buck and prepared the meat for smoking. "What is the best way to use the heart and liver?" Tom asked.

"The heart is best if cubed and used in a stew. The liver you want to slice thin, and if you can get your hands on some fresh wild onion, you can slow-fry them together. It smells to high heaven, but it's a good source of iron to keep you strong."

"That's good to know."

"Hunt and skin what you can. Smithy will take any pelt, and you can use that money to supplement your smoked venison with ham or bacon from the general store. Also, try to keep a few eggs in stock. They are good for protein. You're not done growing yet."

"I hope I can survive without you to teach me."

"There will be plenty time for you to learn from me, and you'll find Smithy a great resource, so if you have questions, ask him."

"I can't thank you enough for all that you've done for me, and talking me out of getting my fool-self killed in the gold fields."

"I'll get plenty of labor out of you for payment." Nat slapped him on the back. "Are you ready to eat?"

"I'm always ready to eat."

"Let's go see what Marissa has heated up for us."

Marissa was setting the table when they walked in. "Get washed up and grab a fresh bucket of water. Then we'll be ready to eat."

Tom followed Nat to the pump and filled the bucket when they had finished washing the blood from their hands and arms. Marissa was placing a fresh-baked cherry pie on the table when they returned.

"Oh my, that looks good." Nat took a seat.

"I baked an extra one today to bring home."

Nat smiled at Marissa. "A very fine treat after a good day's work."

"When will you be heading home tomorrow?"

"I'll leave after you go to work at the hotel," she answered. "I've got several new projects to start on for the shopkeeper. I'm hoping I can stay busy so the time will pass quickly."

"I'll be home before you know it."

"I'm going to miss you two," Tom said.

"You're welcome to visit any time you can."

"You can count on that. Smithy says we work six days a week, but I can leave early on Saturday if I'm going out to visit."

"After the fall rush of trappers trying to beat the weather, business will slow down. You will be free to visit longer if you're willing to fight the cold and snow."

"That would be nice. How do you expect the winter to be at the shore?"

"The winds will be cold, and the rains will be miserable, but I expect the snow at a minimum around the cabin."

"Do you have enough wood cut?"

"Not near enough, which is another reason I need to be back soon. Fall doesn't last long here, and the summer is coming to a close."

"If you will fell as many trees as you need, I will cut as much as I can when I bring Marissa home while she and Maggie unload. I'll have a full day to cut with you and I reckon we can get a good pile growing for you."

"I'd like to cut a path to the lake, so maybe I can use Quincy to bring the downed trees to the clearing. Between projects, I can trim off the branches and stack them for the smokehouse."

"Save some work for me," Marissa added.

"No worries, there will be plenty to do."

"What will you do when the snow comes?" Tom asked.

"I'll still venture out to hunt for fresh meat when possible. Marissa and Maggie will be working on projects used for bartering in the spring." She paused for a second. "I hope to bring down several moose and deer quickly when I return, and Maggie will use the pelts to sew new breeches during the snowy days. The small antlers we can slice for her to use for buttons after holes are drilled."

"You seem to have it all planned out."

"Yes, but there are so many things that we hadn't planned for that could go wrong. We'll need to stay alert and shift plans as needed."

"I reckon you'll know more after the first winter."

"That we will, my friend."

†

Nat snuggled into Marissa, waking her early the next morning before the sun rose. Marissa kissed her lover awake and they made love as the morning broke. "I will miss you," Nat told her.

"I will be there as fast as I can."

"I know, but any day without you is torture for me."

"Just think of it this way. When I move we will have all those days ahead of us. Heck, you might be tired of me after the winter."

"I doubt I could ever tire of you, my love."

"You better stop before I cry."

Nat pulled her close and held her for several minutes. "Do you want me to cook breakfast?"

"No, you get your roll packed for the trip home. We have biscuits left over. I thought I'd whip up some gravy and a few of the linked sausages. That should be enough to hold you until you make it home."

"Yes, it will." Nat tossed back the covers and stepped into her breeches. "I'll get the fire stoked, and then pack."

Marissa washed her face and slipped into a clean dress. "I'll start cooking." She kissed Nat one last time in the privacy of their bedroom. Marissa rushed from the room.

Nat could see that Marissa was holding back her tears. She sighed and pulled on her work shirt and fastened her suspenders before stepping outside to bring in wood to stoke the fire. She carried extra to store in the bedroom so Marissa would not have to carry in wood later. She finished packing her roll and walked to the barn to saddle Hardy. Tom was already awake and was in the barn tending to the animals.

"I fed Hardy a bucket of oats for your journey home."

"Thanks, I know he enjoyed those." She led Hardy from the stall and brushed his coat before slipping the saddle blanket on his back and then the saddle. She bridled him and they walked together to the front yard where she tied him to the hitching post. "Breakfast will be ready soon."

"I need to get Marissa to teach me how to make her biscuits," Tom said, walking into the cabin with Nat.

"I'm sure she would teach you."

"Teach him what?" Marissa asked from the kitchen.

"How to make your biscuits." Nat grinned.

"We can do that tonight." She placed a frying pan with sausage in the fireplace.

"There you are. You have a week to practice." Marissa looked at Tom.

"I think I can learn in that amount of time." He grinned.

"I think so, too and I can teach you a few other basics."

"I'd appreciate that. My cooking skills aren't that good. I'd get tired of beans real quick."

"That sounds like someone else I know." She shot Nat a wink. "Whatever you do, don't try her camp stew."

"I survived many months a year eating my own cooking in the woods," Nat said in her defense.

"When she got back she was twenty pounds lighter, too."

"That was from all the hard work."

"The first time we met, I thought it was going to take a side of beef to fill her belly."

"That is still one of the best steaks I've ever eaten."

Marissa placed a plate of biscuits on the table and a jar of warm gravy. "You can start with these and the sausage will be ready soon."

Nat and Tom broke open two of the large biscuits and poured the warm gravy over them. The aroma of sausage filled the cabin while they ate. When Marissa brought the frying pan to the table and split the sausages between the three plates, Nat noticed Marissa's plate was short.

"Are you cutting back?" Nat asked.

"There's plenty, but I don't need as much as the two of you," Marissa answered.

"Thanks for a good breakfast," Tom said.

"You're welcome."

When the dishes were clean, Marissa and Nat walked outside together. Tom had already left for town, giving them a few minutes alone together. "May I offer you a ride to town ma'am?"

"Thanks, but the sooner you get home the better. I miss you already."

Nat took her in her arms and held her close. "Just remember how much I love you."

"I love you, too." Marissa was clearly struggling to hold back her tears.

Nat nodded and mounted Hardy as Marissa started the short walk to town. She watched until Marissa disappeared from view and turned Hardy toward the road to the south. "Let's go home." She nudged his flanks, urging him forward.

Chapter Twenty-seven

Traveling alone and without a wagon, Nat knew she would make good time and hoped to be home by mid-morning. Hardy settled into a smooth canter and she became lost in her thoughts as the miles disappeared behind them.

Nat smelled the smoke from the wash pot as she grew closer to the cabin. She began catching glimpses of Maggie working in the garden and Gyp stretched out by the smokehouse with her puppies sleeping soundly beside her. Gyp raised her head, let out a sharp yip, and ran to greet Nat.

Nat dismounted and knelt to welcome Gyp, who seemed like her old playful self now that she had whelped.

"Hey there, mama." She hugged her canine friend close. "How are those pups of yours?" she asked while walking into the yard.

"Welcome back," Maggie hollered from the garden.

"Thanks, it's good to be home. Come take a break while I catch you up on the news from town." Nat untied the two bags of apples Maggie had asked for and handed them to her.

Maggie smiled. "I'm glad you remembered." She took the bags, set them on the porch, and pumped two cups of water.

"Richard plans to keep us busy this fall. He has requested we make jerky from moose and deer to sell to the men traveling to the gold fields, and promises to supply the materials and trade us pound for pound for ham and bacon. He also wants to try selling dried fish, too."

"That sounds like a good deal. I can use the hides for breeches if you have no other plans for them."

"That's what I was thinking, too. He also wants as much jelly, honey, and all the berries we can gather, and will be adding extra cases of jars and bags of sugar for the jelly."

"You better get to hunting then."

"I thought I'd go out today and see if I can run up a moose. I'm also going to down some trees. When Tom brings Marissa in a week, he will help me cut more firewood."

"A week? That's good news."

"The woman that only worked the afternoons wanted more hours, so Marissa's leaving worked out well."

Gyp was sitting at Nat's feet until the puppies started to wake and whine. She trotted over to nurse them.

"How are they doing?"

"Well, they should have their eyes open in a few days. They've been eating well and stumbling around the inside of the cabin. I thought it would be nice to let them enjoy the sunshine this morning while I tended the garden."

"How are things growing?"

"Doing well. I finished digging out the troughs, too, and they work well."

Nat grinned. "I'm getting pretty ripe, so I'll need a bath soon. We can try out the drainage system completely then."

"Maybe tonight after dinner. What would you like to eat?"

"I'll bring up some clams if you'll make chowder, and fry bread, unless there is something else you want."

"No, that sounds good. I will fix that while I get a pie ready to cook."

Nat grinned. "Let me get Hardy settled in and then I'll get the clams."

"Would you like some ham biscuits before you go?"

"I'll take one with me when I go hunting. You can fill a canteen for me, too?" She handed her empty canteen to Maggie.

Nat took Hardy to the barn, unsaddled him, and brushed him down. Then after filling his feed and hay bins she filled the water troughs with fresh water. She took her rifle out of the sheath and placed it across her shoulder before walking to the cabin. After placing the rifle by the door, she picked up a bucket and a rake, heading to the shore. Gyp stood to follow her, but Nat shook her head. "You need to stay with the pups."

"Oh go ahead and take her," Maggie called from the back door. "I'll carry the pups inside to keep an eye on them. She's missed you."

"All right, let's go then, girl." Gyp rushed to her.

†

Nat searched a spot they hadn't harvested lately and the clams were large and plentiful. It didn't take her long to fill the bucket and head back up the trail. Gyp chased the surf and barked to alert Nat to the presence of a group of whales passing by on their journey south. The huge creatures amazed Nat and she stood to watch them pass, wondering where they were heading. When she reached the cabin, she covered the clams in fresh cold water and placed the bucket on the porch.

Maggie must have heard her return because she arrived next to her with a biscuit filled with a thick slice of ham. "If I hear a shot, do you want me to get Quincy ready for you?"

"Yes, that would be a big help. Marissa is going to teach Tom how to make biscuits tonight." She was smiling at the thought of her lover. "I bet he'll never make them this good." She took a bite and let out a sigh.

"Did things go well in town?"

"Yes, he started with Smithy today, and understands what he needs to get done before winter hits."

"That's good. I'm going to miss having him around though."

"I think you'll be seeing a good bit of him. He seems to really like it here, too."

"Maybe one day he will have a place of his own out here." Maggie sat down on the steps and began to prepare the clams for boiling.

"Maybe so. Hopefully I'll see you soon." Nat placed the canteen strap over her head and picked up the rifle.

"Good luck," Maggie called, watching her go. Gyp whined, but sat beside Maggie, seeming to understand it was her time to stay at home.

Nat cleared the yard and began the short walk to the lake, hoping a large bull would come for a drink in the later afternoon. She reached a small hilltop and sat with her back propped against a tree. The afternoon sun on her skin felt good. Her eyes searched the surrounding area for game, and she saw several rabbits making their way to the lake for a quick drink, nervously watching for any signs of a predator. They drank, then scurried back into the dense brush. Several young does also arrived to drink, and the lake filled with waterfowl of all types. A smile grew on her face. She had made a good decision to build a homestead here, where the land, Sound, and wildlife would keep her well fed and provide the items she needed to barter.

She was enjoying the feel of Marissa wrapped in her arms in her mind when the approach of a larger beast alerted her. She waited for several moments to get a glimpse of the animal that approached, and she felt her heart race when a huge bull moose stepped into a clearing. He was in range of her rifle and she lifted it to her shoulder and took aim. She took a deep breath before her finger gently squeezed the trigger and the shot echoed around the lake. The moose took two steps and fell to his knees, then keeled over on his side.

Maggie heard the shot ring out, and with a smile, she left the porch to get Quincy rigged to pull the small wagon. She was just finished hitching him to the wagon when Nat came rushing back.

"I didn't take something into consideration."

"What's that?"

"The size of a bull moose." She chuckled. "I need your help to get him into the wagon."

"That's no problem. Start back and I'll put Gyp in the house with the pups and meet you at the lake."

"Bring a sharp knife and we'll bleed and gut him there to reduce some of the weight on Quincy."

Maggie nodded and watched Nat lead Quincy down to the lake before heading back to the cabin.

The bull was still warm when Nat began processing the meat. Several minutes later, Maggie arrived.

"He is a big one."

Nat took the large knife from Maggie. She removed the still warm heart and liver, and handed them to Maggie to place in the back of the wagon. "This large rack will probably weigh fifty pounds or more."

"Smithy is going to love this one," Maggie said. "He'll be perfect for mounting."

"He's a prime specimen. Probably six hundred pounds of meat." Nat ran a hand over the moose, assessing it. "Let's get him on the wagon and I'll use Hardy to pull him up for skinning and butchering."

They worked together to wrestle the carcass onto the wagon. Breathing hard, Nat reached for the canteen, offered Maggie a drink, and then took a long drink, too. "Let's go home, Quincy." She took his lead and they all headed for home.

When they returned, Maggie walked to the cabin to let Gyp outside and to check on the cooking chowder.

Nat used Hardy's strength to hoist the moose in the air for processing. Once done, she returned Hardy to the barn and placed a feedbag on Quincy, leaving him hitched to the wagon. She removed the hide and draped it across the wagon for later processing. She carefully quartered the carcass, removing large sections of meat to cut into slices for making jerky.

Maggie returned just as Nat cut the first of the large roasts. She handed it to Maggie to carry to the pump to rinse before taking it inside to begin slicing it in thick strips. Later, once all the meat was processed and sliced, they would soak it in a special marinade and then season it with salt and pepper before placing it in the smokehouse to be made into jerky.

They took a short break to eat a meal of chowder and fry bread before returning to the job at hand, which lasted late into the night. After placing the last of the meat in the smokehouse, and tending to the animals, they washed up at the pump before walking inside together.

Nat sank down into a chair with a loud sigh. "I don't know about you, but I'm whipped."

"You've had a long, busy day. Why don't you turn in and I'll finish up here?"

"I can help." Nat stood.

Maggie chuckled. "You're like a bull in the kitchen. It will be faster and easier for me to do it alone."

"I guess you're right. I'll turn in and see you in the morning." Nat started to walk to the bedroom before stopping and turning back to Maggie. "Thanks for your help. We did good work today."

"Yes, we did." Maggie smiled. "Sleep well, my friend."

"You too. Good night." In the bedroom, Nat slipped out of her clothing and barely made it to the bed before the exhaustion took her for the night.

Chapter Twenty-eight

Nat spent the next morning cutting down trees. With Quincy's help, she dragged them into the clearing while Maggie used the hatchet to trim the smaller branches. She made a sizeable pile for the smokehouse and laughed at Gyp who took small branches in her mouth and dragged them behind her to help. The pups were curled up in the bed Maggie carried out to the porch, dozing in the morning sun. By lunchtime, they had a dozen large trees trimmed and ready to cut into firewood. That would keep Tom and Nat busy all day when he brought Marissa home.

"What do you want for supper tonight?" Nat asked after they finished off the chowder and fry bread.

"I was thinking I could clean out the wash pot for a seafood boil if you will harvest a few crabs and some shrimp later today."

"That sounds wonderful. I wanted to return to the lake and see if I can get us another goose or two. I thought they'd make a nice addition to the smokehouse."

"I could use the extra feathers, too. I meant to ask you last night if you have plans for the moose hide?"

Nat sensed that Maggie had something in mind for the hide. "Not really. What do you have in mind?" Her eyes instinctively traveled to the hide they had stretched and nailed onto the outer barn wall for drying.

"Since it seems young Tom will be spending some time out here with us, I thought it would be nice if we made him a folding cot to sleep on instead of the cold floor. We could use the hide and some young saplings to make it, and I'll use the goose feathers to make him a pillow."

Nat smiled. "You're always thinking of others, aren't you?"

"Well, he works hard, and I know how uncomfortable a cold floor can get."

"Yes, it does. Are you going down for berries later?"

"Yes. I thought I'd pick the ripe ones."

"I'll go with you then and see if I can get at least one goose. They will scatter at the sound of a shot, so I'll come back and go to the beach to catch supper, and then loop back around to see if I can get another goose. They should have settled back on the lake by then."

"That's a good plan. I'll pick some berries and prepare the goose breasts for the smokehouse. I'd like to use the rest for a stew for Gyp."

"Good idea. She needs the extra protein right now," Nat agreed. "I plan to check traps today, too, so I may be able to add some beaver meat to that stew."

"That would be good."

"I'd better get started then." Nat drained her cup.

"I'll wait here until you get back with a goose, and process it before picking berries."

Nat stood and looked at Gyp. "You ready for a swim?"

Gyp jumped to her feet and rushed to the back door. Nat chuckled. "I guess her answer is *yes*."

"I reckon so." Maggie was laughing. "Hurry back."

"This shouldn't take long. Let's go, little mama."

✝

Nat noticed a crispness in the air as she walked to the lake. Fall would be here soon and hot on its heels would be winter. She was anxious to see what winter would hold for them and hoped she would be prepared to meet the uncertain winter challenge at the shore. The half-day trip to town would likely take longer due to wet and muddy conditions, so trips to town for supplies would be minimal during the winter season. She wasn't concerned about feeding Marissa and Maggie, for there was a healthy amount stored in the smokehouse already, and she could trade with the shopkeeper for bacon, ham, and other supplies to keep them fed. She worried about the animals' survival the most, and wondered if it wouldn't be smarter to send Rusty and Quincy back to town with Tom. The cabin was closer to town, and he would have easier access to feed during the winter months. She would have to give this more thought in the coming weeks and make a decision.

She reached the clearing and saw a large flock of geese on the far side of the lake.

"Let's get us a bird." Gyp licked her lips and followed Nat quietly around the lake until they were close enough for a shot. Nat lifted the rifle to her shoulder and took aim on a large bird. The crack echoed and the waterfowl took flight from the lake in a noisy explosion of flapping wings and cries of panic. The bird she shot was floating twenty feet from shore. "Go get our bird." Gyp ran into the lake and swam to the bird.

Nat watched with pride when Gyp swam to the bird and placed the neck in her mouth before turning and swimming to shore.

"Good girl." Gyp shook the water from her coat, giving Nat an unexpected shower of lake water. She took the bird from Gyp's mouth and carried it by the feet back to the cabin.

"He's a beauty." Maggie handed Nat a cup of cold water."

Nat nodded and drained the water before picking up two buckets. "Let's go, Gyp."

Gyp hesitated and looked toward the cabin. "Go check on your babies. I'll be back shortly."

She walked down to the pool and placed her buckets on the sand, pulled her boots and socks off, and then rolled her breeches to her knees. The water was refreshingly cool as she waded into the first of the pools. There were several large fish swimming in the shallow waters that reminded her that the shopkeeper also wanted smoked fish. She would come back later for the fish after she checked her traps and found a second goose. Nat filled a bucket with shrimp and placed crabs in another bucket before moving to the next pool. She placed several crabs in her bucket, thinking that they would not be around much longer. Once the seasons changed, the crabs would move to deeper waters. They would miss the sweet tasting meat, but Nat would harvest as many as possible, to store them in one of the barrels on the back porch. They wouldn't survive the winter, but she was sure they'd be gone by the time the cold temperatures and rain arrived.

She picked up the other bucket and walked to the pulley line, fastening the buckets to clips to hold them in place. She picked up her boots and rifle to start back up the hill and Gyp came racing toward her.

She dropped her boots on the porch and placed her rifle against the railing, then went to pull the buckets up from the shore. She smiled seeing that her system worked perfectly.

Maggie was almost finished plucking the feathers from the large bird when Nat carried the buckets to the back of the cabin. She peered inside and looked up at Nat. "You did well."

"We won't starve tonight." Nat sat on the steps for a short break after rinsing the salt water from her feet and pouring a cup to drink. "I was reminded that the shopkeeper wants all the smoked fish we can bring him when I saw the fish in the pool."

"Those are probably the easiest to process," Maggie said. "Don't worry over those."

"I was thinking we may need a second smokehouse though."

"That may be a good thing. We could build it on the other side of the chicken coop, so it would get warmth from both sides."

"I hadn't thought of that! Maggie, you're a genius."

"Just practical."

"I'll send an order for lumber back with Tom when he comes out later this week. That will give him a good reason to visit again, to deliver the wood and help build a new smokehouse." Nat finished the water and walked through the cabin to get her boots and rifle. "Are you ready for another goose?"

"I will be by the time you return." Maggie nodded and smiled.

Maggie watched Nat and Gyp disappear and took the breast meat into the cabin to season it before carrying it to the smokehouse. She hung the meat and turned the jerky on the drying racks. There was room still for several dozen fish on the higher racks. She would get Gyp's stew started and walk to the shore while Nat was gone checking her traps. She reasoned that Nat would have walked many miles by the time she returned, and would probably welcome a rest by then. She left the smokehouse and carried the drumsticks and wings into the cabin to start the stew.

Nat noticed several fresh tracks leading to the lake that were too large for a buck and knew there were only moose in the area. She would finish today's work and give the jerky another day to dry before thinking about taking another moose. She was pleased, though, with the plethora of game in the area.

She and Gyp stalked a nervous flock of geese. When Nat took the shot, Gyp flew into the water to retrieve the bird.

"We're getting good at this," she told Gyp when she returned with the bird. "Thanks, girl," she praised when Gyp dropped the bird at her feet.

†

Marissa was peeling apples when she heard the clunk of Tom's boots on the front porch. The door opened and he walked inside.

"Hey."

"How was your day?" Marissa asked.

"Fine. I think I moved every stack of pelts in the store at least once today. Smithy is getting ready to send an order down south, so we've been sorting. Tomorrow, the wagon will arrive and we'll load it to go to the port for shipment."

"You better get a good night's sleep then. I've got a venison roast cooking. Do you feel up to trying biscuits on your own tonight?"

"I think I can do that. Let me wash up a bit first."

"Take your time." Marissa let a little grin crease her lips.

"I wonder what Nat and Maggie did today," he asked when he walked back into the kitchen.

"Hunting and preparing for winter I would assume."

"She's something else." Tom pulled out a bag of flour.

"Yes, she is." Marissa dropped the last peeled apple into the bowl and dumped the peelings into the fireplace.

†

"Do you really need to check your traps today?" Maggie asked.

"It's not critical. What do you need?"

"I turned the jerky today and there's probably enough room for a couple dozen fish in the smokehouse. I thought that maybe we could go fishing before I cook supper. You've already done a lot of physical labor the last two days so you deserve some time off."

"Are you saying I need some fun?"

"Yeah, something like that." Maggie grinned. "You keep up this pace and I'll be needing to make you a new pair of boots."

"You finish the bird and I'll make us some spears." Nat walked to the brush pile for a few straight limbs and sat beside Maggie, using her knife to sharpen the ends into points.

When she finished plucking the feathers and butchering the goose, Maggie handed the breasts to Nat. "Will you rinse these, season them, and hang them in the smokehouse while I clean up?"

"Sure thing," Nat took the two large breasts.

When she finished in the smokehouse, Nat returned to the porch where Maggie was waiting for her, "You're right about the smokehouse. Let's fill it up."

"Should we leave our boots here?"

"Would make sense. That way we don't have to carry them back too."

They removed their boots and socks, leaving them on the back steps. After rolling their pants up, they picked up the spears and a bucket and walked to the shore. "If you want to spear them, I'll get them ready for the smokehouse and use the remains to bait the pools for crab."

Nat nodded and walked to the first pool with the four spears she had made. She took aim and speared a large fish in the head. When Nat lifted the spear, the fish struggled a few seconds and then collapsed. She planted the unsharpened end of the spear in the sand, picked up another spear, and repeated the process. When all four had fish on them, she carried them to the shore where Maggie waited. Nat shook the spears until the fish tumbled onto the packed sand.

"I'll get more if you'll start with these."

They repeated the process until Nat had cleared the pool of the largest salmon and rockfish, and then she moved to the next. In the end, they had almost two dozen large fish, mostly chinook salmon that were quite a load to carry back up the hill.

Once back at the house, they worked together to rinse the fish, season them in the smokehouse, and place them on the racks.

Nat sat down on the porch steps. "Now, I'm ready for a break."

"Well deserved, too, my friend. Why don't you relax and do some carving while I prepare some dinner for us?"

"You'll get no argument from me." Nat got up and walked inside for her knife and the carving she was working on.

"Do you know what it is yet?" Maggie asked.

"It will be a whale when I'm finished."

"That will be nice." Maggie added some brush to the wash pot fire to get the water boiling. She poured in some seasoning into the cook pot and turned to Nat. "Do you want to start with the shrimp?"

"That's fine."

Maggie took the shrimp from the bucket and dropped them into the cook pot.

"How did you get that wash pot off there by yourself?"

"I'm stronger than you think."

"I reckon so." Nat grinned and continued whittling.

Maggie entered the house to stir the stew she was cooking for Gyp. She picked up a clean bowl, and a large dipper to remove the shrimp when they finished cooking. When the shrimp were cooked, Maggie put them in the bowl, brought them over, and sat down next to Nat. They peeled the shrimp and feasted in relative silence, except for the soft moans that escaped Nat as she took bites of the tasty treat.

"I thought I had truly lived until I found seafood."

"It does add some variety from what you can hunt and kill. It's satisfying, too."

The last of the shrimp disappeared and Nat looked at Maggie. "Do you want me to melt some butter inside when you drop the crabs in the pot?"

"There should be some keeping warm on the hearth." Maggie smiled.

"I should have known you'd be a step ahead of me." Nat picked up the bucket of shrimp husks, carried them to the garden, and took a few minutes to inspect the growing crops. The rich soil and Maggie's tending had several of the crops growing quickly, and she knew there would be fresh vegetables on the table in the coming months. She rinsed out the bucket and placed it on the porch as Maggie dropped the crabs into the boiling water.

Nat entered the cabin and stopped at the doorway to her room to see Gyp nursing the pups. "You're such a good mama," she said, continuing to the hearth to retrieve the melted butter and a small hammer to use in cracking the claws. The sweet, tender meat in the claws had quickly become her favorite.

Maggie scooped out the four large crabs from the cook pot and placed them in the bucket to cool. She carried them to the cabin porch and placed the bucket between them. Nat reached to pick up one of the steamy creatures.

"You'd better let them cool for a few minutes," Maggie warned.

"This is torture." Nat groaned, her mouthwatering as she looked at the brilliant red of the cooked crabs.

"Go take a bowl of the stew out for Gyp then and let it cool. By the time you get back, it should be safe to pick up a crab."

Nat looked longingly at the crabs then nodded. The shrimp had been tasty, but the true delicacy of the night's meal was the crab. She walked back into the cabin and took Gyp's bowl, breaking a biscuit into pieces before dipping out some of the stew Maggie had cooked. The gravy soaked into the biscuit and Nat used her knife to cut the meat into smaller pieces. She carried the bowl onto the back porch, placed it beside her chair, and took her seat beside Maggie.

"Now?"

"Yes, but be careful of the water. It may still be hot."

Nat reached in and pulled out a steaming crab. "Damn, it's still too hot to touch." She dropped it on the makeshift table between them.

"One would think you hadn't eaten all day the way you're acting."

"I just can't wait to sink my teeth into that crab."

Maggie chuckled and shook her head. "I'll check the pools in the morning and see if I can collect some for the barrels. I'm sure Tom and Marissa would like some before the crab move to warmer waters."

"I'll keep an eye on the pools, too." Nat carefully picked up the crab and broke the legs apart to help it cool. Nat took the small hammer to crack open the thicker shell of the claws. She was becoming proficient in the art of eating crab. She pulled out another crab to cool. She used her knife to cut through the shell and groaned when the sweet meat came into view after she peeled the shell open.

"You're getting really good at that."

Nat looked up when Maggie made the comment. "I had a good teacher. Dig in."

"You first." Maggie pointed to the bowl of drawn butter.

Nat didn't need a second invitation and picked up the chunk of meat, dipped it into the butter, and took a bite. A loud moan followed. "I think this is the best yet."

Maggie took a bite and nodded. "I have to agree with you there. These are especially sweet."

As they finished the last of the crab, Gyp joined them on the porch to eat her meal. The sun was nearly beyond the horizon when she finished, and Nat followed the line of Gyp's view to see the silver wolf at the edge of the forest.

"Go see him and tell him about the pups," she told Gyp, who bounded off the edge of the porch and disappeared into the forest.

They watched as she disappeared and Maggie turned to Nat. "She's turned into a good mother."

"Yes, she has. I couldn't be prouder. You know, both Tom and Smithy have asked for a pup, but I want you to have first pick of the litter."

Maggie smiled. "I was hoping I could have one. I've taken a shine to the silver male pup. I thought I'd call him Luna."

"That's a great name. They should have their eyes open soon, and then I think we'll all have our hands full."

"You are probably right. They are already starting to wander about."

"Should we take advantage of Gyp being gone to go play with them a bit?"

"I thought you'd never ask." She dropped the shells in the bucket. "I'll take care of these later."

They went inside and sprawled out on the bedroom floor playing with the puppies. They laughed at the pups playing, growling, and wrestling together. When they tired, Nat picked up two, and Maggie picked up Luna, and kept them warm until they fell asleep.

Carefully placing the pups into the bed, Nat turned to reach for Luna. Maggie kissed the pup's head and handed him to Nat to snuggle in with his siblings. "I think we should get some sleep, too. That danged rooster will have us awake at the crack of dawn."

Nat chuckled. "Yes, he will. I'm really reconsidering putting him in your cook pot."

"He'd probably be too tough to eat." Maggie stood. "Will you check your traps in the morning?"

"Yes, I thought I'd do that first and then collect some honey."

"I thought I'd pick some more berries and make more jelly, unless there is something else you'd rather I do."

"That would be good. Check our jerky and see how it's coming. If it's close to being done, I'll try for another moose or a buck tomorrow."

"I'll see if I can find some saplings to use for Tom's cot, and make him a pillow while the berries are cooking down."

"How do you suggest we attach the hide?"

"I thought we could double it and then use some short nails to attach it to the saplings," Maggie answered.

"When I get done with the honey, I'll chop the saplings you pick out and get them ready. Maybe tonight we can work on the base. We need to boil that hide to get the musky scent out of it and let it dry."

"I'll put it on to boil when you check the traps, and then I'll go pick berries."

"That should keep us busy tomorrow, especially if I take down a moose or buck."

"I'll see you in the morning, then." Maggie left the room. She heard Gyp scratching at the back door and opened it to let her in then watched as she trotted into the bedroom and curled around her pups.

"Goodnight," she said, passing the room.

"Sleep well, my friend," Nat answered.

Chapter Twenty-nine

Nat and Maggie stayed busy, and the rest of the week passed quickly. They had slain another moose and processed the meat into strips of jerky, keeping back several large roasts to smoke for themselves. Cases of honey and jelly were also ready to send to town to the shopkeeper. Nat would send these back with Tom along with the two moose heads and several additional antler racks for Smithy.

When Saturday morning arrived, Nat paced nervously waiting for Tom and Marissa to arrive with the wagon. She had felled another dozen trees and had blazed a nice trail down to the lake, making it easier for her to take Quincy and the small wagon down to carry back the items they gathered.

"I think I'll go check the pools for crab and dig two buckets of clams if you'll send some chowder back with Tom. We can have fried shrimp and crab for dinner if you'd like."

The mention of crab was all it took to get Maggie focused. "That sounds good. Give me a whistle when you get the buckets on the line and I'll pull them up and empty them before sending them back down."

Nat rushed to remove her boots and socks and then hurried down to the beach. She quickly filled three buckets with crabs and hooked them to the line and gave a whistle for Maggie. Then she started digging the clams. She had two buckets filled when Maggie sent the empty buckets down, so she exchanged them and went to the pools for shrimp. Spying several large fish, she decided to spear a few to fry after the shrimp. Tonight they would feast after a hard afternoon of work. She carried the speared fish up the hill and joined Maggie on the porch.

"You must be hungry already." Maggie took the fish from Nat.

"I have a plan. If the rest of you get full on fish and shrimp, then that leaves more crab for me."

Maggie shook her head and laughed. "I've heard it all now."

Nat smiled back at her and shelled the boiled clams while Maggie cleaned and fileted the fish. "This will make some fine eating with the shrimp and crabs."

They had just finished cleaning the shrimp when the jingle of metal caught their attention. Nat's head whipped up at the sound. She reached for her socks and boots, and hurriedly put them on.

"She's here."

Gyp raced off the porch. Nat barely waited for Maggie to step off the porch before heading down the trail. She was eager to see Marissa and Tom, and she met them at the base of the trail.

"Welcome home." Nat smiled at Marissa. "I thought you'd never get here."

"She had us up way before dawn and I thought we'd made good time." Tom frowned, somewhat confused by Nat's statement.

"You did good, Tom," Maggie said. "Nat just doesn't wait well."

He smiled and pulled Rusty to a stop.

Marissa climbed down into Nat's arms for a warm embrace.

Maggie smiled and took Rusty by his halter. "Let's take the wagon up the hill. We have a lot to get started on," she told Tom.

Nat and Marissa were still embracing when Maggie and Tom started up the hill. Once Tom was out of sight, Nat kissed Marissa. "I've missed you terribly."

"I can tell." Marissa smiled. "I thought this day would never arrive, but now I'm home."

"Yes, you are." Nat agreed and finally released her from the embrace, but she still held Marissa's hand as they turned to follow the wagon. "We have a busy day planned and a feast for later. Would you mind helping Maggie unload the wagon while Tom and I get started on the outside work?"

"Not at all. We'll unload the household goods and I'll take Rusty to the barn. You and Tom can unload the rest."

Nothing could erase the smile from Nat's face when they crested the hill, and walked to the cabin.

Tom and Maggie were nowhere in sight, so they stepped inside the cabin and heard them laughing in their bedroom. They entered the room to find Tom and Maggie sitting on the floor, playing with the puppies.

"Is it true that I can really have this little girl?" Tom asked, holding up the silver pup.

"As long as Gyp does not have any objections," Nat answered. Gyp licked his face when he stroked the puppy. "I think that's a *yes*."

"I promise I'll take such good care of her," he said to Gyp. "We will come often to visit, so you can see for yourself."

Touched by the genuine excitement he exuded holding the pup, Nat knew they would make a good pair. "It'll be a few weeks yet, before they are weaned and ready. Maybe you and Smithy can ride out together and claim your pups."

"I'd really like that. I can't tell you how thankful I am for you introducing me to Smithy. He works me like a dog, but I'm learning so much from him."

"He's a good man, and speaking of working, are you ready to get started? We have a lot of wood to cut today."

"Yes, ma'am," he answered. He kissed the pup on the head and placed it down with her siblings. "I'll see you later, little Moonshine."

"Moonshine?" Nat asked.

"Her coat reminds me of the moon shining bright in the sky. I thought I'd call her Shine for short."

"Moonshine it is then. Go hitch up Quincy to the small wagon and I'll get the axes. Get a drink before we get started. It's going to be a long, hot day."

Tom nodded and left the room.

Nat looked at Maggie. "Will you make ham and biscuits for lunch?"

"Yes. I'll get them started once we have the wagon unloaded."

"We'll be back later then."

†

Tom was leading Quincy from the barn when Nat arrived carrying the tools. "Do you think you could return the end of next week?"

"Yes, Smithy told me I could come whenever you needed me. What do you want to do?"

"I want to build another smokehouse on the other side of the chicken coop. We'll be able to smoke more meat, and it will help keep the chickens alive during the winter. I've got a list of lumber and supplies I'll need, if you'll bring them out and help me build it."

"I'll be back as soon as I can." He grinned.

They hitched Quincy and walked over to the trees she had cut earlier in the week.

"You've been busy," Tom said.

"It's been a very productive week. I have a load of goods for you to take back to town with you when you go."

Tom took his shirt off and Nat could see the growth of muscles that had already begun to form. She pulled off her work shirt and they began to cut wood. They chopped sections and placed the logs onto the wagon for Quincy to carry to the back of the cabin. She and Tom stacked the smaller logs on the woodpile and left the larger sections to split on a stump Nat used for a base.

Nat glanced at the wagon on each trip to the house to find that Maggie and Marissa were making good progress on the unloading. She and Tom were taking a water break between trips when Marissa stepped out to the porch.

"Will you be ready to eat soon?"

"Let us bring one more load in and we'll break for lunch."

"I'll let Maggie know," Marissa said and returned inside with two bags of flour in her arms.

Nat nodded to Tom and he led Quincy back to the trees they were cutting. Together they had cut six of the two dozen trees she had downed. If their energy held out, she hoped to have a dozen more cut by the end of the day.

"If you want to haul the last load, I'll continue to chop."

"That sounds like a plan." Nat began placing the logs in the back of the wagon. When it was loaded to capacity, she looked back at Tom. "Let's get this unloaded and go eat. I'm starving."

"Me, too." Tom lifted his arms and buried the axe into the tree he was chopping.

"Let me get a feed bag for Quincy and Rusty and I'll meet you."

Tom nodded and led Quincy to the woodpile and began unloading while Nat filled two feedbags and carried them to the cabin. She placed one on Rusty and the other on Quincy before helping Tom unload the wagon. When they finished, Maggie fed them a hearty lunch.

They worked on the wood until it became too dark to see. Nat lit a lantern in the barn and fed the animals while Tom carried in the last of the feed supplies from the wagon. When they were finished, she draped an arm across Tom's shoulders as they walked to the cabin. "We got a lot done today."

"Yeah we did. I think we'll be able to finish cutting and stacking tomorrow morning if we start early enough."

"Early won't be a problem. That damned rooster beats the sun up here."

"Do you have much for me to take back?"

Nat nodded. "Quite a bit actually, if you don't mind."

"Not at all. Smithy can't wait to see what you have for him."

"I think he'll be pleased."

Their timing was perfect. After they washed up at the pump, they went inside just as Maggie was placing a mound of steaming crab on the table. Fried shrimp and fish accompanied a pile of fry bread and glasses of cold water.

"I was about to come get you," Marissa said when they entered the room. "Maggie was worried you were going to work poor Tom all night."

"It was too dark to see or I might have."

"Thank goodness for the sunset," Tom replied. "I haven't worked that hard in my life."

"Come reap your reward then," Maggie said, and they all sat around the table.

"That was a fantastic meal." Nat pushed her plate away.

"You two deserved every bite," Maggie said. "I've also made several jars of chowder for you to take back with you, Tom."

"Thanks. I brought a nice buck pelt that Smithy helped me tan. Nat says you make the best breeches around, so I was hoping you would make me a pair."

"Was it a large buck?"

"Yes, he was huge," Nat said. "I bet you can get two from the hide."

"I'll measure you in the morning and see what we can do."

"Just let me know how much."

"You're coming back next week, is that right?"

"Yes, ma'am, as soon as I can."

"Two bags of apples then, so I can make a few pies."

"That's too good of a deal to pass up." Tom yawned.

"I do believe Maggie has another surprise for you," Nat said.

Tom looked expectantly at Maggie.

"Come with me."

Marissa looked at Nat who only smiled as they left the kitchen and went to Maggie's room. They emerged moments later with the folding cot and Tom's face filled with a smile.

"See what they made for me?" Tom opened the cot for her to see. He was beaming. "No more sleeping on the floor. Maggie even made me a nice pillow."

"Maggie and I figured you would visit more if you had something comfortable to sleep on."

"What kind of hide is that?" Marissa asked.

"That's the first bull moose Nat killed here," Maggie answered.

"You'll be taking two moose heads and a bunch of jerky back when you go, along with other goods," Nat added.

"Smithy is going to go crazy for those heads."

"Just be sure to get a good price for them."

"Yes, ma'am." He set up his bed near the fireplace.

"I don't think any of us will have trouble sleeping tonight." Nat opened the door to let Gyp back inside.

"We have a full day tomorrow, too," Maggie reminded them. "Do you want some breakfast in the morning?"

"We want to get an early start, but we'd gladly stop for food," Nat answered. "Some eggs and flapjacks with bacon would give us energy to burn."

"We'll cook while you two get started."

"I'm sure Rufus will have us up early," Nat said. "So we'll say goodnight."

Nat closed the door behind them and began to strip out of her clothes. She slipped on a nightshirt and climbed into the bed while Marissa brushed out her hair. Nat felt her eyes growing heavy and struggled to hold them open. The next thing she saw when she opened her eyes again was that the lantern was out and Marissa was snuggled close to her keeping her warm.

†

Rufus did not disappoint them the next morning, filling the air with his crowing before the first rays of sunlight crossed the horizon. Nat made a motion to stretch her arms above her head and groaned from the soreness in her muscles.

Marissa felt her movements and cracked her eyes open. "Good morning, my love," she said, a bit too cheerfully.

"It is morning." Nat groaned, sitting up on the bed.

"Are you sore this morning?"

"Yeah, you could say that." Nat bent down to pull on her pants. She picked up her boots and clean socks, and then sat on the edge of the bed.

"I think it's time for you to take a hot, soaking bath after Tom leaves. It will be time to wash these clothes too." She tossed Nat her work shirt.

"They are getting a bit fragrant."

"You've been working really hard."

"Yes, I won't argue that, but there's still much to do to prepare for winter. I thought while you and Maggie cook breakfast, I'll start cutting some kindling if you don't need the hatchet."

"I'll bring you some coffee when it's ready."

Nat leaned down to kiss her. "Sorry I fell asleep on you last night."

"We have the rest of our lives together." Marissa hugged Nat and kissed her again.

†

Tom had already placed the rigging on Quincy and was walking him to the wagon when Nat arrived at the barn. "Good morning."

"Morning. I see you're ready to chop this morning."

"I'm a bit stiff, but I'm sure it will go away when we get warmed up."

"Let's get to it then."

They fell into a rhythm, the sounds of their axes echoing in the cool morning air. The weather had definitely begun to turn. Soon the nights would become colder, and they would need to keep the fires burning inside the cabin. Nat already had woodpiles two times larger than she had at Marissa's cabin, but she still feared it would not be enough. They would easily finish the trees this morning, and she would continue to cut until she was satisfied they'd have plenty for the winter. As promised, Marissa arrived carrying cups of hot coffee and they took a short break. "You two have nearly made it through the trees that were downed."

"We should finish it by mid-morning," Nat said.

"Do you want me to cut a few more for you before I need to go?" Tom asked.

"No, the days are becoming shorter. You'll need to leave by midday to still be able to deliver the goods we send back with you. I'll cut as much as I can this coming week, and if there's time after we finish the smokehouse, we can chop more firewood."

"With Smithy's help, we should be able to build the smokehouse quickly and get back to the wood," Tom said.

"You know, Maggie and I could help Smithy with the smokehouse, and you two could continue bringing in wood." Marissa said. "I know how concerned you are about having enough wood to make it through the winter, Nat."

Nat looked at Tom and he nodded. "That would be good. I'd rather have too much than to run out, and then have to try to cut more in the dead of winter."

"It's settled then." Marissa took their empty cups. "I'll give a holler when breakfast is ready."

A hearty breakfast fueled Nat and Tom's bodies enough to finish the cutting. After cleaning the dishes, Maggie and Marissa helped them, loading the wagon and taking the wood to the piles while Tom and Nat finished the cutting.

After they delivered the last logs to the house, everyone took a short water break before continuing to work. Tom pulled Rusty from the stall and hitched him to the wagon while Nat cared for Quincy.

"You did good work." Nat brushed Quincy, and gave him an extra portion of grain. She turned to Tom. "If you'll load the pelts, I'll grab the moose heads and then we can head up to the cabin. I want to clear the back porch of antlers so I can stack some split wood."

They loaded the antlers and then filled several wooden crates with smoked fish. Maggie had filled six flour bags with the jerky, which she carried out to the wagon.

"Be sure to bring these bags back so I can refill them," Maggie told him. "Any others he can spare would also help."

"Yes, ma'am." Tom took the cases of jelly from Marissa and placed them in the bed of the wagon along with the crates filled with honey. "You're turning into a regular bee charmer aren't you?" he asked.

"That I am." Nat grinned.

"I've packed some bacon biscuits and filled your canteen for the ride," Maggie told him.

"Here are the supply lists for the cabin and smokehouse." Marissa handed the paper to him.

Nat disappeared inside and returned handing Tom two gold pieces. "This should be enough to cover the lumber and supplies. The shopkeeper will give you bacon and ham in trade for the fish and jerky. The berries can be applied to the bill along with the jelly and honey," she instructed.

"What about the items you're sending Smithy?"

"Smithy will deposit the money into the bank for me."

"I think I'm all set then." Tom climbed onto the wagon.

"On second thought, have Smithy give you enough money to buy a dozen boxes of shells for the rifle. I need to stock up on those."

Tom nodded and waited for any other instructions.

"We'll have a load of seafood to take back with you when you return. There will probably only be one or two more after that before the weather starts to get miserable. We'll get as much as we can."

"I'll be sure to tell the hotel manager that I'll be bringing a load back next time."

"I can't think of anything else. Be safe, and we'll see you soon."

"Wait, weren't you sending the moose hide to Smithy?" Maggie asked.

"You're right, Maggie. I'll be right back." Nat walked to the barn, returning moments later with the large hide.

"Now, I think you're ready. How are you for feed and hay for the animals?"

"I'm good for a while yet."

Tom released the wagon brake and slapped the reins on Rusty's shoulder. "Let's go, Rusty."

The women stood together and watched him disappear down the trail and the jingle of the metal faded away.

"So what's next?" Maggie asked.

†

Nat spent the afternoon splitting wood while Marissa and Maggie went to the lake to check for berries. They returned with full bags of blackberries and a bucket full of blueberries. Nat stopped splitting long enough to take a handful of the blueberries to snack on. "Those are really tasty."

"These are the last of the blackberries, so after we finish this jelly, we can start on the blueberries."

"Can you get these rinsed and in the pot to boil?" Marissa asked.

"I think I can manage," Maggie answered.

"I'll start carrying this split wood for Nat then."

"Place it on the end of the porch where the antlers were," Nat requested, and resumed splitting wood.

Marissa started carrying the wood onto the porch, and when Maggie had the berries boiling, she came out to help as well. By the end of the day, the logs were split, stacked, and Nat was near exhaustion.

"I can see how weary you are," Maggie said. "You go take your boots and socks off and relax. Marissa and I will carry some water in from the pump and get the wash pot boiling, so you can take a nice, long bath. You deserve it after all your hard work."

"I won't argue with you tonight." Nat slumped on the porch steps.

"Let me get those boots and socks off for you." Marissa knelt and pulled a boot off.

"Thanks." Nat leaned back against the railing and let out a long sigh. She watched Maggie stoking the fire beneath the wash pot and Marissa carrying in buckets of water from the pump. Her eyes grew heavy and she closed them.

"It looks like she's asleep. She works too hard sometimes." Maggie smiled at Marissa.

"Now that I'm here, maybe I can do more to help the two of you."

"I'm sure we will all be just fine," Maggie said. "I'll get supper started while you get her in the bath."

They allowed Nat to nap while they prepared the bath for her.

"Come on, sleepyhead, your bath is ready," Marissa gently said. When she saw Nat's eyes open she helped her up before settling her in the tub.

"This feels really good," Nat said. "I can feel the hot water easing the weariness in my muscles already."

"I'm taking these to the wash pot." Marissa held up the sweat-stained clothing, wrinkling her nose. "I'll put a clean pair of breeches and one of the new work shirts on the bed for you."

"Thanks. Will you wash my back when you come back in?"

"Of course I will. Would you rather I do it now?"

"No, let me soak a bit first."

Marissa left the room just as she saw Nat lean back against the tub and close her eyes.

Chapter Thirty

The following week passed quickly. They stayed busy harvesting seafood, and each day Nat cut down several trees and used Quincy to pull them into the yard. Marissa and Maggie finished more jelly and returned to the lake for fresh blueberries. They feasted on blueberry flapjacks in the morning to start their days, and then worked until returning for a late lunch.

Maggie and Marissa were cleaning fish to prepare for smoking when they heard the crack of Nat's rifle in the distance. "It sounds like we will have fresh meat tonight," Maggie stated.

"I hope she killed a buck. I could go for a thick steak," Marissa said. "When will the carrots and onions be ready to harvest?"

"In a month or so," Maggie answered. "Have patience."

"I'd like to make a rabbit stew when we get some vegetables."

"That sounds good, and a nice change for us."

When Nat approached, Gyp's ears perked up and she bounded off the porch. Several minutes later, Nat appeared around the side of the cabin. "Here you are. I've killed a nice buck and will take Quincy down to bring him back."

"Marissa was just saying she hoped you got a buck. She wants a nice steak tonight."

"Then a nice steak you shall have."

"I can finish here and get this fish in the smokehouse, if you need Maggie's help," Marissa offered.

"I'll always take her help," Nat answered. "We'll see you shortly."

Marissa watched them leave with Gyp close on their heels. The pups had played themselves out earlier and were piled up, taking a nap, so the only sound she heard was the pounding of the surf as the tide was coming in. She had to admit she was just as in love with the area as Nat was. She watched a pair of dolphins playing in the water. She had worried she would miss the conveniences of being near town, but there wasn't a moment yet that she regretted her decision to move.

Once finished with the last of the fish, Marissa took them to the pump to rinse them before carrying them to the smokehouse where she also turned the strips of jerky. She made a mental note to tell Nat the latest batch was ready. She would ask if they could use some of the venison from today's kill for jerky as well. Nat refused to waste any space she had in the smokehouse. They had a good stock of meat for their consumption, so they continued to work on the jerky for trade.

By the week's end, Nat had killed another buck and a bull moose, filling the smokehouse with jerky and smoked fish. The barrels were full of seafood, and the jelly, berries, and honey were ready to send to town. Nat had collected her traps and would not set them again until next spring. Marissa knew they would now focus on the final preparations for winter. Once the second smokehouse was built, Nat would hunt daily to fill the racks with meat for barter. They would send it in with Tom with the last delivery of seafood after his next visit.

†

The day that Tom and Smithy were to arrive was spent preparing for the build. Nat and Maggie had cut logs and buried them for the corner posts, finishing the last post that morning. Nat would spend the morning trimming the branches from the remaining trees she had cut, while Maggie and Marissa hitched Quincy to the wagon to go to the boneyard—the area where the antlers were found—to harvest as many as they could find.

She heard the jingling of Quincy's rigging and then the laughter of the two women coming into view. "Welcome back."

"Where do you want these?" Maggie asked pointing to a large load of antlers.

"Pull the wagon up closer to the cabin and unhitch Quincy from the wagon. Have you picked out the ones you want to use for buttons?"

"I have several racks I'd like to use."

"Place them in the barn then so they don't get taken by mistake."

"What can I do?" Marissa asked, after Maggie led Quincy away.

"You can carry these smaller limbs to the pile by the smokehouse."

Maggie cared for Quincy and then pitched in to help Marissa with the branches. When done, they took a short water break.

"What would you like to have for dinner, tonight?" Maggie asked.

"Do we have some corn ready, and some potatoes?" Nat asked.

"Yes, to both."

"It will be a few hours yet before the men arrive. Let's go down and see if we can find enough shrimp to fill up the cook pot with some corn and potatoes."

"That sounds good to me," Marissa said.

They stripped their boots and socks and then rolled their pants to their knees and picked up a bucket each. Gyp and the pups rushed out of the house and followed them down to the shore. Gyp stretched out in the sun while the pups raced the water under her watchful eye.

They are getting big and it won't be much longer before she has them weaned. Nat watched them play. *They will be ready to go to their new homes soon.* Nat felt a twinge of sorrow about the pups leaving, but she knew they would be well cared for, and good company to Tom and Smithy.

She pulled her thoughts back to the task and waded into one of the tidal pools in search of shrimp. The temperature of the water had definitely dropped. It was normally cool, but it was rapidly turning colder. This would probably be the last of their seafood until the spring. Maggie had assured her that the clams would be plentiful throughout the winter months, buried deeper in the sand, but Nat would miss the sweet crab and the crunchy fried shrimp they had feasted on since arriving.

Maggie was the first to fill her bucket, and with her help, the other two buckets were filled quickly, and they started back up the hill. Nat pulled her boots back on and returned to cutting wood, while Marissa and Maggie pulled the heads off the shrimp.

†

Nat was finished cutting a tree into sections when she heard the jingling of Rusty's rigging as he plodded down the trail. She buried the axe in the log and walked to the cabin to meet the men. Maggie called Gyp and the puppies to her so they would not be underfoot when Rusty pulled the wagon next to the cabin.

"Hello," Smithy bellowed, when they came into sight. He was grinning from ear to ear. He jumped down from the wagon and pulled Nat into a bear hug. "I've missed seeing you." He looked toward the finished cabin. "The cabin looks great."

"I've missed you, too," Nat said.

"You all need to come to town more often and not rely on Tom to do all the work." He hugged Marissa. "Boy, do I miss your cooking at the hotel." He then turned to Maggie. "I haven't seen you since you moved out here. Are these ladies taking good care of you?" He hugged her too.

"She takes good care of us," Nat corrected him. "Come and I'll show you around the cabin."

"I'll start unloading the lumber and then we can get to work on that firewood." Tom jumped down from the wagon.

"I think you need to come visit your daughter first," Maggie told him. The silver pup he had picked out was wiggling excitedly.

"My, she has grown." Tom bent down to pick her up. The puppy licked his face as he hugged her close. "Is it time yet?"

"Just a few more weeks," Maggie answered. "Then she'll be ready."

"Did Tom tell you I wanted the blue pup?" Smithy asked.

"He did. Have you picked out a name?" Marissa asked.

"Blue. Simple and easy for me to remember." He knelt to pet the pup.

"Original." Nat smiled, and waited for the big man to follow her into the house.

"We'll help with the lumber," Maggie said.

"No, ma'am," Tom replied, "you can take these." He walked back to the wagon and took out four bags of apples. "I brought an extra bag of sugar, too. Charlie returned your flour bags and added a dozen more. He said to tell you the fish were delicious and he can't keep the jerky in stock."

"That's good news," Marissa replied.

"Let me get the lumber and you ladies can take the rest of the supplies inside. Then, when the grand tour is over, we can get down to the real work." Tom turned back to the wagon.

"You have a deal." Maggie carried two of the bags inside, smiling at the extra apples. She'd bake a pie later if they finished early.

Tom was halfway through unloading the boards when Smithy and Nat emerged from the cabin.

"I thought he'd have it unloaded by now," Smithy said.

"We can pitch in and finish it in no time," Nat told him, and lifted a stack of boards onto her shoulder.

When the wagon was unloaded, Tom unhitched Rusty and took him to the barn to remove the rigging and get him settled in. Nat described what she wanted Smithy to build, with Maggie and Marissa's assistance.

"With two helpers I'll have this up in no time at all." Smithy looked at Marissa and Maggie. "Ready ladies?"

Maggie and Marissa began carrying the boards and holding them in place while Smithy hammered the nails into the posts, they had set. Nat returned to her axe, and Tom joined her with his axe and fell into rhythm with her.

By mid-afternoon, Nat called a break. Two sides of the smokehouse were up and they were halfway through a third. The group gathered around the water pump. "Do we want to stop for some lunch?" she asked.

"I'm good if you want to keep working," Smithy said.

"We have a nice supper planned for tonight," Maggie said.

"Let's work on then and get as much done today as we can," Smithy said. "We can have the walls up today and the door cut and hung, then finish off with the roof tomorrow."

Nat eyed the work they had already completed. This smokehouse was bigger, but she had no doubt she could keep it filled with meat. "It looks good so far."

"That should hold at least twice the meat you can smoke in the other house," Smithy stated.

"That won't be a problem at all," Maggie assured him. "With Nat's hunting skills and the fish we can spear, we won't go hungry, that's for certain."

"The shopkeeper just raves about the meats you have sent him. He says that's the best jerky he's ever eaten. It's selling well and I hear the townsfolk keep an eye out for the wagon when it comes to town, hoping you've brought in more smoked fish."

"Those are the easiest to make," Nat replied. "As long as we can keep getting fish, we'll continue to smoke them."

"We have some ready to go back with y'all tomorrow, along with the hotel's seafood and more jerky."

"I saw that wagon load of antlers. Are those for me?" Smithy asked.

"Yes, they are, and I have the last of the beaver pelts for this season for you as well."

"Do you have another moose head?" he asked.

"I do indeed, and two nice bucks. Are you interested in the hides?"

"Silly question. I'll take any hide you can spare."

"With this new smokehouse to fill, I should have plenty for you in a few weeks."

Smithy shuffled his feet and then looked up at Nat. "Tom and I would like to give you a housewarming gift, but we thought we'd better ask you first."

"That's not necessary," Nat said.

"It's something we want to do for y'all," Tom told her. "We've spotted an indoor wood-burning stove that you can use for cooking as well as heating. I know how to put one in if y'all will accept it as a gift from us."

Nat was sure her mouth hung open, listening to Tom. She'd often thought of a stove for Marissa and Maggie, but hadn't gotten around to buying one. She looked at both women who looked excited about the prospect, and she knew she couldn't disappoint them. It would make cooking this winter so much easier for them both.

"I don't see how we could refuse such a generous offer." Nat saw the other faces fill with delight.

"Fine, I'll bring it out in two weeks and get it set up for you. We will need to split smaller sections to fit the stove," Tom said.

"I'll take care of that," Marissa said. "I'm getting good at splitting wood."

"No more than a foot long then," Tom said.

"I can handle that."

"Let's get back to work then," Nat said. "We can plan for the stove tonight over dinner."

By late afternoon, they had finished chopping the trees into sections, and the walls of the smokehouse were done and the door hung. With Smithy's help, Tom and Nat loaded the barrels of seafood into the back of the wagon, and added the antlers from the small wagon, while Maggie and Marissa started cooking supper. Maggie had baked a blackberry pie from the last of the fresh berries, and she put Smithy to work peeling apples while she prepared crusts for apple pies for the next day.

"Should we haul some of the wood until supper is ready?" Tom asked Nat.

"Let's see what we can get done. Go ahead and get Quincy ready." Nat drank another cup of water.

Tom trotted down to the barn and Nat sat with Smithy for a few minutes. "I wish I had his energy."

"He's been a great addition to the store. The customers like him and he works until I make him stop. Heck, just watching him makes me tired. I can't thank you enough for sending him to me."

"He's a good young man."

"Yes, he is. Are you worried about the winter?"

"I reckon it's just fear of what I don't know. I'm not worried about food, but I don't know how we will fare in the winter isolated from town, and I want to have enough wood to keep us warm."

Smithy looked at the two large woodpiles and the stacked split wood on the porch. "With what you have to finish cutting, I'd think you have enough, but you can never be sure."

"I'll feel much better after this first winter," she admitted.

"You know, you could cut down some saplings and stack them behind the chicken coop. It will provide a wind break and the heat from the smokehouses will keep them from being covered with snow, so if you were to run short you have some extra close at hand."

"That's a good idea. I can work on that next week."

Tom led Quincy from the barn and hitched him to the wagon. "Ready?"

"I'm on my way." Nat drained her cup and got up.

Maggie took the apple peels and dumped them in the fireplace. Their smell would fill the rooms with their pleasant fragrance. She went outside for the apples and asked Smithy to stoke the fire and replace the wash pot with the cook pot filled with fresh water.

She carried the apples inside to the kitchen and she and Marissa sliced them for boiling. "Let's keep some of these seeds," Maggie stated. "I'd love to be able to have a few apple trees to grow our own."

"That would be nice," Marissa agreed, and they separated the seeds from the cores.

Smithy stoked the fire and then walked down to help Tom and Nat with the wood. Working together, they got all of the wood moved and the smaller logs added to the pile. Nat would split the rest in the coming weeks.

Maggie dropped the corn and potatoes into the boiling water, and stepped onto the porch where Tom and Smithy were playing with the pups. She passed them and walked inside to her room. When she returned to the porch moments later, she carried out the two pair of breeches she had sewn for Tom. When he looked up, she handed him the breeches.

Tom jumped to his feet and opened the folded material. "These are almost too nice to wear." He leaned down to wrap Maggie in his arms. "Thank you."

"You're welcome. Try them on later to make sure they fit."

"Yes, ma'am, I will." He placed the breeches on the railing out of reach of sharp puppy teeth, and knelt to play with Shine and her siblings.

"When you come back next, the puppies will be weaned and ready to go," Nat told Tom.

"I can't wait. It gets lonesome at the cabin by myself."

"If she's half the pup her mama is, she will become your best friend," Nat promised.

He smiled and laughed rolling on the ground covered by playful puppies.

Gyp was lying with her head in Nat's lap, watching them play while Nat stroked her head. She knew Gyp would be sad to see them go, but hopefully she could tell how much Tom and Smithy would love and care for them. Even Smithy, at his age, was down on the ground playing tug of war with Blue, who had found one of Nat's old socks.

Maggie returned inside and brought a bucket filled with shrimp to dump into the boiling water, and then she added some seasoning. "These will be ready soon if you want to go ahead and set the table," she said to Marissa.

"Do you want some help?" Nat asked.

"No, you and Gyp look comfortable. It won't take me long."

†

With everyone working together, the smokehouse was finished by mid-morning. Tom, Smithy, and Nat cut and trimmed saplings to store behind the chicken coop while Maggie and Marissa installed the drying racks.

The hard work done, Nat looked at the men. "Do you have time for a hunt?"

Their eyes glowed with excitement. "We have time before we need to leave for town. Let's see what we can get to put in that new smokehouse," Smithy answered.

They retrieved their rifles and walked to the lake. Large groups of moose were grazing on the supple grasses along the edge of the lake. Two large bulls were staring at each other, deciding whether to fight over the prime grazing areas. There were several young males in the herds, so Nat was not worried about next year's reproduction. "See if you can take the two bulls and I'll start back for Quincy."

Both men nodded and began to stalk closer for a better shot, while Nat began walking back to the barn. Nat knew that neither of the men had the opportunity to hunt as often as she, so she'd allow them to bring down the bulls. With Quincy's help, they would dress out the animals and carry the carcasses back to be processed. She, Marissa, and Maggie could slice the meat into the thin strips and marinate them for the jerky while the men headed back to town with two fresh moose heads. They could both brag in town that they took down the beasts to boost their egos and make them eager for the hunt next spring. She smiled when she heard the cracks of two rifle shots and knew her plan was working out beautifully.

When she walked back into the clearing, Marissa and Maggie were splitting wood. They stopped when they saw her approach. "Sharpen your knives ladies. I do believe we will have two large bulls to process shortly."

"We'll be ready," Maggie said.

Nat walked into the barn and placed the rigging on Quincy, then hitched him to the small wagon. She waved and left the clearing, leading him down to the lake's edge. Smithy and Tom had already removed the heads, to bleed out the bulls.

They worked quickly and had the bulls quartered and the large roasts carved out to make the jerky. "Would you mind if Tom and I took the other quarters for our smokehouses?"

"Not at all, they are your kills after all. I've already got several quarters smoking for our use, so take them all."

"Maybe when we bring the stove out we can get a few bucks," Tom said. "I've got plenty of room in the smokehouse."

"That shouldn't be a problem." They loaded the meat into the wagon and walked back to the cabin.

Nat was surprised to find that Maggie and Marissa had set up a cutting table made of two large sections of tree trunks and some of the leftover boards from the smokehouse.

"That's a good idea," Nat said when they pulled Quincy up next to the makeshift table. "Tom, grab the hammer and some nails and we'll make this a bit more secure." He raced to the barn for the supplies.

The women began unloading the large roasts and rinsing them at the pump before positioning them on the table for slicing, while Tom secured the boards, and Smithy loaded the heads and other quarters onto the large wagon. When Quincy's wagon was empty, Tom rinsed the blood from the wood and took him back to the barn. After caring for Quincy, he brought Rusty out and hitched him to the wagon.

"What else can we do before we start back to town?" Smithy asked.

"We can take it from here," Nat said. "Thanks for all your help."

"It was a pleasure." Smithy hugged Nat goodbye. "Are there other supplies you will need when we come back?"

"Tom has a standard list. I can't think of anything else we need."

"We'll see you in a few weeks then." Smithy climbed onto the wagon bench followed by Tom.

"Be safe and we'll see you soon."

Tom nodded, got Rusty moving, and within minutes, they were out of sight.

"I'll get a fire going if you want to whip up a batch of marinade," Nat said to Maggie.

"As usual, Maggie's already a step ahead of you." Marissa smiled. "Start slicing and I'll go get the bowls."

Nat chuckled. After starting the fire in the new smokehouse, she pulled out her knife and cut a large roast into sections that were more manageable.

"I thought we'd have some of this liver with some onions for supper," Maggie said.

"That would be tasty." Nat dropped slices of the meat into the bowl Marissa placed between them.

"This will take up several of the racks. What do you want to fill the rest with?" Maggie asked.

"I thought we would smoke more fish, and I'll see what else I can hunt to give us some variety. I was thinking I'd take Quincy and scout farther south, to see what other types of game are available."

"You could do that while we prepare the fish," Marissa suggested.

"She also has a special request," Maggie said.

"What might that be?" Nat asked Marissa.

"I thought, since we have fresh vegetables, I could make us some nice rabbit stew if you'd bring in a nice meaty rabbit."

"That should not be a problem." Nat smiled. "A few rabbits would be nice to have in our smokehouse for the winter too. I'm sure we'll tire of moose and venison before spring arrives."

"A few more geese and some duck would be fine, too," Maggie added. "We have room for more now."

"That we do." Nat smiled glancing over at the brand new smokehouse. "How are we doing for eggs?"

"The hens are laying well," Maggie, answered. "We have several dozen in the pantry already."

They continued slicing the meat in silence until Maggie looked at Nat. "What do you think about making a root cellar?"

"I'll be honest. I know nothing about them."

"I can use the wood scraps from the smokehouse to make one under the back porch. That should be dark enough and cool enough to store some of the potatoes, cabbages, and other vegetables."

"Do you need my help?"

"No, I'm sure Marissa and I can handle this on our own. There won't be much digging to do, and I can manage that."

Nat nodded and smiled at her friend. "Use whatever you need, and if we need more supplies I'll go to town and get them."

Darkness had fallen by the time they had all the jerky processed and placed on the racks. Marissa had left them earlier to start cooking, and supper was almost ready when Nat and Maggie returned inside.

"It won't be much longer if you want to relax a bit."

Nat picked up the block of wood she had been carving and walked out the front door. She sat in her favorite chair and lit a lantern. A cool breeze bathed the porch. When she looked out across the water, the reflection of the moon rippled and danced across the surface while the waves were lapping at the shore. *This is truly beautiful.* Her hands smoothed the block of wood and she began to carve. The head of the whale was finished, and she was working the wood down to his tail. She smiled, pleased with the creature that was appearing under her knife.

Nat wanted to travel south to scout out the area, but with so much left to do to prepare for winter, she had decided to wait. Now, with the addition of Smithy and Tom's help, she felt they were as ready as they could be and she could afford to spend a few days away from the cabin.

She would collect her pack and supplies and leave in the morning. The nights were turning cooler, so the time was right. Gyp wouldn't be happy to stay behind, but she needed to stay near her pups. She, Hardy, and Quincy would go alone.

Maggie opened the door and joined her on the porch. "You look deep in thought."

"I was planning out my scouting trip. I thought to leave in the morning."

"The sooner the better," she agreed. "We will miss you."

"I won't be gone long, just a few days."

Marissa came out on the porch. "Dinner's ready."

"After you, ma'am." Nat held the door open for Maggie.

Nat looked back into the darkness. The wild was calling her and tomorrow she would answer that call.

Chapter Thirty-one

Nat woke before Rufus had the opportunity to wake her and dressed quickly. She was leading Hardy and Quincy to the back of the cabin when the door opened and Marissa and Gyp came outside. Gyp danced around excitedly. Nat knelt to her and buried her hands in the fur surrounding Gyp's face. "You have to stay this time, my friend. You have pups to care for and you need to protect the cabin."

Gyp whined softly and Nat knew she would probably spend the morning pouting, but she would obey her master and guard the cabin well.

"She's not the only one who's going to miss you," Marissa said.

"I'm going to miss you, too. I won't be long." She tied her bedroll to the back of the saddle and dropped her rifle into the sheath.

Maggie stepped outside carrying a flour bag, canteen, and Nat's duster and hat. "There's rain in the air, so you better take these." She handed the items to Nat. "I packed you some ham and biscuits for breakfast, and some jerky for later."

"Thanks," Nat hugged Maggie close. "I'll see you soon."

Maggie nodded and disappeared into the house. Nat turned to Marissa. "Keep the bed warm." She smiled pulling her close and kissing her deeply.

"Be safe and hurry home to us." Marissa had tears in her eyes.

"I will." Nat turned to mount Hardy. She looked back at Marissa and waved goodbye before turning Hardy toward the lake trail.

Maggie was right—the mist began to fall and then turned into raindrops as Hardy plodded along the coastline. Nat pulled the brim of her hat down and raised the collar of her duster to cover her neck. Away from the smoke of the cabin, the scents of the wild called to her even more. The smell of the rain mixed with the salt from the Sound was overpowering, along with the aroma of the aspen trees that filled the forest along the coast. In the months to come, there would be a blanket of a different color, as the trees farther inland became cloaked with leaves of burnt orange and brilliant reds. Nat relaxed completely, listening to the creaking of the leather with each step Hardy took.

She retrieved a biscuit from the food sack and took a bite as she turned away from the coast to follow a game trail leading deeper into the forest. Her ears strained listening for movement and calls from the animals in the area. A variety of birds filled the morning air with song, celebrating the falling rain. The underbrush rustled with squirrels and small animals foraging for nuts and roots to add to their winter stash. It reminded her of her own frenzy to prepare for the coming winter and brought a smile to her face. She noticed paw prints from a wolf pack and she wondered if it was the pack where Gyp's lone wolf had once belonged. The tracks appeared several days old. The pack stalking a split-hooved animal, probably a deer, down the game trail.

Nat continued south, and she followed the trail for several hours. She noticed when rocky outcroppings became more prevalent and her eyes searched the slippery slopes for signs of life. She heard the clicking of hooves on the hard rock and strained her eyes to catch a glimpse of movement. Nat spotted her first mountain goat trotting along a narrow ledge of rock, the color of its coat camouflaging the animal from predator's eyes. Only the shimmering movement of the goat gave away its location, as it blended in with the color of the rock formations. The horns on the creature were thick curls of gray and tan, massive in size. She could just imagine Smithy's mouthwatering to get his hands on a set of those.

The thick cloud cover and falling rain made it difficult to determine the time of day, so Nat kept riding until she found the mouth of a cave. She pulled Hardy to a halt, tied him off to a branch near the entrance, and slid her rifle from its sheath. Nat would need to be very careful entering a cave this late in the season. Bears would be preparing for winter hibernation and the last thing she needed was to become a last meal for a hungry grizzly or walk in on a bear already nesting.

She carefully crept inside the large opening and released a sigh of relief. The opening was wide, but not deep enough to attract a bear as a den. It was plenty deep enough for her and the animals to escape the worst of the weather, though, and she returned for Hardy and Quincy.

Nat collected a small mound of dry branches to build a fire, and then foraged for larger pieces to keep the fire burning throughout the night. The wood was damp, but should dry out next to the small fire. She placed the feedbags on Hardy and Quincy and took a bucket from Quincy's pack to go in search of fresh water.

A short walk around the rock outcropping brought Nat to a fast-moving stream where she filled her bucket and canteen before returning to the cave. Hardy and Quincy drank deeply, so she returned for a second bucket. Nat knelt, filling the bucket, when movement ahead of her caught her attention. She slowly lifted her head and spotted a mountain lion fifty feet ahead of her. She froze in place. The cat watched her curiously and Nat speculated that she was possibly the first human it had seen. Nat cursed her failure to bring her rifle with her. Life at the cabin had dulled her sense of caution, and her hand slipped down to her boot to pull out her knife. It was a poor choice of weapon against razor sharp teeth and claws, but it was the only resource available to her now. Her instinct kicked in and she moved slowly to stand to her full height, hoping her size would intimidate the cat. The cat sat watching her. She fought the urge to turn and run, but her experience in the wild knew that the cat would be on her before she could reach the cave. Instead, she slowly backed away, keeping her eyes on the cat, who calmly lifted a paw and began bathing.

When she could no longer see the cat, Nat turned and rushed back to the cave. Her heart was racing when she picked up her rifle and placed the bucket of water on the ground for the animals. She moved to the mouth of the cave, watching for any signs the cat had followed. Her senses acutely searching the falling darkness. Once she could no longer see, Nat turned back to her fire and sat on her bedroll, her rifle close at hand.

She took out another biscuit and two strips of jerky to munch on as the rain continued to fall. Nat decided she would ride south one more day, and then circle back, deeper into the forest if the rain let up. The sound of a howl filled the air and Hardy anxiously stomped his feet.

"Relax, boy," she said to calm him. "It sounds like they are moving away from us." She prayed her instincts were right and they would be safe for the night.

Nat woke from a fitful night's sleep to eat the last of the biscuits before saddling Hardy and replacing her pack on Quincy's rigging. The rain had stopped, and the sun was climbing above the horizon. She dowsed the fire and led the animals to the mouth of the cave where she stopped and knelt. Deep in the soft mud were imprints of the mountain lion's paws and Nat cautiously surveyed the area. The cat had visited them to check out who was in her domain.

Nat mounted Hardy and made a rapid exit from the cave, keeping an eye open for the mountain lion or signs of the wolves. She moved deeper into the forest and her spirits lifted, moving away from the rock formations into an immense aspen forest. The rains had washed the earth clean and the strong scent of the aspens filled the air. She breathed deeply, filling her lungs with the scent, and her anxiety of the morning faded away.

She noted the ample signs of wildlife in the area and promised herself to return in the spring to take advantage of the variety of animals to hunt. She stopped at a stream to take a long drink and Nat pulled out a piece of the jerky. She was surprised with the sweet peppery taste and fully understood why it had become a favorite at the general store in town. It tasted good and provided energy to weary muscles, a dynamic combination in the pioneer environment.

Hardy crested a hill and Nat pulled him to a halt. Below them lay a fertile valley filled with large, woolly bison. Her fingers ached to remove her rifle and take aim on one of the beasts. Common sense prevailed and she realized the weight of one of the beasts would be too much for Quincy to carry for the distance they would need to travel. Rusty, however, was a different story. If she could find a trail wide enough for the wagon, she would return next season for several of the bison. Two of the animals could easily fill the smaller smokehouse with the tasty lean meat. She would bring Maggie, Smithy, and Tom for the hunt.

She sat and watched the herd grazing in the north, and she wondered how far north they would migrate. She could see a trail they had blazed and she knew it would be wide enough for the wagon. Nat urged Hardy forward trailing the herd from one large meadow to the next.

By the time the sun began to sink, the herd had traveled several hours north, which would put them only two days from the cabin. She turned away from the herd to find a place to rest for the night. She had moved far away from the outcropping, but she found a small area next to a stream that was sheltered by large trees. She tied off the animals and built a fire before darkness closed around them.

It had been a long time since she had spent a night in the open under the stars. She found her eyes attracted to the stars in the open sky and felt at peace. She ate the last of the biscuits and drank cool water from her canteen while the animals fed from the feedbags. She removed their bags, filled the bucket with water, and settled down under a big tree. The trickle of the stream relaxed her and with the fire blazing, she crawled inside her bedroll and drifted off to sleep.

Hardy's soft muzzle against her cheek woke her the next morning, and she was surprised at how late she had slept. The sun was well above the horizon and the herd of bison had moved away to the east. She climbed from her bedroll and stretched, her eyes gazing into the morning sky. There was a slight chill in the air that turned her breath into smoke, but the blue skies promised a brilliant day. Nat shook out her bedroll and stored it on the back of her saddle, followed by her rifle. Hardy stomped his feet, eager to start the day, while Quincy lazily grazed on sweet grass.

Nat was pleased with the discoveries of her trip and turned toward home, eager to share her news with Marissa and Maggie. She decided to head back north and follow the shoreline back to the cabin. If she made good time, she would be back in Marissa's arms by the time the moon rose the following night.

The miles drifted away on the salty breeze while Nat was lost in her thoughts. The blast of an air hole brought her back to reality and she turned her head to see a group of whales swimming south.

"To warmer waters," she said with a smile. The seasons were rapidly changing and she finally accepted the fact that she was ready for anything that the pending winter would throw her way. She was strong, and together with Marissa and Maggie, she could accomplish anything.

That night when she bedded down, she dreamed of being in Marissa's arms.

✝

Hardy could sense they were getting close, and even Quincy picked up his pace, eager to be home. When the smell of the fireplace smoke reached them, Nat knew she was close. They raced up the hill, and Marissa and Maggie met them in the back yard.

"Welcome home," Marissa said.

Maggie reached for Hardy's bridle.

"Thanks. It's good to be here."

"Did you have a good trip?" Maggie asked.

"It went well. Let me take care of the animals and I'll tell you what I found."

"Have you eaten yet?" Marissa asked.

"No, I was hoping you'd have some leftovers."

"I'll make some fresh fry bread," Maggie replied, and returned inside the cabin.

"There is plenty of chowder." Marissa took Nat in her arms and kissed her. "I missed you."

"I missed you, too."

"Do you need some help?"

"No, I've got this. See you in a few minutes."

Nat walked Hardy and Quincy to the barn and removed their tack. She brushed them both, and placed them in their stalls, before adding extra portions of grain to their bins and filling the trough with fresh water.

"You both did well."

She heard the cabin's back door push open and, halfway across the clearing, Gyp rushed to her. She knelt to hug her and received several licks of Gyp's warm tongue to her cheek.

"I missed you, too, my friend. It felt strange to be in the woods without you."

Marissa was standing at the door and watched the exchange. "Come get washed up a bit and supper will be ready in a few minutes."

Gyp danced around her as she walked to the cabin and climbed the steps. Nat weaved through the three growing pups.

"Whoa, you all are growing." She knelt and was covered in puppies instantly. "What have you been feeding them?"

"They love goose stew," Marissa said. "But they have nearly wiped us out. Will you see if you can shoot a couple more tomorrow?"

"That shouldn't be a problem and I owe you a couple of rabbits, too." Nat smiled.

"I haven't forgotten. I will get the vegetables from the garden tomorrow."

Nat broke free from the pups and went into the bedroom to clean up. When she started toward the kitchen, the silver male grabbed onto her pants leg and shook his head as she drug him forward with each step. Marissa and Maggie were in the kitchen, laughing at the pups' antics.

"I think we all missed you." Maggie placed a plate of fresh fry bread on the table. "Come while it's still hot."

Maggie and Marissa sat while she ate and then they all shared coffee and fresh apple pie for dessert.

"So tell us what you found in the south."

Nat told them of finding the rock outcroppings, seeing the mountain goat, and fresh water streams. Marissa was scared when Nat told them of her encounter with the mountain lion. "The next morning, when I turned east, I crested a hill and saw the most amazing sight."

"What was it?" Maggie asked.

"I came upon a valley dotted with large brown and black masses, moving so slowly, I thought I was dreaming. Then a giant bull lifted his head to the wind and scented me, and the herd trotted ahead a few hundred yards."

"Bison?" Maggie asked. "I haven't seen them since I was a young woman."

"Yes, bison, and they were so big, I was afraid Quincy could not carry the weight of even one of the smaller animals. I was hoping that, with your help, we could go back next spring and bring a few home. I think two would fill a smokehouse."

"I would like that. The meat is so lean and the steaks are mighty tasty." Maggie grinned.

"I tracked them for a day before they turned back east and I think they would only be a day or day and a half ride from here with the wagon. There are a few sections we may have to down some trees to get the wagon through, but I think we can get close."

"I can just imagine Smithy's excitement to see a bison head and hide," Marissa said.

"Have you ever seen them?"

"Only in the drawings in magazines back east," Marissa answered.

"They are majestic creatures," Nat spoke with a dreamy quality to her voice. "I can't wait to hunt them."

"They are challenging prey to hunt," Maggie replied. "I doubt you would have difficulty, though, with your skill."

"I will dream of them for nights to come." Nat grinned before yawning. "So what have you two accomplished while I was gone?"

"We've filled the new smokehouse with fish, and bagged nearly thirty pounds of jerky," Marissa said.

"We've harvested the last of the berries and put up more jelly than we can possibly eat over the winter, and we built the root cellar and have it partially filled," Maggie added.

"How do the pools look?" Nat asked.

"Less plentiful than we are used to, but we may get one more decent harvest for the hotel," Maggie said.

"We can work on the barrels in a few days. I think we could all use a day or two of rest."

"Are you finally confident we are ready for winter?" Marissa asked.

"Yes, I think we are. I don't know of anything else we can do to prepare. I will hunt in the morning, and then we can have a leisurely afternoon while your stews are cooking."

"On that note then, I'm going to call it a night." Maggie yawned and stood.

"I'm looking forward to a soft bed. I think I've gotten too old to sleep on the ground for long."

"Come then and let's get you to bed." Marissa pulled her up from her chair.

In the bedroom, Marissa undressed Nat and gave her a proper welcome back into their bed. As they lay with bodies entwined, searching for breath, Nat turned to her. "I love you so and am happy you have joined me here."

"I've finally found where I belong."

"Where might that be, my love?"

"In the strong arms of my brave bee charmer," Marissa answered.

Nat chuckled. "I will forever be your bee charmer."

Chapter Thirty-two

They managed to take two leisurely days before Nat decided it was time to begin the final harvest. She and Marissa waded through the pools to capture shrimp and the few remaining crabs while Maggie emptied the buckets they sent up the line.

Tom and Smithy would arrive again in two days to install the stove, and collect the last of the seafood for the hotel and goods for the shopkeeper. After they finished at the pools, Nat looked at Maggie and Marissa. "Are you up for a walk through the woods?"

They both nodded as Nat pulled on her boots. "What did you have in mind?" Marissa asked.

"I thought we would hitch Quincy to the wagon and see if we can find any fresh antlers to send back with Smithy. We haven't searched the woods south of the lake for antlers."

"That sounds fine to me. Let me get my boots back on."

"Maggie, will you get the rifle, while I hitch Quincy?"

"Yes, I will. You know you have four others that are dying to go, too, right?"

Nat smiled. "Let them come. We can all use the exercise."

Nat had barely made ten strides toward the barn when Gyp and the pups came racing after her. "Whoa, slow down." The puppies surrounded her. She walked inside the barn, took Quincy from his stall, and placed the rigging over his head and shoulders before leading him to the wagon. Maggie and Marissa joined her as she hitched Quincy to the wagon.

"Are we ready?"

"I do believe we are." Maggie had the rifle resting on her shoulder.

Nat took Quincy's lead and they walked toward the lake. The pups ran ahead of them, and when they got too far away, Gyp would bark for them and they'd come lumbering back. They all arrived at the lake to find the surface covered with waterfowl, and they found evidence that moose or large elk had come to drink just a short time before. The jingling of Quincy's gear would alert any animal in the area to their presence, so Nat wasn't worried about startling any large prey. She pulled Quincy into the forest on the far side of the lake and tied his lead to a tree.

"Let's fan out and see what we can find," she said. She took off to the right followed by Gyp and the pups. The scent of the forest filled the cool air as she walked nearly silently through the forest. The pups raced ahead, growling and tackling one another until the blue female scented something and froze. Several feet from her was a rack of elk antlers, the last velvet of the season blowing in the wind. Cautious of the strange sight, but not intimidated, she approached the rack and sniffed the antlers.

"Good girl. You found a nice rack." Nat petted the pup's head, picked the rack from the ground, and hoisted it to her shoulder. They moved forward and located several smaller sets of deer antlers, and with her arms full, she walked back to the wagon to deposit her finds. Either Maggie or Marissa had found a huge moose rack and had already placed it in the wagon. She could hear Maggie and Marissa walking in the distance.

Nat returned to her search and heard the pups growling. When she reached them, they were playing tug of war over a tree branch. She chuckled and continued her search.

When they gathered back at the wagon later in the afternoon, they had amassed a full load of antlers. Maggie was the last to arrive. "I have something I want to show you."

They followed her for several hundred yards into the woods until they came upon a large turtle shell. The puppies sniffed at it and then ran off to play. "I don't think I've ever seen a turtle this big," Nat said.

"It's strange to see one this far from the water. It's a sea turtle and it must have come ashore to die."

Nat bent over to examine the thick shell. "Can you think of a use for this?" she asked Maggie.

"Not at the moment, but it's such an oddity, I think we need to take it."

"Agreed, but we may have to fight Smithy to keep it. You know how he likes unique things."

"That's true, but I'd give him a good fight."

"There would be no fight. It's your find to do with what you wish. Come, let's see if we can haul this thing to the wagon."

†

When they returned to the cabin, they unloaded the turtle shell by the wash pot and pulled the wagon to the back porch. The pups' curiosity got the better of them, and they explored the inside of the large shell. Even their razor sharp teeth could not penetrate the surface. It did however give Nat an idea. She took a small saw from the barn when she returned Quincy to his stall and walked to the large smokehouse. There were several venison quarters smoking and she used the saw to cut the hooves from the legs. This would give the pups something to chew on besides her boots or the chair legs that seemed to be their favorite targets. She carried them to the back steps, sat down, and called the pups to her. She gave each one of them a hoof to chew on, and they happily accepted their gifts and settled under a tree to gnaw on their treats.

"Do you want me to slice some buttons for you while I have the bone saw?" Nat asked Maggie.

"That would be nice," Maggie answered. "I've got a stack by the wood pile on the porch that are the right size."

"I think there may be others on the wagon you can use, if you want to sort through them." Nat got up to walk to the woodpile on the back porch. She picked up the first set of antlers, and using a split log as a base, began cutting antler rounds for buttons.

Marissa returned to help Maggie sort through the wagon and they came up with several smaller sets of antlers, and then joined Nat on the porch.

"These should keep you busy for a while," Marissa said. "I'm going to go check on the stew and start some bread."

"I'll check the smokehouse and then see if there's anything in the garden that needs to be picked," Maggie said.

Nat sawed buttons until she had filled a half bowl and her hands were beginning to cramp. She walked down to the barn to care for the animals and put the saw away. Gyp trotted along behind her and sat to wait for her to finish. When Nat finished, she walked back to the porch and sat on the steps. Gyp laid down beside her and placed her head in Nat's lap while they watched the pups play.

Maggie joined her after placing several heads of cabbage and carrots in the root cellar. "It's a beautiful day, isn't it?"

"Yes, but I'm afraid we won't have many more like this."

Nat was watching the puppies intently with a smile on her face. "I'm going to miss those two. Tom and Smithy will take them back when they leave."

"You'll see them again," Maggie reminded her. "They will have good homes and will be treated like queens."

"Yes, you're right about that. They'll make good companions."

"Luna has already found his way onto the foot of my bed. He will make a good foot warmer this winter."

"Would you look at that?" Nat nodded toward the trail to the lake. Gyp raised her head.

Maggie squinted through the sunlight to see the gray wolf sitting at the edge of the trees watching the pups play.

"Go get him girl." Nat watched Gyp run across the clearing followed by the pups.

They watched the wolf sniff at the pups and lick them on the tops of their heads, marking them as his offspring, and then he lay down next to Gyp, letting the pups climb all over him in play.

"That's interesting," Marissa said coming out the door. "Are you two ready to eat or do you want to watch the happy family?"

"I think we can eat and let them enjoy one another for a while." Nat stood and offered Maggie a hand.

†

Nat spent the rest of the week splitting wood, while Maggie and Marissa cut the sections into smaller logs for the cook stove. By week's end, they had a sizeable pile on both porches for the stove, and a stack of fireplace lengths along the side of the cabin. When the sun was warmest, Maggie and Nat walked down to the pools, but the pools were often bare as the seafood harvest ended.

The wolf spent late afternoons playing with the pups while the women looked on. They were growing quickly, and feeding them was becoming a challenge. Gyp would lead them into the forest to teach them to hunt, but they were still more interested in playing than hunting, so Nat would hunt for rabbits and other small game. Her stack of rabbit pelts was growing, much to Maggie's delight. Maggie had decided to sew a coat with the soft, warm pelts to trade in the spring. She spent nights after dinner on the porch or by the fire, sewing while Nat carved and Marissa made buttons.

Nat had finished the whale carving and it sat proudly on the hearth. A bison was taking form from the block of wood she was whittling on, and she intended to have a small herd at winter's end. A mountain lion and goat would also join them on the hearth.

When the day arrived for Tom and Smithy to return, Nat woke up with a sadness. She was excited to see her friends and to have them install the stove, but she dreaded the following day, when they would leave taking Blue and Shine with them. A part of her deep inside regretted agreeing to their requests for a puppy. She knew the men would love them, but it felt like a small part of her would be empty without them. That morning, she took an extra-long walk in the woods with them, cherishing their time together. When they emerged from the forest, they found Tom and Smithy had arrived and were busy unloading the stove and supplies from the wagon. When the pups saw them, they raced across the clearing to welcome their new friends.

"These pups are huge. What have you been feeding them?" Smithy asked when he saw them.

"Anything they can sink their teeth into." Nat grinned. "They seem to really enjoy rabbit and squirrel."

"They are beautiful," Tom said. "I promise I'll take great care of Shine."

"I know you'll be great companions, and I expect them to visit when you return next spring."

"I'll guarantee that as soon as the weather permits, I'll be here."

Nat helped them finish unloading. They watched Tom and Smithy install the new stove. Tom climbed onto the roof and cut a hole for the stovepipe, sealing the edges with a sticky black resin that would prevent any water leakage.

Maggie and Marissa marveled at the size of the cook top, remarking how much easier cooking would be with the stove. They would cook up a batch of fresh vegetables and fry bread for lunch while Nat and the men walked down to the shore to dig clams to fry for dinner. Nat told them of her trip to the south, and both their eyes lit up when she told them of the bison herd.

"I was hoping maybe the two of you could spend a week or so down here, and we could have a proper hunt."

"That would be fine with me," Smithy replied. "We can get one of the others to mind the store for us. I'd love to hunt the bison with you."

"Maggie says they are challenging prey, and I can certainly understand that after seeing how big they were."

"Is it spring yet?" Tom asked.

Both Nat and Smithy laughed with him.

"I'm sure we'll all be ready for a good hunt after winter arrives," Smithy said.

"No doubt," Nat agreed. "On the milder days, if we have some, I hope to see what the winter brings as far as game is concerned. I think I'd probably drive Marissa and Maggie crazy if I stayed cooped inside all winter."

"I bet you would." Smithy knelt down to pluck the clams from the wet sand. "I couldn't help but notice your growing collection of carvings on the mantel. Would you consider doing some for sale? It would give you something to work on during those long winter nights."

"Yes, I could do that. I've got a few saplings I want to take down and cut into lengths for carving."

"I would love to see you carve some walking sticks too. I bet they would sell well," he added. "Everyone raved about the one you did for Maggie."

"That would keep me busy. I'll see what I can do."

Tom noticed the fish spears stuck in the sand. "Do you want me to wade out to the pools to see if I can get a fish or two to go with these clams?"

"Knock yourself out."

Gyp and the pups came rushing down to the shore just as he sat to remove his boots and socks. The puppies sniffed the socks and threatened to take off with his boots, so Nat picked them up out of the puppies reach. Tom took up several spears and headed into the chilly water, followed close by the pups.

"Lordy, this water has turned cold."

"Yes, it has, so don't spend much time in it," Nat warned.

"No worries there." He hurried over to the pool.

The puppies whined at the edge of the water, wanting to follow him, but the water was too cold for them to enter. He moved to the second pool when the first was empty. Tom turned back to find Smithy and Nat watching. He smiled and speared the first of four large fish from the pool, then turned to rush back to the shore.

Nat and Smithy had already attached the buckets of clams to the line while Tom was fishing. Smithy reached for the fish and Nat handed Tom the boots she had rescued from the pups. "Run ahead and get your feet dry and warm. We'll be right behind you."

They could see the smoke trailing from the stovepipe as she and Smithy walked up the hill. "I guess they are breaking in the stove. Thank you for such a great gift."

"It's the least we could do for y'all."

The next morning they woke to a gray sky. The threat of rain prompted the group to get busy. Nat and the men loaded the last of the seafood in the barrels onto the wagon, then the antlers, bags of jerky, and smoked fish. Maggie and Marissa cooked ham steaks and flapjacks with the last of the blueberries to give them a hearty breakfast for the road.

Tom and Nat walked to the barn to get Rusty, and she fed Hardy and Quincy while Tom hitched Rusty to the wagon. "I'm going to miss seeing you," he said, walking back to the cabin.

"Hopefully it will be a short winter." Nat placed her arm around his shoulder.

"We can only hope."

"Let's go eat so you can get on the road before the weather gets any worse." Nat led him back inside.

After breakfast, the men pulled on their coats and walked out to the wagon. Nat and the ladies followed them out. Tom looked almost guilty when he called Shine to him and lifted her onto the wagon, followed by Blue. Gyp looked on with what looked like an anxious expression as Smithy and Tom hugged everyone goodbye.

"We will take good care of your babies, Gyp," Smithy promised.

"You better go before we change our minds," Nat warned. "I'll be back as soon as I can with a wagon loaded with supplies." Tom climbed onto the wagon.

"Be safe, my friend, and don't drive these two crazy this winter," Smithy told her. With a final hug, he climbed in beside Blue.

Tom picked up the reins and they started down the hill.

Gyp whined softly. Nat knelt beside her, a single tear sliding down her face. "I'll miss them, too, but the boys will give them good homes." She buried her face into Gyp's coat.

Maggie tapped Marissa on the shoulder and nodded toward the cabin. Marissa nodded and quietly followed her inside, leaving Gyp and Nat to share a moment together. Luna had also watched the wagon pull away with his sisters, and he ran to the edge of the clearing before Nat's whistle brought him back. He looked confused and sad, bringing more tears to Nat's eyes, and she included him in their embrace. "We'll see them again." Luna shook his tail so hard he wiggled, and licked the salty tears from her face.

When Nat could no longer hear the wagon, she turned to go back inside. "Let's go," she called and Luna raced passed her to the door. Gyp stood looking into the forest for several long seconds, then turned, and walked with Nat into the cabin.

Chapter Thirty-three

Winter arrived, covering the ground in several inches of snow. Nat would travel to the barn several times per day to tend the animals and keep a path open. The wind off the water kept the front yard cleared of snow, but the ground crunched under her boots as she walked to inspect the outside of the cabin. The water rippled in the cold wind and even the shore birds tucked safely away in a warm nest away from the cold.

Weeks turned into months. Nat wandered outside often to escape the confines of the cabin. She needed the scent of the fresh, cold air, and the wide-open spaces to calm her soul. On one bright morning, she and Gyp walked down to the lake. The trees creaked in the soft wind, their branches coated with thin ice from a freezing rain from the night before, but the rest of the air was silent. The ground and everything in sight, was covered in a light dusting of snow, and she could smell more snow in the air. Gone were the flocks of geese and ducks, having fled south to warmer climates. Even though she spotted tracks of larger animals on occasion, it was rare that any other living creature was in sight on her walks. She and Gyp were totally alone in the chilly outdoor wonderland.

Maggie and Marissa stayed busy during those months, and Nat frequently returned to the cabin to the aroma of a cake or pie baking and filling the cabin with a wondrous scent. The woodpiles were still plentiful and the smokehouses filled with meats, so there was little need for Nat to worry.

The carvings grew on the mantel and she found great enjoyment in carving the walking sticks. She had filled one of the barrels on the front porch with lengths of wood she had cut to use, and settled in close to the fireplace to carve them. After carving them, she dried them in front of the fireplace and Maggie showed her how she could use ash and animal fat to stain the wood a variety of colors.

Gyp's wolf visited them often and Nat tried to befriend him. He became comfortable in her presence and was thankful for the meals of leftover stews, but he kept a safe distance from her. Nat became increasingly concerned with how skinny he had become and asked

Maggie to cook some of her beaver stew with some of the carcasses she had in the smokehouse.

Nat made him a warm bed of feedbags inside the barn, and she left bowls of food there for him in hopes he would bed down there out of the worst of the weather. It took several days, but he began spending nights in the barn. Nat would return to find the bowls and bed empty the next morning.

Under Maggie's constant prompting, Nat parted with an old work shirt that had become so worn it was impossible to mend. She placed it in the bed to provide extra insulation and to desensitize him to her scent.

A week later, when she entered the barn with a bowl of stew to feed the wolf, and tend to the horses, she was surprised to find him curled up in the bed. He made no move to escape, so she calmly placed the bowl on the ground and went to work tending to Hardy and Quincy. When she finished, she sat on a bale of hay and watched the wolf lap at the gravy in the nearly empty bowl.

He raised his head and fixed his golden brown eyes on her.

"I will tell Maggie how much you enjoy her stew," she told him.

She was even more surprised when he took a tentative step toward her and then another. Nat desperately wanted to reach out to pet him, but she knew the wolf would need to trust her first, so she waited. He crept a few more steps closer and sat on his haunches. They studied each other for several minutes before he turned and trotted into the forest.

"Well, that's a start." She picked up the empty bowl and walked back to the cabin.

So began the routine they would follow for several weeks. Each day he would cautiously approach a bit closer as they became accustomed to one another. When the day came that he finally sat in front of her, Nat slowly offered him her hand to smell. For several long seconds he seemed to be contemplating her before he lifted his muzzle to her hand and softly licked the top. "Good, boy," she whispered softly. He turned and trotted into the forest.

Nat was sitting on the front porch one mild morning, working on her latest carving, when she heard the sound of dripping water. She looked up to the roofline to see the slow drip of the melting frost. *Spring was finally on its way*. A smile grew on her face.

†

The first steamship of the spring brought two loads of goods to Smithy's store. New traps, mining equipment, and hunting supplies filled the crates Smithy and Tom unloaded. It was well after dark that evening before they had emptied the last of the crates and Tom sloshed home through the muddy trail. He was startled to see smoke coming from the chimney of his cabin. He knew the fire from the morning should have long died down to ash. He wondered if Nat had surprised him by coming to town. He rushed into the yard expecting to see Hardy tied to the hitch or grazing near the barn. He was nowhere in sight. Shine, who was matching his pace stride for stride, started growling as they approached the door.

Tom could see footprints in the mud and knew they were too large for Nat. Clearly, it was a man's foot. He bent down and retrieved his knife from his boot as he crept onto the porch. Tom pushed the door open and Shine, rushing through, nearly sent him flying as she searched the cabin for an intruder. There was evidence someone had been there, but the cabin was empty. Tom rushed back outside and circled the cabin. Whoever had invaded his space had spent time investigating the property, evident by the prints leading to the barn and smokehouse.

Who the heck? He circled back around to the front and caught a glimpse of movement from the corner of his eye. He rushed forward, but found nothing but growing darkness.

He reentered the cabin and felt like something was crawling on his skin. He took the rifle down from the mantel to check to make sure it was loaded and walked through the rooms. Someone had been lying on Marissa's bed. Displaced covers and the pillows stacked atop one another made his anger grow. He walked to his room to find someone had moved items around the room. His growl filled the air as he paced back through the house.

Tom tossed and turned all night, waking at the smallest sounds to get up only to find he was alone in the cabin. When the sun rose, he pulled on his boots, picked up the rifle and headed to town. Shine danced along beside him, unaware of the peril her master was facing.

"You're in early this morning. Is everything alright?" Smithy asked.

"I didn't sleep well last night. Smithy, someone was in the cabin yesterday."

"What do you mean?"

"When I arrived home, the fireplace was burning, and there was evidence someone had been in there."

"What the hell?"

"That's what I said. I think I saw someone in the shadows, but I couldn't find anything but footprints."

"Go home early today before it gets dark. Do you want me to go with you?"

"No, I've come prepared today." He held up the rifle.

Tom finished his work and headed for the door.

"Are you sure you don't want some company?" Smithy asked.

"Thanks, but I'm good, Smithy. Let's go, Shine." Shine crept from the bed she was sharing with her sister, Blue, stretched, and trotted over to her master.

"See you in the morning, boss."

"Goodnight, Tom."

Tom, anxious to reach home, walked swiftly until he reached the top of a hill and saw smoke coming from his chimney.

"What the hell." He pushed forward with his rifle cocked and ready.

Tom rushed inside and came to a halt when he saw a well-dressed man sitting at his kitchen table, drinking his coffee. The man, startled by Tom's sudden appearance, spilled coffee down his shirt. His eyes shifted from Tom to Shine, who was now baring her teeth with a low growl filling the air.

"Who the hell are you and what are you doing in my cabin?" Tom demanded as he approached.

"I could ask the same of you, young man. My name is James Mason and my wife, Marissa, and I own this cabin."

Tom was dumbfounded. "Marissa's husband is dead. He died in the war."

"I can assure you, young man, I am quite alive. You are?"

"My name is Tom and I rent the cabin from Marissa."

"So where is my wife?"

"She doesn't live here anymore."

"Where might I find her?"

"You won't, but I can get a message to her in a day or so. Until then, I'd suggest you get a room at the hotel." Tom shifted the rifle in his direction sending the man a clear message.

"Very well, young man, but I'd appreciate you contacting my wife and telling her I'm here to take her back east."

"Yeah, I'll do that." Tom bent down and tossed the man his bag. "The hotel isn't hard to find," he said and opened the door.

"Thanks. I hope to see you soon. Are you interested in buying the cabin since Marissa will no longer need it?"

"I'll have to give that some thought," Tom said. "Goodnight."

James smiled and then tipped his hat before walking out the door. Tom closed it behind him and then sank onto a kitchen chair. "What the hell is happening here?"

Shine, sitting at his feet looking up at him, whined. "I've got to talk to Smithy. He'll know what to do," he told Shine. "Let's go, girl."

The stranger was nowhere in sight when he reached town, which was a relief to Tom. He walked on toward Smithy's small house on the edge of town. He knocked on the door and waited for Smithy to answer.

"Come in," Smithy bellowed from inside the cabin.

When Tom and Shine entered the cabin, Shine rushed over to Blue and they began to wrestle.

"What's wrong? You look like you've seen a ghost," Smithy said. "Sit down." He pointed to a chair.

Tom slid into the chair and looked up at Smithy who was now frowning with concern. "I think I may have seen a ghost."

"Take a deep breath and tell me what on earth you're talking about." Smithy gave him a cup of water before sitting beside him.

"There was a fire burning in the cabin when I got home again. When I rushed inside there was a man sitting at the table." Tom took a drink of the water. "He claims to be James Mason, Marissa's husband."

"That's impossible. Her husband died in the war. I read the cable from the war department with my own eyes."

"He claims he's come to take Marissa back east to their new home."

"What did you tell him?"

"That Marissa did not live there anymore, that I was renting the cabin from her."

"Did you tell him where she was?"

"No. I told him I'd get a message to her, but didn't tell him where she lives. I sent him to the hotel."

"You did a good job."

"What can we do, Smithy? He can't take Marissa away, can he? What about Nat and their home?"

"Relax, Tom, we will think of something. Only Marissa will know if he is really her husband or not." Smithy was quiet for several long seconds, deep in thought. "Here's what I want you to do. Hitch up Rusty at first light and drive out to the cabin. Make sure Marissa is sitting down when you tell her the news of the man who claims to be her husband. Bring the women with you back to town and we will sort this matter out."

"Can he really force her to leave?" Tom's bottom lip was quivering.

"He's officially dead, according to the government, so I really don't know. The mayor will be back in town tomorrow, and I'll talk with him to get his advice while you go for the women."

"Smithy, I'm afraid of how Nat will react. Do you think she would kill him for trying to take Marissa from her?"

"That is something to be considered, so we'll have to keep a close eye on her when she's around the man."

"Oh, Lordy. I'd hate to see that happen, but I know in my bones she isn't going to react well." Tom blew out a breath.

"I know, but we'll deal with it if it happens. When you return, drop the ladies at the cabin and come get me. I don't want them meeting up with him alone." Smithy paced the floor of his cabin. "I will come up with a solution to the problem of James Mason, I promise. Go now and get some rest, so you can head out at first light."

Tom got up and left He rushed back to the cabin, and ate a quick meal before climbing into bed to get some rest. Haunted by nightmares, he finally gave up on sleep. He was dressed and driving the wagon out of town when the first rays of light reached the horizon.

†

Nat had finished her breakfast and was sipping on coffee while Maggie sat with her. "What are your plans for the day?

"I thought I'd pull out the traps for an inspection and oil them. It won't be long before the streams are full again."

"I can help if you'd like. I'm getting a case of cabin fever." Maggie grinned.

"I'd love your help."

"What would you two like for supper?" Marissa asked.

"I think there is some venison steaks left in the smokehouse," Nat said. "I think they'd go well with some of the pickled cabbage and some canned green beans."

"That does sound good," Maggie agreed.

"Let's go and check on those traps."

Nat nodded and she and Maggie stepped onto the back porch to walk to the barn. When they heard the approach of a wagon, Maggie looked at her. "It's too soon for Tom to be coming, isn't it?"

"Yes, I wasn't expecting him for another week. I wonder what's going on."

"I reckon we are about to find out." The wagon came into view.

The back door opened and Marissa stepped outside. "Is that a wagon?"

"Yes, it appears young Tom is visiting early," Nat told her.

The group stepped out into the yard to wait for Tom's arrival.

Tom saw the three women standing in the yard waiting for him. He took several deep breaths to calm his nerves and drove Rusty up the hill.

"Good morning, ladies." He pulled Rusty to a stop.

"Welcome, Tom. We didn't expect you before next week. You must have left before the sunrise to be here this early. Is everything all right?"

"Yes, I left before breakfast. I could use a cup of coffee to warm me." He grinned.

"Come inside then. I think we have some ham and biscuits left, too." A frown reached Nat's face.

Tom sat at the table with the ladies waiting patiently for him to tell the news he was obviously carrying since he wasn't due to arrive for another week. He sipped on his coffee and braced his courage.

"I wish I could tell you that I was here to help you get started laying traps, but I've been sent by Smithy."

"Is he sick or injured?" Nat asked, sounding alarmed.

"No, no, Smithy is well. I do have news though that has been upsetting to both of us, but let me start from the beginning."

"Please do." Nat looked truly worried.

"When I returned home yesterday, I smelled smoke from the fire and I knew the morning fire would have been long expired. I walked into the cabin expecting to find you. Instead I found a man sitting at the kitchen table."

"What the heck?" Nat said.

"Yeah, that's basically what I said." Tom paused and looked at Nat and then at Marissa. "The man claims to be James Mason, your husband."

Marissa turned white at the mention of the man's name and fainted.

"Oh shit." Tom lurched forward to catch her.

Both Nat and Maggie sat motionless. "I could use some help here." Tom was struggling to hold Marissa's head off the table at the odd angle.

"Of course." Nat moved beside Marissa and gently patted her face. "Marissa, Marissa, wake up, honey." She looked at Maggie. "Will you break off some ice in the barrel and wrap it in a rag for her?"

Maggie grabbed a rag from the counter and rushed to the front porch.

"I'm sorry, I didn't know how else to tell her."

"You're fine. I don't know any other way to do it either, Tom, so relax."

Maggie returned and rubbed Marissa's face with the icy rag until she began to stir.

When her eyes fluttered open, she looked at the others with embarrassment on her face. "Oh my, did I faint?"

"Yes, you did, but you're fine," Nat said.

Marissa looked at Tom. "Did I hear you correctly? Did you say James is alive?"

"He claims he is your husband, and he's here to take you back east with him."

"The hell he is." Nat jumped to her feet.

"It can't be him. My husband was killed in the war." Marissa had tears in her eyes.

"I sent him to the hotel. Smithy asked me to come get you and bring you both to town. We will meet at the cabin so we can plan what to do."

"Nat, try to relax and wait to find everything out before getting so upset," Maggie said. "Come, I'll help you saddle Hardy."

Tom watched the two women leave. Maggie was a calming influence for Nat who, he suspected, was about to erupt. He looked at Marissa who was still looking dumbstruck.

"I'll get us a bag together," Marissa said absently before leaving the room too.

Tom wiped his brow with his shirtsleeve, steadying himself for what was to come.

Nat stormed out of the cabin with Gyp and Maggie hot on her heels.

"You need to get ahold of yourself," Maggie said, when she caught up to her.

Nat wheeled on her friend with rage burning inside her. "How am I to do that when the woman I love is being claimed by a dead husband?" She immediately regretted her tone. "I'm sorry. I didn't mean to yell at you."

"I understand, but Marissa needs you to be calm for her right now. Just try to imagine how she feels."

"I can't feel anything but anger, right now."

"She loved him enough once to marry him and now, like a ghost, he's returned from the dead," Maggie replied. "It's no wonder she fainted. I would have, too."

Nat nodded and stalked to the barn to saddle Hardy. Maggie fed and watered Quincy who stomped his feet at being left behind.

Maggie wiped away the tears from her eyes as Nat pulled Hardy from his stall. "You have to believe everything will turn out for the best."

Anger flashed again in Nat's eyes. "I'll see him dead before he takes her against her will."

"You can't think like that, Nat. If the law recognizes him as her legal husband, there may not be any other option." Maggie grabbed Nat by her shirt. "Marissa would never want that. She loves you as dearly as you love her, so stop thinking like that."

Nat covered Maggie's hands with her own. "I know you're right, but I can't live without her in my life."

"Things will work out. I don't know how, but they will. I've seen the two of you as old women together in my dreams."

Nat hugged her smaller friend. "You've never told me that before."

"I never had a need to tell you. Now, will you let me go before you break me in half?"

Nat chuckled as she released Maggie. "I'm sorry. I didn't realize you had gotten fragile in your old age."

"Keep that up and I'll show you just how fragile I am," Maggie warned. "Come, let's get this nonsense over. I'll take Hardy and wait at the wagon with Tom while you go get Marissa."

Nat walked inside and heard Marissa crying in their bedroom. She rushed to brush away her tears and took Marissa in her arms, feeling the sobs racking her.

"This is too much all at once," Marissa cried into Nat's chest.

"I know. Everything will turn out for the best. We just have to believe that."

"I love you, Nat, and even if it really is James, I've grieved his death, and my love for him is gone. I'm here with you and that's where I belong."

"Yes it is." Nat's confidence bolstered by Marissa's affirmation. "We will put an end to this nonsense together."

Marissa leaned back in her arms and looked into her face. "Promise me one thing."

"What?"

"That no matter what happens, you won't kill James."

"It might be difficult, but I promise."

"Thank you, Nat. I do love you."

"I know." Nat kissed Marissa deeply. "Let's go put this matter to bed."

Nat took her hand and led her out to the wagon. She helped Marissa onto the wagon seat and handed her the small bag. "We'll be back as soon as we can. Any special requests from town?" she asked Maggie.

"Nothing but for the two of you to hurry home."

"We will." Nat mounted Hardy. "Let's go."

Maggie called Luna back to her side as the wagon turned and Gyp trotted along beside Hardy. "You need to keep me company, my big boy." She scratched behind his ears.

†

"So let me get this straight, this man comes to town and claims he is Marissa's dead husband?" Mayor Turner asked.

"Yes, and he intends to take her back east to their new home. Is she still legally bound to him as his wife?" Smithy asked.

"I don't know for sure. I'll have to do some research. I'll meet with them in a few days when I have more information. This may take a day or so, and a few cables with the Marshall in Wyoming."

Smithy nodded his comprehension. "I hope you understand Marissa's current position."

"While I don't agree with the nature of the relationship, who am I to question true love? It's obvious how much in love they are. Regardless, there may not be another option if the law is on his side."

Smithy nodded even though he didn't like the comment. "Thank you." He left the office no more confident than when he entered. He walked back to the store and paced the morning away, trying to come up with a brilliant idea for making James disappear if the law said he could force Marissa to leave with him.

†

The ride to town seemed longer than usual to Nat who, riding beside the wagon, was deep in her thoughts. Tom had tried his best to engage them in conversation, but their limited responses made it evident that neither was in a mood to talk. When they stopped to water the horses, Tom took Hardy's reins and led him and Rusty to the creek. Nat took Marissa's hand and they walked upstream of the animals for a drink.

"How are you feeling? Are you warm enough?" Nat asked.

"Yes, darling, I'm fine." Marissa took the cup of cold water Nat offered. She drank it and handed the cup back to her. "That tastes so good."

"Yes, it does." Nat took a deep drink. "We should be there soon, and we'll meet with Smithy. How do you want to meet with James?"

"To be honest, I don't know yet. I think it would be best to meet him at the cabin instead of at the hotel. I don't want the entire town knowing our business."

"I agree. We will do whatever you wish."

"Thanks." Marissa snuck a kiss before they walked back to the wagon.

When they arrived at the cabin, Tom jumped down and helped Marissa from the wagon.

"Go ahead into town to get Smithy, and I'll take care of the horses," Nat said.

Tom nodded and rushed into town.

"I'll help you." Marissa took Hardy's reins while Nat unhitched Rusty. They led the horses back to the barn and fed them.

Nat checked on Buck and added hay to his bin before going inside. She stoked the fire and added logs to the fireplace to warm the cabin while Marissa put on a pot of coffee.

†

Smithy met Tom on the porch of the store. "How'd they take the news?"

"Better than I imagined, except for Marissa fainting."

"Did you have them sitting down?"

"Yes, I did. Thank you for telling me to do that. It was hard enough catching her in a chair."

"Are they at the cabin?"

"They are. Nat's settling the horses while waiting to talk to you. Do you have a plan?"

"Not much of one, but it's better than nothing. Let's go," he said and they left town.

†

Marissa poured them all a cup of coffee as they sat around the table. "So what do we need to do?" Nat asked.

"I met with the Mayor. He is doing some research and will meet with us in a few days to discuss the circumstances."

319

"I need to see him to make sure it is James we are talking to. I need to know why he is just now making an appearance, nearly three years after his death."

"That will be interesting to find out. Especially why he didn't return immediately," Smithy agreed.

"Can he really claim me as his wife?"

"I don't know. That's part of what the Mayor is researching."

"I don't love him anymore, and I don't want to go with him. My home is here."

Smithy could see she was about to cry. When he looked over at Nat, he could see she was beginning to boil with anger. "We'll all do our best to see that doesn't happen." He tried to make his voice sound reassuring, even though he had his doubts.

"I guess I need to see him then."

"Are you sure you're ready for this?" Nat asked.

Marissa nodded slowly. "I have to know."

Smithy turned to Tom. "Will you go to the hotel and get him?"

"Sure," he replied before leaving the cabin.

Marissa turned to Smithy. "I made Nat promise not to hurt him. Do I need to have you make the same promise?"

"You said *kill him*," Nat reminded her. "I still might hurt him."

"Only if it needs to be done, but no, I don't think we'll need to kill him." Smithy was doubtful.

"That's comforting to hear," Marissa answered, sounding nervous.

Smithy looked up at Nat, hoping he could keep his word to Marissa. He knew what Nat was capable of if challenged, and he feared a city slicker would not fare well under her wrath. *I may have no other choice.*

When the door opened and Tom led a man inside the cabin, Marissa knew instantly he was indeed her husband. She looked at him, surprised by his lack of size. She didn't recall him to be a small man, but Nat towered over him when they were introduced.

"James, these are my friends, Smithy and Nat. You've already met Tom. Have a seat and I'll pour you a coffee."

James made a move to hug his wife, but Marissa raised a hand to stop him.

"I don't even get an embrace?" he asked.

She could tell he was slighted by her behavior, but she didn't care. "You have a lot of explaining to do." Marissa took her seat.

"Yes, we have a lot to catch up on, my love, but do we really need an audience?"

Marissa glared at him. "These are my friends and family. What you have to say to me can be spoken in front of them."

James looked at the people gathered around the table. "You have a strange sense of family."

Marissa could feel the tension as Nat frowned across the table. "They have never abandoned me and I can't claim that of you," she shot back at him.

James visibly reeled back from the barb Marissa had thrown at him. Nat sat straighter in her seat, pride evident on her face, and she eased back in her seat.

Marissa was holding her own against the man claiming to be her husband.

"I am still your husband and you need to give me more respect than this." The veins were popping out in James's neck.

"My husband is dead. I received a cable from the War Department that you died in action over three years ago. I grieved for your loss and put the love we shared to rest with your memory."

"I cannot account for the error from the government. I was wounded in battle, and I recuperated in a field hospital for three weeks, but I assure you, dear lady, I am alive and well. I traveled to Boston when I was well enough to travel. I started a small shipping business to secure our future. Now I've come to collect my wife and take you home."

Marissa lashed out and slapped the startled man across his face. "Do you really think you can waltz in just like that? Are you really that dense, James?"

"You do not speak to your husband in that manner," James growled grabbing for Marissa's arm.

Nat's reactions were lightning fast. She took her knife from inside her boot and rose to her feet. The blade flashed in the light as she placed it against the man's throat. "I'd drop that hand if I were you," she growled through gritted teeth. "We don't treat our women folk that way here.

"You have no right to prevent me from touching my wife. Who do you think you are, some type of protector for her, or some impersonation of a man with your short hair and manly dress?"

"I'm someone who loves Marissa for who she is, not what she can do for me."

"No matter. She is my wife and legally my property to do with as I wish," he growled back.

Smithy stepped between them. "That is still to be determined. We will meet with the Mayor in two days. He will hear both sides of this issue and give his verdict. He is the law in this territory."

Nat added enough pressure to the knife to make the man swallow hard. "Unhand her," she repeated.

James relented and removed his hand from Marissa's arm. "In a civilized world, that would be considered assault." He glared at Nat.

"I never claimed to be civilized. In my world, a man could be killed for assaulting a woman."

Smithy cleared his throat and looked at James. "Look, I can feel the tension escalating and it is time to stop before something happens that we will regret. There will be no resolution tonight, so I'd suggest you head back to the hotel and meet us at the Mayor's office in two days. The front desk can give you directions."

James, his face flushed with anger, stood and straightened the lapels on his coat. "Fine then, I shall see you in the morning," he snarled. "I plan to spend the rest of my visit in our home."

"Like hell you will," Tom growled. "I am legally renting this homestead from Marissa, the owner of this property, and you are not welcome here. You'll stay at the hotel or find some other arrangement."

Marissa smiled at Tom, proud that he was standing up for her. "He's correct. He rents this property from me every month and his payment is current, so he has the say of who remains under this roof."

"Damn," James cursed under his breath. "Fine then, I'll stay in the hotel. This isn't over, and I will come again tomorrow, to see if I can talk some sense into you, my wife."

"I will be here, but I doubt anything you can say will change my mind."

"We will see about that." He stormed out the door.

Tom, who had returned to pacing in front of the fireplace, looked at Smithy.

Smithy tossed him a bag of coins. "Follow him back to the hotel and bring us some supper back."

Tom caught the bag and left, following James into town.

Smithy let out a deep sigh. "That was intense. How are you holding up?" he asked Marissa.

"I'm fine. I don't see what I ever loved in that man. He's not the man I married. There is no way I will go anywhere with him."

"The only place you are going is back home," Nat replied.

"That's right," Smithy agreed. "Soon this whole mess will be done."

Silently, Smithy prayed that his words were true and the nightmare for Marissa and Nat would be over.

"I'll pump some fresh water, if you two will set the table," he stated, and left the room.

Nat stood and pulled Marissa into her arms. "I love you and will never let anything or anyone come between us."

"I love you, too," Marissa said. "I just want to go home and forget this ever happened."

"We will. I promise."

Nat released her and went to the pantry for plates and cups while Marissa pulled out forks and spoons.

Smithy returned, and dipped out cups of the cold water. "I'm going to suggest Tom come home with me tonight to give you two some privacy."

"Thanks Smithy," Nat replied. "I don't think there will be much sleeping done tonight."

Tom returned with a crate full of food, topped off with a fresh pie. Marissa, who had regained her appetite was eating as well as Tom and Smithy. They all laughed at Nat's stories of their first winter at the cabin.

"I'm glad you ladies made it through safely. I'll have to admit there were several storms that moved through that had me worried," Smithy told them.

"We survived so well, I was beginning to have difficulty fitting into my breeches," Nat told him. "I had to get outside and burn some energy to be able to fit in my clothes."

"How did your wood pile hold out?"

"We still have one large stack of split wood and logs. I did have to chop more of the smaller wood for the stove, but that was easy."

"How did the chickens fare?"

"We only lost one hen to the cold. The extra smokehouse really sheltered the coop and added extra warmth. They continued laying most of the winter."

"What will you do differently next winter?" Tom asked.

Nat thought for a few seconds. "I think I'd like to have a couple of split pigs in the smokehouse. The ham and bacon didn't last as long as I'd hoped."

"It was a nice break from the moose, venison, and smoked fish," Marissa said. "I think some sausage links and maybe some beef would be nice too."

"Yes, a steak would have been nice on those cold nights."

"The bison will be a nice addition," Smithy said. "I look forward to trying the meat."

Nat smiled. "I can't wait until it warms enough for us to travel south."

"It will be here before we know it," Smithy told her.

The conversation kept the focus off the problem at hand and everyone was relaxed and enjoyed a hearty meal. When the food was gone and the dishes cleaned, Tom and Smithy left to head back to town.

"Keep your ears open tonight," Smithy whispered to Nat. "I don't think he'd be stupid enough to try anything, but you never know for sure."

"I'll be ready if he pays us a visit."

"We'll see you in the morning," Smithy said.

Nat and Marissa watched their friends disappear into the darkness, and then went back inside the cabin. Nat bolted the door behind them and then joined Marissa by the fire. It was still cool enough at night to give them a good chill. "This feels good." She warmed her backside at the fireplace.

Marissa smiled. "Do you want some coffee?"

"I'd love a cup with you." Nat returned to the kitchen table and Gyp positioned herself between the table and the door. Her sharp hearing would alert Nat if anyone paid them a visit during the night.

Nat blew out the lantern flame and climbed into the bed beside Marissa. She pulled her into her arms and held her close. She felt Marissa shivering and she lifted her face to look at her. "Are you chilled?" she asked.

"No, I'm toasty warm with you next to me. I'm fearful of what the future will bring."

"Time and patience will bring an end to this madness, and we will go on with our lives."

"I wish I had your confidence," Marissa sighed.

"Trust me."

"I do, with my life." Marissa snuggled back into Nat.

Marissa turned toward Nat. "Will you make love with me tonight?"

"I'd love to." Nat climbed from the bed. She added a log to the fireplace and walked back to the bed.

She sat Marissa on the edge of the bed and lifted the nightshirt above her head as Marissa's hands caressed the length of Nat's long muscular legs. Marissa's hands on her made her burn with desire and she reached behind her head to remove her nightshirt, leaving her naked in front of her lover. Nat smiled down at Marissa her hands moving around to fondle the cheeks of her ass while her tongue trailed from one hipbone to the other. Nat buried her hands in Marissa's long hair as Marissa's hands moved between them to cup Nat's small breasts, causing her lover to moan with pleasure.

"I need you," Marissa breathed against Nat's skin.

Nat pulled back the covers on the bed and then joined Marissa on the bed. Marissa rolled her onto her back and straddled Nat's waist. As she leaned forward, her hair cascaded down across Nat's bare skin, leaving a trail of fire burning down her body. Nat moaned loudly as Marissa kissed down her chest and her hair floated across Nat's hard nipples.

"You like that feeling, hmm?" Marissa whispered against her skin.

"Oh yes, Marissa." Nat's voice was full of her passion.

"Then you should really like this." Marissa moved her right breast between Nat's legs, dragging her nipple up Nat's lips and across her aching clit, and then moved down to repeat her movements.

"That feels so good," Nat groaned.

Marissa felt Nat's wetness coating her breast as she moved against her. "I am going to make you feel so much better."

Marissa moved farther down Nat's body, her tongue tracing small circles around Nat's clit, teasing her lover to the brink of climax, only to back off and allow Nat to release the breath she was holding.

"Marissa, please," Nat begged.

Marissa's fingers gently parted Nat's lips and her tongue lavished slow kisses on Nat as she drank in Nat's juices. When Marissa's tongue finally entered Nat, she shook uncontrollably and flooded Marissa's face with her sweetness. Marissa climbed up Nat's body, licking her lips and her eyes smiling at Nat.

"You taste so sweet, my love," Marissa whispered in Nat's ear.

"Not near as sweet as you." Nat rolled Marissa onto her back. She took her time, teasing Marissa. When finally released, Marissa's voice echoed in the room, calling Nat's name.

Nat smiled and pulled her into her arms.

Nat held her until Marissa fell asleep, but sleep would not come easily for her. Her ears were vigilant for any sounds that were unusual, and her mind wandered through different scenarios of the meeting with the Mayor. She finally settled on a plan. If the law prevailed and Marissa was still the property of her husband, Nat would challenge James to a duel. It was the only chivalrous way for her to confront him that was legal. She would kill him or die trying to protect her love.

✝

When she awoke and stretched, Nat turned to look at Marissa who was already wide-awake.

"I will never admit to saying this, but I almost missed Rufus waking me this morning with that awful crowing of his."

Marissa chuckled. "I can't believe you admitted to that."

"He keeps me from sleeping through these special moments with you." Nat leaned over and kissed her. "How did you sleep?"

"Surprisingly well, but then I always sleep well next to you."

Nat smiled. "You always say the sweetest things."

"Only for you, my bee charmer." Marissa grinned.

Later that morning, James came to the cabin to try to convince Marissa to return east with him and start a life anew. Nat was proud of Marissa when she stood up to him and gave in to no part of his pleading.

When a frustrated James stalked out of the cabin, Nat pulled Marissa into her arms. "I love you."

"I love you, too, and won't let him come between us." Marissa kissed her soundly, erasing all doubt in Nat's mind.

✝

The next day, Smithy walked a customer out the front door and turned the wood sign to *Closed*.

"What are you doing?" Tom asked.

"I'm closing the store until we get back from the Mayor's office. Let's go."

Tom was proud to be included in the morning's events. He loved the ladies like family, and was happy Smithy saw him as such.

They met Nat and Marissa at the edge of town and found James already waiting in the foyer of the Mayor's office. They exchanged nods, but remained silent.

Promptly at nine, the Mayor opened the door to his office and welcomed the group inside. Smithy introduced James and they all took a seat around a large table.

The expression on the Mayor's face was solemn. Nat could see the worry on Smithy's face. Mayor Turner was normally a jovial, fun-loving man, and his serious demeanor was worrisome to her.

"I have been made aware of the basics of this situation, and have completed research into the circumstances, but I would love to hear from both parties and get their versions of events." He settled at the head of the table.

"Ladies first," he said, turning to Marissa.

"Thank you, Mayor Turner. My husband and I moved here nearly five years ago and rented the cabin that young Tom here now rents from me. My husband wanted to move west to have a fresh start after the war ended. We moved here, and then he went back east to join the war effort."

"That was very admirable of him," the Mayor stated.

The comment brought a smile to James' face.

"Months passed and I hadn't heard anything from my husband since the day he left. No letter or cable from him, nothing to let me know his whereabouts or any news of his health." She looked at Smithy and then the Mayor. "I hadn't any information regarding my husband until the morning you and Smithy turned up at my cabin with the cable from the War Department."

"I remember that now. It came to my office as the Mayor to break the news of your husband's death to you. It read that he died valiantly serving his country."

"Yes, I still have the cable tucked away in my belongings. So, you see, I mourned the death of my husband, believing him deceased, and after several years I've moved on with my life."

"As I also recall, you received a small widow's benefit from the army. Is my memory correct?"

"Yes, you are. I did receive a small sum from the government in consolation for the death of my husband. I used it for a down payment on the cabin, and have since paid the mortgage in full."

"So the cabin is solely in your name on the deed?"

"That is correct."

James, obviously growing impatient with the questioning, barked out, "What does this have to do with anything?"

"I must insist you stop interrupting, Mr. Mason. You will have your opportunity to speak in just a moment."

James said nothing more, but Nat could see his ire growing. She couldn't resist a sweet smile when he looked her way and fixed her with a glare. The skin on his neck was turning red, and the flush was moving up to his face as she held his stare.

The Mayor cleared his throat and continued. "So, by notification of the government of this country, and having no other news of your husband, you were given the status of widow. Is this correct?"

"Yes, it is," Marissa proudly answered.

"But I am alive and well, by damned. Can you not see me sitting right here?" James roared.

Nat could see that the Mayor was clearly losing his patience. "Mr. Mason, we only have one small cage we use for a jail cell in this town, and it is not the most pleasant of locations, but as God is my witness, I will send you there for the day if you do not shut that yap of yours."

She smiled, watching James turn from scarlet to a deep shade of crimson, but keeping his mouth shut.

The Mayor turned back to Marissa. "Is this man the one you married nearly five years ago?"

"His name is the same, but the man I married would never have acted in this manner. He was a sweet, gentle man, who only treated me with love and kindness."

The Mayor then turned his gaze back to James. "Now, Mr. Mason, we will hear your version of this story."

"Finally," James cried. "I have returned to claim possession of this woman, my legally married wife."

Nat tensed at his claim. It took great restraint to keep from reaching for her knife and gutting the beast right where he sat. Smithy placed his hand on her shoulder and it was enough of a distraction to keep her hand at bay.

"Claim possession, that's sounds remotely like a wife is some form of indentured servant or even a slave." The Mayor raised his brow in astonishment.

"That's right. By law, she's still my property," James crowed.

"Correct me if I'm wrong, Mr. Mason." Mayor Turner gave him a curious look. "Did you not go to war to free this country of the very same servitude you wish to impart to your reported wife?"

James stammered for a few seconds. "She's still my wife and I plan to leave here today with her by my side."

The Mayor ran his fingers through his hair. "So, let's get back to your story, Mr. Mason. You left your wife here to join the army. Is this correct?"

"Yes, it is. I am proud to have served and received a battle wound for my country."

"Where was this injury?" the Mayor asked.

"I was wounded by gunshot to my leg." James pointed to his lower right leg. "I was in the hospital for several weeks."

"Show me this injury," the Mayor requested.

"What?" James asked.

"I want to see your injury from the war," the Mayor explained.

James hesitated, but then stood and moved several feet away from the table and began to roll up his pant leg. The skin on the outside of his calf looked bruised in a line of discoloration.

"That is your war wound? A grazing from a bullet." The Mayor's voice was full of disbelief.

"Yes, it is, and might I add it was very painful. It was several weeks before I could bear weight on my leg again."

Nat could see that the Mayor was furious. "You coward! Boys and men were losing limbs to the field surgeons, while thousands gave their lives, and you received a scratch and claimed it to be a war wound?"

"It was a wound I received in battle." James lunged forward.

Both Nat and Smithy jumped to their feet ready to restrain him if necessary.

"Take your seat, Mr. Mason." The Mayor restored his emotions and held his hand up. "So, after your injury, you were hospitalized for several weeks. Is this correct?"

"It is, sir," James agreed.

"What happened after your release?"

"I had given my service to my country, so I traveled to Boston."

"Boston? Why Boston? Was your unit in Boston?"

"No, they went on to Gettysburg. I used the money I had saved from my service and bought a small building which I've turned into a shipping business on the Boston Harbor," he reported proudly.

"So, instead of returning to your company, you deserted your service to this country?"

James' eyes bugged out at the Mayor in disbelief. "It wasn't like that. The war was almost over by then, so I didn't feel my services were needed any longer."

Nat looked at Marissa whose mouth was hanging open as she listened to the story James was weaving. It was obvious to Nat that she was in shock at the words coming out of his mouth.

"You spineless coward." Marissa slapped his face.

"You will pay for that," James threatened.

Nat flew to her feet, striding toward the man, hell bent on doing serious damage to him when the Mayor spoke.

"Miss St. Croix, please return to your seat until we are finished."

Nat hesitated and then returned to her seat.

The Mayor looked at Smithy. "What time is the next steamship?"

"At noon, Mayor," he answered.

The Mayor looked at the clock on the mantel over his fireplace. Eleven-thirty. A half-hour until the next steamship departure. "I am ready to make my ruling."

Nat held her breath as everyone turned toward him. The air felt sucked from the room.

"In the eyes of this office, which is the legal equivalent of a marshal's office, I find you to be a fraud and a coward, Mr. Mason. In the eyes of our government, you are dead and your wife is a widow."

Nat released the breath and began to relax.

"I have two solutions you can choose from for your actions," said the Mayor continued. "First, you can rush back to the hotel to collect your bags, buy passage on the next steamship, and never return to our fair town. Or, I can have your sorry ass, pardon the language, ladies, thrown into our one, aforementioned, less-than-adequate jail cell to await four months for the arrival of the Wyoming Marshal to face charges for desertion of duties and defrauding the government."

"Are you insane?" James lunged to his feet. "She is my wife and, therefore, my property."

"Did you make any attempt to notify her that you were still alive?"

"No."

"So, for over three years, she thought you had died, and then you just show up out of the blue and expect her to take you back as her husband?"

"I am her husband," he shouted.

"No, sir, you are not in the eyes of the law." The Mayor turned back to Smithy. "Smithy, Tom, will you escort this man to the hotel to pay his bill and collect his baggage, then see that he gets on the ship?"

"With pleasure," Smithy replied. "Let's go." He glared at James.

"You will regret this." James climbed to his feet shaking his fist at them.

"Should I add a charge of threatening an officer of the law, and toss your sorry ass in jail?" Mayor Turner asked.

"No, there will be no need for that," James answered.

"Then I wish you the best for your future. Let me remind you once again that you are not welcome here."

"You can't do this. This is illegal," James sputtered.

"I doubt that." Smithy pushed him toward the door.

Tom followed them from the room, leaving Nat and Marissa with the Mayor.

"Thank you for your assistance in clearing this up. He once was a good man," Marissa told the Mayor.

"You were right in burying that man years ago. The man he is today isn't worth having. I would recommend you ladies stay out of sight until he is safely aboard the ship. Please feel free to stay here in my office as long as you'd like."

He started to turn away and stopped, turning back to them. "By the way, I just wanted to say that moose jerky you make is the best I've ever tasted."

Nat grinned. "Thank you, sir. I'm glad you enjoy it."

"Have a nice day, ladies," he said, and left the office.

Marissa collapsed into Nat's arms. "I'm so glad that is over."

"Everything will be back to normal soon." Nat stroked her lover's hair. "He will be gone for good and we can get on with our lives."

They watched from the front window as Smithy and Tom emerged from the hotel and marched James toward the harbor. James looked toward the Mayor's office and Tom promptly urged him forward. Dwarfed between the two large men, James could do nothing but comply with the Mayor's command.

When the men were out of sight, Nat walked outside with Marissa and they sat on a bench outside of the Mayor's office to wait for Tom and Smithy to return. Nat looked over at the general store across the street.

"Since we're in town, would you mind if we pick up a wagon load of supplies?"

"It seems a waste if we don't," Marissa replied.

"I'll go order if you'll wait for the boys to return. I think we owe them a lunch."

"We'll wait for you at the hotel then." Marissa walked across the street and Nat went inside the store.

†

The steamship was just arriving when the men made it to the harbor. Smithy placed his hand on James' shoulder and the smaller man did everything he could to shake it off, but Smithy firmly gripped his shoulder.

"Take your hand off me," James sneered.

"I wanted to give you a piece of friendly advice. If you value what's left of your miserable life, don't ever return here," Smithy warned. "If Nat's blade doesn't slit your throat, I will make sure you stumble into an accident and I guarantee your body will never be found."

"You can't threaten me like this."

"These aren't threats. We promise that you will regret ever stepping foot on this ground if you return." Tom gave him a smack on the back.

Tethered onto the pier, the steamship was ready for the two passengers who waited for boarding. Tom picked up the bag and pushed it into James' chest.

"Let's go." He urged James forward.

"Hey there, Smithy," the boatman called out.

"Hey, Bobby, I need a favor from you."

"Anything."

"Make sure this one makes it across the harbor and he doesn't return." Smithy pointed to James.

"Do you want me to drop him halfway across the bay?"

"You wouldn't dare." James eyed the man.

Bobby pinned James with a look that Smithy could tell easily relayed to James that Bobby wouldn't hesitate for a breath to send him overboard.

"That's not a bad idea," Smithy agreed. "We promised him safe passage on the ship though. He is to never return, so make sure he gets off across the way."

"No worries, Smithy. The only way he'll make it back here is if he swims. I doubt this little bit of man could outswim the sharks."

James's face blanched while clutching his bag to his chest.

"Thanks, Bobby." Smithy tossed him a coin for the trip.

Bobby caught the coin and tossed it back to him. "Mr. Fancy Pants can pay his own passage or swim," he added with a grin.

James rummaged through his coin purse to dig out a coin and handed it carefully to Bobby.

Bobby took the coin and placed it in his pocket, then shoved off from the pier. Tom could hear him telling James, "I don't know what you did to irritate those two, but if you plan to see your next birthday, I would stay far, far away from them. Those men can make a man disappear." Bobby shot a wink to Tom.

"My business isn't done here," James shouted from the safety of the departing ferry.

"Yes, it is, if you know what's in your best interest," Bobby warned.

Smithy and Tom turned away from the harbor and chuckled. "I almost wished he would have put up a struggle. I would have taken great pleasure in pounding him to the ground."

"I don't think you'll ever get that opportunity again," Tom said, while they were walking back to join the ladies.

"Let's hope not."

✝

After lunch, Nat and Tom walked back to the cabin to hitch Rusty to the wagon to return to town for the supplies she had ordered.

Smithy and Marissa went back to his store. "Are you feeling relieved?"

"Very much so. This all happened so fast, but I'm glad it's over. You do think it's over, don't you?" Marissa asked.

"By all means. I don't think James Mason will ever show his face around here again. If he did, he would meet with an accident, or at least that's what young Tom promised him."

"Did he really?"

"Yes, he did, and I believed him."

"He's a good young man." Marissa smiled.

"That he is. Would you mind if he traveled back with y'all for a few days? He's been chomping at the bit to get out there after being cooped up all winter."

"We'd love to have him for a visit. You too, if you can spare the time."

"Not just yet, but I guarantee I'll be there in time for the big hunt."

Marissa smiled. "Nat's been dreaming of that all winter."

"She's not the only one. We are both excited to be included."

Tom entered the store and walked over to them.

Smithy looked at him. "I thought you might stay and help them get loaded?"

"Nat sent me over to get a dozen new traps from you."

"Go ahead, you know where they are."

"Would you like to spend the rest of the week with us?" Marissa asked.

Tom turned back to Smithy. "Would that be all right with you?"

"It was his idea," Marissa said.

"I can survive for a few days. Bring back a load of goods if Nat has some ready."

"Yes, sir." Tom rushed over and picked out the traps Nat needed and walked to the counter. "She asked for us to put these on her account."

"She's got more credit than that on her account," Smithy replied. "Ask her if we can get together for a steak dinner at the hotel tonight."

"Will do." Tom smiled and went on his way.

"That does sound good," Marissa agreed. "Let me go see if I can help out. See you later."

†

It was just after dark when the wagon was covered and unhitched in front of the cabin. Rusty was returned to his stall and all the horses were cared for. With the chores done, Tom, Nat, and Marissa walked back to town to meet Smithy for supper.

Joseph met them in the dining room. "I am excited to hear that you will soon have seafood for me to serve to my guests. Tom shared that you hope to hunt bison this spring. I will gladly buy any bison you can bring me."

"Have you eaten it before?" Nat asked.

"Yes, down in San Francisco a few years ago. It's even better than that steak you are eating."

"That's mighty tasty then." Nat turned to Tom and Smithy. "It looks like we may need to plan several hunting trips this spring."

"That wouldn't bother me at all," Tom replied.

Smithy grinned. "More meat, more hides, what's not to like about that?"

"You three can hunt all you want. I prefer a nice soft bed." Marissa smiled at them.

"You can hold down the fort at the cabin while we're gone," Nat told her. "I'm sure there will be plenty to keep you busy."

"I hope we'll have a garden to tend by then and there's always wood to chop for the stove."

"You're right about that," Nat agreed.

Gyp, Blue, and Shine gnawed on steak bones under the table. "We'll leave the dogs with you for protection and some company while we're gone. It'd be too dangerous to have them around the bison."

"I'll let you explain that to her when the time comes." Marissa looked at Gyp.

Nat chuckled. "She'll pout, but it really would be safer."

"What time do you plan to head back in the morning?" Smithy asked.

"Early, so we can make it home and unload by lunchtime. I hope to get some traps set before nightfall."

"I can help and you can teach me," Tom reminded her.

"That was the plan." Nat smiled.

Smithy paid for dinner even though Nat offered. "We needed to celebrate," he told her. "I won't see you in the morning, but I'll see you when you come back to town."

"Thanks for everything." Nat hugged him.

"I'm glad everything turned out well."

"Me, too." Marissa kissed him on the cheek.

"I'll see you next week, boss," Tom told him.

"Have fun and bring me something nice."

"I will." Tom shook Smithy's hand and walked home with the women.

Tom added wood to the fire to take the chill off the air. "I'll get up early, get Rusty hitched and the horses ready, if you promise to make some ham to go with the biscuits," he told Marissa. "I figured we could eat on the way."

"You're not excited are you?" Nat asked with a grin.

"Naw, not me."

"Get some sleep then and we'll head out at first light." She and Marissa retired for the evening. Nat hadn't realized how tired she was until she lay down. "We can all relax now," she told Marissa.

"Yes, we can," Marissa replied. "I love you, bee charmer."

"I love you, too." Nat wrapped a protective arm around Marissa and fell asleep.

Chapter Thirty-four

Tom's bustling around woke them the next morning, and when they climbed out of bed he had already stoked the fire and laid ham out on the counter to be warmed.

"I'll get to cooking if you want to help Tom get the horses ready," Marissa said.

"I'll be back soon then." Nat kissed her sweetly and then left.

Tom had placed the rigging on Rusty, and was leaving the barn when Nat arrived. "Good morning."

"Morning." Tom greeted her with a smile. "I hope I didn't wake you."

"No, I was awake, just not quite ready to get out of the warm bed."

"There's still a chill in the air."

"Makes for good traveling weather. Be sure to bring a warm coat since it's still cooler by the coast."

"Yes, ma'am." Tom led Rusty to the wagon with Shine following along.

Nat went inside to saddle Hardy and take Buck out of the stall. She was preparing to saddle him when Tom returned.

"I'll get him saddled if you want to check on breakfast."

Nat nodded and walked Hardy to the front yard and tied him to the hitching post. She stepped back inside as Marissa was pulling the fry pan off the fire.

"Will you put up the fireplace screen and scatter the logs while I make our biscuits?" Marissa asked.

"No problem." Nat used the poker to separate the burning logs and then fastened a wire screen to the mouth of the fireplace, allowing the fire to burn out on its own. Gyp stretched lazily on the hearth.

"Are you ready to go home, Gyp?" Nat knelt to scratch her head. Gyp licked her hand. "I think you just stayed inside hoping for a bite of ham."

"Well, it worked. I gave her some scraps," Marissa admitted.

"You are spoiling my dog."

Marissa chuckled. "Like she could get any more spoiled."

Gyp yawned and stretched out even more in front of the fire.

"Have you filled our canteens?"

"I'm on my way to do that." Nat left the cabin.

Nat filled two canteens and when Tom approached with Buck, she reminded him to fill his. She placed one on the wagon bench and the other around her saddle horn. "Do you have your bag packed?"

"It's already on the wagon and my rifle is under the seat." Tom tied Buck to the back of the wagon.

"I reckon you're all set then. Will you go get our bag on the bed and put it on the wagon while I check on Marissa?"

Tom flew past her into the cabin.

Marissa was filling a tin plate with a stack of ham biscuits when Nat returned.

She took one of the biscuits and bit off a large bite. "These are tasty."

"Let's go home." Marissa handed Nat the plate to carry to the wagon. Gyp raced them to the door and Tom followed them out, carrying the bag to the back of the wagon.

Nat placed the plate on the bench and helped Marissa climb into the wagon. She took another biscuit and mounted Hardy. Gyp ran to the edge of the yard with Shine hot on her heels as Tom released the brake and Rusty started walking.

†

They made a brief stop to water the animals and made it back home before the sun rose to its midday height. Tom pulled the wagon to a halt at the back of the cabin and jumped to the ground. He stretched and then reached to help Marissa down from the wagon.

"You made good time." Maggie stepped out onto the porch and smiled.

"We left at the crack of dawn." Nat smiled back.

Maggie hugged Marissa. "I'm very happy to see you return. You can tell me all about it while we put away the supplies."

"It's good to be home." Marissa returned the hug.

"Will you take our bags inside while we unload the cabin supplies and take the rest to the barn?" Nat handed bags to the other two women.

"Let's get to work," Nat told Tom. She loaded his arms with bags of flour, meal, and sugar. When Maggie and Marissa returned to help, she gave them smaller bags of supplies. She held out a small bag for last and when Maggie returned for more, Nat held it out to her. "This one is for you."

Maggie grinned, opening the cloth sack to find several smaller bags. "Seed corn," she said excitedly.

"There are also seeds for beans, squash, and cabbage. The potato slips haven't arrived yet, but I let him know we wanted some."

"Thanks," Maggie replied. "Quincy and I began turning the soil in the garden. I was wondering if we could clear more rocks to have a bigger garden."

"I don't see why not. Now that we have Rusty, he can pull the plow much more easily than Quincy can. We can still use him to pull the small wagon, and we can put the rocks in the wagon to add to our rock base in the front yard."

"Maybe one day we will have a rock fence," Maggie said.

"I'd be glad to plow for you." Tom looked at them with a serious expression.

"The rest of us will load the rocks, and chop the larger clumps of earth the plow doesn't break," Nat said.

"Do you want to plow today since Rusty is already rigged for pulling?" Tom asked.

"We could. It shouldn't take long to finish unloading the supplies."

"Maggie and I will put away the cabin supplies and be ready when you are." Marissa winked at Nat, then returned inside the cabin.

"Are you sure you don't mind plowing?" Nat asked Tom. "I didn't invite you out to work you to death."

"I actually miss that part of farming," he admitted. "There's nothing like the smell of fresh-turned earth to a farm boy."

Nat smiled at him, fully understanding how he felt. She felt the same way about the scent of the forest. It was in her blood and gave her comfort.

Tom led Rusty to the barn and began to unload the wagon while Nat cared for Buck and Hardy. When he had the supplies stored, he placed the plow in the back of the wagon and walked Rusty back to the cabin to unhitch him. Quincy was eager to work and stepped quickly out of his stall as Nat slipped the rigging over his shoulders and led him to the cabin. She took several shovels and a rake from the barn and leaned them against the porch railing. Then she hitched Quincy to the wagon.

Maggie handed them all work gloves and when Tom was ready, he took up Rusty's reins and they began to plow. When he reached the end of the first row, he turned to Maggie. "How much farther do you want to go?"

"I'd like to double the size, if the ground isn't too rocky," she answered.

"Only one way to find out." He urged Rusty forward.

The strength of the horse and the young man made the work look effortless, but Nat knew how physically demanding plowing could be. They followed along beside him and picked up the larger rocks he uncovered with the plow. The soil was dark and rich, but filled with rocks. It only took two turns of the plow to fill the small wagon and Nat walked Quincy to the front yard to unload. Maggie helped while Marissa carried a cup of cold water to Tom and made him take a break.

Tom removed his work shirt and hung it on a low branch. He and Rusty had worked up a lather.

"What would you like for supper tonight?" Maggie asked.

"I'd love some of your chowder and fry bread." Tom had a bashful look on his face. "If it's not too much of a problem."

"You're earning every bite of it," Maggie told him. "The least I can do is feed you well."

"Thanks, Maggie." He smiled and picked up the reins returning to the plowing.

"I'm good here, if you two want to go to the beach to see if there are clams," Nat said.

"With two of us digging, it shouldn't take long." Marissa patted Nat's shoulder.

"Hurry back then." Nat picked up the large rocks Tom had uncovered with the plow.

Tom made it through two more rows of the new earth before the plow banged into a large stone. Nat was just returning from emptying a load of rocks when she heard the sound.

"That sounds like a solid one," she told him. "Take a break and grab some water while I see how big that rock is." Nat picked up a shovel and began digging around the edge of the rock.

Tom walked to the pump, drank two cups of water, and brought a bucket for Rusty and Quincy. "How big is it?"

"It's good-sized and solid. This one's going to take some digging to unearth."

"Do you need my help?"

"Not yet. Let me dig around it a bit and we can use a sapling to pry it from the ground."

"Just holler when you're ready." Tom returned to plowing.

Nat removed the soil from the perimeter of the rock to find it was nearly three feet wide. She concentrated on the lowest point of the small boulder and began digging, trying to locate the bottom of the rock. When she was a foot below the surface, Nat walked to the chicken coop, picked up one of the small saplings in the pile, and carried it to the rock. She placed one end in the hole, wedged it beneath the rock, and placed all her weight on the lever. The rock didn't budge. Nat dug out holes on each side and the back of the rock, trying the sapling wedge in each hole with minimal movement. Not to be defeated, Nat walked to the woodpile for three more saplings.

Maggie and Marissa had returned with the clams and she called out to them. "Ladies, can I get your help?"

Tom stopped Rusty and walked to where Nat was working. "That looks pretty stubborn."

"It's pretty solid." Nat scratched her head. "I figured we could work together to see if we can at least get some movement. If we can get a turn on it, we can use Rusty to pull it the rest of the way."

Tom nodded. "That sounds like a reasonable plan."

With all four of them working in unison, they were able to break the seal the earth had on the rock and lift one edge that was big enough to hook to Rusty. Tom backed him into position and tied off a rigging strap around the rock. Maggie would guide Rusty forward while Nat and Tom pried with the saplings.

"When we get this out, I say we drag it to the side of the smokehouse. It can be my rest spot when I'm working in the garden this spring and summer," Maggie said.

"That sounds good to me. I hope we can get it that far," Tom replied.

"We will. Once we get it broken free, Rusty will pull it easily." Nat stood next to the rock.

"Let's give it a try then," Tom said.

Tom and Nat took up their positions and Maggie walked to Rusty. When they nodded they were ready, Maggie took his reins and urged him forward while Tom and Nat strained with all their might to pry the rock from Mother Earth's grasp. The ground suddenly gave up its grip and the rock slowly edged forward.

"Keep him moving forward," Nat yelled.

Once freed from the earth, Rusty pulled the boulder into the position Maggie wanted, leaving a gaping hole in the earth.

Nat looked at Tom and smiled. "That was even bigger than I thought."

"Amen," he said. "We can use some soil from the pile to fill in the hole and bring it up level with the rest."

"I believe we all deserve a break after that." Nat eyed them all. "Let's get some water."

"I have biscuits left from breakfast, and either jelly or honey to go with them," Maggie said.

"Honey would give us energy," Nat said.

"Have a seat and I'll be back." Maggie turned to leave with Marissa walking with her.

"We might finish this today." Nat wiped the sweat from her brow.

"As long as we don't run into any more boulders." Tom grinned.

"Let's hope not." She took a cup of water he offered.

They shared a quick meal and then went back to work. Fortune smiled on them and there were no other boulders lying hidden under the soil. Rusty and Tom made quick work of breaking the ground for the new plot, and then finished by breaking ground on last year's plot. Nat and Marissa moved the rocks while Maggie started supper.

Tom and Nat tended the animals before stretching out on the front porch while Marissa went inside to help Maggie.

"Look," Tom pointed across the water.

Nat turned to see what he had spotted. "Those are whales," she told him, "heading back north for the warmer season."

"They are huge." Tom's eyes trailed them until they disappeared.

"That they are. Maggie says one of the creatures could feed a village for months."

"I can believe that." Tom looked once more, but they had disappeared.

Nat was nodding off when Maggie called them to supper. She and Tom entered the cabin and took seats around the table.

"I don't think any of us will have trouble sleeping tonight." Marissa placed bowls of the thick chowder on the table.

"We got a lot done today, didn't we?" Tom asked.

"Yes, we did, thanks to your help. It would have taken at least two days for me to get the garden plowed."

Tom beamed with pride and took a bite of the chowder. "What do you want to get done tomorrow?"

"I thought we could set some traps in the morning, and then take a ride down the coast. I spotted some other pools that I would like to take a look at."

"I'd also like to help you bring in some fresh firewood before I go back to town."

"We can do that." Nat looked at Tom. "Good idea. It won't hurt to get ahead of next winter."

"Keep your eyes open for a nice buck," Maggie said. "I need more buckskin and a nice steak or roast would be good."

"I think we can handle that request." Nat smiled at her.

"With Marissa's help, I'd like to go ahead and get some seeds planted in the garden, and maybe get a few apple trees planted."

"Where did you find apple trees?" Tom asked.

"Maggie has managed to get some seeds to sprout this winter," Marissa told him. "If we're lucky, in a few years we'll have our own apples."

"Until then, I promise to keep you stocked in apples if you'll continue to bake pies." Tom looked at Maggie hopefully.

"You have a deal, young man."

Tom looked at Maggie bashfully. "I was hoping you'd make me a new pair of boots this spring," he said. "I'd pay whatever it costs."

"Better add a moose to my request then. The moose hide will make fine boots. Nat's are starting to get thin in spots too."

"We have a busy few days ahead of us, so we better get a good sleep tonight." Nat yawned and stretched her arms above her head.

†

Maggie and Tom were awake and cooking breakfast when Nat and Marissa emerged from the bedroom. Tom was toasting slices of the bread Maggie had baked over the fireplace while Maggie warmed bacon and ham slices.

"How would you like your eggs?" Maggie asked.

"Some dippers for me please," Nat requested.

"That sounds good." Tom turned the toasted bread.

"That's no problem. Marissa, would you bring butter and jelly from the pantry?"

"Yes, I will."

Fortified with a hearty breakfast, Tom and Nat saddled up and hitched Quincy to the small wagon. They filled it with the new traps and with the well-seasoned traps and started into the forest. Tom was excited to learn about setting traps and proved a good student. By midmorning, they had set all the traps and decided to go to the lake to see if they could get a buck or a bull moose.

They tied Quincy and the horses near the lake and approached as quietly as possible. The lake area was full of animal activity and several moose and deer were present.

"You get the moose and I'll take a buck," Nat whispered. "Let me know when you're ready."

Tom set his sights on a large bull and he slowly counted down from three. Their rifles cracked, filling the air with a loud pop and the smell of burnt powder. Both animals stumbled and fell to the ground, sending the rest of the herds fleeing from the lake.

"Good shot. Let's get the horses and Quincy and get to work."

After field dressing their kills, they loaded the carcasses across the wagon and returned to the cabin.

Maggie and Marissa heard their approach and took a break from planting to help with the butchering and skinning. Marissa took a moose roast and some venison chops into the cabin for supper. Tom and Nat stretched the hides on the barn wall and then continued processing the meat. Quarters were hung in the smokehouse, and loins were sliced for jerky.

"We still have time for a short ride, if you're up to it," Nat told Tom.

"Let me put Quincy in the barn and I'll be ready."

"Go ahead, Tom, I'll care for Quincy," Maggie told him.

"We'll see you in a bit then," Nat replied.

†

Gyp, Shine, and Luna ran along with them as they cantered down the beach. The tide had gone out when they reached the pools Nat had spotted on her trip south. They directed the horses into the shallow water. The three pools were well formed, the shell walls sufficiently high to trap sea creatures when the tides retreated. It was still too early for the abundance of sea life to have returned, but Nat was pleased to have found additional pools if they needed a larger supply source.

"When the weather warms, these will be filled," she told Tom. "It's a short ride, so I was thinking we could use these pools for our food and the others for bartering."

"I'd like to fill my smokehouse this year, too," Tom said. "About halfway through last winter, I would have loved to have some of the smoked fish."

"Get another barrel from the general store and we will use that one exclusively for you. There's no reason we can't fill your smokehouse and Smithy's too."

"How long do you think the bison will be close enough to hunt?"

"At least through the summer. If we could hunt at least once per month, we should bring in plenty of meat." Nat turned her horse and they headed back to the cabin.

When they smelled the smoke from the cabin, Tom looked over at her. "Something sure smells good."

"Yes, my mouth is watering too."

"We still have some daylight, if you want to cut some trees."

"Tom, are you reading my mind again?"

Tom smiled and they started up the hill together.

✝

When Tom got ready to return to town later that week, a fresh pile of wood was cut and the first string of pelts were drying. The wagon was loaded down with jerky, smoked fish, and a few sets of antlers for Smithy. The barrels were stored on the front porch ready to fill when the waters warmed enough to begin harvesting seafood.

Maggie carried out a small bundle and handed it to Tom. "We've almost forgotten to send these to Smithy."

Tom unwrapped the bundle and found a dozen knives with bone and antler handles. The blades gleamed in the sunlight. "He's going to love these. Heck, I might even break down and buy one."

"Don't," Nat told him. "We are still working on yours. It will be ready by the time you return." Nat was carving one of the smaller whalebones for a handle on Tom's knife. Maggie had already honed the blade to a razor's edge and it would soon be ready.

Tom grinned at the women and unlocked the brake. "I'll be back in two weeks with the wagon, to hunt with Nat and to bring a fresh load of supplies from town." He gave them a wave, snapped the reins, and headed away from the cabin and his friends.

✝

Several days after Tom returned to town, Nat decided that she would raid the honey tree to fill the jars they had emptied during the winter. Maggie was tending to the garden, so Marissa decided she would go with Nat.

Nat carried a case of jars and Marissa carried Nat's rifle. Nat had seen signs of a bear in the area, and decided she would stay armed while in the forest until the threat of a hungry bear had passed. After a long winter of hibernation, bears would be hungry—a hungry bear was an aggressive animal and she would take no risks.

When they reached the honey tree, Nat got Marissa settled next to a tree a safe distance from the buzzing bees. She lit her torch to get it smoking and picked up a pair of jars. "I'll be right back." She kissed Marissa.

Marissa watched Nat work her magic with the swarming bees and she quickly filled two jars before returning for the rest of the crate. She placed them at the base of the honey tree and dipped out the precious, golden liquid. Over the winter, the comb had depleted, so she only took a small portion that she carried back to Marissa. She dowsed her torch and joined Marissa under the tree.

They worked together to cover the jars and then Nat split the comb into two sections. "A treat for you, my love." She offered the comb to Marissa. She placed the remaining piece of comb inside the crate, intending to give it to Maggie when they returned. She licked the honey off her fingers and leaned back against the tree.

"This is as good as I remember." Marissa offered Nat a bite.

Nat took a small bite and moaned at the sweetness. "That is good."

"My bee charmer. Have I told you lately how proud I am of you?"

"For what?"

"Working so hard to provide for all of us this winter, and making us such a wonderful home. And, for bringing me such a nice treat." She ate the last bite.

"You make me happy and all the hard work is worth the effort. You and Maggie are a large part of our success, too. I may do the hunting and the more physical chores, but you two keep us fed, clothed, and provided with the goods for us to trade in town."

"We make a good team."

"That we do." She looked into Marissa's shining eyes. "Do you have any regrets about moving out here?"

"Not a single one. I love being with you and Maggie, working side by side."

"I love the two of you being here. I can still trap and hunt, then come home to hold you in my arms almost every night."

"So no regrets for you, either?"

"Only that my father didn't live long enough to be here with us. Nathan would have enjoyed living here."

"I wish I could have met him. He must have been really special to have raised such a fine young woman."

"He was and he would have loved you, too." The cry of a hawk caught her attention as it circled about the lake. "Maybe he is here with us after all." Nat pointed out the hawk.

Marissa snuggled into Nat, watching the hawk swoop down near the lake's edge, and take flight with a small rodent in its talons. They watched as animals came to the lake to water and hunt, enjoying a peaceful time together before the sun began to sink.

"Let's go home." Nat stood and offered her hand to Marissa. She picked up the crate filled with honey and took Marissa's hand, and they returned to the cabin after another successful day in the woods.

That evening, Nat sat on the porch carving her latest walking stick, while Maggie and Marissa cleaned the dishes from supper and prepared a pan of biscuits for the next day.

She felt a smile growing on her face thinking about all they had accomplished since she decided to leave her life as a trapper behind. Once, she had questioned her ability to settle into one spot and carve out a life for herself, but now she thought of how proud Nathan would be of her decision and the life she had created.

When the darkness fell around her, Nat walked inside the cabin and hugged the two women she loved. "Thank you for being here with me." Tears were filling her eyes.

"There's no place we'd rather be," Maggie replied. "This is home."

About the Author

Ali Spooner

Ali Spooner, a native of Florida, calls Pensacola her forever home. Ali has been writing for many years as a hobby, and with the assistance of the Affinity team, she has taken her love of storytelling to a new level.

Ali's characters range from cowgirls and psychics to a healthy dose of supernatural beings. She has written stand-alone titles as well as series. Ali is an avid reader and her other hobbies include photography, outdoor activities, and watching college sports.

Other Affinity Rainbow Publications Books

The Organization by Annette Mori & Erin O'Reilly
The feisty, fiery women from Asset Management are back for another heart-stopping adventure! This time, their sights are set on a new mob boss Leonid Petrov. Val is tagged as the go-to member to infiltrate Leonid's inner circle. Tasked with keeping Leonid's impossible new wife, Gina, safe, Val encounters more problems than solutions. Will wild card Gina be Val's Achilles heel and lead to her demise, or will it fill her with a strength she didn't know she had?

Jeager's by JM Dragon
When your world turns upside down and all your safe secure yearnings are thrown to the wind what happens? What would you do? University lecturer Dr. Kirsten Van De Pelt shortly due to retire early from her academic life is about to find the answers to those questions when Corley Anders, a TV star, enters her life. Will Kirsten take an opportunity of a lifetime or simply settle for the safety net that has been her life?

Running From Love by Jen Silver
Sam Wade returns home from a business trip to discover her wife, Beth left her for another woman, Lydia. To take her mind off the break-up Sam accepts an assignment to learn to play golf at the newly opened Temperley Cliffs Golf Resort in Cornwall not knowing that is where Beth and Lydia plan to go too. There is more than one way to run from love; from never having to make a commitment and say those magical three words, "I love you." Find out what happens when they find themselves together—sport, betrayal, jealousy, and love form an unforgettable fusion of emotions.

Specter of Fear by Erin O'Reilly
Anne and Bailey are in love and planning a future together. Only the letters that Anne keeps getting are filling her with fear and doubt. Could the love they share really be a sham? Or is there something more behind

the letters? Is the sender of the letters after Anne, Bailey or both women? Find out in this suspenseful tale...or is it a real story?

Back in the Saddle by Ali Spooner
The crew from *Cowgirl Up* are back in the saddle for more fun. In their new adventure, Coal, Stormy, and Gene get the chance to be part of something they have always dreamed of—a cattle drive. Even without the gang being at the MC2 ranch, there's still plenty of action going on with a new addition, Doc Bo, bringing a hint of jealousy and maybe the start of a new romance. Pull on your boots and hats, and hold on tight as you ride along with the crew of the MC2.

Faith in Rayne by Dannie Marsden
Welcome back Rayne and Lisbet from *Rayne Comes to Town* and *Rayne's New Beginnings*. Their life has flourished since meeting. Rayne ventures to Telluride, Colorado, where both adventure and trouble land at her feet. Lisbet heads to Telluride to reunite with Rayne, her head filled with dreams of their future only to have her dreams come crashing down. Can she find the strength to fight for Rayne, allowing her faith to guide them back to their love?

Ruined by Ali Spooner
Kade, a seasoned battlefield soldier has had enough, refusing to fight for greed. Now on a quest to return to her homeland she meets Iza. Iza, a slave from the army defeated by Kade, begs the warrior to take her on as a servant. Kade, sympathetic to the slave's request, allows her to travel as a companion and a friendship begins to form.

Refractions Trilogy by Angela Koenig
Follow the adventures of Rhodes Scholar Jeri O'Donnell who becomes embroiled in Ulster's fight for independence from Britain. Later Jeri travels through the Himalayan highlands where she meets Kelly Corcoran, a tourist from the United States. Kelly is willing to gamble her heart, as Jeri struggles against involving anyone in her perilous and chaotic life. For Jeri, the true battle is confronting her attraction to violence as she struggles against losing herself in the exhilaration of combat.

Affinity
Rainbow Publications

E-Books, Print, Free e-books

Visit our website for more publications available online.

www.affinityebooks.com

Published by Affinity E-Book Press NZ LTD
Canterbury, New Zealand

Registered Company 2517228